"I spend many of the clear nights in the study of astronomy.
There is a sense of infinite peace and protection
in the glittering hosts of heaven."
-- H.G. Wells, *The Island of Dr. Moreau*

"With infinite complacency men went to and fro over this globe
about their little affairs, serene in their assurance
of their empire over matter. It is possible that the infusoria
under the microscope do the same.
No one gave a thought to the older worlds of space
as sources of human danger."
-- H.G. Wells, *The War of The Worlds*

"Man, proud man,
Dressed in a little brief authority,
Most ignorant of what he's most assured,
His glassy essence, like an angry ape,
Plays such fantastic tricks before high heaven
As make the angels weep."
-- William Shakespeare, *Measure for Measure*

"It takes great courage to see the world
in all its tainted glory,
and still to love it."
-- Oscar Wilde

# Paragon
# of the
# Eccentric

Terry Kroenung

Rare Moon Press

**Paragon of the Eccentric**
Copyright 2021 © by Terry Kroenung
www.terrykroenung.com

**Cover design by VixyDesign**
**www.fiverr.com/share/d65dpa**

Printed in the United States of America
Library of Congress Cataloging-in-Publication Data on file.

ISBN: 978-1-7378947-0-4

To Janet

You're the paragon,
I'm the eccentric

# Paragon
# of the
# Eccentric

# Act One

~

## A Tempestuous Noise

*Above the English Channel, Dorset coast, July 1887*

"Boatswain!"

The sturdy fellow rushed to his commander's side, wobbling as the ship careened again. "Aye, sir!"

His superior turned, glossy black leather coat catching the flash of another tremendous lightning strike. Those disturbing pale blue eyes seemed to spark. "See to your men. You must all do your utmost, or this storm will undo us."

Saluting, the boatswain hurried aft to secure the rigging. It wouldn't do to explode now, with land so near.

"Remember who you have aboard," a tall Confederate captain reminded the commander.

"It is ever in my thoughts, Carter. Precious cargo if ever there was." He ran nervous fingers through his white-blonde hair. His accent seemed born in Donegal, but hinted also of something else, the flat tones of America, perhaps. "But so is my own arse."

"I trust a man more who thinks of his own survival ahead of some damn fool mission." The darkly handsome Carter's voice was pure Virginia.

"As do I, but if harm comes to our eerie friend, her inbound mates will be spectacularly and gruesomely unforgiving."

Another blue-white bolt slashed across their bow. "A direct hit will do us for sure."

"Unlikely. Our metal frame is essentially a giant Faraday cage. The wind is more of a danger. That, and…"

He jerked his head toward the stern. Carter craned his neck to peer out the window. When the next lighting flared, an enormous airship filled the entire sky, several times larger than theirs. "He's going to ram us!"

"Sebastian is insane, but not foolhardy. He needs to get our prize back from us intact. More likely he's lowering grapples to snare our rudder." The commander snapped to his helmsman, "Hard to port!"

The gondola lurched as the little ship swerved, but the maneuver was never completed. Something had jammed the steering mechanism.

"Too late!" Carter growled.

"Damn!" The commander moved in close and whispered to him. "Get our slimy friend into one of the beetles, with a driver. Ensure her enclosure shield is sound, else she'll hijack his mind. Ready another for you and me."

Carter nodded and hurried aft, gripping the walls as the ship bucked like a frightened horse. Behind him the helmsman cried, "Controls are lost, sir! I can't steer her."

*"Very well, son. You've done your best. Better brace yourself. We've a hard landing ahead. I only hope it's a dry one."* He fingered a photograph hung around his neck and muttered, *"If you had just let her go, they'd both be alive, and it wouldn't have come to this."*

Atop the white chalk cliff, a handful of dark figures in oilcloth watched for the result of the chase. For a long time, it seemed that the smaller ship would escape, but then the great *Giffard* had shot lines down into her tail. Now she fishtailed like a jig in a storm, losing height every second.

*"Will she at least make it to land?"* asked one in a curiously emotionless tone.

*"If she don't, we all's lookin' fer new jobs come mornin',"* another said in the same manner.

Their leader, peering at the oncoming behemoths through binoculars that emitted a greenish glow, said, *"She'll get here. Be a damned near thing, though."*

Tall and thin, in an old plaid coat, his jaw jutted out like the prow of a ship. He turned to his men. Another storm burst showed them to be a pair of most disturbing individuals. One bore an unhealed but bloodless bullet wound above his right eye. His partner's face was a smallpox-destroyed horror show. Their eyes were mildly clouded.

*"Stand ready to get the boss clear if they make it. If he don't, well…then we scarper off before we're something's dinner."*

In the end, the first airship did get clear of the Channel, by a whisker. It struck the muddy ground with a crumping sound. Before its gas bag could begin to sag, two round horseless vehicles burst out of it and bounced inland. Close behind came three eerie figures from the other ship, vaguely human in shape, but running on all fours like predators of the veldt. They swarmed the rear car, rolling it on its back and plucking a large squarish object from it. In another moment, a rotor-aero picked them up and returned to the *Giffard*, which kept on to the north. As it glided overhead, the lantern-jawed fellow trained his binoculars on its nose, where the name **Prosper** could be seen for a moment before the darkness absorbed it all.

*"Off we go, boys. Let's hope Jimmy was in that other beetle. But it's a foul mood he'll be in."*

# 1 / "ANY STRANGE BEAST THERE MAKES A MAN

*London; October 1887*

*When a Whitechapel whore waves her tentacles at you, attention must be paid.*

Normally he would have passed on by, of course. It would not be wise to permit her to lure him in with her soft words and body. Before he knew it, he would find himself reeled in like a foolish trout. Yanked from his element and skinned. Boned, possibly, if her pimp lurked in the alley and was more than usually desperate. Best to just tip one's hat and keep on walking, particularly after midnight in such a foul area.

*Tentacles, though. Not your everyday dollymop, this one.*

He slowed, turned. The gears in his left leg were new and well-oiled, but he could still hear them whirring. Most people could not, but then most people had not spent seven years being hunted across the globe. It had honed his senses, that. And an excellent thing, too, because his pricked ears detected tiny gasps coming from somewhere behind him. *Some fellow's trying to mask his breathing. But this bloody yellow fog is playing the devil with his lungs. He snorts like an animal.*

Reserving a corner of his mind for that potential threat, he saluted her with the smooth steel head of his stick, touching it to the brim of his bowler. A few feet away a dim gaslight gave off the feeblest of glows. Beauty did not live in her features, of course. The comely ones easily found indoor work and better pay. This girl -- and she was no more than twenty, though she looked twice that -- wore the drawn look that spoke of too much gin and too little food. None of her clothes matched, coming from a variety of second-hand shops and trash heaps. Covered in sad, soggy flowers, her hat was a milliner's nightmare. But even without those disadvantages, she had never turned heads. Her eyes were a trifle lopsided, the nose over-long, the chin too pointed. One canine was missing.

"Evenin', m'lord," she croaked, voice as dry as a mummy's. "Fancy some company? Dreadful night to be alone, ain't it?"

"Dreadful it is," he agreed. His eyes scanned her thin form. The tentacles had disappeared, tucked out of sight now that she had hooked him. "But I'm no lord."

"A gentleman, at least, though, with togs like yours. And such refined speech."

A corner of his mouth twitched beneath the fair mustache. *Oh, you should've heard me at Isandlwana, missy, with my Yorkshire accent and pauper's manners. I swore like a thousand demons when the Zulus took my leg. Pissed myself, too.*

"Hush," he said with a smile. "You'll turn my head."

"Oh, I can do more than that, love." She slid toward him, putting on her best 'come-hither' gaze. "For the right price Millie can turn yer inside-out."

*Yes, and your partner back there will do the same to my pockets, no doubt.*

A brewery wagon rumbled past, empty kegs making a terrible racket as it bounced along the cobbled street. When it had gone, he cocked his head to pick up the suspicious breather again. No sound could be heard now. The man had scooted away under cover of the noise. *Ah. Aren't you the clever one?*

"Well, Millie, I must be honest with you," he told the trollop, "I'm not the sort of man who patronizes a working girl on the street."

She smiled and waved a dirty hand at him. "Aw, if I had a shillin' for every time I've heard that ---"

Returning her smile, he nodded while scanning about for sign of the missing stalker. But the labored breather had gone. No strange odor gave him away, either. *Hardly surprising, with the stench of so much filth this near the Thames. Plays hell with one's defenses.*

"I imagine so," he agreed. "Nevertheless, you intrigue me." His voice dropped to a whisper. "My Millie can tease her man in a rather unique way, yes?"

Millie tried to wrap her tongue around the unfamiliar word. "Yew-neeke?" She made a sour face. "Don't know about that one, dearie. Whatever 'tis, cost yer extra, it will."

Her new customer did his best not to make an eye-roll at such tragic ignorance. "It means one of a kind. Exceptional. Rare."

Understanding lit her plain face. "Aw, yer mean me wigglers?"

"Quite. Are they real?"

That earned him an affronted frown. "Course they's real. I gives honest value. Whaddya take me for?"

"Well, that's what we're negotiating, isn't it?"

"Two bob, love. That includes Millie's bonus treatment."

With that she glanced about, then shook her head. Two slim snakes, perhaps eighteen inches long and thick as a thumb, slid across her prominent collarbones. Mottled gray and green, they seemed to grow from the base of her skull. Small pink suckers ran along the undersides. At the end of one was a mouth with tiny, curved teeth, while the other sported a lovely blue eye with a vertical iris. It raised itself up and blinked at him.

"That's quite the bonus," he breathed, squinting back at the eye. His callused hand dipped into a pocket of his brocade vest. He held out two silver coins, one on either side of an ivory calling card. "And a bargain, I'd say."

She peered at the card. Its writing was difficult to see by the muted glimmer of the gaslight. The fog had grown worse. Now it resembled oolong tea tainted with sulphur. A storm-driven south wind was coming in now, but it did nothing to thin the muck. After taking a long moment to sound out the words in her head, she read the card aloud. "Montague Paragon." Millie raised an eyebrow at him. "This yer name?" He nodded once, still captivated by her wriggling tentacles. "The Ogilvy Theatre." Her head came up again. "Yer an actor, then?"

"Of modest reputation only. I'm no David Garrick."

The whore frowned. "Who?"

A sigh. "Not important."

"What's this at the bottom? The Eccentric Club, 67b Shaftsbury Avenue, Soho? Sounds dodgy to me."

He laughed aloud at that. "And to many others, I daresay. That's where you can locate me tomorrow afternoon."

She took a suspicious step back. "And why would I do that?"

"Because, my dear precious Millicent -- that is your given name, yes? -- if you present this card there at two o'clock, I will hand you five guineas for your trouble."

Her tired eyes grew to the size of carriage wheels at such an immense sum, as much as a tradesman earned in a year. "Pull the other one!"

"You are right to be circumspect." Paragon produced a gold sovereign. "Here is proof of my good intentions."

The coin vanished, snatched up by the toothed tentacle, which tucked the loot down her failed bosom. "Ooh! What did I do to deserve meetin' yer tonight?"

*What, indeed? My imagination deserts me.* "Promptly at two o'clock ring at the servants' entrance, show the clockwork man this card, and say 'Namaste.' He will escort you directly to me. Can you remember that?"

Her brow furrowed as she concentrated, tongue peeking between her chapped lips. "Nah-mah-stay." Fresh suspicion darkened her brow. "Yer doesn't want a tumble tonight? What game yer playin' at?"

"No game at all. I merely want a professor friend from the Royal Society to examine your, um, wigglers. All very innocent, I assure you."

Millie giggled. "I ain't precisely in the innocent business."

Paragon winced as his mind flickered an image of poor Sergeant Brutte's pale, dead face on that African killing ground. "None of us is, I fear." Once more he raised his walking stick in salute.

And in the polished head he saw two rough men with knives creeping up on him. *Ah, well. I came to Whitechapel to be killed. This is as good a spot as any.*

The rowdies were stout fellows, but Paragon was no willowy reed himself. Years of wandering Africa and Asia after Isandlwana, working with his hands and back in exchange for the secrets of each new combat master, had hardened his six-foot tall body into oak. It had also taught him to embrace the calm at every storm's center, to permit the winds to whirl past him. In the seconds before the first attacker arrived, he took a cleansing breath and sank his soul into the earth.

Perhaps Millie was in on the assault from the first. Or perhaps they merely took advantage of the opportunity his whisper of a limp suggested. It mattered not to Paragon. These were just the sort of men he would have sought out anyway. Hard lads who could offer him the kind of atonement he craved.

He shoved Millie back against the wall. Her tentacles jerked back into her hair as if by steam-driven pulleys. From the look on her face, the knifemen were no friends of hers. *That's nice. I'm developing a fondness for the girl.* With a wink, he slid hard left just as the lead man laid a heavy hand on his right shoulder and pulled. With his balance too far back, a firm elbow easily shoved the thug away.

The dollymop clung to the grimy wall, too shocked to run. Paragon placed himself in front of her. *See, m'lady? Chivalry lives, even here.* Exaggerating his limp, he played the part of a pathetic cripple, just as he had on stage earlier that month in Avery's over-written melodrama. Now he played Caliban at the Ogilvy with the stump in plain view.

One man with a blade was a hazard worth avoiding. Two of them were death on winged feet. No sane man would invite them to waltz. But then, all sane men in London were a-bed this night. Only the suicidally guilty walked abroad. Wobbling dramatically, black stick held behind him, Paragon oozed false fear. His opponents looked at one another and smiled. Though he expected them to insist that he empty his pockets, they set their ugly faces into grim masks and advanced.

*No robbery, this. Just murder. So much the better. I hope you're up to it, gents. I grow tired of waiting to join Brutte, but I won't just lie down for you, either.*

The fellow on the right proved to be a bit lighter on his feet than his partner. Less gin in his system, perhaps. He arrived a few steps ahead of the other chap, much to his immediate chagrin. As his knife slashed at the arm Paragon offered, it met only fog. A neat pivot on the front leg had removed the target. With a blurred snap the stick rapped the man's knife hand. His blade bounced on the cobbles. When he yowled and yanked the bruised member away, Paragon kicked the second rowdy in the knee with his rear leg…the aluminum one. A high-pitched hiss left the killer's lips. He hopped back out of range, clutching his wrecked joint.

Paragon put his weight on both feet now that the ruse had played itself out. The complex system of gears, chains, and clockwork that Queue had installed in the new limb barely groaned as he pushed off toward the first man. *Splendid that it's worked so well in its first trial-by-combat. The bloody thing's worth its weight in silver, I'm told. I'll wager that this strange metal is the coming thing.*

Right then the first assassin was the coming thing. He had taken great offense at having his knuckles rapped. He rushed in hard and fast. The actor let him get a good grip on the lapels of his frock coat. Then he thrust his stick between the man's arms and across his thick neck while twisting the grasping wrist. In a single heartbeat the fellow found himself levered face-first onto the cobblestones, Paragon's cane grinding the elbow in a direction nature had never intended. His victim screeched and crawled off.

An ornithopter rattled overhead, almost close enough to spit at. Its fabric wings clattered and jangled as they beat back and forth, nearly smothering the sound of the small paraffin engine. *Who in blazes is flying in this beastly fog? And so low! Is he mad?* Distracted, Paragon learned too late that the man he had kicked possessed great powers of recovery. His wicked blade just missed Paragon's cravat, and the vulnerable throat beneath it. Hurling himself backward, Millie's newest friend managed to block the second and third strikes with instinctive flicks of his stick. He skidded backward to gain some breathing space. When his grunting foe kept advancing, though favoring his damaged knee, Paragon sighed and pulled thirty inches of Sheffield steel from the black body of his cane, an advantage he had not wished to employ. Something gave him pause.

*Grunting? Really?*

Now that the assailant had skidded to a stop, the sword point mere inches from his nose, Paragon took the time to get a good look at the fellow's face. He had to blink and stare again. There was no mistake. The knifeman did not have a nose per se. Rather, he had a snout. An actual pig's snout. Oink-oink and all that.

Paragon let out the sort of disbelieving laugh a bloke might make if he had come face-to-face with a unicorn. Edging to his right, he gazed at the other assassin, who held the outraged arm while scrambling to his feet. That man had a normal human nose, but his ears boasted points, while patches of reptilian scales covered his cheeks and neck.

*What the devil…? And All-Hallow's Eve is still a fortnight off. Sorry, Brutte old chap, our reunion will have to be postponed. I simply must know what this is all about.*

Scaly-bloke hissed, a forked tongue flicking out of his thin mouth. Grimacing, he hefted his blade with his undamaged arm. With a sideways glance at his fellow slayer, he began to slide to Paragon's right. Swine-boy eased around the other way, hoping to position himself where his enemy could not see both foes at once. Paragon kept the sword aimed at the first man and the heavy cane body at the second one. He scooted backward to defeat their plan, keeping his eyes on the lizard and his ears on the hog. This time he would use the new metal leg to put them down for good.

But as he tensed his muscles to interdict the attack, the ornithopter returned. This time it flew much lower. In fact, it landed right on top of them.

The thing was a tiny single-seater, a Hargrave 300. It took up so little space that the pilot almost wore the machine, rather than sat in it. Even with its graceful, curved wings flapping away it still had room to maneuver in the narrow London street. How the operator could see in this abysmal chocolate soup was anyone's guess. Before diving out of its way to pull the screaming Millie down and cover her, Paragon caught sight of him. A slotted breath shield with filigree silver accents hid his face. Instead of the standard two lenses a single great pane of curved and mirrored glass covered the eyes. One hand worked the stick, while the other brandished a queer-looking pistol with brass fins and a fluted glass barrel.

The animal abominations also launched themselves out of the flying machine's path. As it lurched to a clumsy stop, they did not run away, nor did they attack the pilot. Instead, each knifeman knelt before the sputtering contraption, placed his weapon on the ground, and then touched his beastly forehead to the stones in a sort of worship.

A metallic whine came from the weapon, connected by a metal hose to a flat wooden box on his back. Its translucent barrel gave off a pulsing aquamarine light. As the stranger unbuckled himself from his seat harness, he leveled the gun at the pig-man. Neither of Paragon's would-be slayers had raised his head yet. Clearly, they knew this person, to be kowtowing so. The object of their veneration stepped into the murky street, walking with a pronounced and unfeigned limp. Long white hair stuck out beneath the back of the mask. He wore tall boots with puttees, canvas jodhpurs, and a tweed Norfolk jacket with a bandoleer across the chest. It held what seemed to be narrow glass tubes full of a mercury-like fluid.

"What is the Law?" croaked the pilot. His mask garbled the words, making it sound like a speaking tube from one's servants' quarters.

The piggish fellow glanced sideways at his partner, then whispered in a growl, "Not to hunt other Men. That is the Law."

"That is the Law," the scaly chap echoed, not lifting his head.

"What else?" demanded the stranger with a wave of his pistol.

"Not to shed blood," the swine-man continued. "That is the Law."

Again, the reptilian repeated the odd refrain. "That is the Law."

"For are we not Men?" cried the pilot.

"Are we not Men?" the assassins chanted in unison.

Millie tried to shove Paragon away from her so she could see. "Look here!" she complained. "What's he on about? Who is that bloke anyway?"

Paragon slapped a firm hand over her mouth. "Shush!" An instant later her toothed tentacle nipped at his fingers. Its teeth felt like straight razors dipped in acid. He released her out of pure reflex.

"Don't shush me, mate."

He whispered directly into her ear. "A thousand pardons, my marvelous Millicent. But as this mysterious gentleman is in possession of a firearm I've never seen the like of -- and I am unusually well-traveled -- perhaps it's best we lie low until we have a firmer grip on the situation."

She turned up a corner of her mouth at that. "A firm grip, eh? Now yer speakin' me language, gov." Her bony hand reached low to give him a rather more intimate squeeze than he might have expected in their present situation.

*How can this blasted woman think of coupling in these circumstances?* Paragon glared at her. "I meant what I said." He grabbed her wrist and yanked it from his expensively tailored trousers. *Bad enough they're suffering the indignity of this East End sludge we're lying in. Soiling them from the inside would be more than my poor valet could bear.* It occurred to him that only a year earlier the thought of possessing any sort of bespoke tailoring, let alone a servant, would have been laughable.

Millie's other tentacle, the one with the eye, jerked back. It tapped her on the shoulder and pointed toward the scene in the street. Both snaky appendages vanished beneath her hat. Paragon looked behind him.

And stared into the glowing maw of the outlandish pistol. *Ah. He's not here to rescue us, then. More's the pity.*

Its unearthly whine grew louder. A blaze like Satan's flash powder obscured gun and shooter. Instead of a sharp report like a normal weapon, it made a triple boing like a great clock spring snapping. The very air seemed to melt as rings of chartreuse energy burned the stones and wall where Paragon and Millie lay, obliterating the streetlamp. In its place remained a plume of burning gas, throwing flickering lights that made the scene even more disturbing. If they had stayed put, only a scorched shadow would have remained of them.

But Montague Paragon had not survived Zulus, Thuggees, Cantonese Triads, and Parisian Apache by debating with himself on courses of action. With no conscious thought his clockwork leg had kicked against the wall and propelled them both out of range. As masonry rained down upon them, he threw the shrieking and cursing woman into the alley. He pulled himself up with his cane body, useless sword at the ready. Jaw set, he waited for obliteration. No second shot followed, however.

The flyer turned away from Paragon, sensing that Millie's savior posed no imminent threat. He reloaded with a glass charge from his bandoleer and stared down at the fawning beast-men, who had not stirred from their subservient positions. His voice crackled again.

"When the Law is transgressed, what must occur?" No reply. "Speak!"

"Chastisement," hissed the reptilian one.

"And why is this?"

"That Chaos may not reign. That Order may prevail in house and field."

"Is your offense a minor one?"

Neither replied. They only shook their heads in rough unison. The pilot holstered his terrible pistol and approached the pair of unnaturals. He put a gloved hand on each bowed neck, a tender gesture out of keeping with his prior harsh words. "It is a hard thing for a father to lose even a single child, let alone two."

Paragon blinked. *Father?*

"Yet an example must be set," the stranger continued. "No one may override the Law." His voice seemed to almost break. "For are we not…Men?"

"Are we not Men?" the odd pair echoed again.

They picked up their knives together, as if they had received some secret signal. For the first time Paragon noticed that their blades were not of steel. Rather, they were some sort of curved animal tusk, each a good twelve inches long, with a serrated inner edge. Rawhide wrapping served as a handle. No animal Paragon had ever seen or heard of produced a tusk of that precise size and shape.

The pilot spoke to each man in turn, saying the same thing in a soft tone. "Go in peace, my son. I do this out of love, not anger."

The pig-man cut the throat of his partner, just as the snake-man did the same for him. Scarlet jetted onto the filthy cobblestones, collecting in the joints and sliding into the gutter. With their last breaths the dying men staggered toward the pilot, arms outstretched, pleading. They sagged to the ground, still imploring him with those limp hands. He never moved, even when a stream of blood pooled beneath one boot.

Paragon remained frozen, watching, listening. There were times when a man of action needed to embrace stillness. He did not yet have enough information to choose a proper course. *All of this will have to be recalled later. I must collect and record, not strike out of ignorance.*

But the unknown man did not pause. Once the bodies had ceased twitching, he thrust a hand into his jacket pocket and produced a large steel flask. With an unhurried motion, as if there were neither witnesses nor any potential for a bobby to show up, he shook a coarse powder over the still forms. Then he unholstered the deadly pistol and turned a knob on its breech. A casual shot, much weaker than the one launched at Paragon, sent sparks onto the fresh corpses. Painfully bright blue-white light flared up from them, supremely harsh in the fogged darkness. Paragon clenched his eyes to protect them. His sensitive nose, though, was soon overwhelmed with the sweet stench of roasting pork.

In moments, the street lay dark again. Though the powder burned with a terrifying ferocity, its life was brief. Paragon opened his eyes, but of course his night vision had been destroyed. He might as well have been holding a white cane and an alms cup for all the good looking did him. Realizing his vulnerability, he scooted sideways until he found the alley. The smallsword slid back into its housing with an oiled snick.

In the street the masked pilot let out a metallic wail. He cried to the surrounding buildings, "I know you're watching, Jimmy! This was your doing! Seducer of children!" He hobbled toward his aero, voice sagging like an old roof. "Dragged them back to the jungle, you did." Strapping into the Hargrave, he added, "Do you think she would have wanted you to do this? How are you honoring her memory – *their* memory – by corrupting our work so? Once you made men, now you make monsters. That must stop. I'm coming to take them all. Even your harmless whore. And then you. Our business will finally be resolved."

The ornithopter chuff-chuffed into life again. In half a minute the wings began to beat. With a bit more grace than it had shown on landing, the flying machine rattled off and lumbered into the air once more. Moments later the street lay silent. Nothing remained of the two creatures, only heaps of steaming ash.

Paragon looked down, feeling blindly with his stick. The gas flare did his sight no favors. Millie had fled, of course. No one with sense would have remained. Perhaps she might still turn up at the club tomorrow. Five guineas was an unobtainable fortune to her sort. Professor Jekyll would positively coo with delight when she displayed her wigglers for him. After a proper bath, though, so as not to offend the famed physician's delicate sensibilities.

Blinking as some of his vision returned, the actor brushed off as much street muck as he could. His pale gray kid gloves would have to be seen to by Mervyn, who would give him a disappointed shake of his brass head. *Best not to think how he'll react to the ruined trousers, not to mention the scuffed toes of your boots. Probably a metallic shudder of horror. I wonder, do they build that response into all the artificial valets at the manufactory, or is mine just a bit odd?*

A police whistle tweeted in the near distance. Even in crime-riddled Whitechapel the festivities had drawn notice. From inside the frock coat Paragon produced another of Queue's new toys, a brass wind-up torch. Several strong turns of the crank produced a serviceable light for about one minute. With speed born of urgency he hurried into the street to stand at the blackened site of the beast-men's immolation. At first, he thought that all remnants of them had been consumed, but upon close examination with his monocle magnifier he spied a sliver of bone with perhaps a square inch of attached flesh. His prize went into a tiny, corked vial. He fled back into the alley before a copper could spot him, head throbbing from having sucked in so much wretched air. Just visible on the brick wall were fresh-painted words that had not been present even two minutes before: RIOT ARMY. That phrase had been cropping up all over London of late. No one knew what it meant. Beneath it, "The red plague rid you…." had been scraped into the wall with a knife. It occurred to Paragon that finding a quote from the play he had performed that very night stretched the bounds of coincidence.

All the way home to Soho his mind tried to juggle what had happened. *Monty, Monty, Monty…quite the puzzle, this is. Your alienist will charge you double for tomorrow's session.*

## 2 / "SUCH STUFF AS DREAMS ARE MADE ON"

"Sir...sir...please awake," said a metallic voice. "I fear you are having the Zulu nightmare again."

Paragon struggled a while longer against the unyielding hands. Gasping, icy perspiration gluing his nightshirt to his pebbled flesh, reality crept back. Yes, he lay in his own bed. His familiar possessions were just visible in the dim gaslight. Most prominent was the small Buddha statuette in the far corner.

Looming above him stood his clockwork man, Mervyn. Clad in standard valet's livery, the automaton wore as concerned an expression as his brass features would permit. His face had been constructed to look reassuring, capable, calm. The head and jaw were square and firm, the nose strong. Blue crystal eyes looked benignly back at him with a faint chemical glow.

"Are you quite recovered, sir?" the machine man asked. The sound that came out was clearly not made by a human, yet its timbre soothed the ear. Paragon did not reply, still staring with wide eyes like a hare that had just dodged a falcon. "Shall I make tea? Perhaps the lavender jasmine?" Mervyn turned toward the door.

The actor buried his face in his hands and shook his head. "Laudanum."

Mervyn stopped. His head rotated all the way back around, though his body did not move. "Is that wise, sir?"

"Laudanum."

"May I remind you of the sad events precipitated by your most recent foray into the world of opiates?"

"Laudanum."

"Please, sir, I---"

Paragon snapped, "Imperative!"

The clocker's eyes flared yellow. His head jerked back to the front and he proceeded out the door, making the floor shudder. "At once, sir."

His master slid to the edge of the bed, the toes of his only foot settling onto the plush Saraband carpet. The terrifying images of the African massacre, made even worse when commingled with the memories of that night's bizarre events, still slithered through his mind.

"Zulus in 'thopters, grunting like swine," he sighed, shaking his aching head. They had been terrifying enough before, charging bare footed across those Isandlwana rocks like some black torrent, pounding on their cowhide shields as they defended their sacred land. Even now he could still hear that deadly rhythm, the heartbeat of the demon that had slain his regiment.

And poor Albert Brutte, as near to a father as any man, savior of his very soul. Sometimes he fancied he saw his friend in the flesh, lurking in a corner, that knowing smile in a corner of his mouth, like a silent guardian angel. But the shade evaporated when he tried to look at it directly.

Paragon stood, wobbling. His aluminum limb leaned against a chair beside the footboard. He felt as tense and sore as if he had been training with Queue. *That's the ticket. A sweaty session of savate and stick-play to work these kinks out.*

The clock on the washstand insisted that it was 5 a.m. Paragon hopped over to it and splashed cold water on his face. He peered into the mirror, half-expecting to see old Zulu King Cetshwayo in a breath-mask. Instead, he saw his own bloodshot blue eyes, dark circles beneath them. His short sandy hair resembled a handful of hay stubble. *I might have to take heroic measures with the macassar oil this morning.* The nose had once been a fine specimen but had been somewhat ruined by a pair of breaks. One had been the result of an ill-advised shortcut through a Tangiers alley, where a pair of the usual assassins had lurked; the other had come from a Tibetan monk who had unceremoniously ejected him from a Lhasa temple where foreigners had been forbidden.

Paragon fingered the moustache that matched his hair. *Wants trimming.* Forcing a grin, he examined his teeth. They were straight enough. A miracle, considering all the blows to the face he had taken. Below them hung the strong cleft chin which so enamored him to women and assured him of getting cast in all the right sort of plays. *Ought to have that fellow covered by Lloyd's.* It had not been so prominent in his youth when he had weighed but eight stone and nearly blew away in a Yorkshire breeze. Being six feet in height by age twelve, he had resembled a pencil. Years of hard training and better nutrition had filled him out now to a solid fourteen stone.

And the scar.

His most evident reminder of Zululand, apart from the regrettable deficit of legs. The gouge ran from the center of his sharp left cheekbone, up past the eye which the spear tip had just missed, and along his temple to vanish into his hairline. It had been a fearsome thing, but a surgeon in Kashmir had opened the wound anew and worked wonders with needle and herbs. Now the scar resembled a pale line painted with the tiniest of brushes. That stirred the ladies' hearts, as well. No doubt they imagined him to be a grand war hero.

*If only that could be true. Then perhaps I would lie in the arid Natal soil and Albert could be here in my place, saving mankind from unimaginable perils. Heaven knows he would be immeasurably better suited for the task. Her Majesty's Extraordinary Clandestine Service runs quite the risk, depending on such a brittle instrument.*

He carried even uglier wounds, of course, hollowing him as if by a tropical parasite. One from Brutte's death, always festering, never succumbing to lancet or suture. The older one bestowed by the ironically named Peaceful Manners, his mother's bedmate. Despite her occasional second sight, which she called moonmagic, she had never known that her gold-toothed man had had an eye for her delicate son, for sad little Michael Parsons.

*"Our little secret, Mikey. Tell yer Mum and I'll have to cut your pretty white throat. Such a shame that'd be. Now hoist your nightshirt. There's a good lad."*

Paragon gasped and whipped his head about as he shrank from those searching coal-stained hands.

He spotted the white jade Buddha. Its placid image calmed the storm in his mind. Only six inches tall, it had been a parting gift from his first guru. Through all the travels since he had managed to keep it with him, along with the brass vajra and tribu which lay beside it. No matter what travails he endured, what battles, what assumed identities, what hurried escapes, always he packed those items first. And well aware was he of the irony clinging to them, since the Buddha taught that attachment caused suffering.

*Ah, well. Just one more aspect of life I'm terrible at, along with soldiering, friendship, and table manners.*

With some agile one-footed dancing he maneuvered himself to his small shrine. On the low table, atop a gold brocade cloth, sat the statue and his vajra, a small double-headed brass scepter only seven inches long. Paragon gave the Buddha a tiny smile, as he would do an old friend. Growing up, he had been as friendless as a boy could be. After that, any companions worthy of the name lay in a mass grave in Africa or had been abandoned across three continents for their own protection. Did his London guru count as a friend? Or his alienist, Madame Bernays, who struggled to repair his broken soul? His fellow actors and Eccentric Club members would likely shed no more than a perfunctory tear if an enemy succeeded in dispatching him.

With a head shake to clear his jumbled mind, Paragon sat before the altar to light the candles and sandalwood incense. While taking cleansing circular breaths, vajra in his right hand and the bell in his left, he began to chant. *Om mani peme hum, om mani peme hum.* For several minutes he maintained the hypnotic rhythm, ritually moving the vajra and tribu, thunderbolt and emptiness, male and female, wisdom and compassion. All the shame and terror of the dream grew transparent. It fled toward the horizon, leaving a long faint shadow behind.

Until from the Buddha's mouth came a tentacle with a blue eye and vertical iris. Its delicate pink suckers pulsed like sea anemones. With a cry the tormented actor flung himself away from the altar onto the carpet.

Mirror-shined shoes and white spats stopped inches from his crooked nose. "You are incommoded, sir?"

Mervyn held a tiny blue-white china cup, a spotless tea towel across his other forearm. The automaton's free hand gripped Paragon's bicep. Although he clearly could have crushed the bone to powder, instead he lifted the prone man as gently as one would a fragile butterfly, depositing him back onto the bed.

Paragon rubbed his eyes. A look back across the room showed that the statue wore its accustomed placid expression. He held out his hand for the tea like drowning man might reach for a rope.

"Excellent choice, sir," said Mervyn.

For a long moment he sat still, taking in the delicate floral notes of the golden liquid. His foolish peers had no idea what they missed, slurping away at the horrid sugary black stuff they adulterated with milk. *Barbarians, all.*

After two sips of the lifesaving drink, he scowled. "Did I not give you an imperative command?"

"Correct, sir, but you did not specify that I was to actually pour the laudanum into your tea." His great hand held up a tiny flask between thumb and forefinger.

"Too clever by half, you are. Equivocation will undo us." Just as he was about to snatch the glass vial, he thought of the last time he had dosed himself with the stuff. He had awakened with a mouth full of raw cotton, itching all over. Not to mention clogged bowels and melancholia. *Desire does cause suffering, after all.* His hand eased away.

Paragon drank the tea down. He pointed to his metal leg. "Help me get this wretched contraption on. I believe I shall attempt some exercise before resorting to nepenthe."

Mervyn bowed with a slight squeak. "Most perspicacious of you, sir. The mark of a man of maturity and good sense."

"The mark of a man who can ill-afford to be further lectured by his gentleman's gentleman, you mean."

"As you say, sir."

The surgeons had fitted a brass cup-and-plate arrangement directly onto his shin bone. Queue had installed clever clamps so that the metal leg would seal as tight as the hand of man could manage. When they had tested it in the laboratory, the device had remained snug even when hammered upon by Queue's clockie, a forty-stone behemoth named Walther.

They managed to get the leg in place. To Mervyn's credit, he took no notice of his master's creative use of the Anglo-Saxon language. Once on two feet, Paragon flexed the metal limb in all directions to activate the self-sensing gears, cables, and hinges. Exactly how it all worked he had no more idea than he did about the mechanics that made Mervyn function. If either of them broke down he would have to resort to fervent prayer, because repairing them was far beyond his ken. At any rate, tinkering with a clockwork man's working was a felony. All work had to be done in secret by the Ministry's hand-picked technicians.

Paragon clad himself in his favorite silk trousers, picked up the vajra, and went into the hall. He had insisted on converting two bedrooms into a single large training area. With wrestling mats, Indian clubs, pulley weight systems, wall-length mirror, and other amenities, it was the equal of any such facility in London. Queue had even designed a clockwork opponent of sorts.

He plucked a practice stick of sturdy ash from the weapons rack and belabored the air. He always began with a set of drills that kept the most essential moves of offense and defense embedded in his muscles. Many of these patterns he had picked up perforce as a means of survival in his years of Asian travel, pursued by bounty hunters of every stripe. Having an enormous price on one's head was not to be recommended, but it did encourage one to acquire a lethal set of skills, innate pacifism notwithstanding. Paragon thrust, cut, parried, swept his feet in elegant circles of avoidance, blocked phantom attacks with every limb, kicked out at invisible foes with strikes an asp would envy. He mixed pugilistics and stick-play with Oriental wrestling and the art of yielding. To the uninitiated he merely seemed a bee-stung Morris dancer, but on countless occasions he had walked away from a deadly encounter thanks to these drills.

Perspiring in the windowless room despite the autumn chill, Paragon set the stick aside and pummeled the heavy bag hanging in a corner. While employing standard English boxing techniques, he also struck with his elbows, knees, feet, even his head. He added the vajra, holding it in his fist and striking with the inch or so sticking out of each side. At the same time Mervyn flung hollow rubber balls at him without warning. Killers seldom worked alone. After years of practice with live partners, and aided by meditation and other mental practices, Paragon had developed a keen awareness of his surroundings. Though not a true sixth sense, as some of his more bruised fellows at the Eccentric Club claimed, it served him well enough. At times he would simply dodge the sneak attack or strike the ball while still engaging his primary opponent. Twice he spun his main enemy into the ambush, using the bag's own momentum.

Finally, Paragon defended himself against Queue's toy, a pulley-operated mannequin nicknamed Mr. Fleming which traveled on ceiling rails. Partially clockworked, it possessed a certain variety of attacks which it might randomly employ as Mervyn sent it hurtling at him in an imitation of an onrushing foe. Once it caught Paragon a solid blow to the ribs with its oaken foot. Twice it had almost knocked his head off with surprise arm sweeps. Only gymnastic flips and cartwheels saved him.

During one frenzied defense against a particularly devilish assault, Mr. Fleming reached out for him with lustful arms and a golden front tooth, warning him again not to betray their 'special secret.' As pitiful Michael Parsons flailed in the thing's grasp, tears welling in his eyes, it grunted like a laughing pig. Moments later Paragon found himself on the drawing room settee, tended to by a concerned Mervyn.

"Arduous night," Paragon observed.

"Indeed, sir. More tea?"

"With the added Afghan flavoring this time, if you please."

"Only if you permit me to measure out said flavoring, sir."

Paragon stared at the bottle for a long while, then shifted his gaze to the automaton's crystalline eyes. No bad dreams or hallucinations ever seemed to arise when he looked at Mervyn. "As you think best, old man."

As the drug began to relax him, his bliss turned sour with the usual remonstrance. *I am the worst Buddhist in Britain.*

*2 a.m., Brighton coast*

"*Cor! Can't the slimy little bastards shoot no better than this? Nearly put it in the sea.*"

The speaker's beefy hands seized the steaming metal cylinder and dragged it toward him. With a low sucking sound, the marshy mud yielded its odd prize. It resembled a small beer keg, only narrower and smoother. No markings could be seen on its silvery surface.

With a snort muffled by a thick scarf the man's thin blonde partner said, "*I'd like to see you do any better, mate.*" His unnerving pale blue eyes sparkled even on such a foggy night. "*From a hundred million bloody miles off it's a fookin' miracle they managed to even strike the right planet.*"

The big fellow's clouded eyes narrowed. "*Eh? What you on about? They chuck these in from a mortar boat in the Channel.*"

The lanky one backed away as a gruesome shadow appeared above his associate. His voice became much more refined. A hint of Ireland crept in. "*Strictly speaking, old cock, they lob them from a canal.*"

Frowning, the other man half-turned as something heavy dropped from the sky. Great scaled talons tore his throat out. Dark blood jetted onto the cylinder like so much spilled porter.

"*His time was short anyhow. Starting to stink. Resurrection is still an imperfect method for obtaining servants. Snack on the choice bits, then take the carcass out to the sharks.*" He rinsed off the gore with a flask of water from his overcoat pocket.

Leathery wings carried the dead load up and away. As it vanished, he poked an odd corkscrew-shaped key into the end of the cylinder where no hole could be seen. An instant later some interior mechanism engaged, and the end of the missile turned and dropped off. He stuck an expensively gloved hand inside and rummaged about.

The man approaching from his right found himself nose-to-muzzle with a derringer even stranger in design than the key. Its barrel also twisted. A vial of milky fluid sat atop it.

"*Whoa there! It's only me,*" said a southern American voice. A man in a gray military greatcoat held up his hands, a ring with the Greek letter omega on one finger. "*A mite jumpy this evening.*"

"*Stealing from monsters has that effect on a man, Captain Carter.*" The hand in the cylinder brought out a long leather case. Like the key and gun, its shape held an impractical spin. A tap at its end opened it with a hiss.

"*Gold,*" observed the new arrival. "*And diamonds. Your intelligence was spot-on, as always.*"

The Irishman pocketed handfuls of gems and small gleaming yellow plates. After them came a glass vial full of orange fluid, as well as papers covered in diagrams, written in a bizarre script which resembled the scrawlings of crazed elves.

Carter indicated the frosted glass container and said, "*More sanity serum from your distant friends?"*

His partner shrugged. *"If it isn't, then they'll soon be finding more dead whores in Whitechapel. Give me your fakes."*

In a trice, replicas of the precious items went back into the box, along with documents which also seemed authentic. They replaced the plug, and the cylinder went back into its impact crater.

*"Those plans will give them fits. If we're lucky, the device will take a few of them with it when it blows. If Dame Fortune had favored us, then that meddling Paragon would also have been disposed of by the bestial blokes I suborned. Ah, well. C'est la guerre."* He searched the barren beach with anxious eyes. *"You'd best get back before they miss you. Wouldn't do to get caught working both sides of the street. Let us go…before Sebastian's thugs arrive and eat us."*

## 3 / "A KIND OF EXCELLENT DUMB DISCOURSE"

"We missed you after the play last night, darling," purred the small man in the powder-blue velvet suit as he dipped a strawberry in Devonshire cream. "Had a better offer, did you?"

Phoenix Dardanelles so reeked of gardenia that Paragon feared he would need a deep-sea diving helmet to survive breakfast. The surfeit of scent made the actor's eggs taste like a French whorehouse. A very particular Marseilles establishment, in fact, where he had once prevailed against a pair of savateur assassins by employing a whalebone corset as a deadly weapon. With oiled black ringlets, slightly olive skin inherited from his Syrian mother, and unsubtle make-up, the wealthy theatrical producer was a walking advertisement for the love that, in his case, not only dared to speak its name but sang it out as an aria from every rooftop in London.

"I was otherwise engaged, alas," Paragon whispered. His laudanum hangover amplified every sensation. Even the delicate clinking of tableware sounded like gunfire.

"More's the pity," said Oscar Wilde, his broad face hidden behind that day's *Freemen's Journal.*

London's leading personality lowered the Irish Nationalist sheet, which bore a headline about the latest Breaker controversy. The mysterious machine-smashers stood accused of trying to blow up the Queen, the Prince Consort, and fifty kings and princes of Europe at her Golden Jubilee that summer. Now the more excitable members of the press claimed that Parnell and his Irish cohorts had conspired with them.

"Phoenix outdid himself for my birthday," Wilde continued. "After all, a fellow only turns three-and-thirty once. He presented a classical tableau at his digs. A bevy of handsome lads from the chorus at Covent Garden portrayed the Nine Muses. Seldom has art inspired me more."

Dardanelles let his fork linger on his full lips. "Inspired by the *Laocoon*, it was. Gave me a cramp in the…thigh just to watch it. Required six men, a pint of olive oil, and a pry bar to untangle them."

While his colleagues waffled on about the usual inanities that Aesthetes tended to indulge in, Paragon yawned and gave the Eccentric Club a look. Even though the club was undoubtedly one of the most secure spots in Britain, it would never do to let one's guard down.

They sat in the atypically sunny breakfast room, decorated in terra cotta and gold.

Over the door to the bar was a clock that ran backward, one of the club's two best-known symbols. The other perched above it, a stuffed white owl in a glass case. In its beak it held a large pocket watch with the hands set to four o'clock. Since the primary membership of the Eccentric Club, at least as far as the public were concerned, was actors and other artistic folk, the dead of night tended to be the busiest.

Paragon glanced down at the black onyx ring on the little finger of his left hand. Beneath the gemstone, in a hinged compartment, sat a tiny silver owl, copied from the Athenian obol coin. Greek dead were buried with an obol in the mouth as payment for the Styx' ferryman. And it was no coincidence that the basement of the Eccentric Club, mockingly called Hades, was only open to those who wore an owl ring. None but operatives of the Extraordinary Clandestine Service wore them. Oscar Wilde had one. So did that fop Phoenix Dardenelles. In fact, gardenia and all, he was the chief officer of the ECS, answering only to the Home Secretary.

*Hold on…that blonde waiter seems out of place. Odd eyes. Almost colorless blue. Cold as a wolf's gaze. Surely, I would have noticed him before.*

"Is our stalwart Paragon lost in contemplation of the applause he received last night for his Caliban?" asked Wilde in his deep voice. "Well-deserved, what? Particularly that 'be not afear'd' scene. Chilling."

"Oh, come back to earth, Monty!" Phoenix exclaimed. "You look like you're in orbit around Mars. Here's a scone. Forget your Buddhist self-denial and have a go."

Shaking himself loose from his suspicions, Paragon accepted the scone and picked up his knife. The conversation had drifted away from well-muscled young torsos in writhing tableaux.

"You look dreadful. I've seen better specimens of humanity in my beloved pussy's litter box," Phoenix said.

This was too much even for Wilde. He held up a large palm. Oscar stood at least three inches over six feet and was not in any sense a frail reed. That put him nearly a hand taller than Paragon and a foot above the petite Dardanelles.

"Phoenix, I beg you, some moderation. Poor Montague has clearly had a rough night."

Dardanelle knew when to drop his effeminate pose and get down to business. His voice dropped half an octave and lost its froth. "My apologies, Paragon. Eat, damn it, and regale us with the tale of your sordid evening's adventures."

Paragon, glad to have something to think about beyond lost comrades, related the events of the previous night. Since only this band of the club members was with the ECS, he kept his voice low. Wilde and Dardanelles leaned in to catch every word. To their credit they did not interrupt him with questions but trusted him to give a full and detailed accounting.

As Paragon finished the tale, Oscar frowned. "Who the deuce would risk his neck in an ornithopter in such conditions?"

"The whole affair had the appearance of a pressing event," Paragon replied, munching on the scone and praying it would stay down. "This fellow didn't have a care for who might see him blasting away with that bizarre pistol of his and had less of a care for his ordering the suicide of two of his own men, if I may use that term for those things. Took off again almost before their blood stopped flowing."

"So, you just chanced to take a stroll in the most murderous part of town, after midnight?" Phoenix asked, though perhaps not as idly as he might have wished to sound.

*Ah. Should have known that the old boy would see through that. Careless, Monty, careless.*

With a shrug and a sheepish smile Paragon said, "You know me, the funks I get into. I'm not the social butterfly you two are."

Wilde snorted and sipped his tea. "An understatement if ever there was one. You're without a doubt the most people-averse actor in London. How you ever managed to get onto the stage at all is a complete mystery to me."

*But not to me. Pretending to be someone else is much preferable to being Michael Parsons.*

"We cannot have you ambling about in a trance," said Dardanelles. "Despite the merely pedestrian danger of your falling into the Thames, there is something more bothersome to consider. Anyone with an ounce of sense can see that you are being hunted."

Paragon laughed. "By animals? What a novel idea. Did they have gun-bearers and native porters, do you think?"

"Oh, don't be flip. That is my portfolio. We have lost two operatives in the past week in suspicious circumstances. A supposed gyrocar accident and an overwound clocker. Now a Clandestine man happens upon a soiled dove with -- I can hardly believe I'm saying this – tentacles and is instantly fallen upon by two bestial individuals. Wake up, Monty! A year with us and you miss such clear signs of enemy action?"

"Enemy action, eh?" a high youthful voice cried. "Splendid! I've been languishing for far too long, all my sinews decaying."

All three men turned toward the new arrival, a crisp vision in silken top hat, tailcoat, and monocle. An opera cape lined in white satin hung from his narrow shoulders. With a sharp nod of his handsome head, he touched his gold-headed stick to his brim and grinned. Small-headed and large-eyed, no taller than Phoenix, a kind of lovable energy seemed to radiate from him.

The others made as if to stand, but the youth waved them back down. "Oh, no. There will be none of that. I'm in training, don't you know? Been out all night like this, in my newest incarnation. Fog cleared off enough just before dawn so that I had a fine view of that Orionid meteor shower the astro chaps are all in love with."

Phoenix sat down, chuckling. "Who are you this time, then?"

"I fancy I'm a cruel wrecker of maiden reputations." The youth, who looked to be no more than twenty, pulled a gold-banded cigarette from an engraved case and slid it between his lovely lips. "A cad, a bounder. Choose any repellant term you like."

"However…" Wilde urged.

"However, I expect that in the end the love of a pure woman shall reform me."

"In the end of the second act, you mean."

Their guest beamed again. "Ah, you know me too well, Oscar. It would never do for the scoundrel to remain unrepentant and unredeemed. I'd be torn to pieces by the outraged audience."

"Sit down, Vesta," said Wilde. He gestured to the empty seat.

The young man removed his topper and set it on the floor beside him, tossing his gloves inside. "Perhaps you should introduce me to the perplexed gentleman in the green morning coat. If he scowls any more fiercely, he may do himself an injury."

Dardanelles laughed. "Mercy, where are my manners? Montague Paragon, London's newest Caliban, may I present Vesta Tilley, London's foremost male impersonator…after myself, of course."

Only Paragon's iron self-control, acquired through years of pretending to be someone he was not, permitted him to keep his face still at this revelation. *This is the toast of the music halls?* After a subtle catch-breath he relaxed his features into the sort of bland man-about-town mask he had spent the last year perfecting.

"The pleasure is all mine…sir," he said, shaking Vesta's hand. For someone so slight, she had a grip he would not soon forget. Her onyx ring left a white mark on his knuckle. *Oho, so she's ours, too. Interesting casting decisions you make, Phoenix.*

Tilley plopped down into the chair, holding her head and body so like a man that after only a few moments Paragon forgot that she was no such thing. Immediately the table returned to a male domain, complete with rude jokes and talk of horse racing. She plunged into the conversation with all the gusto expected of a young blade. Paragon had to admit that she displayed great calm under fire. *More than I managed to do in Africa.*

"Oscar, where do you stand on the issue of the Irish and the Breakers?" She tapped his paper with an elegant finger. "I see that Fleet Street is doing its level best to implicate Parnell."

Wilde snorted with the derision of a tiger for a mongoose. "Fatuous drivel, of course. As usual, there is a magnificent paucity of evidence. Parnell is simply the most obvious target for the Erin-haters, being our voice in the Commons."

"Blame notwithstanding, that plot came damned near to succeeding," mused Vesta. "Sharp work there, Paragon. Took some nerve to disarm that infernal clockwork dynamite device while those Breakers tried to knife you."

Many disaffected groups liked to express their displeasure with the recent astonishing pace of mechanistic progress. The faceless Breakers styled themselves new Luddites for the new age. Their symbol was the Greek letter omega, signifying the end of the Empire if machines were not ended first. Using a clockwork bomb had been their idea of a joke.

Paragon waved off the praise. "I merely plucked wires like a frantic fool. Might have set the thing off myself in my ignorance."

"But you didn't," said Phoenix. "Lucky is the mistress of the good in our business, particularly while belaboring three masked lunatics with your stick at the same time."

Vesta wiped her monocle with a silk handkerchief. "Ambushing automatons, tipping over gyrocars, taking potshots at airships. If it had not been for the Jubilee incident, one would think them merely university pranksters."

"The chaps I fought were no callow students," Paragon said. "They possessed nerve and skill. Someone had trained them well."

"Luckily, the blokes who jumped you last night were less so," said Dardanelles. He laid his napkin across his plate. "Now, let us have a peek at your evidence."

One of Paragon's eyebrows lifted. "What, here and now?" He looked about the room for anyone with too great an interest in their table. *Such as that vulpine waiter.*

"Yes," his superior sighed with an eye roll. "And while we're about it we shall dance a jig and proclaim our every national secret in an improvised patter song." The whole table tittered. "Down to Hades. I'll have Professor Jekyll meet us in the laboratory."

The small dapper gent flew out of the room as if on fairy wings. More than one set of shoulders in the breakfast room shook in silent laughter as he passed. Dardanelles gave the impression of being lighter than air, but he was no pushover. Not two months earlier Paragon had watched him subdue a brace of surly young drunks in the bar and escort them outside, employing no other weapon than a judicious come-along hold. They had mistaken his elaborate and silly demeanor for true coin.

Oscar cooed, folding his newspaper, "I say, is that outlandish Tilley girl still being paid court to by every young jackanapes in London?"

"So I hear. Who would ever have thought that a pair of breeches and a waistcoat would prove so alluring?" She smirked as Wilde licked his lips. "And what about the stout Mr. Paragon here? Surely with that chin and scar he collects feminine sighs wherever he goes?"

The young woman posing as a lad kept on speaking, but her face and voice changed. While Paragon watched in fascinated horror her features melted like wax under a paraffin blowlamp. They rearranged into the Apollonian countenance of Sergeant Albert Brutte, blood from assegai wounds streaming from his body. All the club's background chatter faded, replaced by the screams of the dying and the crash of Martini-Henry rifles.

*"Run, lad! Save yourself! Live a long happy life and make me proud!"*

Only a miracle prevented young Parsons from blubbering until snot stained his tunic, as he had in 1879. For a long moment he sat at that elegantly laid table, fists clenched until the nails drew blood in his palms. Galaxies of stars burst behind his pounding eyes. Paragon mumbled an unheard excuse and fled into the bar.

"I say, what all that was about?" gasped the startled Vesta Tilley. "Have you any idea?"

"None," said Wilde.

"Poor man. I hope Phoenix has not placed his trust in a weak vessel."

At the bar Paragon ordered a double brandy and sank into a seat at a corner table. For a moment, his old guru's voice urged moderation and meditation, but the shade of Brutte chased that worthy teacher out of Paragon's head. He tossed off half of the drink at a single go. The alcohol's heat replaced the nervous energy in short order, as usual with his panics.

*Bloody fool! They're only phantasms. Throttle them with your will and act like a man. People depend on you.*

Feeling as wretched as if he had been carousing in low taverns all night, Paragon longed for a comforting word from Mervyn. Somehow the automaton could soothe him when no living human could. Had that not always been the case? Even as a young boy he had turned to clockwork dolls and toys. They had never beaten him, abandoned him, taken liberties with him. No harsh judgments ever came from their brassy mouths. *Perhaps we should just turn this dreadful world over to them. Let them police us, since we clearly have failed to do so ourselves. Giant metal men with the power to forestall wars and other foolishness. How could it be any worse than endless imperialism and crime?*

The earth seemed to stand still as Paragon considered that dream. Deciding that he could jump to Mars before it would ever come to pass, he shook the idle fancy from his whirling brain, stiffened his spine, and returned to the breakfast room. Dardanelles had also come back and stood beside Wilde. They held a whispered conference while Vesta squinted through her monocle at Oscar's paper.

"Ah! All better, then?" she asked.

Phoenix stared at him for a long moment, as if thumbing through the catalog cards in Paragon's mental library. Apparently deciding that whatever he found there could wait, he said, "Shall we all travel to the sunny underworld? All the best sort of people will be there, you know."

"Spies, assassins, inscrutable Asiatics, decadent Aesthetes, fetching transvestites... everyone who keeps the British Empire humming along," Wilde added.

Passing through the marble-tiled lobby, the band ducked under the grand stairs and into a doorway hidden behind a stand of ferns so high that one almost needed a native guide. A narrow iron circular stair took them down to the unfashionable part of the club's basement, where sooty men stoked boilers and repaired machinery. A few flickering gaslights threw demonic shadows on grimy walls. In contrast to the fresh morning air above, down here the closeness of the foul atmosphere reminded Paragon of a volcanic cavern near Naples where he had once spent three miserable days, hiding from the Cosa Nostra. He coughed. The air was hardly better than on the London streets. *No wonder the old Clandestine hands call it 'Hades.'*

At the far end of the worst passage, Dardanelles halted before a neglected door that read "Custodian's Office" in green peeling paint. Below that was the long-dead man's name: Herbert Lochmoor. He produced a strange brass key from his waistcoat. It had a webbed crystal at its tip. Phoenix slid it along a small section of the door's hinge side. Through some magnetic process Paragon did not understand, three sharp snaps released the mysterious inner locks. With a hiss the door popped open the wrong way, pivoting at the knob side. Inside was yet another circular stair.

At the bottom they encountered a door like that on the watertight compartment of an ironclad man-of-war. Phoenix inserted his owl ring into a notch and twisted his fist. That alerted someone inside to spin the inner wheel. Bright light flooded the cramped entryway. Paragon squinted and shaded his eyes. *This is new. Where are all the gas lamps?*

"We've made some improvements," said the grandmotherly, pistol-armed greeter with pride as they all stumbled blindly in. Her accent and complexion had been crafted in Bombay, as had her scarlet sari. She shut and locked the door behind Phoenix. "Good morning, sir."

"Good morning to you, Mrs. Patel. Everything tip-top with the new filaments?"

Patel, round and cheery, but with an edge of danger in her eye, grinned. "Aye, they're right as rain. Carbonized bamboo does work the best."

"That fellow Edison knew what he was about, then. Too bad he didn't live to see his invention put to practical use."

They stood in a waiting room such as could be found in any solicitor's office. A pair of ordinary doors with frosted glass panels faced the group. One read Director and the other read Research.

"Electric lamps," Phoenix explained, removing his low-crowned topper. "Fascinating things. Bright, even light. No smell or mess as with gas. Someday you'll see them in every home, mark my words."

"Who is this Edison chap?" asked Paragon.

"American bloke. Murdered nine years ago, December '78. Cleverly made to look like an accident. Shocked to death as he sat in his chair, tinkering with a motor. Never solved, though the police suspected a rival inventor. Brilliant bloke named Westinghouse. Leaped, more likely pushed, from the roof of his laboratory as the detectives closed in. Pity. Who knows what wonders they might have produced? Why don't you all go say hello to Queue while I check my pneumo messages?"

The other three passed through the Research door, better known as the Wizard Shop, to a cluttered laboratory the size of two squash courts. At scorched tables rubber apron-clad technicians worked at their arcane craft, most with goggles on their faces. Sparks flew, beakers and retorts bubbled, and blue clouds of smoke hung in the air. Paragon had little idea what any of them were doing. One corner was biological, another chemical, a third mechanical. A fourth held firearms and other more experimental weapons.

"Queue?" Wilde shouted above the din of the machines. A serious little fellow jerked his balding head at a door marked Tactical. The writer waved his stick in thanks and pushed through it. Paragon let Tilley go ahead of him, partly because a gentleman should do so, but primarily because he knew what was coming.

A bass-note *oof!* announced that Wilde had become the first victim. Over Vesta's head Paragon saw his hat, coat, and stick fly in three different directions. Fortunately for Oscar, the floor was covered in thick wrestling mats. His sack-coated bulk lay in a panting heap fifteen feet inside the door. Paragon took a deep breath and held back.

*You knew better than to go in first, Wilde. Being overly chivalrous to the lady?*

Tilley yelped like a terrier as she was snatched from view, pinned to the mat as if the force of gravity had increased five-fold. The cause of that corruption of nature turned out to be a five-foot tall Chinese woman, barely thirty years of age, who could have weighed seven stone only if anvils were in her pockets. A tight-wound black braid hung to her waist. She wore a loose blue silk tunic and trousers and sat half on the white canvas mat, half on Vesta. One of her legs trapped the victim's throat and chin. Miss Tilley's arm was stretched across the other woman's knee, elbow joint bent in the wrong direction to the point of danger yet not of damage.

"I say, could you help a fellow out here?" Vesta asked of Paragon.

"If I do that, she'll only thrash me as well," the actor replied. "As things stand, she can't come for me as long as she restrains you."

The assailant laughed like a crystalline bell. "Oh, doesn't that sound like a challenge, Mr. Paragon?" Her accent was pure Cambridge, without a hint of any foreign tones. Queue had arrived in England as an infant, brought from Shanghai by                                                                                    missionaries.

She rose from the floor like a sapphire whirlwind, keeping hold of Vesta's coat. Before Paragon could take a breath, Miss Tilley's slender form had trapped him against the wall.

"What now, Montague?" Queue teased from behind Vesta. "Your opponent has used your own partner against you? How might you rectify such a predicament without damaging him?"

He had known a test was coming, of course. She never missed an opportunity to hone him to a keener edge. Despite all his previous training, all the skills he had acquired from the great masters of Tibet, India, and Africa, she wanted him to better himself.

And that was why he had selected a crook-handled stick that morning…just in case.

"Partner? I scarcely know the lad. His bad luck, I'm afraid."

As he had expected, Tilley gasped in outrage and shoved herself away from him. That opened enough of a gap for Paragon to slip his crook between her trousered legs and snare Queue's knee. As Vesta continued moving backward to crash into her, Paragon gave his stick a mighty jerk, ruining Queue's balance just enough for Tilley to take her down as they both fell. Like some feral cat, Queue twisted, rolled with the barest whisper of fabric, and avoided the falling Vesta, who landed like a felled tree. By the time Tilly hit the mat, Queue was up on her bare feet again, moving away from the two overdressed forms and inviting Paragon to the center of the training area.

"May I?" she asked Oscar, indicating his fallen walking stick.

He shrugged and sat up, fussing with his hair. "Try not to get any of his blood on it."

"Your confidence in me is touching," Paragon said with a wry smile.

Wilde's response was to playfully mis-quote *Hamlet* as he struggled to his feet. "Since she has gone into France she has been in continual practice. You are fat and scant of breath."

Queue tossed the polished brown stick into her hand with a flip of her foot. As soon as it landed in her slender palm, she feinted toward Paragon's face with its tip and sent a cobra-fast kick at his thigh. Expecting that combination, he raised his own stick into high guard and pivoted on his aluminum foot, withdrawing the other leg. Despite his anticipation, she still landed a glancing blow. With some hope that he could catch her before she regained perfect balance, he tried a wrist cut at the crown of her head. It might have landed if she had remained there, but all he caught was the tip of her long braid as her head snapped aside.

His punishment for missing was a burning slap of her stick against the back of his knee. She had pulled most of the blow's force, but it stung like the devil, nonetheless. After giving her a nod of acknowledgement, he stepped away and hefted his own stick, mind racing with all the possible combinations he might try against her. The trouble was that none of them had ever worked before, so he had precious little confidence in them now.

*It's a bloody good thing that most of my opponents are unskilled hoodlums. If they were as good as this lass, I'd have to look for a new situation in the Times. Copying the Encyclopedia Britannica, perhaps.*

She tossed the stick back to Wilde and let him attack again. Though that might have seemed a kindness to an untrained observer, Paragon knew better. Their system of antagonistics was largely based on redirecting an attacker's momentum and using it to subdue him. *Oh, well. Let's not disappoint her.* Ten seconds after advancing, he found himself face-down on the mat, her knee in his back, that braid wrapped around his throat. Just as he began to see black spots and fade out, Dardanelles' voice rescued him.

"How I love to watch my children romp. Everyone dust yourselves off now and come into the laboratory." He giggled. "Professor Jekyll is fairly drooling to see Monty's bone."

## 4 / "ALL THY VEXATIONS WERE BUT TRIALS OF THY LOVE"

They sat in the biological section, awaiting the verdict of the Royal Society's top man. Henry Jekyll looked as though he himself had been created in a laboratory, as the Platonic ideal of what a great and kind doctor should be. Tall, handsome, barely fifty, dressed in morning coat and striped trousers, he clucked over his microscope.

"Most peculiar," he muttered. "You say this fellow stood before you, living and breathing? Decidedly impossible, yet here it is."

"What, exactly, is so impossible about it?" asked Wilde.

"Why, sir, the cells! The cells! I have never seen their like. It is as if someone elbowed God aside and tinkered with his handiwork."

Jekyll looked up from his instrument's eyepiece, blinking like a mole suddenly dragged into the light. "Whoever did this has re-wrought the nucleus of every cell, tampered with its very essence. Somehow, he has thrust bits of lizard and man together. A gross corruption of nature, this is." He slapped his thigh. "And deuced clever, too! Why, he has ---"

Paragon cut in before the physician could launch himself into one of his endless expository rambles. "Are there any biologists known to you who possess this sort of perverse skill?"

The great mind screwed up his noble face as he considered. "There is always some young jackanapes who thinks his insignificant knowledge of Huxley Cell Attributes gives him the right to break every law of nature. They pull pranks in the medical colleges. Transparent eels, winged goldfish, that sort of thing. We rap their knuckles sharply for it and they move on to worthier pursuits." Jekyll shook his head and waved a hand at the slide. "But this is far beyond any of that. Blending human and animal HCA so successfully. It requires a master's touch. And a ruthless willingness to thumb one's nose at the Creator. There lies madness and horror, as that poor Swiss fellow discovered all those years ago when he attempted to make a man in his laboratory."

Dardanelles and Wilde exchanged a knowing glance at the mention of the Frankenstein affair, for they knew the truth behind it. Phoenix leaned in close. "But if you were forced to hazard a guess?"

"I would not like to accuse a colleague of this sort of thing." His voice dropped to the merest whisper. "It would be like indicting a member of one's own family." The professor looked all around the cluttered room, but not into any of their eyes.

Vesta had coolly absorbed Jekyll's distracted manner. "Yet if my own brother was a known malefactor, causing suffering to others and bringing obloquy to the family, at the least I might consider suggesting that the authorities make inquiries in a particular direction."

Their expert witness sighed, ran a hand across his sleek head. "You are astute beyond your years, young man." Jekyll rose and shuffled to the door, where Mrs. Patel waited to blindfold him before escorting him upstairs. He turned back, pointing at them with his whippet-headed stick. "If I were you, I would visit the Royal Society. Room 42-B. Much wisdom to be found there, for the clever investigator."

He snapped his fingers. "Oh, another thing. That fallen woman with the unusual appendages? I am still most eager to examine her this afternoon. There is only one other case like hers in all of London that I am aware of. Good day."

When he had gone, to be deposited by Lochmoor underlings some three blocks from the Eccentric Club, a smug Tilley said, "He called me 'young man.' Did you notice?"

"I noticed that he could easily have given us the name of the blackguard who designs monsters like my tailor designs suits," fumed Dardanelles. "Yet he gives us this Royal Society run-around instead. Clearly, he's protecting this man."

Paragon picked lint from his coat sleeve and shook his head. "No, it isn't that. It's fear. The good doctor is terrified of what might happen to him if he reveals too much. I've seen that furtive look before."

*In my own mirror, after Peaceful Manners had done with me.*

"I'll put a man on him, see what's threatening him and what it may be making him do," Phoenix said.

Wilde plopped a bowler onto his head. The long hair he cultivated stuck out oddly beneath it. "Then we shall make discrete inquiries at the Royal Society. To see if he is being honest with us."

Phoenix agreed. "Do so at once. Take this handsome lad with you. Let him get his elegant feet wet. Monty, Queue needs you here. When she's done, please collect your dollymop of the wriggling appendages and interrogate her. I have a long morning of blasted paperwork. How I long for the old days of field duty, where all I had to worry about were Tong wars and stiletto wounds."

While everyone had scattered to their various tasks, Paragon ambled across the laboratory to Tactical. Instead of returning to the combatives gymnasium, he entered a room beside it. This sound-proofed chamber ran a good thirty yards long and perhaps twenty wide. At the far end were targets on pulleys. A cluttered workbench filled a corner.

"Did this unworthy one task white devil too hard, Par A Gon?" Queue asked in an atrocious pidgin accent, hands tucked inside her sleeves and her eyes lowered. It took all her considerable self-control to maintain a straight face…a face stolen from a Tang Dynasty painting.

"One of the days the white devil will turn you across his knee for a firm spanking," Paragon replied. The thought of that warped his moustache with a smile and his trousers with something more.

Queue oozed over to him like a mongoose on the hunt. "Perhaps this lowly servant would have her hands full, in that case."

Imagining how full his own hands might be in such a case nearly caused Paragon to faint from the misdirection of blood flow. He stomped on his good foot with his metal one. The pain brought him back to reality and the proper cut of his breeches was restored. His Chinese tutor could no longer maintain her demure guise and burst out laughing.

"You ascetics are all alike," she informed him in her normal cultured tones. "So easily controlled with just a hint of sensuality. What will you do if an enemy tries to exploit that weakness to advantage?"

"Close my eyes and think of England?"

"All well and good, until she slits your foolish throat mid-rapture."

Paragon sighed and followed her to the workbench. As he got to within four feet of her, she spun toward him, empty hand leading. In reflex he blocked with his stick, and a good thing, too. A steel baton two feet long snapped out of her fist and nearly broke his nose again.

"Careful!" he exploded. "It's suffered enough, don't you think?"

She snickered and handed the weapon to him. "A collapsible baton. Same principle as a telescope, really. One sharp snap of the wrist extends and locks it. Eminently concealable. Can snap a femur."

He raised an eyebrow and waggled his cane. "But not my manly shaft, it would seem."

"Don't flatter yourself. I did not give you my full blow."

Paragon bit the inside of his cheek so hard he winced. She patted him on the shoulder while collapsing the weapon.

"Here, put this in a pocket. Play with it at your leisure."

More biting, more wincing. *She must have studied with a master torturer of the East.*

Queue put on a gray bowler. Somehow the man's hat on her sleek-haired head only heightened her glorious face. She tapped the crown. "Here. While you still have that toy. Wallop me a good one."

He nearly choked. "Are you mad? You just said this thing could break a man's leg."

"And so it can, employed properly. Go on, show me what you can do with your burly baton, Mr. Paragon." She leaned back against the workbench. To accent her demand, she blew him a kiss.

"Priscilla, I am not about to ---"

With a frustrated groan she snatched the club away from him, snapped it open with a crack of her wrist, and pummeled her own head thrice. Anticipating having to catch her unconscious form, he lurched at her, arms outstretched. All he ended up catching was the knob at the baton's tip as she poked it into the soft flesh beneath his jaw.

"Do not call me Priscilla," she told him in measured tones between clenched teeth.

Paragon gulped. As Her Majesty was rumored to say to a luckless minister, she was not amused. "But that is your name, Miss Ang."

"Not in Lochmoor." Cold fire in her eye, she pounded the tip of the club onto the workbench, reducing its impressive size to a mere shadow of its former self. Paragon knew how it felt. "Not here. Not ever."

She tapped the hat's crown on the edge of the bench. Instead of the expected soft thump, it made a solid clank.

"Steel, between two layers of an especially-dense fabric the lab wizards came up with. In tests it stopped a revolver bullet at close range. Rings like the devil when you get hit, and the concussion nearly fractures your skull, but it's certainly better than the alternative." Queue turned to give a nearby wooden mannequin a tremendous clout with the hat. The poor artificial man's head and neck cracked with a gunshot sound.

"As a bonus, it makes a wonderful sap. Take it."

Paragon removed his own hat and set the new one in its place. "Not as heavy as I expected. Still, it might become a bother after a few hours."

"Oddly enough, that's what everyone says of you," she retorted. But the twinkle had returned to her obsidian eyes.

He gave her a wide smile. Queue making jokes was immeasurably preferable to Queue in anger. "Any other marvels for me to ogle?"

She turned to lean over the bench. It took her a long moment to locate what she wanted. Accustomed to multi-layered skirts, Paragon found her thin silk trousers to be one more example of her heartless cruelty.

Queue turned back around, face as innocent as a newborn lamb's. She held out an umbrella, a standard black-fabric model with a crook handle. It looked to be a bit thicker than the usual bumbershoot. The grip was covered in India rubber. A long, insulated wire ran out of the handle, ending in something that resembled a tiny foot pump for a church organ.

"This will make you see stars as your every muscle clenches."

"Really? How delightful. And might I say ---"

Without batting an eye, she plunged the umbrella tip onto his right ankle. Exquisite pain bit into his flesh. Spasms racked his frame, bright lights shot across his vision before darkness fell. When it all ceased, he found himself sprawled upon the filthy stone floor, drooling from a corner of his mouth, aching in every fiber.

"Sorry about messing your trousers."

To his relief, and annoyance, she had only been referring to the dirt on the flagstones.

"Surely you could have demonstrated that on a rat or some other vermin," he suggested in a sour voice as he took her hand and stood.

"Oh, no. I'm choosy about the vermin I torment."

*Lord, I implore you, please get me out of here in one piece and back to battling beast-men and ray guns.*

Queue invited him to examine the brolly. "The wonders of electricity. Storage batteries in the shaft, augmented with things called capacitors, oscillators, and a host of other gadgetry. You'll have to ask the fellows at Tesla's workshop if you really want the details. We stole the plans from them when he went into hiding."

Paragon peered at the thing but remained ready to leap away, as if it were a sleeping black mamba. Two metal electrodes projected half an inch from the tip. Clearly, they were the source of his late misery. The rubber handle served to insulate the user. But the reason for the small pump eluded him.

"Recharger," Queue answered. "Attaches to a boot heel and you build up a reserve of electricity in the batteries with every step. It will hold its charge even if you activate the quick-release."

Paragon snorted. "So essentially it's a one-off weapon? Seems quite a bit of effort for so little return."

She laughed. "Says the man whose leg is still twitching."

"Fair enough." He swung the umbrella in a few standard saber-drill arcs. The thing was not very maneuverable, but it would fetch an enemy a memorable blow even without the electrical surprise. "Will it prove efficacious even on one of those twenty-stone rowdies who work the docks?"

"Do I look like a tyro at this? It will drop a charging African rhinoceros."

"You tested it at the Zoological Gardens?"

"On the contrary, I relied upon it when I locked myself in a cell with a man who had murdered seven women with an ice pick. Somewhat more than twenty stone he was. In lieu of his scheduled execution, he chose to have a go at number eight."

"And given that you stand here before me I gather ---"

"Her Majesty's government has been saved the bother of a hanging, yes. We must all do our part for Queen and country, you know."

Paragon felt his body temperature drop five degrees upon imagining the delicate Priscilla Ang so coolly dispatching such a monster, armed only with an experimental bumbershoot.

"Why, Montague," she said, "you have gone quite pale. Have I distressed you?"

He swallowed. "Enlightened me, would perhaps be more accurate."

"I hope you have not been under the impression that I possess merely theoretical knowledge. The late Mr. Hallward was not the first man to succumb to my more shall we say, prejudicial, charms. In fact, he was not even the fifth."

A frozen centipede skittered down Paragon's spine. He stepped away from her without meaning to.

Queue saw his reaction but made no mention of it. A queer look came across her features, though. A mix of pride, longing, and disappointment.

Paragon moved to the firing range while taking a few deep breaths. He felt as if he had been lured into a cobra's lair. "Have you any other gadgets for me today?"

"None that are properly ready for use. We do have some modifications that should augment the performance of your existing items. Drop by tomorrow and I'll show them to you."

He pulled his pistol from its shoulder holster. "I should give my Bulldog a workout, while I'm here."

"In your dreams," Queue chuckled. "Ah, your gun. My mistake. Go ahead, then." She tapped his artificial leg with an elegant toe. "How is the new appendage faring? I hear you wasted no time giving it a combat test."

"That I did." He wondered if she knew what his plans had really been the night before. "This little lovely is a wonder. Light, strong, quick. Turns are never a problem. No torquing at the joint. No pain."

"I'm glad to hear it. Tomorrow we will put it through some rather more vigorous testing than you had before. And the wizards have already concocted several improvements for it. Tailored packages for specific tactical uses."

"You know how much I enjoy it when you play with me. How you leave me all hot, sweaty, exhausted ---"

"--- battered, bruised, bleeding, humiliated," she finished with a coy lip. Queue indicated a target some twelve paces away. "There. Blaze away, Renowned Agent of the Empire."

Paragon snatched his pistol from its shoulder holster and snapped off five quick shots. The Bulldog barked. Thanks to the new cordite gunpowder little smoke hung in the air. He recalled how hazy the battlefields of his youth had been, and how a sharpshooter had always been wary of giving away his position.

"Not precisely awful," Queue observed. His shot group looked to be about eighteen inches across, mostly in the center.

"What do you mean?" he protested. "That's about as well as I've ever shot."

"Which is my point. That tiny thing is good for jamming in someone's ribs and not much else."

"I happen to love it. What's wrong with it?"

She lay a hand on his shoulder and looked as if she were about to break the news of a family member's demise. "It's a lady's gun."

Paragon's manly chin nearly bounced off his aluminum foot in astonishment.

"Eminently concealable, yes," Queue went on, "but you have to be so close to count on a hit that you might as well use your sword cane. A 2 ½ –inch barrel! And only five shots. We can do better. Here." She handed him a large pistol with unusual zig-zag grooves on its heavy cylinder. "Since you venerate your blessed Webley so much, try the next generation."

He hefted the gun, which made the Bulldog look like a derringer. It was nearly a foot long. "What's this?"

"Webley-Fosbury Automatic Revolver. Prototype. .38 caliber, eight-shots, six-inch barrel. The only one in existence."

"An automatic revolver? Oxymoronic, don't you think?"

"The only thing moronic here at the moment is you. Cocking the hammer does not charge the weapon. You must slide the entire barrel and cylinder assembly all the way to the rear the first time." The pistol made a satisfying click as she demonstrated. "After that initial cocking the pistol fires, advances the cylinder, and re-cocks the hammer through recoil. That gives a gentle trigger pull, unlike on a double-action revolver."

Queue gestured downrange at a target twenty paces away. "See for yourself."

Placing himself side-on, Paragon sighted down the long barrel. He cleansed his mind with circular breaths and pulled the trigger eight times in three seconds.

And thus, a love affair was born.

He obliterated its center ring with a three-inch grouping. The weight and smaller caliber of the gun made for more stable shooting than with the stubby .455 Bulldog.

"I may have to buy this revolver dinner," he sighed. "Declare my intentions to its father. Even waive its dowry."

"Good. Now that you have a fiancé, perhaps you'll leave me be for a while." Queue's tone was intended to be cutting but did not quite succeed.

He extracted the shells and returned the weapon to her. "But you're aware of the rumors about Lochmoor operatives. Girl in every port. Love them and leave them."

"Well, don't leave this one after you've, um, shot off. It cost the government more than you make in a year." She set it aside. "Sign it out tomorrow."

"I'll just keep my effeminate Bulldog a while longer, then. Perhaps sleep with it under my pillow one last time, before our tearful parting."

"You do that. Before you go, have a look at this." Queue led him to an iron cauldron filled with sand. A rusty granular substance lay in its center. "According to your report on last night's incident, the pilot burned the bodies with a powder ignited by his flash gun. Yes?"

"Quite. Damnedest thing."

"Did it look like this?" She handed him thick smoked-glass goggles. No sooner did he hold them up to his face than a dazzling white light burst out of the cauldron, a near-copy of the beast-men's pyre.

"Aluminum and iron oxide, ignited with a magnesium fuse. Efficient stuff. I believe he's improved the formula to make it even more frightful."

Patel knocked twice and stuck her head in. "Excuse me, Mr. Paragon, sir, but you're wanted upstairs. A somewhat disreputable young man. Says he has news of a young lady named Millie."

Frowning, Paragon said, "Hair like a scorched haystack? A squint in his right eye?"

"That's just the lad. You know him, then? Friend of yours?"

"In a manner of speaking. He leads the Esteemed Punques."

The doorkeeper nodded, sighing as if the Huns were at her gates. "Then I'd best tell the club manager to put a guard on the plate."

Paragon took his leave of Queue with a bow and a wink, then returned upstairs, searching for but not finding the strange blonde waiter, until he stood in the club's cheery morning room. Its crème walls and gold wainscoting served to accent the French-made carpets and rose brocade drapes. These last had been pulled back to let in the rare morning sun. The disheveled boy standing in the center of the place seemed in awe. Munching on the last crumb of a biscuit, teacup in hand, he held himself as if he feared that the slightest wrong move would cause an explosion.

"Relax, Griffin," Paragon told him. "It's just furniture."

"Beggin' yer pardon, sir. Never thought to find mese'f in such a posh place."

The lad guzzled his tea as if afraid someone would realize their error and snatch it away from him. Sooty and scuffed, perhaps thirteen, he was tall for his age but skinnier than a fence picket. His hair was longer than the current fashion and so tangled that a comb would never get through it. Perched atop that dull yellow rat's nest was a tiny topper, a fascinator, like ladies would sometimes wear. It had not only seen better days but better years. A threadbare tweed affair, his waistcoat hung on him like a shawl on a broomstick. To make it worse, he had no shirt. Not a square inch of his bare arms or neck had been spared a covering of filth. Here and there a white scar showed through. So full of holes that they resembled musket targets, the young man's trousers were a loud orange check pattern that clashed abominably with his waistcoat. Strange to say, though, his boots were brand-new, just off a cobbler's shelf.

*Well, well. Griffin's done some business, and recently, too. Those boots cost him much more than his typical rate for information.*

For that was Griffin's stock in trade. Knowledge. Which, as every good spy knows, is power.

"What do you have for me, my man?" Paragon asked, treating him like an adult. As leader of the Esteemed Punques and thus answering to no one, he deserved that much.

Griffin smiled at that, revealing the expected crooked teeth. One of the lower ones in front was missing. "Well, yer said to come 'round if anything out o' the ordin'ry 'appened."

"So I did. Tell me all about it. And sit down before you fall down."

"No, sir. Me filthy arse would be the ruin of these fine chairs."

Paragon shoved the wavering child until he plopped on the settee. "Let me worry about the cleaning bill. Pray, spin your tale."

"Some o' the lads was scoutin' out the East End a bit. Never know what might be a saleable commodity. P'raps a bloke changin' his daily routine, not goin' 'ome from his employment at the usual time or route. Might indicate an engagement with somebody not his wife, eh? Could be worth his while to toss us a few bob to ferget all about it."

"Yes, you fellows are quite the businessmen, I hear."

"Beats mudlarkin', don't it? Anyways, the Whitechapel crew meets up with Millie. Sweet bird, that one. Never a kick or a curse. But today she's wearin' a reg'lar hangman's frown, she is. Lookin' all about as if she's bein' followed. Even more queer, she keeps lookin' straight up into the bloomin' sky, like a crackin' great bird might swoop down and snatch 'er."

"Did your lads speak to her?"

"She spoke to them. Spotted Manticore and strolled up to him like he was her best customer. Took him by the arm and said that things were followin' her and she needed help."

Paragon jumped a bit at that, his interest finally piqued. "Things? That's the precise word she used? You're sure?"

"Manty was real particular about it. 'Things, awful things, is after me.' White as chalk, she was. Never stopped glancin' about the whole time she talked to him."

"When was this?"

"Early this mornin'. We thought it were odd because it weren't her normal routine. Street girls tend to sleep late."

"What else did she say? Be specific now."

"Gave Manty two bob and asked him and his boys to watch over her place while she slept."

*My two bob, you mean.* "Odd, isn't it? Doesn't she have a cash-carrier?"

"Yer mean Pockmark Pete? That's another funny thing. Ain't nobody seen him in three days. One minute he's hangin' on his girl's arse like a second shadow and then poof! Vanished."

"So Millie's only protector, such as he is, disappears, and now she's being pursued by…things. Hardly likely to be a coincidence." *Particularly considering last night's little dance. Was she the target after all?* "Anything else?"

"Yes, sir. She gave Manty a message fer you. Said to tell you that she's sorry, but she can't make her two o'clock appointment. In fact, she ain't gonna leave her room till you say it's safe."

"She must truly fear for her life if she won't travel here to collect five guineas. Did your lads go around to her building?"

"That they did. After all, we took her two shillings. The Esteemed Punques is solid once the money changes hands."

"And?"

"At first they thought she was 'avin' us on. Nobody lingerin' about that they could see. But then Manty remembers how she looked into the air, so he sends a couple of lads onto her roof. What they found up there fairly chilled their blood, they said." Griffin paused, crust of toast in hand.

"Quit playing for effect, you rascal, and speak plainly. What was so terrifying to the likes of you?"

"Animal tracks in the soot, big as pie plates. Claws like a lizard, but it walked on two legs. Drag marks of a great whoppin' tail, too. Whatever they are, they 'ave a taste fer cats. Chunks o' dead kitties everyplace, all chewed up."

*Someone is violating the Law. Their father will not be happy about that.*

"You have done well," Paragon told Griffin. "Maintain your vigilance. Tell Millie to stay put. I'll cover her lost wages. And as of now I am paying for your surveillance." Paragon gave him several more shillings. "You'll get that much every day until this is settled."

"Blimey!" the boy said, eyes aglow. "I hope she has this sort o' trouble fer the next month."

"Well, I don't. Have you seen any ornithopters about, especially single-seaters?"

"Manty didn't mention no flappers."

"The pilot I'm looking for is oddly-dressed." Paragon described the flyer in detail. "Do not attempt to capture him. Don't even let him know you're watching. That gun is a horror. It nearly did for me last night."

"Don't worry, guv. The Punques are men of stealth, after all. He'll never know we're there."

"I do not doubt that." Paragon frowned. "I say, do you chaps know anything about this Riot Army business?"

"You mean them writin's on walls and trains and such? Probably some new ruddy gang tryin' to set themselves up. You want us to look into that, too?"

"No, concentrate on Millie's safety first."

When Griffin departed, he did so with an air of a gentleman, nose in the air and back ramrod straight. To Paragon he cut a better figure than some of the drunken louts and cruel cardsharps who counted themselves true members of the club. *All I know is that when I was his age, I crawled about like a kicked cur. This boy lives in the streets yet carries himself like a lord.*

Since Millie could not keep her appointment, Paragon had unexpected time to himself. He decided to take the gyrocar home, dine on a light lunch prepared by Mervyn's talented metal hands, and try for a nap. Some dreamless, drugless sleep to atone for the previous night's disaster would be bliss.

The horrid hallucinations tended to come in spurts. For weeks he might go without a single bad dream, then there would be several straight days of unrelenting misery. So far, he had suffered three days on this current round of nightmares. Well he knew that the laudanum was a weak crutch that would collapse under his weight someday, precipitating him into madness or death. And if Shakespeare's insights held true, shuffling off this mortal coil might be as bad as staying, his eager trips to the East End notwithstanding. That left Madame Bernays and her mesmeric sessions.

On the monorail home, Paragon marveled at the smooth ride and tight turns. Gyroscopes in each car kept the vehicle upright on its single metal rail, steam puffing out of the top. Traditional two-track railways were still in wide use outside of cities, but gyrocars were increasing in popularity due to their universal gauge. Overhead, large ornithopters and even more massive airships traveled to and from London's unfortunately titled Foulness Aerodrome. Since the great breakthrough discoveries in aviation in the 1850's, by Cayley and Stringfellow in particular, civilian travel had become more accepted. But the expense, coupled with the occasional spectacular fatal accident, kept most travelers on the ground.

Or beneath it. The Tube was a marvel, but the ever-present smoke forced many potential passengers onto the streets, rather than beneath them. Those who found the discomfort worth the benefits of speed and convenience were easy to spot. They wore tight-fitting goggles with large lenses that made them look like an odd species of fish. Over their mouths would be chemically treated cloth masks or activated-charcoal rubber faceguards to permit easier breathing. Some citizens had taken to these precautions above ground, so horrendous was the city's air at times. Many people kept canaries, like the coal mines did, to warn them of imminent breathing dangers.

But even on splendid days like this, Paragon spotted mask-wearers on his gyrocar. They were the flash young elites called Arsethetes -- in parody of Oscar Wilde -- who set fashion for their peers. And the current vogue was for ornate, vastly over-decorated breath-masks and goggles. Begun as a protest against government inaction toward setting clean-air standards, it had been transformed into wearable art. In contrast to the purely functional versions for everyday use, the Arsethetes' covered their masks in etched brass, exotic wood veneers, rare metals. Insect and other animal designs were popular. Many were bejeweled and were worth small fortunes. Some had been made into one-piece affairs, mask and goggles combined.

Absurd clothes went with the masks, of course. Toppers with colorful scarves. Garish pith helmets covered in pointless clock gears. Leather 18th century breeches with tall, brass-buckled boots. Shockingly revealing corsets worn on the outside of young ladies' shirtwaists, along with equally risqué skirts which barely covered their stockinged thighs.

Paragon shook his head at the pretentious youths and hopped from the car at his Soho stop. Already anticipating a lunch of curried vegetables, daal, and naan, he lost himself in a pleasant daydream and nearly missed the six-foot-long gray-green lizard tail that whipped out of sight around the corner of his house.

# Act Two

~

# The Goddess on Whom
# These Airs Attend

*Islington*

"You're late," complained the impatient metallic voice from the pilot's breath-mask. Wisps of steam puffed out of silver slots in the cheeks. As he limped heavily away from the machine shop door, he supported himself with a tall staff covered in South Pacific native carvings. It was seldom out of his grip.

The new arrival, a portly fellow with a prominent beak and salt-and-pepper side whiskers, shrugged and fiddled with his watch before tucking it into a waistcoat pocket. A sprig of strange red leaves was pinned there. "My time is not entirely my own, MP or not. There was a meeting of the Conservatives about the Jubilee affair. I was obliged to attend."

"I trust you are managing to maintain the focus of culpability upon the hapless Irish."

"Of course. I am not such a fool as to disobey orders."

His hand resting lightly on the mahogany butt of his strange glass-barreled pistol, the masked man let out a chilling chuckle. "Disobey? No, only inventors seem to do that. The list of those we have had to extinguish is long. Bell, Sprague, Hertz, Edison, Maxim, Benz, Westinghouse, Bell, Browning. Pity we've failed with Tesla, and that Nobel chap. Our distant friends would have greatly desired that high explosives not been developed. What is it about the mechanistically-inclined personality which is so resistant to control?"

"I shall leave that to the alienists to determine. Though I do marvel that so many dead inventors has not raised suspicion."

"It isn't difficult to arrange convincing accidents when dealing with a population so given to tinkering with machinery. Gears snatch at clothing. Fuel explodes. Wires get crossed. Dangerous stuff to be working with."

"Particularly if you stupidly tell our employers to sod off."

"Indeed." The white-haired man in the Norfolk jacket looked hard at the politician. "I hope that you are not about to do the same."

"Heavens no. But…I require more funds."

Steam poured out of the mask. Its owner said nothing.

"I…I understand our agreement. The gold and jewels were more than generous. But I may have to flee to the Continent. There have been inconvenient questions."

More steam. More silence.

"It's Lochmoor. The Eccentric Club. The same bastards who queered the Jubilee business. I fear that they are onto me."

A white cloud nearly hid the other man now. Still he remained mute.

"Perhaps all shall yet be well. But Dardanelles is being a nosey parker at my bank and with my *staff. If he manages to connect me to you, or to the cylinders…"*

The masked chin inclined. *"You are correct in your desire to be cautious. That is why we are eager to send that Paragon to his ancestors, before he does us any more injury. Would another thousand pounds suffice?"*

A long, relieved breath left the MP. *"Why, yes. And let us hope than I never need use it. Perhaps I am over-worried about Lochmoor, eh?"*

*"Their prodding may come to nothing. But it is best for you to have an escape plan. Come back here tonight at twelve o'clock to collect it. And take no further action until we are assured of the operation's safety."*

*"Of course. But what about our golden-haired friend? Your disappointing brother, after a fashion?"*

*"My…hounds…are on his scent, as they are on Paragon's. He shall be run to ground shortly and then his interfering with my organization will be no more."*

*"A bitter pill when one of your own turns on you, eh?"*

The giant mirrored eyeplate fixed on the whiskered gentleman. *"Quite."*

When the nervous politician had departed, a shrew-faced little man with green triple-lensed spectacles and a leather apron emerged from a sort of indoor greenhouse affair against the wall.

*"It's been assembled,"* he croaked. *"The toy performs splendidly, just as Fthosa Wold-Rarwe claimed it would. The imported tools are a marvel. At full size it will be terrifying. We have to check the projector mechanism is all. The cylinder's plans for it are more complex than usual."*

*"We shall field-test it tonight. It will give us the opportunity to see if our suborning of Jimmy's abominations has succeeded. Turnabout is fair play. Pneumo the good doctor and tell him to mix up his monster-serum again, and to scare up a couple of bully boys for Mr. Paragon's entertainment. If he escapes our gadget, they will do for him. Meanwhile, our other test subject shall arrive at midnight, eager to embrace his fate."*

*"Outlived his usefulness, has he?"*

*"As do they all. Our masters are most exacting in their expectations. This one has been remarkably inept. Selling mechanistic secrets to all and sundry for years. Seems to believe that the invasion shall occur before his malfeasance can be discovered. I leave you to your playthings."* His breaths rattling as if an engine was wearing out, he opened his watch and gazed at a tiny photograph of a woman and small girl. He brought to his mask to where his lips would be. *"I have a family reunion to arrange. My prodigal child has been hiding in plain sight, it seems."*

## 5 / "SHE WILL OUTSTRIP ALL PRAISE"

It slithered out of sight toward the rear of the brick building. He had it trapped. To get to the alley and escape it would have to climb an eight-foot wall. *Time to test the leg's running capabilities.*

So much extra stress on the gears and cables slowed down the mechanism. Covering the fifty yards to his property seemed to take an eternity, not dissimilar to how he ran from the Zulus in his nightmares. Paragon looked all around, panting.

The garden was empty.

Hiding places were few. Some pokes with his stick satisfied him that no one lurked in the shrubbery or behind the locked shed. Clawed footprints, long and narrow, ran toward the wall. The gate was still locked. And the prints did not come anywhere near the wall. Rather, they stopped ten feet short of it.

"What the devil---? Did a pocket airship collect him?"

Ridiculous as that idea was, it made him stand and begin to look up out of reflex. Something heavy fetched his skull a tremendous blow. An enormous weight, accompanied by a hissing, almost steam-whistle screech, drove him to the ground. By the time he recovered the attack had ended. Nothing but birdsong remained.

Paragon flexed his strained neck. He removed his new hat to see how it had fared. Sharp talons had shredded the felt. His assailant's bulk had put a barely visible dent into the steel casing. *What may have happened without this beauty doesn't bear thinking about. Well done, Priscilla.*

The kitchen door banged open. Mervyn's great mass filled the opening, apron around his waist and chef's hat atop his round brass brow. In one hand he held a silver serving spoon. The hidden plate in his other iron forearm had opened and the ten-gauge shotgun installed there scanned the garden. A glass gun sight hung over his right eye, which glowed dull orange in his merciless protective modality.

"Footsteps on the roof, sir."

"Yes, I know," said Paragon, walking toward the house. "He bounded onto my poor pate as he made good his escape."

"Ah." The automaton continued to search, the deadly gun aimed at the top of the wall. Something whirred and the eyes returned to their pacifistic blue shade. His cross-haired reticle disappeared into a slot on the skull. Mervyn's gun cranked back up into his arm and vanished. Now he looked like any other gentleman's gentleman, apart from being somewhat larger. "Tossed salad, then, sir?"

"Thank you. With the mango vinegar dressing, I think."

"Excellent choice, if I may say so. Please wash up. I put out fresh towels."

They were in the kitchen now. Paragon set the scarred bowler on a side table. "Mervyn, old stick, we are being watched, if not actively hunted."

The servant tore lettuce into a wooden bowl. "So it would seem, sir. Shall I remain on Defensive Alert tonight?"

"Please do. In fact, you should probably be on DA whenever I'm absent, until we sort this out."

After a splendid lunch and mercifully dreamless nap, Paragon changed into a charcoal-gray sack coat, matching trousers, and a double-breasted blue waistcoat. As always, changing garments required attention to those special items that a Lochmoor man required. His brass pocket watch, owl fob, multi-bladed pen knife, and silver stickpin were adornments that any man in London might carry. But thanks to Queue's mechanical wizards, each article possessed special features that could be of use to him in the field. The same was true of his buttons, collars, cuffs, hatband, spats, shoes, even the heavy belt buckle. Paragon almost certainly boasted the deadliest tailoring in Europe.

Selecting a straw boater as a replacement for his honorable but wounded bowler, Paragon took a light-colored malacca stick from the stand at his front door. Before venturing out, Paragon uncapped the speaking tube to the left of his door, a disguised periscope. He could scan the entire front of the house without exposing himself. A lever served as a remote-control trigger for the hidden scatterguns buried amongst the flowerpots which ran along the brick walkway.

Nothing untoward was visible. His hand on the latch, Paragon told Mervyn to send a pneumo to Lochmoor detailing his reptilian encounter. The valet bowed and said that he would endeavor to give satisfaction. Of that his master had not the slightest doubt. Any intruder unwise enough to attempt a forced entry would find himself in the unenviable position of facing a Mark 007C automaton. Outlawed for civilian use, they were normally found only as sentries at selected sites of national importance.

Escaping Madame Bernays' hypnosis with some of his dignity intact, Paragon arrived at the Ogilvy Theatre by six o'clock. Dardanelles had taken on the faded gem as a pet project, with decorating assistance from Wilde. As frothy as his supervisor pretended to be, once their theatrical business got underway the man proved as hard as a cast-iron bridge support. Decisions were made with resolution, schedules religiously kept, bills paid on time, financial negotiations undertaken with firmness of purpose. Now the Ogilvy's seats were again full.

Paragon reluctantly entered the dressing room. He unnerved his fellow actors. At first, he had believed that it was due to the leg. As a representation of Caliban's damaged personality and status, Dardanelles insisted that he perform the role half-naked, with the stump showing, like a wounded animal. Though incredibly effective with audiences, who always shrank with horror when he first entered, it had the same repulsive effect on the cast.

"Something inside of you creates Caliban afresh every time you step on that stage," Phoenix had explained. "With most actors a role is a mask they don, a false surface only. But you...your half-human creature's torment comes from within. You don't put it on like a frockcoat, you let it ooze out of your pores from some dark cavern in your soul."

*Hmm. I seem to be paying the wrong alienist.*

Caliban's makeup took a good while to apply. Two artists spent ninety minutes covering him with fish scales, gills, creased leather, tangled hair, crooked reptile teeth, and claws. In his contorted pose -- spiraled spine, shoulders askew, head bent, leg gone -- indicative of the monster's abhorrent birth from the demon Sycorax, little of his humanity remained. In gaslight and shadow the impact on an unsuspecting audience was truly unsettling.

*Like some man from Mars. Or even one of the beast-men running amok about town lately. There's a lovely thought.*

"Are we not Men?" Paragon growled.

The prop man handed Paragon the crutch that he used backstage. When he went on, he would crawl most of the time, though occasionally Dardanelles had him supporting himself with a crooked staff in mockery of Prospero's magical one. No matter what he did, though, revenge on the world that had doomed him to his wretched, crippled, loathed fate animated every fiber of his being.

Paragon stood in the wings stage right, stretching and unkinking his muscles while waiting for the curtain to rise. A heavy hand on his shoulder caused him to jump. It required all his self-control not to seize it in a joint lock and subdue the man. But it was only the assistant stage manager, Mr. Henley.

"Beg your pardon, Mr. Paragon, sir," he whispered. "Three minutes to curtain it is. And take a peep at the bird o' paradise in the stage left box first chance you get. Beautiful plumage, if you take my meanin'."

"She must be quite the eyeful in this assemblage. Everyone here is dressed to the nines."

"Oh, it ain't just her fancy rags, sir. This lady has that quality what commands attention. Spy her out for yourself later and see if I ain't tellin' the truth."

Paragon could just see the box in question, but he had little interest in some strange woman and put the thing out of his mind. Concentrating on the task at hand would be difficult enough after his recent bizarre adventures. The disturbing session with Madame Bernays had not helped. *I'd rather she had consulted me before ending the mesmerism without the usual memory block. Now I have poor dead Brutte's face in my mind instead of Caliban's thoughts.*

Brought out of his reverie and back into the world of Shakespeare's genius, he had little difficulty becoming fully Caliban by the time the embittered monster slithered onto the stage and croaked his first words.

The audience's reaction was palpable. High-pitched gasps from the ladies were accompanied by the rustle of hundreds of skirts as they involuntarily shrank back. So unexpectedly horrid was his appearance, so inhuman, that he hardly needed a leg stump to terrify them. Dardanelles had instructed Paragon to crawl to the lip of the stage early and often. Hanging over the pit, he delivered his first real speech straight at the cringing crowd.

> "This island's mine, by Sycorax my mother,
> Which thou takest from me. When thou camest first,
> Thou strokedst me and madest much of me,
>   And then I loved thee."

Spoken by such a contorted, pained creature, the words set the hook early. Despite their revulsion, he engaged their sympathy. Even while every sentiment told them that Caliban was a vile animal, their hearts bled a little for the circumstances that had made him so.

*Not unlike that mad Frankenstein fellow's tormented creation.*

Monsters of all sorts had crowded his mind of late. Adam Franklin, Frankenstein's seventy-year-old creature, hiding in a Lochmoor safe house in Bloomsbury. Consumptive Millie using her marvelous tentacles to sell her poor flesh in Whitechapel. Beast-men cutting one another's throats at the command of a mysterious aviator. Taloned something-or-others pouncing upon him from his own roof.

*That's a great deal of 'queer' for one man to encounter in a day.*

After his first appearance he had a long wait until going back out. Paragon hobbled to stage right to get a look at the much-praised feminine wonder.

She appeared to be made of brass.

Paragon shook his head and looked again. No, it was her dour clocker he had spotted, standing at attention to one side of the loge. The lady in question sat back in the shadows, only a slender dark outline silhouetted against the pale entry door.

He turned to head back to his dressing room for a sit. Just then the woman chose to lean forward as if to stop his departure with her gaze, as surely as if she had snagged him with a stout fishing line.

"Ah, Henley," Paragon sighed, "you badly understated your case."

Only visible above the waist, the vision wore a pale grey sleeveless silk dress, trimmed in tiny violet flowers. The bodice was low cut, and her magnificent bosom was bathed in a shimmer of translucent white chiffon which did precious little to conceal her charms. Her slender but strong arms were accented by long black gloves. A matching velvet choker with cameo decorated her throat. Just as black, her hair, clearly waist-length but swept up and knotted behind, was worn in a wispy fringe across her high forehead. She affected a tiny top hat, cocked to one side and sporting a peacock feather.

Spectacular as her expensive couture was, it was the mysterious lady's face that made her a swan trooping with crows. Smooth, even-featured, with a delicate point to the chin and lips full of honeymoon promises. Her fine nose ran straight, an Alexandrian wonder with small, flared nostrils. Those eyes, which seemed to have locked onto him even though he hid in the blackest of shadows, rivaled Cleopatra's for clarity and purpose. Yet they were not precisely Greek or Egyptian. Something else lurked there. South seas islander, perhaps? That would explain her decidedly un-English complexion, a rich shade something between café au lait and ghee, the clarified butter he had devoured in Asia. Never had he seen skin that color.

"You look as if you were assembled by a team of woman-worshiping scientists, my lady," Paragon whispered, feeling kinship with Romeo as he stared up at that tiny balcony space. '*Arise, fair sun, and kill the envious moon...*'

As if on cue, the woman smiled.

'*A rich jewel in an Ethiop's*' --- *great thunder, Paragon, get hold of yourself, man!*

Her lovely even teeth disappeared behind a condescending little pout. Could she read his mind? With what he had experienced of late, Paragon could hardly afford to dismiss telepathy.

He had thought she held a fan, but when she lifted one slim hand to her stunning and exotic face the long brass object unfolded itself with springs and gears to cover her features with a pair of powerful lenses. Opera glasses, yes, but of no common design. They seemed to glow from within with a man-made light. *Some sort of night-seeing device? If true, Queue would dearly love to relieve her of it.* As she looked at him from across the theatre, resembling a mechanical owl, the woman spoke into a tiny ivory box strapped to the inside of her wrist. A wax-cylinder recorder? Impossible. Much too small.

"My lady, though I admit to the insufficiency of the statement…you do intrigue me."

With that he saluted the overdressed spy and thumped off on his crutch to enter for his first scene with the fools. It seemed that he could still feel those remarkable eyes of hers following his every move, as if he were caught in a Mauser's crosshairs. Her tangy memory tingled his brain at inopportune times as he played with Stephano and Trinculo.

Somehow, he managed to get through to the end of the thing without embarrassing himself. The audience applauded with typical gusto as the curtain fell for the interval. Though many in the company offered him congratulations for the scene, he accepted them with only a curt wave of one hand.

*Bloody woman…is she a witch? Do they exist, too? Did her minions slip me a drug to make me susceptible to her charms? This is how agents end up dead, you know. Mooning over a skirt.*

He continued to fume while his make-up artist Jaffers touched up his elaborate guise. As he continued to think on the rest of his role, the snit began to fade, and he looked forward to dazzling his public again.

Until her note arrived.

Henley delivered it on a silver tray as if he was an aristo's footman. He nodded at the card. "It's from her, you know. Looked you over as if she planned to buy you and perch you on her mantle. Wish the missus would do the same for me. We'd never leave the house."

Of the finest linen stock, bordered in violet accents, the card read simply, "Lady Ambergris Kalmaar, Largo House, Belgravia." Nothing more. But on the reverse side, written in pale purple ink, she had added, "Mr. Paragon, forgive my boldness, but I have information which may preserve your very existence…and mine. Please deign to meet me in the manager's office after the play." The handwriting bore the same elegance and perfection of proportion as the lady herself.

Paragon pondered the note. 'Preserve your very existence'? An odd thing to say. Was it just a ploy to meet him? If so, the woman needed better advice. The only men in London who might refuse to meet with her were those who held one another's hands in Hyde Park after midnight.

Paragon continued his drunken, innocent, yet murderous portrayal of the wronged island creature. His brief session of meditation during the interval helped to steady his nerves. Now even the disturbing words of Lady Kalmaar's note, and her even more distracting person, could not deflect him from his purpose. By the time the scene reached its end, with Caliban's famous short speech about the island, he was more than ready to deliver it. Its irony, though, was not lost on him.

> "Be not afeard; the isle is full of noises,
> Sounds and sweet airs, that give delight and hurt not.
> Sometimes a thousand twangling instruments
> Will hum about mine ears, and sometime voices
> That, if I then had waked after long sleep,
> Will make me sleep again: and then, in dreaming,
> The clouds methought would open and show riches
> Ready to drop upon me that, when I waked,
> I cried to dream again."

*Oh, don't you wish you had those sorts of dreams?*

The play ended as it always did, with the audience on its feet, blistering their palms with applause. As he rose from his bow, arms about Stephano and Trinculo for balance, Paragon spared a glance at the lady's box, but it stood empty. He wondered if she would keep her appointment. But he also considered the play's final words, spoken by Prospero in the Epilogue:

> "As you from crimes would pardon'd be,
> Let your indulgence set me free."

*They'll carve that on your tombstone someday. Presuming you even get one.*

With that happy thought he rushed to remove his makeup, don the aluminum leg, and meet his newest admirer. After gliding through the adulatory crowd like an eel through seaweed, Paragon pushed through the door to Phoenix's office and shut it behind him. He put on his best smile and began to step further into the small room.

But the railroad tunnel of a Colt pistol muzzle greeted him.

The revolver rested in the fist of her clockwork servant. Decidedly unlike most such machines, the light in this one's eyes glowed a rich purple.

"Reginald, stand down, please," a warm husky voice commanded from the desk.

At once the massive arm lowered, tucking the pistol inside his perfect tailcoat. The brass man shuffled backward to stand beside his mistress, who sat in Dardanelles' chair as if she owned the theatre.

*Perhaps she does. Someone is paying for all this.*

"My apologies," Lady Kalmaar went on. "Reggie's a dear but his Protect function is somewhat overdeveloped."

Perhaps thirty years of age, though that remained at best a rough estimate with her unusual features and complexion, she filled the room even at rest. Her small, booted feet lay atop the blotter, crossed at the ankles. A thin cigar burned between slim fingers. About her bare shoulders she wore a black velvet, hooded cape, trimmed in the same violet as her dress. *I sense a theme here. Do you wear violet scent as well?* Paragon sniffed as surreptitiously as he could. *Hmmm. No. Something musky yet feminine. Overtones of the sea, as well. Can't place it.*

"Do you snort at all of your new acquaintances like a police hound?" she inquired, a smile threatening on her moist lips.

*So much for being a master of subtlety. Careful, Monty. She's no over-bred fool.*

"Merely wondering what your exquisite perfume might be. I've never encountered it before."

"You would be unlikely to. I wear no perfume."

*That incredible odor is just…her?*

"But kudos to you for noticing it at all. You just may be the first man to do so. And with this delightful cigarillo masking it, as well." She looked him up and down, taking her time.

Paragon held up her card. "You may be the first patron to send me a dire warning at intermission. An impressive flair for the dramatic."

Lady Kalmaar waved that off. "No mere show, I assure you."

"So I assumed. I do not take you for a flighty lover of actors."

She chuckled and blew a smoke ring inside of a larger one, her ripe lips ovaled. Paragon felt like opening a window to cool off. "No, 'flighty' is a word that one should reserve for a more literal use…say, when discussing masked aviators in Whitechapel streets?"

Controlling his surprise, Paragon sat on the corner of the desk, as near her feet as he dared. She made no effort to move them. "Strange. I would not have expected you to be a frequenter of the East End."

"And you would have been correct in that assumption. But I have associates who spend their working lives there."

Now Paragon chuckled. It did not appear to produce the same effect on Lady Kalmaar that her laugh had made on him. "That word. It does seem that its usefulness as a euphemism for 'spies' has just about reached its tired old end."

"Fairly spoken, sir. You are a 'cards on the table' sort of fellow, then? 'No mucking about, spare me your silly games.' All of that?"

"Not at all. I relish games. But playing the same hand too often rarely results in success."

"I promise you this is a game that you have never played before. And it bears little resemblance to whist or euchre. More like chess on a burning barge full of gunpowder."

Paragon feigned the appropriate mix of shock, confusion, and disbelief. "You don't say?" He tapped her card. "Strong stuff, m'lady. What should a poor actor have to fear that is of such moment that one such as yourself goes out of her way to warn him?"

Now her feet slid from the desk. She puffed on the cigarillo and stood. Paragon noticed that inside the collar of her cape she had pinned a tiny sprig of a plant he could not identify. Though it had small leaves that resembled an ivy or creeper, her odd corsage was deep red, as if dipped in old blood. Frowning, he caught sight of the same plant on the lapel of Reginald's coat.

"Oh, tush. You disappoint me. I expected better from the man who made me believe tonight that he was a hybrid monstrosity."

Still he refused to abandon his tack. "My good lady, you have the advantage of me. I ---"

"That I do." The sultry vision blew smoke at him as she advanced. Her walk reminded him of a panther that had once hunted him for two days before he could craft his escape. Moving to his side of the desk, Ambergris Kalmaar moved close enough to mingle their breaths. Paragon's rate of respiration was noticeably faster than hers. *I might enjoy it if I didn't feel so like a mouse being tranced by a cobra.* Now their eyes were on an equal level. She raised an expensively manicured hand toward his face.

*Istanbul!*

Training took over his reflexes. Paragon found himself with his back against the door, stick covering the low space between them and his free hand defending high. The woman had not stirred. Her winder-man, however, clanked into life, taking a step in his direction with a whirring of cogs. Its fiery eyes glowed hot.

"Stand down!" Kalmaar snapped. The thing halted its advance as if it had run into a wall. "Inactive!" Reginald sagged a bit. His head dipped and the light in his eyes faded.

"My lady," Paragon said, still in character, "you startled me."

"Oh, bugger that." She stubbed out her cigar in a ceramic ashtray. "Actor, my eye. A soldier in your youth, that's clear from your carriage. Quite the speedy reaction. They have you trained to a hair-trigger, don't they?" Ambergris opened her hands and spread them wide. "See? Harmless. No assassination tonight." With a shake of her beautiful head, she reached around the desk to retrieve an umbrella that Paragon had not noticed. Its fabric matched her dress, of course. "What was her name?"

"Name?"

"The woman who offered you violence in the guise of love. Naught else could make you spring away from me like a kangaroo rat. And we both of us know that you were in that Whitechapel lane last night when the 'thopter dropped in out of the fog. Don't insult my considerable intelligence by pretending otherwise."

Paragon lowered his defenses, both literally and figuratively. She had him dead to rights, after all. "I blush to admit that I did not know her name. Just some fetching Ottoman lass. Or so I thought at the time."

"Until she tried to cut your throat?"

"Garrote, to be precise. Quick wench, I'll give her that. Got behind me before I could blink."

Lady Kalmaar grinned. "How ever did you escape her evil clutches?"

"When a rear head-butt failed, I dove into a jakes with her riding on my back."

She winced. "What a charming memory. And she let you go?"

"No choice. The opening was only wide enough for me."

"Ouch! You certainly wasted no time in disposing of the threat."

His eyebrows bounced up. "A pun? I would never have suspected you of sinking to such foul linguistic depths."

"But it was you who did the sinking. And to fouler depths than I."

"You have no idea how accurate you are. Twelve hours I spent there, hiding from her employers."

They paused, taking one another's measure. Outside the door, the lobby noise had faded. Few people were left in the building.

Lady Kalmaar shrugged. "This has all been delightful, but sparring loses its charm quickly... particularly when compared to true danger."

"Such as?"

"Monsters that make Caliban seem like a tame kitten. And sorcerers who wield actual magic, not stage effects."

*Is she serious?* "Sorcerers, you say?"

"Near as. Men who have perverted science to the point of being able to laugh at natural law."

"We fly in ornithopters and airships. We travel across London on gyrocars. Mechanical men do our bidding. Are we not all sorcerers, then?"

"I speak of madness beyond the toys of city life. Those who hunt you have twisted natural philosophy much further. Which is why I must insist that you give me the items you scraped from the street last night."

"Items?"

"Come, Mr. Paragon. You have survived two beast-men in the East End and a third at your own home. How long is your good fortune likely to hold? The biological evidence that you secured. Proof that your encounter was no chimera. That aviator will kill to retrieve it. It could lead to his downfall. It will afford me a bit of protection from him if he knows I can give it to the police."

"He pursues you?"

"He does…and you, as well."

"To what end?"

"To your own end, of course. We are a threat to him. I because of my intimate knowledge of his crimes, and you because you could destroy him as you did those Breakers in July. Your success has made you a marked man, and not just by the aviator. The leading criminal mind in London also wants you dispatched. Anyone so feared by these two men must be formidable, indeed."

*So it was Breakers and not the Irish.* "

"As much as I would love to please you (*if you only knew just how much*), such things are not mine to give."

She rolled her amazing eyes. Paragon saw that they were either black, or so deep a blue as to be nearly that. "Ever the good soldier. 'God for Harry, England, and St. George', eh? Fine. I did try. Let the record show that at your coroner's inquest. 'Death by person or monsters unknown' will be the verdict."

Lady Kalmaar marched straight at him. A wave of her intoxicating scent nearly overwhelmed him, like a lethal tide might haul down a struggling swimmer. His hand twitched, on the verge of taking her hand and swearing allegiance. She slowed, as if completely aware of his predicament, and gave him an expectant look. When he mastered the urge and eased aside to open the door for her, she raised her lovely chin in acknowledgement of his will.

"Activate! Accompany!" she called out over her shoulder. Reginald's eye re-kindled. His heavy feet thumped a tattoo across the carpet. A moment later both had left the room.

Walking backward through the empty lobby, Lady Kalmaar warmed him with her smile one last time. "I do not exaggerate. The true Calibans and Prosperos will never abandon the hunt. They have deadly schemes afoot that will brook no interference. If you do not believe me yet, look no further than Parliament. You have men sitting there who love a far distant Other more than they love their Queen. Please call on me. I am always at home…to you."

Alone with her memory lingering in his nostrils, Paragon noticed that he ached all over. Every muscle -- some more than others -- felt near to cramping from resisting Lady Kalmaar. Did she want the bestial sample for herself? To what end?

Merely to deny it to an enemy? Perhaps for someone else, who employed her as a tender trap?

"If that was the creature you were alone with in my office all of this time," said Phoenix Dardanelles as he entered from the house, "all I can say is 'good show!'"

"Not alone, alas," Paragon sighed. "She had her clockie with her."

"Not necessarily an impediment. Some of them are made, shall we say, more accurately than others. I recall a luscious long weekend in Chelsea where a pair of them ---"

"This one pointed a barrel as long as your arm at me."

"Ooh, really? I stand by my statement."

"You would. No, this particular gentleman is a cold defensive model. Too quick on the trigger for my liking."

"That would have positively ruined the holiday in question. Fortunately ---"

"Your happy reminiscences will have to wait. Can you have the team in Research work up a file on someone for me?"

"On that Eurasian lovely? As your superior, it is my duty to observe that it's a sad use of government time, you know. Still, a woman like that could almost convert a sinner like myself back to the, um, true faith."

"I hate to disappoint you when you're imagining such a fine debauch, but this is business."

"How so?"

"She wanted me to give her the bone and skin samples from last night's escapade."

"Indeed? And how might she have come to know of their existence?"

"I gathered she runs some sort of intelligence network. The woman had enough details to prove that she wasn't just fishing. Claimed I was in mortal danger so long as I held onto them."

"I'll put some people onto your dark goddess. Her name would serve as an excellent start, if you managed to pry it out of her while she was ensnaring your soul."

"Lady Ambergris Kalmaar." Paragon showed Phoenix her card.

"Belgravia? Pity she has to suffer so, eh?"

"My very thought. If you install someone there, you'll have to put out a pretty penny for expenses."

"If it comes to that I may go myself. You know how I enjoy field work."

"Yes, so long as none of the field ends up soiling your cuffs."

"Touché."

"Is she at all familiar to you?"

"Afraid not. There are a few Kalmaars, originally from Sweden, but none titled that I'm aware of. Still, anything is possible. The wretched peerage in this country is so complex that you need a Babbage Engine to sort it all out."

"Well, see what you can do. She's our only real clue to last night's events. Oh, she hinted at a Parliamentary plot of some kind. Not sure how it meshes with this other business. Her precise words were 'You have men sitting there who love a distant Other more than they love their Queen.' Does that strike a chord?"

"That could apply to every MP who hides his sterling in an overseas bank. Or who has a mum in Canada, as far as that goes."

"No, she clearly meant some political business. Treason was in her breath but not in her words."

"That's different, of course." Dardanelles grew serious, fey guise fading. His voice sank low. "There are always rumors of that sort of thing. We've ferreted a few out. Those fellows generally choose not to stand for election again, then have tragic fox hunting accidents at home."

Paragon recalled Queue's remark about how often she had employed her 'prejudicial charms' and shivered a bit. "Is there any reason to believe that beast-men and tentacled prostitutes play a part in any of the machinations under investigation?"

"None of which I am aware. But keep poking that handsome nose of yours into it. Depending on what Wilde and Tilley discover, this Lady Kalmaar may turn out to be the stray thread that unravels the whole bally mess. If so, don't let that brass boy get too close."

"Of the two, he's not the one I'm most afraid of."

"Wise words. Women can undo the strongest of men, particularly when they look like your Lady Kalmaar. We've lost more than one good operative that way. Remember young Laughton? No, he was before your time. Envenomed hatpin, straight into the ear. She got him just at the moment of, er, completion. Never knew if he was going or coming."

With that charming image burned into his brain, Paragon left the theatre. The fog had once again fallen upon the city like a giant toxic duvet. For once, coughing like a consumptive, eyes burning, he began to appreciate the chosen costume of the Arsethetes. As he moved along Oxford Street the dreadful atmosphere thinned a bit…which was how he managed to spot the funny little machine before it did him mischief.

Only knee-high, it moved on the north side of the street, paralleling his path. It did not walk on proper feet nor on wheels, but on skinny flexible legs composed of stacked metal discs. Strangely, it had but three, an oddity of construction that gave it a curious rolling gait that defied geometry, burning his brain with peculiarity. The whip-like limbs supported a body that resembled a small boiler with a brass hood, two glass ports giving it an insectoid face. Dangling beneath it, a cluster of steely tentacles fluttered, as if eager to seize upon prey. *More infernal tentacles. I grow weary of the damned things.* Amongst them, larger and less frantic of movement, hung a segmented metallic hose with a green-glowing camera-like lens, looking about with disturbing sentience.

To Paragon the thing seemed an unnerving hybrid of praying mantis and squid. And it could not mean him anything but ill.

Whenever a rare passer-by came along, the dangerous-looking toy always avoided detection. By hiding in a closed shop doorway, ducking behind a dustbin, and once even hiding inside of a hinged sandwich sign, it displayed remarkable cunning. Paragon wondered how it was being controlled and what its power source might be. *Clearly no one can be inside the thing. And I see no smoke, no exhaust. Clockwork, then? Or possibly that novel electrical system that Phoenix loves so much?*

The little machine stopped, then skittered across the street as quick as a terrier. Paragon swore and increased his own pace. He decided to lead it a merry chase away from his residence. *It may be a mere science experiment out for a test. Or a reconnaissance scout. Or an out-and-out assassin. No matter which, it won't do to bring it home.*

A hard turn at a chemist's put him in a narrow alley. The tripod's progress was interrupted by his tossing a crate of ale bottles which he discovered behind a pub. While it tiptoed its three feet amongst the rolling glass objects, he turned left into the next street. His pursuer eased out of the alley. It looked carefully about, like a guilty husband sneaking home, before entering the street.

*Interesting. It cares more about discovery than it does for keeping up with me. Someone wants it to remain a secret.*

Armed with this new intelligence, Paragon knelt behind a red postal box to observe the lash-limbed enemy. Its housing swiveled on silent bearings so that the glass ports could scan the street. The little demon's gaze passed over his motionless form. As a test, Paragon lobbed a fallen chunk of coal so that it fell six feet in front of the machine. Before the black stone landed the dangling lens came to life, its green light changing to blue-white. With a hiss, the ether before the segmented snake shimmered like the African summer air. An instant later the coal burst into flame as if lodged in the center of a superheated furnace.

Paragon's eyes widened, but he took care to stay very still. Clearly the thing was attracted by movement, at least in the foggy night. *Won't do to anger it. Some sort of heat-emitter.*

Recalling that it had not seemed eager to be noticed by anyone but him, the Lochmoor operative abandoned his cover to proceed west at a fast walk. The tripod followed, maintaining a distance of perhaps fifty feet. The emitter hung slack, smoke oozing from it. Occasionally sparks burst out. *Malfunction? Could I be that lucky?* All the exertion in the putrid conditions began to tell on Paragon's lungs and throat. When he reached the Eel and Stones, an Arsethete pub full of effete customers, he mingled with the overflowing crowd before the entrance.

A few shillings purchased him a cheap but serviceable breath mask from the barman. Its filter canister hung from two feet of rubber hose. The cheap glass tended to distort objects somewhat, and disturbed his depth perception, but that could not be helped. Paragon left the establishment, coat slung over one shoulder, behind a pair of well-lubricated young men in toppers and expensive masks.

He crossed the street to head toward the thing. With dozens of witnesses in a well-lit area, he expected the diminutive demon to attempt escape once he came upon it. If all went well, he might track it back to its operator. But it was nowhere to be seen.

*Blast! What now?*

Stick at the ready, Paragon proceeded back the way they had come. Soon he picked up the deadly toy's tracks in the damp muck. One metal foot seemed to be dragging and dabs of lubricating oil indicated a leak. *Take care. The wretched wee beastie might just be shamming to ambush you. It won't do to have that in your obituary notice: 'Dispatched by a three-legged iron milking stool with a heat-ray John Thomas.'*

So obsessed was he with seeking the metal dwarf that he almost let the normal humans take him. The usual homeless lads had returned to the Oxford Street alley. Paragon noted their drunken snores and detoured around them. Within four paces of exiting the narrow passage, what little light that had been visible at its opening vanished. An immense figure blocked his way there. Then the supposedly sleeping pair he had just passed scrambled to hobnailed feet. One glance over his shoulder revealed stout cudgels and handkerchiefs across their faces.

These were no beast-men. Merely hired London rowdies. Still, Paragon did not quite manage to evade the blow aimed at his right ear. He pivoted left, but still caught it on the shoulder. His malacca stick clattered to the ground as his arm went numb. On his left the other man swung his cudgel at his exposed temple.

Paragon stepped inside the arc of the arm, tossing his coat in the man's face, and used his own impetus to fling him into his partner. With no feeling in his right arm yet, and his stick out of reach in any event, he had to rely on some particularly unsavory Parisian street fighting.

Whenever traveling in dangerous areas Paragon liked to slip on his Apache ring. A complex steel Medusa's head with a small grip that rested against his palm, he had removed it from a deceased French gangster in Montemarte who had endeavored to knife him. Before the attackers could recover from his counterstroke, he snapped a *coup de pied bas* into the knee of one with his aluminum foot. The vicious low kick brought the wincing man's face down to the perfect height for a powerful left cross to his jaw. Paragon's dreadful ring left Medusa's bloody portrait on his face as it put him down and out.

His opposite number tried to sneak in a killing blow to the crown of the actor's head, since the boater offered little protection. Sliding left, Paragon let the fellow's cruel cudgel spend itself on empty air. With the rowdy's balance upset the fellow could not evade a powerful metal side kick to his ribs. The hapless villain's body smote the unforgiving wall with a wet smack. As the fellow bounced from it, Paragon elbowed his throat and turned to engage the giant who blocked his escape.

But he had gone.

The one he had hit with the ring lay on his side, moaning and clutching his knee and jaw. Paragon kicked the cudgel out of reach and pressed him hard against the grimy wall with the false limb.

"Yer broke me knee," whimpered the beaten fellow in a muddy voice.

"And possibly your jaw, sounds like."

"Gonner give me up to the peelers, then?"

"That depends on how forthcoming you are."

"Ain't gonner peach, if that's what yer thinkin', mate."

"You prefer a cell? Don't look for prompt medical attention from the Metropolitan Police. Most likely they'll laugh at you for being unable to handle one man between the pair of you."

"Weren't takin' no chances. They said yer was a tough nut, they did."

"Who said?"

All he received in reply was a slow shake of the head. "There's worse things than a beatin' from a toff. Go ahead and kick me again if yer want. At least I'll still be human in the mornin'."

"What's that supposed to mean?" Paragon backed away to pick up his stick coat and shake feeling back into his arm. He had a machine to catch.

Paragon darted into Oxford Street. His new breath mask itched and peering through its goggle eyes gave him a headache. Only one vehicle was visible. A good hundred yards east a steam-powered penny farthing bicycle, of all things, puffed along. It towed a small canvas-covered cart behind it.

*What sort of grand scientific conspiracy uses such an absurd conveyance for its henchmen and their wonder-weapons?* Paragon had almost talked himself into ignoring the contraption when a last look changed his mind.

A single metallic tentacle slipped from beneath the wagon cover, hanging limp as an elderly willie.

*Ah! Never underestimate the ability of mankind to settle for the ridiculous in pursuit of the sublime.* Setting his jaw, Paragon set out to catch the bicycle and its weird cargo. Now he saw that the big chap drove the cycle, making the sight even more ridiculous. This would be quite the test of his new leg. There were certainly no other options but to run it down. Not a cab in sight.

He lost it in Whitehall, of all places. The dreadful breath mask proved to be quite the hindrance. *How on earth does anyone function in these abominations?* Horse Guards and the Banqueting House shimmered and distorted as in a bad opium dream. When buildings began to imitate ocean waves, it was time to consider going home. With a sigh that fogged his mask's lenses, he turned back north, taking care to remain vigilant in case his luck turned and the motorized bicycle crossed his path.

It did not. In fact, nothing caught his eye all the way home. Since his leg sang so out-of-tune, Paragon longed for a double gin and tonic as a doubly medicinal solution to his day's difficulties. It would also address the bit of old malaria that he fancied he could feel in his bones.

He made it home just before his leg gave out from overuse or his lungs collapsed from the Mask of Torquemada. His shoulder throbbed now. Mervyn clucked over him like a giant brass hen. So thorough was the clockwork valet, so assiduous in his ministrations, that he managed to ease his master into bed without resorting to the poppy.

While sleep knitted up the ragged sleeve of care, Paragon spent his dreamtime running from those three-legged war machines, dodging that awful heat ray. Only this time they were thirty yards tall, destroying most of London. Pure fantasy, of course.

### 6 / "LIKE POISON GIVEN..."

Balance...control...patience.

All three were needed in equal measure as Paragon stood on Queue's canvas training mat the next morning. Balance he needed because Queue had removed his leg to make some needed modifications to it. Control was essential because he would only have one opportunity to make an effective strike. Patience would permit him to calm his mind and allow the moment to present itself. Wearing only a pair of loose black cotton trousers, he regulated his breathing while remaining aware of his opponent. Eyes half-closed, senses reaching all about him like the searching arms of a giant octopus, he tried to project an image of weakness and torpor.

The short but solid Aero Marine George Herbert had at first attempted to circle around to Paragon's left, hoping to overbalance him on his supposedly weaker side. That had earned him a heel-snap to the thigh when his sparring partner dropped onto his hands to let Herbert's punch pass overhead. Wiser the second go-round, George had tried to sweep the taller man's foot. But Paragon had deftly hopped over the kick as if reading his attacker's mind. Two seconds later the luckless Herbert had been snared in a torturous twisting arm lock.

So now he orbited Paragon like one of the moons of Mars. Despite having just the single leg as a support, Paragon showed not the slightest waver or tremor. Untold hours of yogic meditation gave him the stability of a tree long rooted to Mother Earth. Heightened hearing told him that his opponent continued to move around him clockwise. *Breathing's a bit more labored than before. Catch breaths signal indecision.*

Subtle vibrations tingling up his foot added to the story. *His strides are more hesitant now. Schemes are being evaluated and discarded.*

Paragon's flared nostrils detected something he had been expecting: a whisper of a change in the composition of the man's perspiration. Now it gave off a sharp tang. Fear and anger. *Good.*

Herbert's paces grew more determined. Both knotty fists rose and began milling before his face, hoping to confuse Paragon as to which would strike first.

*Ah. Pugilism it is, then. A sound choice. But is that your true aim, I wonder?*

Paragon lifted his own hands in defense. He swatted away a pair of experimental jabs, then cocked his head to dodge a hard right cross. Hopping forward, Paragon wrapped that fearsome arm with his own and tried for the choke hold with his left that would put the man to sleep.

Except that young Herbert had learned from his earlier miscues. As Paragon reached for the throat, he ducked his head and let the arm pass over. Using the leverage provided by his thick neck, he smashed the attacking arm against its owner's jaw, pinning it there. At the same time, he grasped the other arm in a wolf-trap grip and pulled. This peeled Paragon from him as if he were an annoying cobweb. For a long moment, the one-legged man sensed only silence, peace, calm. Then he saw angry colors as he crashed spine-first into the weapons rack.

Lying there, tangled in ash sticks of varying lengths, Paragon observed that a meteor flying from outer space might feel the same indignant pain upon striking the Earth.

He rolled a short staff across the mat. Herbert stopped it with one foot. When Queue smiled from her workbench and nodded assent, he picked up the stick and rushed at Paragon, screaming like the proverbial banshee.

It worked only too well.

Stunned, worn raw from two late nights in a row, covered in fresh injuries, and still suffering from the lingering effects of his alienist's rough treatment the day before, Paragon's composure crumbled. His vision narrowed until all he saw was a near-naked giant rushing him with an assegai. *You won't take me, bloody savages! I'll not join poor Albert! I'll show you some goddamned grace under pressure, I will!*

The hapless George Herbert never had a chance. His descending blow landed smartly where Paragon lay. Unluckily for him the frenzied operative slid forward so that the stick struck nothing. Flat on his back, young Michael Parsons drove his only heel into the big Zulu's sternum. Like a sixteen-stone mortar shell, Herbert flew halfway across the mat. A bass-note boom shook the training room as he landed. Before he could recover his wits or his breath the shrieking Paragon had scooted across the mat to belabor him with his own fallen staff.

"One for Brutte! And for Sergeant Bigglesworth! And Curran! And Weems!" He grunted with the effort of raising the stick and whipping it at Herbert's face and body. With each name he shouted the vengeful thump caromed off the walls.

Strong hands clutched at him, hauled him from the bleeding, motionless form. He writhed beneath the weight of many hostile figures, no doubt reinforcements from his assailant's marauding impi. Some sort of unyielding fabric encased him until he could move no more. *My winding sheet, no doubt. I've fallen to the dusky hordes at last. I've come to join you, Albert! Sorry for the long wait!*

"What the devil happened?" demanded Phoenix, his sartorial perfection marred with the strain of subduing his operative. Beside him lay Oscar Wilde, who used his considerable bulk -- and his cape – to render Paragon immobile.

Queue knelt beside the savaged Herbert. "No idea. The sparring was sharp, no doubt of that, but why he lost all control ---"

Vesta motioned toward a knot of curious researchers who had come from the lab. "You! Fetch a litter! And you, send word to the infirmary."

Like a disturbed anthill, the room burst into furious movement. In perhaps two minutes the luckless Herbert was whisked away to the aid station. Paragon was kept immobile by Tilley and Wilde. Back at the weapons workstation, Dardanelles and Queue conversed in whispered concern.

"Sorry business, this," said Phoenix, biting his lower lip. "He seemed to be progressing so nicely. You saw the whole affair?"

"He betrayed a certain anxiety at first, but once the training commenced, he settled into his usual serenity. It is only in battle that he is ever at ease." She squinted hard through her spectacles at him. "This could have been even more tragic, you know. What if we had been handling firearms? I need to know what his torments are, else I cannot work with him."

The small man fluttered his kid-gloved hands. "Oh, very well. He has been seeing an alienist. She aids him with certain…issues of a passionate nature. Paragon was in the Zulu Wars, you know."

"Many men can say the same and none of them ---"

"None of them survived Isandlwana, I'll wager."

Queue's eyes widened a bit. "Ah."

"Naturally, I have been monitoring the sessions. Apparently, he was saved more than once by a dear friend who fell on that dreadful field. His only friend, to hear her tell it. Worshiped him like a father. Enormous guilt for surviving. Yesterday the alienist mesmerized him, made him relive the whole bally thing, and then left him with the fresh memory of it seared into his unwelcoming brain."

An unfamiliar maternal twitch flashed across Queue's face. "I see. That sort of thing has broken stronger men."

"So that, in addition to the usual Lochmoor stresses, plus some of the oddities we have been experiencing of late…not to mention crawling about my stage each night portraying Caliban. It's a wonder he hasn't flung himself into the Thames."

Queue raised a finger. "Perhaps he has been doing just that, but in his own way."

"How do you mean?"

"I mean every month or so he comes in with significant battle damage, even when no operation is afoot. Bruises, cuts, the odd puncture."

"You believe he has been courting death in combat, rather than by suicide?"

"I do. Perhaps we should not leave him alone until he sorts himself out."

"Did you not see what he did to our poor little Georgie? Nearly pulped the man. You desire me to just send him on his merry way to wreak more carnage?"

"Leaving him in some madhouse to rot will do no one any good. How long do you think he would last in inactivity? With nothing to do but dwell on his supposed culpability?"

Dardanelles fussed with his velvet lapel. "Your point is taken. Truth be told, I did know that he was damaged goods when I recruited him. And damn me, the man has a knack for slicing through Gordian knots." He let out an almost girlish giggle. "Do you recall the Myddleton affair? How no one had any inkling that the cipher was based on the addresses of brothels?"

That earned a rare smile from Queue. "Until he underwent heroic…research to make the connection."

"All the more remarkable since he avoids sexual congress except in the line of duty. How he avoided the pox is a complete mystery. Loins of iron."

"Not quite iron. I recall him emptying ice from the club's champagne buckets and slyly dumping it into his trousers."

"Ah! So that's why my champers was so deuced vile last year. I suppose now I must apologize for venting my wrath on the sommelier."

As they moved toward the stricken operative, Phoenix frowned. "We daren't send him out on his own. Not until we assure ourselves that he won't explode again."

"Agreed. Partner him with Wilde. Keep him focused on the task at hand and I believe he will be less likely to allow his emotions to subvert his judgment again. Idle hands, devil's playground, all that."

"You say 'devil's playground' like it is a bad thing, darling Priscilla."

"No, calling me Priscilla is a bad thing. Do try it again."

Paragon felt as if he had been tagged by Queue's diabolical electric bumbershoot. Every sinew strained, twisted, and complaining. It seemed as if his throat had been scoured with a wire brush. *What just happened? Where's George? And whose blood are they mopping up?*

A forest of woolen legs rose about him, interrupted only by Queue's slim silken ones. Concerned faces stared down at him. One was his mother in a green plaid dress, a concerned look in her dead eyes, but she faded like mist as he spoke.

"What have I done now?"

Vesta Tilley squinted at him through her monocle. "No memory of it then?"

"What might it be? I recall being tossed across the mat like a puppet, then waking up here with you lot glaring at me as if I had dropped in from another planet."

"Well, you did behave as abominably as some otherworldly creature might," Wilde informed him.

Queue explained precisely what had happened. By the time she finished relating the sad events Paragon's head lay atop his crossed arms. "Bloody hell," he mumbled.

Phoenix tried his usual tack. "Quite. And I may be out a considerable expenditure for a new training mat. Perhaps I shall take it from your salary, Mr. Paragon. Now if you are quite recovered from bashing my operatives about, I would appreciate it if you would get back into the game. The blasted world won't save itself, you know."

Wilde and Tilley hauled Paragon to a wobbly standing position. They asked him a few more probing questions, then left him in Queue's care. Once they had left the training room, she lay a warm hand along his cheek.

"Not good," she sighed.

"So I hear," he said, voice hoarse from screaming at Herbert. "Whatever will you do with me? The birch rod this time?"

She dug her thumb into his cheek just below his left eye, until he winced. "I suggest you embrace sobriety right now. Phoenix nearly had you put away. Would have done, too, if I had not counseled otherwise."

Paragon lay a rough hand across hers. His trembled a bit. "Too good to me, you are."

"Let us see if you sing the same tune when next we spar, infuriating man."

Supported by Queue, he hopped over to the workbench to don his new leg. When he hefted it, he frowned and cocked his head at her. "Seems a trifle heavier. What hath God wrought now, I wonder?"

"If by 'God' you mean the lads in the Wizard Shop, I'll explain later. We need to get you reassembled and dressed. Oscar is waiting for you upstairs. He's to be your nanny until Phoenix trusts that you won't go berserk on another innocent."

After he had dressed – a Mervyn-approved ensemble of blue frock coat, gray trousers, spatterdashes, crème waistcoat, and a new armored bowler – he presented himself back to Queue for her approval before departing. She brushed him down and picked at lint and ash as if sending him off to the City to pore over ledgers. Paragon said as much to her.

"Indeed. However, when Mr. Paragon sallies forth on his typical job of work, that might involve reanimated badgers, or submarine saboteurs assaulting the trans-Atlantic cable."

"Those badgers were quite the handful, weren't they?"

She rolled her eyes at the shared memory of one of their most absurd cases. "And on the off chance that they return, let us examine the delightful refinements which modern science has added to Her Majesty's limb. Try not to wreck the thing before luncheon, eh?"

After cutting off Paragon's next attempted witticism, Queue explained how to employ the new weaponry and other toys his metal leg now contained.

"Added less than two pounds, actually. We simplified the mechanism while maintaining proper function."

Paragon swiveled his head about, searching the work area. "Now that we speak of proper function, where's my new mistress?"

She fetched the Webley-Fosbury pistol from a drawer and presented it to him with a small flourish. "Why do I feel as if I should have wrapped it with a velvet bow?"

"I'm a bit put out that you didn't." He hefted it, then stroked its barrel as if touching a new lover for the first time.

Queue's mouth turned up at one corner. "Should I leave you two alone for a bit?"

"We'll leave that discussion for another day. Oscar is waiting…impatiently, I expect. "

Paragon scooped up his stick, a proper brass-headed combat model this time, containing as many surprises as his leg, and eased toward the door. Halfway there he spun on one expensive shoe. "What do you know of communication mechanistics?"

Her brows lifted at that. "Quite an expansive and daunting subject. Please specify."

"At the theatre last night someone spoke into a box on her wrist. It appeared to be made of ivory and polished brass. Almost like a tiny steamer trunk, perhaps three inches long and two wide."

Queue's brows moved in the opposite direction. "There have been wireless telegraph experiments, but with nothing like so small a housing. And no cables? No evident power source?"

"None."

"If a true wireless, then she has achieved quite the feat. Will you see her again, do you think?"

Paragon's tiny hesitation brought forth a cackle, that most rare of Queue's expressions. "Say no more! She is clearly in Paragon's gun sight. May your beaters soon drive her within range. Try not to leave her so exhausted that she cannot speak of her mysterious bauble."

Aware that he blushed like a maiden, Paragon once more moved to the exit. But again, he whirled to face Queue.

"You'll never get to your assignment at this rate," she observed. "I begin to think you are about to declare your intentions to me."

He felt himself flush even hotter at that. *Infernal woman! Have I not suffered enough today?* "My intention is to suggest a rationale for her speaking into that thing." Quickly he told her everything pertinent about the odd events of the previous evening.

"Amazing. I agree that it would strain credulity to believe that this Lady Kalmaar would warn you off, then a war machine would promptly appear."

"Might she have been giving instructions to the device's operator? Or controlling the thing directly somehow?"

"Anything is possible. And you say the machine clearly saw you, and fired a heat emitter?"

"Oh, yes. And unless some clever wizard has managed to miniaturize people as well as machinery, it had to be controlled from afar."

"Meaning he must have been following you the entire time, keeping both you and his mechanical pest in sight."

Paragon shook his head. "Not possible. I would have spotted him. Too much running, too many changes of direction, not enough places to hide."

"Then the device must have some sort of wireless spyglass, as well. I confess that I am positively enthralled with this achievement." Queue's face bore much the same look that Paragon's had when she had given him the Webley to fondle.

"You bloody well would have sung a different tune last night while it skittered after you with that blasted volcano-gun."

"Perhaps. Still, if you come across it again, try to take notes while dodging thermal death, eh? As a favor to me?"

"I shall keep that in mind." Paragon saluted her with the golden head of his stick and backed toward the door for the third time. "And I really am going now, before Wilde eats his absurd buttonhole in frustration."

"Happy hunting." She tossed him a tangle of black leather straps and buckles which he snared with his stick. "You'll need this. The Bulldog's holster will never serve for that howitzer. Four full clips are already in it." Queue snapped her fingers. "Oh! And take this." The fearsome electrified umbrella flew at him. "The weather around you can be unpredictable."

He plucked it from the air and grinned at her. "Other mothers send their little boys off to school with a sack lunch and a fresh pencil."

After donning the new holster and stowing the Webley in it, Paragon made his way up to the Eccentric Club lobby. There Wilde did indeed seem ready to gnaw on the ridiculous white lily adorning the lapel of his equally silly green velvet suit. Only his splendid black overcoat with beaver trim redeemed it. A magnificent silken top hat more suited to the opera than the street completed his ensemble.

"Just to be clear, some of us to have other jobs to do," he sniffed. "My magazine does not edit itself."

"Who dresses you?" Paragon shot back. "Lewis Carroll?"

"Says the chap with a stick **and** an umbrella. I may be occasionally overdressed, but I make up for it by being immensely overeducated."

"Oh, that's good. You should write that down and put it in one of your plays."

"It is splendid, isn't it? Perhaps I shall do that very thing. Whatever is required to elevate the tone of the vulgar babbling that passes for civilized discourse in this city."

"You know, it's that supercilious attitude and scandalous approach to your fellow citizens that has everyone talking about you."

"The only thing worse than being talked about is not being talked about."

"If I'm to be forced to endure listening to you quote yourself, this will prove to be an onerous trip. Where are we going, anyway?"

Wilde shuddered. "Islington."

"And why Islington?" Paragon asked while waving down a cab. "Is the Empire threatened from that sleepy quarter?"

"Only by their taste in architecture," Wilde replied. "But a significant personage has turned up dead there and our illustrious Mr. Dardanelles insists that we make inquiries before Scotland Yard do."

Both men climbed into a glass-fronted mechani-growler. As it lurched forward Paragon continued questioning Wilde about their mission. "And just who has shuffled so precipitately off this mortal coil? He must be someone of note to catch the interest of Lochmoor."

"My understanding is that we are not so concerned by the life of the departed and unlamented MP Grigsby as we are by the manner of his leave-taking," Wilde raised an eyebrow at Paragon. "And speaking of sudden death, I trust that you are not likely to assail me in a frothing fit? I would keen like a bereaved mother at an Irish wake if this fine coat should be creased."

*If I test out my new Webley on him, will any jury in England convict me?*

"Upon my honor as a British gentleman, I swear that I will only venture into the realm of murderous insanity when not in your presence."

"Thank you."

"The sole caveat being that if you ever wear that suit around me again, all bets are off."

"Philistine."

"I have been called worse." *Most often by Peaceful Manners.* "Now, our poor victim?"

Wilde consulted a small red leather notebook. "Samuel Grigsby, sixty-two years of age, father of four. Minor but noisy pro-industry, anti-Irish back-bencher, known for kicking up many a vicious row in Parliament against Parnell and anyone with an O' before his name. Incessantly blaming them for Breaker attacks. By the way, the silence you are hearing is me not mourning his passing."

"You said the manner of his death seemed peculiar. How so?"

The light from fog and chimney smoke left little light for reading. Wilde put his nose nearly against the leaves of the book and squinted. "Constable reports the victim was covered in black dust. Unable to determine the makeup of this material. Decidedly not coal dust. Victim bore no marks of violence upon his person, but a hideous expression of terror was frozen onto his features."

Wilde pocketed his notebook. "That was enough for the estimable Mr. Dardanelles to dispatch one supremely-talented author and one promising stage performer to see what they could see."

"Meaning it sounded a simple enough inquiry to send said performer off as a test of his mental and emotional faculties."

"A safe bet, as the lower orders are wont to say."

Upon disembarking from the clock-horse carriage, they found themselves before a soot-stained brick blacksmith's shop. Wilde wrinkled his nose at the uncollected manure and refuse at their feet. A helmeted constable with impressive side whiskers met them at the shop entrance. Two of his comrades stood on either side to shoo away a crowd of curious citizens.

"Be you the blokes...er, I mean gentlemen, I was instructed to expect? Me sergeant said we was to give you every consideration and support."

"A wise man, your sergeant," Paragon observed, displaying his owl ring. "It is clear that he rose to his exalted position through sharp mental acuity and bountiful perspicacity."

"Now you're out of me depth," said the peeler. "Henry Bottles is the name. Anything you need, give me a bellow." He demonstrated that very technique, aiming it at two of his fellows. "Oi! Muggins, Landsdowne. These is the toffs they told us about. Let 'em through."

The gawkers moved aside as Wilde loomed before them. Most shouted questions. But one woman, shriveled like an old apple, clutched her plaid shawl tight to her bony shoulders and muttered about 'monsters.' Paragon motioned to PC Bottles that he should bring her inside with them. The lady would have scarpered if Muggins had not held her with both thick arms.

"Here! I didn't do nothin'!" she complained. "Leave me be!"

When the sturdy door boomed shut behind them, she whimpered and fell silent. In the front room sat a forge and anvil, along with parts for engines and such. Grime and grease covered every square inch. Wilde tiptoed through the mess as if he feared contagion.

They passed through a great iron door in the sooty back wall. The rear chamber more resembled a surgery than a blacksmith's. Smooth white tile made up the walls and ceiling. Underfoot lay more tile, larger slabs, with India rubber matting in spots and several drains. Enormous lamps hung low over a row of steel tables.

Paragon recognized some of the machinery. Lathes for turning metal. Punches. Drills. Screw-making devices. Riveters. Flywheels to provide smooth power from the bulky steam engines in the corners. Such machine shops were becoming a natural extension of the blacksmith's art as the mechanistics boom accelerated.

Along one wall, however, he saw something novel. Enclosed in a sort of blue-glassed greenhouse affair was a single row of unusual contrivances. So odd was the apparatus that it seemed otherworldly. He could not fathom its purpose, no matter how long he stared at the weirdly shaped wheels, nozzles, and blades. Where the other machines bore the blocky, heavy look of all such practical tools, designed to take a great deal of punishment day in and day out, these had a delicacy and elegance out of place in such an environment.

"Sewing machines for fairies," muttered Wilde, squinting through the half-opaque azure panes.

"Indeed," his partner nodded. "What in blazes is the purpose of these things? They seem more medical than mechanical, but the metal refuse says otherwise. Even the geometry seems wrong, as if the dictates of Euclid don't apply."

"Must be fragile, though. They've been sealed up tighter than a bishop's bum."

"You're right. Triple layered rubber door seals, two sets of glass windows with some sort of bluish jelly in between. A kind of foam insulation on the tables. Must be highly sensitive to dust, light, and vibration."

Paragon shook the handle of the single narrow door. It gave not a bit. There was no play in it at all. "Spectacularly made. And it takes a key shaped like a corkscrew. The lads at Lochmoor will positively soil themselves with delight."

Another door hung ajar in the far outside wall. It resembled the portal of a bank vault. A constable stood just inside in case the fellow sprawled on the floor were to jump up and make a run for it. Lying there was the twisted body of a mutton-chopped elderly man, white hair scattered around his head. An expensive suit of pale gray, once neatly pressed but now disheveled and torn, covered his body. Death's pallor gave him the look of a beached fish. His face, in fact, greatly resembled that of a trout flung ashore to die…bulging eyes, bloated cheeks, and lips gaping to catch elusive oxygen.

All about him, coating the otherwise immaculate white floor tile, lay fine black dust. Paragon had seen plenty of coal dust in his Yorkshire youth and this was assuredly not that. It managed to appear as fine as a lady's face powder but at the same time it behaved more like beach sand. The stuff had much more weight and density than it by rights should have. And it absorbed light as if thirsty for it.

"Doesn't behave like it wants to obey the laws of physics, either," mused Paragon.

No one stood near the body, naturally fearing that the black dust carried the seeds of Grimsby's destruction. The powder covered the entire room in a paper-thin layer. It collected in the irregularities of the dead man's face.

"Who found him?"

Muggins jerked his head at a sturdy fellow lurking in a corner. "The shop owner. He claims not to have been in here the past two years. Leases it out to some American bloke. All this machinery has been added by the renter. Had business in town and happened to be nearby, decided to check on his property. This door has been newly added by the tenants."

"How did he get in then?"

"It seems it did not quite close when this unfortunate chap entered."

"Footprints?"

"Other than his? None."

Paragon looked the room over again. Immense secure doors front and back. No windows or skylights. A pair of vents in the roof, but they were thirty feet above the ground. And no ladder or catwalk connected them to the rest of the shop.

"What about the floor?"

"No trap doors if that's what you're thinkin'. Solid concrete it is, beneath those tiles."

"Has the body been searched, or disturbed in any way?"

"No, sir. The doctor ain't even been here yet. We recognized the deceased from his picture in the newspapers. Haven't so much as turned out his pockets. Sergeant ordered us to leave it all for you gents."

Paragon moved around the walls, searching for anything that should not be there. Near the boilers which served the engines he spotted that very thing.

Tracks. Small, round, three-footed prints.

From the placement of the black dust and the pattern it left on the floor he determined that the stuff had originated from that corner. *Fortunate for me that I stayed out in the open with it.*

No marks of human feet were in evidence, other than between the door and the corpse. The curious owner had mucked things up there so badly that Hannibal's army, elephants and all, might have passed through earlier and no sign would have been seen of them. Paragon crouched over the dead politician. Plucking a small monocle-magnifier from his inner coat pocket, he took pains to scan every square inch of the corpse. Grigsby's silver cravat pin bore an omega in its center. *A Breaker symbol? The plot is thickening like Irish stew.* He emptied the man's pockets. That yielded him some minor treasures: handkerchief, pen knife, pocketbook containing £80 (*not robbery, then*), a little notebook, and two keys. One looked like it might fit the lock of the outside door.

The other was coiled like a corkscrew.

Constructed of an unlikely blend of frosted white glass and some queer metal that resembled brass but contained shiny multicolored flecks, it went into his vest pocket. When the police were no longer underfoot, they would test its efficacy on the greenhouse. *Queue will squeal like a girl at Christmas when she sees those mad contraptions.*

With Muggins' assistance he rolled the late Honorable Samuel Grimsby over. More of the black dust lay beneath him. The man had been overcome by it while standing. Judging by the lack of Grimsby's footprints elsewhere, he had fallen almost instantly. *Wicked stuff, this. Would even a breath mask save one from its lethal effects? And why does it seem harmless now?* While turning that thought over in his mind, Paragon made his second lucky discovery in as many minutes.

A crushed red leaf lay on the smudged tiles…precisely identical to those worn by Lady Ambergris Kalmaar and her pitiless clockwork guardian.

"What a pity," he said aloud. "I was beginning to favor the woman." He pocketed the item. A tiny glass vial of the murderous dust joined it.

Wilde's mirror-shined toe appeared beside Grimsby's head. "Developments, old stick?"

Paragon stood. The gears in his leg whirred with less noise than before. "Several. And you?"

"Uncertain." The Irishman bit his prominent lower lip. "Attend her story and decide for yourself. I confess that if I wrote such a thing, I would never dare print it."

"What does she say then?"

"That demons from the sky killed him."

Paragon's eyebrow lifted. "Did you think to sniff her breath?"

"I did, actually. Not a whiff of gin on her. She insists that she has forsworn the juice of the juniper these seven years. And she has not the look of an imbiber. I gather that her passions tend more toward the heavenly."

"Present me to our good lady witness, Master Wilde. I long to hear her testimony."

Eustachia Ottershaw struggled in the grip of a constable who gratefully released her. For a woman so religious she possessed a remarkable command of biting invective.

"I'll have the lot of you before a magistrate! Abduction, that's what this is!" she declared. "Keeping a poor woman against her will."

"Now, now, mother," cooed Wilde, "do you not wish to help us apprehend the man who did this?"

"Man! Don't you wish it were a man." She shuddered and clung ever more tightly to her shawl.

"Ah, yes," said Paragon. "You mentioned to my associate that demons slew this poor fellow?"

Mrs. Ottershaw's seamed features twisted as she found herself forced to recall the horrors of the previous night. "Demons it was, as I live and breathe."

"But how can you know that? Were you present inside this shop when it happened?"

"Are you saying I'm involved? I'm a good church-going woman I am!"

"Now, now, calm yourself. I merely wish to ascertain how you come by your so-certain knowledge, that's all."

"Certain is the word for it. Didn't I walk straight past this place yesterday near midnight, after my niece's lying-in? Didn't I have to spring aside like a cat to avoid masonry falling upon my poor head? And didn't I see two monsters atop the roof, peering down at me with their glowing green eyes?"

"Monsters, you say?"

She drew herself up to her full five feet and two inches. "Even in the dark fog I could hardly mistake them for chimney sweeps."

"Describe them for us, if it is not too distressing."

"Eyes that bored right through you. Great long dragon snouts. Misshapen bodies, all out of proportion. Arms too long, legs too short. Huge claws on hands and feet. Great wings a-flapping."

"Wings and...snouts, you say?" *Can this business get any stranger?*

"So, demons they certainly were, my good man. Fallen angels out of hell, here to do mischief and murder upon the good folk of Islington. You doubt me?"

Paragon held up his palms to her. "I find your tale utterly convincing."

She turned to Wilde. "Here...is he having me on?"

Oscar shrugged. "Any other day I would say yes, but..."

Paragon pressed her. "What were they doing? Please think carefully."

"Don't have to think at all." She pulled a wrinkled slip of paper from her glove. "Wrote it all down the moment I reached home."

"Mrs. Ottershaw, you rise in my estimation."

"Well, one doesn't see demons in the high street every day, you know." Clearing her throat, she took on the air of a great dame of the stage. "One of the monsters carried a parcel in a potato sack. Size of a small child. The other fussed with the shutter of the ventilation opening. No one was to be seen at the street-level door. In fact, the street was almost devoid of traffic."

"Almost?"

"One can hardly consider that failed teetotaler Neal Bromley as 'traffic.' I mean, the poor man was so inebriated that he strayed directly into the path of a penny-farthing. Though what lunatic would be out riding a bicycle in the dark on such a fog-bound evening I cannot imagine."

"A penny farthing, you say? Employ your considerable powers of remembrance. Was there anything particularly odd about that conveyance?"

"I should say so! It was one of those steamer types, puffing away. Rider was the size of a bull. And the thing had a cart towed behind. Can you believe it? Ought to be a law against them. Dangerous for pedestrians and horses alike."

"I fully sympathize. Is that all?"

"It is. The demons vanished inside the building and I scurried home as fast as my terrified legs could take me. Crawled into bed with tea and my Scriptures to protect me."

"Sound reasoning, ma'am. And may I say what a decided help you have been to our investigation into this sorry affair. The Crown shall not forget it, let me assure you."

Mrs. Ottershaw puffed up with patriotic pride. "Nothing any proper citizen wouldn't do, I'm sure."

After sending the good lady off home, Paragon turned to Wilde. "I think I know what happened. Some of it, anyway. Can you boost me up to the top of that engine's boiler?"

Oscar's face lost all color. "In this suit? Are you mad?"

"I thought we had already established that I. Come on. Close your eyes and think of England."

"I shall be thinking of my tailor, at any rate."

In the event, Wilde's splendid overcoat protected the cherished velvet suit, and a spot of brushing preserved even that expensive item from any lasting indignity. Once atop the slightly rusty boiler, Paragon had no difficulty locating deep scratches in the unmistakable pattern of formidable claws. Since no such marks were evident on the floor, the beast-men had dropped their parcel from that spot.

"Mrs. Ottershaw's demons flew onto the roof with the tripod that attacked me, or one just like it. They released the contraption to do its fatal work on Grimsby, returning to the roof while the black smoke choked the life out of him. Once the murderous mist had settled, they flew back down, retrieved their device, and departed again, shutting the vents as they went."

Wilde stared up at the ceiling. "Let us hope they do not surprise us. The battle may be brief and inglorious."

They left through the rear door and inspected the narrow dirt lane. Here again someone had rudely painted RIOT ARMY on the wall. Paragon showed Wilde the weird key and the red leaf, taking care to explain the significance of the latter as concerned Lady Kalmaar.

"Withholding evidence from the Metropolitan Police again, I see," said Oscar. "And such a frisson of excitement does come with that, let me confess."

Paragon stared hard at the ground between the wall and the street. "Where do you suppose our good friend Inspector Shepperton has gotten himself to? On any other murder of this magnitude, he would already have sealed off the area and held at least two meetings with the gentlemen of the press."

"I imagine he has been unavoidably detained. A pair of pneumos arrived in his office this morning. The first informed him that a mysterious contagious disease of a nasty reproductive nature might be involved in Grimsby's dispatch, while the second ordered him to remain at headquarters pending a surprise visit of inspection by the Home Secretary."

"You sound well-acquainted with these missives."

"As well I should be, having composed them myself. And might I add that they are the two most splendidly-written communications that the CID is likely to see this month."

"Which also means that the author's style shall be immediately recognized. Did you employ the phrase 'profundity of desire' again?"

Wilde pouted. "Hmmm. I might have done."

"In that case, I estimate that we have mere moments to scour the area and make good our escape. The killing of a man of Grimsby's notoriety and importance cannot be kept to ourselves for long."

Paragon held up the curled key. "Keep your elegant Irish nose on the scent. I'll hie myself to that blue-glass shed and see if I can gain entry."

"Righto. Try not to assault any civilians while you're in there. The forms I would be forced to complete in that event would bring an enforced tedium that would markedly reduce my singular intelligence."

Ignoring that remark, Paragon returned to the machine shop. The corkscrew-shaped key threaded so easily into the lock that he thought it had not engaged the mechanism. He turned the key in the opposite direction to withdraw it and try again. No sooner did it come free of the lock than the seal broke with a faint hiss. He swung the door open just wide enough to gain entry. Its hinges operated every bit as smoothly as the lock had.

Nearly opaque from the exterior, inside the glass proved to be perfectly transparent. Adding to the disconcerting strangeness was the surface's resistance to smudging or scratching. Try as he might he could not mark it in any way. No amount of griming, wiping, nor scoring with metal made any impression. He abandoned the effort and turned to the mysterious apparatus on the single table.

They somewhat resembled sewing machines, with slender metallic arms that ended in a variety of narrow hinged attachments. Whatever material they were constructed of gave off a pewter-like sheen with a faint violet undertone. Just as with the door's mechanisms, the contrivances appeared to acknowledge friction only grudgingly. Yet no lubricant of any kind was visible. Bits of worked metal beneath the devices hinted at their function. So far as he could tell with his limited knowledge of mechanistics, some of them could weld steel or iron without heat. Others appeared to cut the finest of lines, in every complex shape imaginable, though no blades could he see. The abilities of most, though, were beyond his ken. Their strangeness made his head swim.

Paragon snuck back out of the little house and relocked it. Despite his inability to comprehend what the machines could do or why they might be hidden in an Islington shop, one thing remained clear. He stood at the center of a profound mystery.

Paragon strolled outside, where Wilde stood idly swinging his stick while improvising verse in Attic Greek. After learning that Oscar had discovered nothing on the hard, dry ground, he led the way out. They hailed another cab and returned to the club. No sooner had they descended than they were swarmed by a gaggle of filthy urchins.

"Mister Paragon, sir!" blurted the tallest and cleanest of them, a husky dark-skinned lad with kinky hair who sported an incongruous monocle. His mother had been an army camp follower in Africa, but the Punques cared nothing for that sort of thing. "Yer has to come quick! Monsters have invaded the East End, they have."

The actor turned up one corner of his mouth. "Have they, now? Quite a lot of that about nowadays. Deuced nuisance, wouldn't you agree, Oscar?"

"Beastly annoyance, these creatures," responded Wilde.

"Are you acquainted with the Esteemed Punques?"

"By reputation only." Oscar tipped his hat. "Pleased to meet you all, my fine gentlemen."

The boy who had spoken rolled his eyes. "Why do all the toffs think we're bloody idiots?" He waved both arms to indicate his disreputable crew. "Gentlemen? Bollocks! Do we look like a mob of Mayfair's finest to you?"

Paragon worked to appear suitably chastened. "That you do not, Master

Manticore. Why would you settle for such a demotion in rank? What about these monsters, then? Why am I so urgently needed this day?"

"Because they've taken the Griffin prisoner! Him and your Millie both."

*London Medical College*

*The pale blue eyes widened as she glided in, Reginald impassive yet lethally observant behind her. She wore bustled burgundy velvet like an empress.*

*"Thank you for answering my summons so quickly." He gave his small ivory box, the twin of the one on her wrist, a dubious look. "I perfectly comprehend even the most arcane biology, but these transmitter things are beyond my ken. Too much like sorcery. Still, this one seems to have called you well enough." Tucking it into a pocket, he forced a sort of smile. "You elevate the tone of this establishment, m'lady." The small room served as a comfortable lounge for the Medical College's lecturers. A pair of snoring and bewhiskered fossils dozed in a corner, their eyebrows in need of mowing. "Pardon the dust on my colleagues."*

*Lady Kalmaar gave him a tight smile. "At least your flattery is spotless, Professor Navita." Her forced pleasantry did little to take the chill out of the stale air.*

*"If you believe me insincere, then I suggest that you spend more time before your looking glass." Navita smoothed his blonde hair and offered her a chair.*

*"Thank you, no. I cannot stay." She eyed him as one might an adder found on the sideboard.*

*"A pity. Was your Shakespearean evening enjoyable?"*

*"Quite. Though not as profitable as I might have liked. He is a tougher nut than you led me to believe."*

*"He would not part with his prize? Your special powers of persuasion notwithstanding?"*

*"I scented him within an inch of his life. For an instant he wavered, but he recovered with aplomb. Someone has trained him well, possibly a great Oriental mystic. Paragon is of those haunted ones who rely upon self-abnegation. He has a wretched and painful past. Caliban is perfect for him."*

*Navita's palm went up. "Unfortunate. But also moot. It would seem that our Henry Jekyll visited the Eccentric Club today. Sadly for us, he wore his socially-proper face."*

*"Then they have already analyzed the tissue?"*

*"Alas, yes. Much good may it do them. They cannot trace it."*

*"You thought that before, remember. And now you are murderously pursued from ten thousand miles away for your arrogance."*

*"A hit, a hit, I do confess it. But the endgame always was to close with Sebastian and dispatch him for **his** arrogance, so…"*

*"And will all this intrigue and murder revive the poor lady…or her daughter? Your daughter?"*

*After a long pause he replied, "Sebastian thinks so. His every moment is dedicated to precisely that. He keeps their remains in preservation, awaiting the day of his breakthrough." He wiped an eye, recovered, gave her a hard look up and down. "It seems that the day is nearly at hand."*

Kalmaar shook her head. *"Men! If you all spent as much time alleviating the world's suffering as you do salving your wretched 'honor'..."*

*"Glass houses, m'lady. Are you not mired in our marriage of convenience for the same reason?"*

*"More an abduction than a marriage. And I see it as justice, not revenge. You well know what a curse he laid on me."*

*"Shall we compare curses? Not only are my darlings dead at his hand, his twisted poison has made me a bloodthirsty fiend. I do not endure those dreadful injections for the sport of it."* He pulled a chain from his pocket as he spoke. On it hung a small, framed photograph of mother and child, identical to Moreau's. *"Let us press on. Can you stay close to him? Learn more of their progress and plans?"*

That earned him a little laugh. *"To judge by the look he gave me as we parted, he may be sleeping on my doorstep tonight."*

*"A crowded location, so rumor has it. Encourage him, then. See what you can discover. We may have an opportunity for Captain Carter to plant some little deceptions upon Dardanelles and his minions."*

*"Very well. And in exchange...?"*

Navita drew an envelope from inside his gray morning coat. *"The paternal loins have settled in the far north, though he ventures away on occasion. Here is the location of his airship's lair. They are to have a meeting of his chiefs. Dally not. He shan't linger. As agreed, so long as you remain loyal to me, I shan't reveal your location to him."*

Lady Kalmaar plucked it from his grasp with two gloved fingers. Her sour expression indicated a desire for a carbolic acid bath. *"Shall we meet here again? In two days' time?"*

He bowed low. *"I look forward to it as might an eager bridegroom."*

*"And I as might a Christian in the arena,"* she muttered as she swooped out.

## 7/ "HELL IS EMPTY AND ALL THE DEVILS ARE HERE"

Paragon stamped the end of his stick on the pavement. "Prisoner, you say? Where?"

"Raven Row. Near the Medical College."

"These monsters. You saw them with your own eyes?"

"Two there were. Right out of Dante's *Inferno*. Remember when you showed me and the Griffin that fancy old book? Devils from the bowels of Hell. 'Twas half a dozen hard fellows what did the real work, though."

"Did you recognize any of these men?" asked Paragon.

The runt of the group, a cross-eyed boy with a constellation of freckles, piped up. "I did. The leader was Humphrey Littlewit."

"The resurrectionist? You're certain?"

"Spent all night spyin' on him in a churchyard once. Ain't likely to ever forget that lumpy phiz. Jaw so long it scrapes his bootlaces."

"But why would a grave robber kidnap ---"

Manticore jumped up and down so hard his weather-beaten derby fell off. "No time for 'why.' Me mate's about to be eaten alive, or worse."

Paragon turned to Wilde. "I've failed poor Millie, it seems. Now Griffin is in for it, too."

Nodding, Oscar said, "I'll gather a team."

"And I'll go on ahead with Manticore here as a guide and sort things out. I'll send word when to move in."

"Alone? Have you taken leave of your ---?" Oscar laughed and shrugged. "Of course, you have. Are you at least armed?"

Paragon grinned and patted his frock coat where the Webley-Fosbury hung, heavy and eager. "Queue has outdone herself."

"Go, then. I should obey orders and accompany you, but this seems to be an instance where madness *should* reign."

To the tiny chap who had identified Humphrey Littlewit, Paragon said, "Master Wyvern! I leave the Esteemed Punques in your capable hands. You have a task of the utmost urgency."

Wyvern saluted as if on a Grenadier Guards parade ground. "Sir! We await your orders, sir!" Behind him the rest of the Punques snapped to attention.

"Good show. My command is that you repair to the Eccentric Club kitchen and stuff yourselves full of sandwiches."

As one man the platoon called out, "Oh, yes!"

"And after that…lead a frontal assault upon the Turkish Delight."

"Rule Britannia!" cried the Punques, fists pumping the sooty air.

With a wink to Wilde, Paragon asked, "Escort the troops to Mrs. O'Grady and see that she feeds them, will you. Make certain that it goes onto my account."

Oscar grinned. "She'll be a hero to this lot today. And to think that someone once termed her a woman of no importance."

Paragon's stick went up to his hat brim. "Splendid. We who are about to die salute you."

"Oi!" blurted Manticore, glaring at them through his monocle. "All this talk of dyin' is makin' the Manticore a bit jittery-like."

"Merely a soldier's expression," Paragon assured him. "Let us be on our way to the nearest Tube station."

"That'd be Oxford Circus." Manticore eyed Paragon and shook his head. "In those togs you'll elevate the tone of the place. Hope yer lovely coat don't get soiled."

Paragon did not tell him that he usually avoided the Underground, because close dark spaces reminded him of the Yorkshire mines where he had briefly toiled. He did not trust himself to maintain good discipline.

Mercifully, the train ran smoothly and on schedule, Paragon's clenched fists and chilled spine notwithstanding. On the way, the odd pair worked out a plan while wearing cheap masks bought at the station. Passing through London Hospital and Medical College they could lose any pursuers, posing as a wealthy philanthropist escorting his latest charity case to treatment. Paragon suggested that Manticore might display feeble-mindedness. The young man countered that perhaps Paragon might bugger himself.

Disembarking at the hospital, they passed beneath the five-arched brick façade. No one gave them more than a passing glance. Pocketing his monocle, supporting himself with Paragon's cane, and twisting one arm into a pained arc, Manticore managed to look so pitiful that Paragon suspected that this was not his first attempt at a pretended malady. Paragon looked for Joseph Merrick, the truly deformed yet charming chap who, along with that too-clever fellow from Baker Street, had aided them on a recent case of organ-snatching. But the famed Elephant Man must have been up in his attic lodging.

No monsters showed themselves in Raven Row, though some grubby children played tag. Most of the buildings were 18th century affairs, three sagging stories with a shop on the ground floor. One sat apart from the others, its neighbors having burnt or been torn down. Though it bore a sign proclaiming that it was the pawn shop of Israel Rabinowitz, no merchandise showed in the dark window. Sparse clumps of weeds, browning in the autumn chill, grew between irregular cracks in the paving stones and steps. An estate agent's placard hung on the door.

"There you are," announced Manticore. "We saw 'em dragged into that place. The Griffin and Millie had sacks over their heads, but it was them, all right. Should I sneak 'round to the back door?"

"Do. Be careful. I believe these fellows took the life of an MP, so don't expect them to value yours any more highly."

"Aw, don't fret about me, gov. You're the one who stands out like a prick in church." With a quick wink he vanished.

Paragon considered his options. Storming the place would likely be suicidal, for him and for the hostages. But he couldn't afford to dawdle. Littlewit had served time in Dartmoor for selling corpses to anatomists and re-animators alike. He might be about to replenish his stock. Manticore's crude observation reminded Paragon of how out-of-place he was in this street. Might that not serve his turn?

His comrade-in-arms appeared beside him as if transported there by witchcraft. "Guard at the back. Pretendin' to be asleep in a chair. Windows all boarded up but one, top floor. West corner."

"That's where they'll be, then. Where are your men?"

"Manticore nodded toward the end of the street. "The not-so-legless beggar at the corner is Lindworm." He indicated the other direction. "Halfway down, the lad bootin' the football against that wall. That would be Cocky…Cockatrice. Across the alleyway we put Basilisk on a roof. Good eyes, that one. I swear she don't blink but once an hour."

"Excellent. Then all that remains is for us to stroll merrily up to the front door and introduce ourselves."

They approached the dilapidated shop. By the time they stood on the top step, the boy had resumed his guise of the sadly twisted orphan. Wearing Manticore's monocle, Paragon rapped thrice upon the door with the handle of his umbrella.

When the door screeched open on neglected hinges, Paragon displayed his 'I-am-put-on-this-Earth-to-rescue-mankind' expression. Beside him, Manticore presented the perfect picture of wretchedness, clearly in so much pain from his palsied, contorted condition that he might expire at any moment.

"And a very good day to you, brother!" chimed Paragon, his voice high-pitched and cheery. "How does this splendid day find you? Well, I hope."

The poor doorman was out of his depth. "I…uh, can't complain." His raspy voice betrayed a northern accent. The sack coat he wore was of patched brown tweed, with pants from an entirely different suit. The worn face sagged. "How might I help you, sir?"

Paragon pointed to the sign as if it promised salvation. "This is how!" He tipped his hat in greeting. "The Right Reverend Basil Bredon at your service. I minister to the suffering people of this district at the newly established Chapel of the Sacred Whimsy. Might I present one of my parishioners? Say hello to the nice gentleman, Peter."

A long string of drool oozed down the chin of 'Peter'. He yowled, "Bleertchooz!" while his limbs twitched. Not making eye contact, instead his gaze traveled in a jerky figure-eight. This disguised the fact that the apparently helpless Peter expertly reconnoitered the interior of the shop.

"One of my unfortunates," sighed Paragon. "But we are all God's children, are we not, sir? And whom do I have the honor of addressing?"

"Oh, um, Smythe. Richard Smythe. Pleased to make your acquaintance, Reverend." He wiped his right hand on his trousers and held it out to Paragon, who seized it with vigor and manipulated it like a recalcitrant pump handle.

"Likewise, likewise! Always a pleasure to meet the good citizens who make me so proud of the Empire." While lingering on his effusive handshake, Paragon employed all his senses to take the man's measure.

*Smells of whiskey…and fear. The pulse in this hand pounds like an overworked steam engine. Unhealthy, desperate, and deathly afraid of failure. His superior is the unforgiving sort. Has a short knife up this sleeve but likely has never used it in anger. A follower, not a leader. And, unless my old nose deceives me, the leader would be the onion-loving bloke hiding behind this door.*

"How may I be of service?" inquired Smythe, freeing his hand.

"I will tell you, my good man. This placard proclaims that one Silas Greene offers this fine old building for sale or rent. It just so happens that we are in sore need of a suitably placed structure to serve as a center of living and worship for lads like Peter here. It is our intention to install a dozen or so boys, along with their adult sponsors, in a healthy and wholesome communal arrangement."

"Well, now, Reverend, I don't ---"

Paragon held up his umbrella to interrupt Smythe's protest. He had shifted forward several inches during his speech. Now his aluminum foot blocked the door. "Now I know such an impressive property will no doubt come at a dear price. Let me assure you that, thanks to many philanthropic men of business, we are in a position to handsomely remunerate the owner."

"E-moon-er-athe," gurgled Manticore, sliding up against the door to put pressure against the man hiding behind it, while seeming to merely be in the throes of a spasm.

"But I ain't the owner," Smythe insisted. "And I don't think he wants to sell."

"And who could blame him? If it were mine, it would require a king's ransom to pry it from my --- I say, will you look at that fine staircase!"

And with the feigned exuberance, Paragon bounded into the dusty foyer, leaving Manticore to maintain his trap of the would-be ambusher. Smythe followed, distress clouding his face even more.

"Sir, I'm not authorized to treat with you about this matter. Perhaps if you inquired at Mr. Greene's office?"

Paragon stroked the oak banister with a beatific smile. "This is wicked of me, I know, but I simply must have a look upstairs. The owner would not begrudge it of me, surely."

With that Paragon bounded up the creaky steps, giggling in false rapture. Before the hapless Smythe could do anything about it, the imposter stood on the landing, fairly quivering with excitement. "This will suit us down to the ground! The boys will have a palace as their abode! A palace!"

Smythe began climbing the stairs, his breathing labored. "I'm begging you, Mr. Bredon. This is not the house for you."

Before he could even catch his breath, he found himself backed up against the rail with the long barrel of the Webley thrust up against his chin.

"On the contrary," whispered Paragon in his normal tone of voice, "it's precisely what I was looking for. It comes furnished with a young lady and a boy, tied up tight. Am I correct?"

When Smythe opened his mouth to speak, the cold steel burrowed farther into his flesh. Understanding, the fellow nodded. His eyes wandered up.

"They shall be leaving with us. Whether you remain here to grow cold and stiff matters not to me. Now, how many of you are there? Use the hand without the secreted knife, if you please. And if you betray any aggression, I shall be forced to splash your brains all over this well-appointed foyer. A pity, that. The carpets are rather fine."

Smythe held up four fingers with a gulp.

"Excellent. Is that Littlewit behind the door, waiting to do me mischief?" A nod. "Now, most important: where are the two 'special' troops who came here with you? The ones you hope to heaven you never have to see again."

One finger pointed directly up twice. To judge by the sudden pallor of Smythe's face, they frightened him much more than the gun.

"Roof?" Smythe nodded again. The Webley's pressure eased a fraction. "One final question and you will be free to dash out of here and, I hope, reform your life altogether. At which door upstairs should I politely inquire?"

The sorry Smythe put up a pair of fingers and motioned left.

"Guards?" Four fingers went up.

"Splendid. Now we are going to continue our charming farce as we descend. Pleasure doing business with you." The pistol disappeared inside the frock coat. Paragon's voice returned to its shrill ministerial note. "Mr. Smythe, you have been more than accommodating. We shan't take up any more of your valuable time."

Smythe led the way down. When they reached the open doorway, Paragon paused. His eye twinkled. Manticore continued to gurgle and twitch as he leaned against it.

"Well, good-day to you, sir. One word of advice, though. I believe that these hinges are rusty. You really ought to have them seen to."

His false leg smashed against the door in a blur. A sharp cry like a kicked dog might make was the reward. The door recoiled and began to close, but not before Smythe squeezed through it on his way to a new life of less crime and fewer demons. Revealed was a tall narrow bloke with a lantern jaw and a plaid coat. Though he held a cosh in one hand, he was in no position to employ it, as all the wind had been knocked out of him.

Paragon lay a hand on Manticore's shoulder. "I use my godly powers to heal thee, unfortunate boy!"

The Esteemed Punque straightened up and stretched his twisted limbs. "Thanks, gov." He nodded at the gasping man. "Looks like a horse, this one. Shall we take him to the glue factory?"

"Tempting, eh? Mr. Humphrey Littlewit, renowned trader in things dead, though they occasionally do not remain so if the price is right."

That seemed to breathe life into the resurrectionist. His club cocked back to deliver a savage blow, but Paragon's armored bowler thumped against his skull. With a sigh, Littlewit slid down the wall and lay still.

"Tie and gag him. Then I need a diversion around back to keep that guard busy. And keep a tight seal on this place so that no reinforcements can interrupt the rescue." Paragon handed the boy one of his cards. "Send a runner to the nearest constable. Tell him a sad tale of white slavery or something suitably lurid. Anything to get him to blow his whistle and come running with several of his friends. By then Oscar should be here with our lads."

Manticore bound Littlewit with the man's own kerchief, stuffing one of his socks in his mouth as a gag. Then he saluted, winked, surrendered the brass-headed cane, and vanished out the front door. Paragon shut it tight. He leaned the umbrella in a corner and moved to the foot of the stairs. Smythe's northern voice croaked from his lips. "Oi! I need some help out 'ere!"

The door opened and a gruff Cockney growled, "Yeah?"

"It's Littlewit. Twisted his bally ankle, he did. Brained himself on the newel post."

The man swore. "Blighter's got the perfect name, that's certain. Half a mo'. I'm comin'."

Booted feet thumped. By the time the fellow arrived at the bottom, Paragon had wrapped his arms around Littlewit's limp form and stood up, hiding himself behind.

The complaining henchman looked like any of the thousands of nondescript laborers one might find milling about the docks. "How in blazes he ever managed to get to be boss of this gang ---"

Paragon flung the bound body at the grumbler, who gasped in surprise and reflexively bear-hugged it. In a matter of seconds, a strong arm vised his throat, putting him to sleep. The victor trussed him just like Littlewit and dragged him out of sight of the stairs.

Pargon called out in the new man's voice this time. "Need another pair of hands down here! He must weigh an extra five stone when he's all limp-like."

A throat which might have belonged to a troll rumbled, "What's the matter? You little girls can't lift one scrawny Welshman?" He spoke to someone in the room. "Keep a sharp eye on 'em, you two. If our customer ain't happy when he comes to collect, well...shit rolls downhill. He'll likely kill you all over again."

Hearing the great stomp of the giant's boots, as well as his locomotive-like breathing, Paragon adjusted his tactics. *A right-good ambushing is what's called for here.* He took a cue from his enemy, opened the door again, and stowed himself behind it, pistol at the ready.

The goliath came into view on the landing, a locomotive of a man, stub of a cigar between his thick froggy lips. His unshaven face looked as though he had fallen directly onto it from a great height. Reminiscent of the simian Missing Link that the evolutionists went on about, his brow and jaw were heavily boned. A weather-beaten coachman's hat clung to his monstrous head. In one great fist he clutched a walking stick that looked familiar to Paragon somehow. Where he had found a tweed overcoat to fit his immense shoulders was past imagining. *Brobdingnag Haberdashers, perhaps.*

Paragon recognized that silhouette at once. It belonged to the mysterious penny-farthing man who shepherded the deadly tripod. The man who had blocked the alley for his ambush.

"Where the bloody hell did you all get to?" he bellowed. The sound shook the foyer like a distant dynamite blast. With a grunt, he bent down, grasped Littlewit under the arms, and flung him over one shoulder like a bag of grain. When he straightened his back, he noticed the muzzle of the Webley pointed directly up at his squashed nose.

"I might have known somethin' was up," said the man-mountain. His lips shifted his cigar to the other side of his mouth. "You a copper?"

"Yes and no," replied Paragon. The cane hung lightly from his left hand. "But we've sent for every constable in the East End. I imagine they take a dim view of kidnapping even in Raven Row. Who do you expect to pay the ransom, anyway?"

That earned a bass-note laugh. "Ransom? For a street rat and a whore?"

"Ah. That would explain the involvement of the loathsome Mr. Littlewit there.

Are the organ-harvesters back in business? Kindly drop that stick, if you please."

The silver-headed cane fell. "I don't know who provides your information, but you ought to ask for your money back."

"Enlighten me. I positively ache for knowledge."

"Oh, you'll ache, alright, when I get done with you."

"I would hurry if I were you. The police are coming. A chap your size will have few places to hide."

The giant guffawed.

Paragon raised an eyebrow. "That was a joke?"

"A sort of pun on my name. Your last, I fancy."

And with that rumbled threat, the ogre pitched the drooping body straight at Paragon and charged with a bear's roar.

Hoist by his own petard and cursing himself for it, Paragon could only brace himself for the impact. It struck his gun arm while the rest of him ducked low. That turned out to be fortunate, for even though the pistol flew from his hand, he managed to just avoid the anvil-sized fist of his attacker. The great mass of bone cracked the old plaster of the wall a bare two inches above his head. Anticipating the next move, he rolled to his left as a ferocious kick came at his ribs.

Paragon came up to his feet without his armored hat or gun, the walking stick over his head in defense. The pistol lay in the far corner, beneath the unmoving Littlewit. *Careful now. This fellow is a good deal faster than his size might indicate.* He took a calming breath and assumed a stance which would let him dance about and not let his immense foe grapple with him. A wrestling match might well be the end of Paragon's career.

Those huge fists milled before the ugly face. Unsurprisingly, the giant had been taught to box once upon a time, to someone's great profit, no doubt. Paragon guessed that most of those bouts had involved a single devastating punch or a sudden 'illness' on the part of the other fighter. As things stood, he sympathized with those unlucky men.

But when the first blow came, he saw that the man's pugilistic instruction had been lacking. He tended to over-swing, too confident in his bulk. And he had likely never encountered a combatant with Paragon's unique skills.

After dodging the third clumsy punch and gauging his opponent's rhythm, Paragon feinted with the tip of the cane. The fellow batted it away with his left hand, making the mistake of looking in that direction as he did so. Paragon slid inside and struck his right temple with the cane head. The shock numbed his hand. His foe scarcely felt it. But at the same time, the metal foot lashed out to crunch the behemoth's knee, making him stumble and curse. But despite his pain the man's speed served him well. His tree limb of a forearm whipped back and knocked Paragon ten feet down the hall.

Out of breath and stunned, the actor had to meet the limping rush of his enemy while kneeling. Just as Queue had drilled him, he spun like a quintain to direct that fearsome energy past him while slashing at his head with the stick. The strike went too low and only slapped the brute's thick shoulders. Momentum forced the beast into a wall. He pushed away from it and turned as Paragon rose, twisting the cane head. A needle-sharp steel point sprung out four inches.

*No more dancing with this great bastard. He may break me in two. And his friends must know something's wrong by now.*

A saber cut from the stick opened the troll's forehead. Stinging blood immediately streamed into his eyes. While his foe cursed and rubbed at his face, Paragon toe-kicked him in the spleen. The blow made him fold with a screech despite his size. An instant later that sound was cut off with a choking gurgle as the massive brass head of the stick smashed his thick throat twice. The monster sank to the floor like a well-shot African rhino.

Panting, Paragon re-capped his stick and picked up his heavy bowler, heart pounding like a locomotive engine. No constables arrived in the nick of time to relieve him of his duty. *That only happens on stage in badly written melodramas. Excelsior, Paragon!*

A sprig of the ubiquitous red weed had fallen from inside the giant's hat. Paragon pocketed it for later examination by Jekyll. With a wince, he retrieved his pistol, brushed his frock coat and trousers, straightened the cravat, and refolded his pocket handkerchief. The flower in his lapel was a tragic loss. His last chore was to retrieve the electric brolly.

He crept up the stairs, stick and umbrella in one hand, gun in the other. No one attacked him. In fact, the prison door hung open. They had fled with their prizes.

"Bollocks!" he hissed, rushing into the empty room. Overturned chairs, an abandoned cap, and half-eaten tins of food testified to the haste of the exit. The other three rooms were also vacant. A line of heel marks indicated that someone had been dragged the length of the passageway and up the stairs. On the top floor the trail ended at the far wall, as if his prey had dematerialized and walked through it. *Unlikely. The only fellow I know who can do that sits in an underwater prison in Scotland. Slippery git he was.*

In the ceiling, disguised amidst the molding, he found a door not quite shut. Leaping up and pulling made steps tumble down with a bang. Taking a deep breath, he swallowed hard as he contemplated the black attic space above.

It was in just such a musty garret that Peaceful Manners had pinned him to a filthy mattress and...

Paragon found himself back on the landing before mastering his fear. It took heroic focus and much consideration of what Madame Bernays had said to him that day to force himself back to the drop-steps.

No bullets rained down. Conscious of the ticking clock, Paragon scurried up the wobbling steps as quickly as he dared. At the top, he paused to permit his eyes to adjust to the darkness. The garret reeked of rodent droppings, piss, sweat, and mildew. Vibrations tingling the palm of his supporting hand indicated many feet ahead. He continued into the gloomy space, braced for defense. Soot-stained windows allowed in a bit of the dim daylight. Antique furniture moldered. There were crates of pawned items that had never been redeemed. Every few moments something with small sharp claws dashed past him. His pulse pounded. Sweat ran inside his linen shirt.

With ambush in his mind, he negotiated the warren with care. Once he nearly fell through a rotten patch of floor but hurled himself aside just in time. When he had progressed past the halfway point, he could make out the angry muffled noises of a pair of gagged individuals. They struggled mightily with their captors.

Paragon rounded a corner and squatted behind an upended armchair. There was a large skylight above, but it was as grime-caked as the rest of the windows and admitted little light. A pistol cracked from some thirty feet away, splintering the molding above him. He lay flat in the inch-thick dust, silently apologizing to Mervyn in advance for the indignity done to his clothes.

The chap with the gun stood behind a stack of moldering steamer trunks. Only a bit of his head and hand could be seen. To Paragon's right another fellow crouched, suffering mightily at Millie's outraged hands. Though tightly bound, her captors had neglected to secure the wigglers. The tentacles struck at him like the hair of Medusa. When he managed to seize both with a triumphant cry, Millie delivered a sound kick that threatened to unman him. Though bent over, he backhanded her. She squealed and fell upon Griffin, who already lay quiet after an earlier correction.

Two rapid shots neatly took down both kidnappers. The man with the gun went down for good, his temple shattered. Needing information, Paragon merely bored the thigh of the other. Just as Paragon congratulated himself, however, a third leaped out from behind a sofa and slashed with a long knife. Having heard him grunt as he raised himself, Paragon managed to impale him on the spike of his stick. He slumped back onto the couch with a gurgle.

The wounded man was still alive, but that did not let him off easy. Millie and the boy rained blows and kicks upon him.

"He can't speak with a pulverized jaw," Paragon pointed out after ensuring that no one else waited for him. He handed the stick to Griffin, retaining the brolly. After noting that the dead men bore ragged rope burns on their throats (*hanged and reanimated*), he removed the gags and restraints of the prisoners.

"I was beginnin' to think you'd scarpered," Millie complained while rubbing her wrists. "Ain't had nothin' but trouble since meetin' you, and that's the truth of it. Two days of no work. They'll turn me out of me rooms at this rate."

Paragon smiled an apology and handed her a gold coin. "Many pardons, dearest lady. Here is another advance on that five guineas. My doctor friend at the Eccentric Club is still interested in you."

The bloke he had wounded laughed at that. Bony and pale, perhaps forty, with eyes the color of ice chips and a shock of nearly white hair, the kidnapper snarled like the cornered animal he was. Griffin searched his rude workman's clothes, coming up with no gun but a pair of wicked knives. There was nothing else on his person. While he bound the clean wound – the bullet had passed through -- Millie turned out the dead men's pockets. From her business-like manner, Paragon deduced that she had handled more than a few corpses in her time.

"What is your purpose in taking these two?" he asked the man while struggling to place his half-familiar face. "Millie works the streets and Griffin lives on them. What profit could you hope to realize from snatching them?"

He spat at Paragon's foot. His untutored voice proclaimed him a Midlands native. "Looks like yer precious beauty sleep's gonna be ruined tonight, wonderin' about me business."

Griffin snickered. "Bold words, as they say in the penny dreadfuls."

"There's the perfect word, brat."

"What? Bold?"

"Oh, no. Dreadful. That's what me friends are."

Paragon smirked. "Littlewit and his mates are hors de combat. That hulking great brute is dead in the foyer, just like this one here, though I'll grant that it required more effort."

The criminal winced in pain. His eyes had a wild, half-mad caste. "I'll wager big Eddie's not as dead as you imagine. Hard to kill, that unnatural bastard is. But them's not the friends I'm talkin' about."

And in the same moment that Paragon cursed his folly, realizing who he meant, the roof exploded down at them. Skylight glass rained, along with a pair of thick leathery bodies. Their cloven feet cracked the floorboards. In the resulting cloud of dust, only their gleaming yellow eyes could be seen. As one they let loose an unearthly screaming.

Mrs. Ottershaw's demons had arrived.

Millie shrieked and dove behind the cooling corpse on the floor. The tough-talking Griffin vaulted behind the wall of crates to be seen no more. Even Paragon, despite having battled the walking dead and many another slithering thing besides, gulped and took a step back.

The monstrosities boasted three rows of teeth the size of hedge shears. Their bulging crossed eyes gleamed like those of animals caught in torchlight. Though scaled like lizards, their bodies more resembled the gorillas Paragon had seen in Africa. Huge, pointed ears, elongated skulls, fearsome claws. Six-foot-long tails lashed the air. Great membranous wings twitched and kicked up a century of dust, half obscuring them.

"Told yer!" cackled the blonde criminal like some Bedlam loony.

Paragon pointed the pistol at him to shut his annoying mouth, while keeping one eye on the new arrivals. "Where is your tiny tin tripod, I wonder?"

Puzzlement clouded the fellow's ferrety face. "Eh? Tripod? What yer on about?"

*He is not allied with the Islington force, then?*

With a horrid screech one of the gargoyles advanced with the caution warranted by a loaded pistol. Paragon gave matching respect to its saber teeth by retreating a step. Though reasonably certain he could put three bullets into the nearest fiend before it could leap upon him, he had no way of knowing what sort of armored bone structure might protect its vitals.

"It's been lovely havin' this little chat," chimed the wounded fellow, struggling to his feet, "but as you can see, the advantage is mine." As he spoke, he pulled out the tails of his shirt. Another crazed giggle escaped him.

"What advantage do you suppose you have?"

A blur. The Webley vanished from his grip as if a genie had taken it. Paragon stared as a gray-black tentacle waved it. That unexpected appendage, and another like it, emerged from the man's abdomen, just above the hips.

"What? You thought this whore had a monopoly on 'em? She were just a trial run."

"Clever. And useful. Perhaps I'll have a set of my own installed."

"New brains, more like. Thinkin' yer's so bloody clever. All yer at that Eccentric Club."

And at that moment Paragon recognized him as the mysterious waiter he had spotted at breakfast. The nose had been different, probably putty, but it was certainly the same man.

The tentacled foe transferred the pistol to his hand. "You'll all be comin' with us now."

Paragon's finely tuned senses detected something that the newly armed chap did not. Many booted feet climbing the stairs. Gruff voices of command. *Just a little more time.* A sneaking shuffle to the left put the nearest gargoyle between him and the pistol. He stamped and twisted on his left heel while fumbling with the umbrella. *Only one shot, Queue said.*

The hinged boot heel came free with a loud pop. Contact with the air detonated the special chemical secreted there. Noise, light, and stinging smoke overwhelmed the unprepared senses of the ruffian and his demonic minions. They wailed. Paragon remained unaffected, Tube mask held to his face. He ducked low beneath the curtain of white vapor, lunged with a fencer's grace, and plunged the tip of the umbrella into the gargoyle's belly. Foul green drool bubbled from the thing's mouth as every sinew spasmed. Like a marble column felled by an earthquake, it crashed nose-first onto the grimy floor and lay still.

Paragon rolled behind the inert demon. The blonde man growled and raised the gun. The attic suddenly grew very dark. All the Webley's remaining shots flew upward, toward the ruined ceiling. *What's that about?* When the hammer clicked with no further result and he tossed the gun, Paragon flew at him.

The second gargoyle's wrecking ball-tail smashed Paragon's abused ribs and launched him across the storeroom. An unforgiving wall interrupted his flight. Multi-colored pain blended with the piercing squeals of police whistles. Men bellowed orders for surrender. Pistols cracked. Strange animal growls, not from the gargoyle. A white-furred foot dashed past his eye. *What new horror is that?* With a sickening gurgle, Millie's terrified caterwauling cut off. Seconds later steam hissed from above and sparks dropped down with a tremendous roar, light returning to the room. Though a constellation of agonized stars danced behind his closed eyes, Paragon had but one distressed thought.

*These splendid trousers are torn. Damnation!*

## 8 / "GOOD WOMBS HAVE BORNE BAD SONS"

Griffin returned, having used the confusion to escape to the street, but Millie had not been so fortunate. Something unnatural had dropped from a giant airship and snatched up the ill-used dollymop, then rocketed away. The tentacled man, unable to walk, was carried into the sky and freedom by his remaining gargoyle. Littlewit and the others had escaped as well.

*Excellent work, Monty. You remain in possession of one unconscious reptile. Phoenix will wet himself with mockery.*

As he leaned on his stick, wincing, Paragon took inventory of his hurts. He foresaw much yoga and meditation – and perhaps a soothing draught of poppy elixir – before his abused corpus would forgive him. *Caliban's misery will entail precious little acting tonight.*

Paragon and Griffin covered the still-stunned gargoyle, now manacled, with a fragment of rotting carpet. The policemen all nodded in polite disbelief as he spun them a hasty tale about a rare hairless baboon stolen from a menagerie by unscrupulous men, who planned to show it abroad for a great profit. But when he displayed his talismanic owl ring to their sergeant, they shrugged and clumped back downstairs to undertake saner pursuits. Soon a Lochmoor detail would arrive to remove the prize for examination. A Metropolitan Police wagon had already fetched off the mortal remains of the now twice-dead kidnapper. When Paragon informed them that there was another body in the entry hall, the bobbies frowned and shook their heads.

*That great brute not only survived two throat strikes, but walked away on his own? Bloody hell...*

Manticore arrived with the Esteemed Punques. Lindworm, Cockatrice, and Basilisk lounged in the remains of the garret battlefield like victorious soldiers who had earned their leisure. Their bizarre appearance -- soot, muck, and cast-off clothing accented with toppers, smoked spectacles, canes, watch chains – served as the perfect accent to what had transpired there. They all puffed on cigars and pipes as if in competition with the foul smokestacks of industrial London. Paragon lit his own miraculously undamaged Kapp & Peterson briar, a gift from Wilde for surviving a particularly dangerous Dublin operation against riverine poltergeists.

Cocky, a broad boy with a missing front tooth, tossed the coin Paragon had given each of them, catching it in a comprehensively unwashed palm. "Don't mean to piss on me client, gov', but you look like shite."

Griffin came to his savior's defense. "He saved me sorry arse. Mr. Paragon, next time you need to call on the Punques, there'll be no charge."

Paragon noticed the horrified expressions on the faces of his troops. "I will pay the standard rate, as always. Call it combat pay. This is hardly a typical spying operation."

"That's certain," agreed Basilisk, her sensitive eyes hidden behind green goggles. "It's a good deal more fun."

"What's next, then?" inquired Manticore as he wiped his monocle on a trouser knee.

Paragon gazed about the room, hunting for anything that might have been missed. He saw that RIOT ARMY had been cut into a crate with a knife. "First, use all of your considerable resources to find Millie. What they may be planning to do to her does not bear thinking about. Second, find out all that you can about any sort of beast-men, demons, or walking metal tripods. Facts, rumors, East End fairy tales, whatever. Third, I have an interest in a certain woman."

Lindworm leered and snickered. "Too bad, gov'. They've just flew off with her!"

"Not Millie, you intolerable scamp. I speak of Lady Ambergris Kalmaar."

"Oooh, posh!" the Esteemed Punques hooted in unison.

"Settin' our sights mighty high, ain't we?" said Griffin. "You bein' a mere actor and all." He appeared to suddenly consider Paragon's recent feats of arms. "Er, no offense."

Paragon smiled as a cat might at a particularly courageous mouse. "None taken. And I have no plans to propose marriage, nor anything else. I know nothing about her, and she keeps appearing in this business. Find out all you can." He pointed at the carved words on the box. "And find out what this bally phrase means and who is behind it. It follows me wherever I go."

As he finished speaking, he also stopped walking. Beneath the aluminum foot lay a rubbery blob. He poked it with the spiked tip of his stick and lifted the wobbly bit to eye level. Less than two inches in length and the color of a dolphin he had once seen in Malaya, one side shone slick and smooth, while the other held a fleshy disk.

"It would appear that our fair-haired friend somehow lost the tip of his wiggler."

Griffin made a pained face. "Knew a Hebrew kid who had that done."

"Perhaps he'll wear it in a sling," said Lindworm. "Make our job easier."

"At any rate, he's made *my* job easier," Paragon concluded. He dropped the meaty item into a corked bottle along with coarse white hairs from whatever had snatched Millie.

The stunned gargoyle stirred beneath its concealing carpet. Soon the room echoed with its outraged roars and thrashings. Paragon recalled a dog in his youth, tormented into savagery by Peaceful Manners. He carefully stroked its snout until the monster quieted. From unholy bellowing, it fell into a pathetic childish whimpering.

"Don't sound so awful now," Basilisk observed. "More like a pup without its mother."

"I daresay you may be more correct than you know," Paragon said, waving to Phoenix's team as it entered with a covered litter. "Unless I miss my guess, these demons are more sinned against than sinning."

Ten minutes later the shackled fiend had been hauled out. *Hopefully, they won't dissect the poor thing.* Paragon relinquished his evidence, instructing them to have the bits analyzed and their Huxley Cells compared to his earlier sample.

He took a gyrocar west to his house. Once home, his clockwork man fussed over him to the point of absurdity. Mervyn bustled about the kitchen with his jerky-jointed motions, employing soapy cloths to cuts and scrapes, sticking plaster to wounds, wrapping his ribs, and applying expensive ice to swellings and bruises. All the while he clucked, sighed, and groaned as if he were a real human. No doubt his master's refusal of any narcotic aid gratified his Puritanical-mechanical soul.

"These are no mean injuries, sir," he pointed out, in case Paragon had grown unaware of the fireworks of pain exploding all over his ill-used body. "If I may be so bold as to say, you do on occasion display an alarmingly precipitate desire to assail the enemy."

"That's why I took the Queen's shilling, you know. I am Her Majesty's blunt instrument."

Mervyn prepared his master's dinner. The eggplant parmesan, fried baby artichokes, and carrot soup a la Crecy were capped with refreshing orange snow. An ambrosial delight, as always. He shuddered to think of what horrors most of the rest of Britain might be eating at that moment.

Leaving the redoubtable Mervyn to burn incense for the deceased trousers, Paragon napped for a blessed bit, then rose and dressed. He selected a flattering burgundy frock coat and his favorite double-breasted black brocade vest. A white hair chain hung from one of Queue's deadly watches. Supposedly it was made from the fur of a yeti (so said the disreputable-looking vendor who had pushed it on him in Lhasa). The protection of the armored bowler he sacrificed for a silk topper. Selection of the proper stick required predicting what arcane assaults might come his way. Deciding on the silver derby handle, he installed a new yellow blossom in his lapel and made his way to the theatre without incident, but not without aching.

Shakespeare proved to be a splendid pain reliever. Once Caliban crawled out and began growling, all thought of his actual misery vanished. The verse squeezed the suffering from him like juice from a berry. What made for an even better tonic was spying Ambergris Kalmaar in the same box she had occupied so magnificently on the night prior.

Lady Kalmaar's couture was more practical this night. A good deal less skin was on display. But her powder-blue satin dress atoned for that by the way it clung to her every corseted curve like rainwater on a Grecian statue. Trimmed with dark-violet lace down the front, the garment's outer skirt was gathered in a small bow at the left hip to display the white diamond-patterned chiffon underskirt. At intermission she stood and turned to speak to her automaton, which displayed her prominent bustle and pearl headdress to fine advantage. The long fan in her white-gloved hand bore a Japanese print, a sea scene featuring an octopus seizing a ship.

"O, brave new world, that has such creatures in it," breathed Paragon, standing on his one leg in the wings. *Careful, old bean. A turned head is all the easier to be struck off.*

The remainder of *The Tempest* proved to be uneventful. Merely a typical night of Calibanic wretchedness, the tumultuous applause, and then the lonely struggle to replace his artificial limb. *I am the only member of the cast who removes his costume to play his role.*

This time she boldly staked her claim to a significant patch of the lobby. Despite the crush of overdressed humanity about them, to Paragon it seemed that she stood alone, bathed in strong light from some singing star. On a little finger, outside the black glove, she wore a blue and silver ring bearing the Greek letter omega. Paragon wondered at the fashion statement, since it was the Breaker sign, but kissed the ring as if he was her acolyte.

She politely declined his offer of a drink at the bar, saying that she only took water most of the time, and guided him toward the main doors. Reginald shadowed them three steps behind. As they passed Phoenix, who spoke to a pair of diamond-encrusted matrons, Paragon felt a calling card thrust into his waistcoat pocket. Dardanelles winked but otherwise did not acknowledge the exchange.

"Where might we be going?" asked Paragon outside. "There are many splendid restaurants nearby."

"Thank you, no. I have already dined. And as scrumptious as was *The Tempest* a second time, I feel the urge to refresh my theatrical palate." She let out a delicate low cough. Paragon instantly reached into his inner coat pocket to offer her the austere breath mask he had procured for the train. "Your consideration is touching, but I have my own."

From her beaded silver reticule, she took a flat oval packet barely larger than a pocket watch. At the press of a hidden latch, it opened like an oyster, then expanded in all directions. To Paragon's amazement her palm now held the smallest, most exquisite of breath masks, a crème-and-gold work of art. Even more astonishing was that it required no straps, adhering to her lovely skin by some mysterious process. It just covered her mouth and nose, while delicate goggles sprung from the top. Nowhere was a filter canister visible, nor a voice emitter. Yet Lady Kalmaar appeared to breathe and speak with perfect ease.

"A splendid bauble, no? All mechanistics fascinate me. The best engender a most deplorable acquisitiveness."

After fumbling with the straps of his own mask and getting the blasted uncomfortable thing around his face, he asked, "So...this theatrical palate cleansing. What might it entail?"

"Why, a music hall, of course. And if we hurry, we can just make the late showing. There is a particular performance I am most curious about."

That proved, oddly and suspiciously enough, to be a musical performance by Vesta Tilley at Mornington's Temple of Varieties, where they were surrounded by a noisome and raucous crowd. The patrons roared their appreciation of the 'handsome lad's' soprano. Paragon naturally viewed the adventure as Lady Kalmaar's subtle announcement that she knew all about him and Lochmoor. His suspicions were immediately confirmed.

He frowned as a corpulent fellow deep in the throes of inebriation jostled him, then vomited a few feet away. "Must we endure the press of this feculent mob?"

"Come, Mr. Paragon, where is your vaunted intrepidity? We are come to experience how the stout yeomanry of England choose to spend what little free time we so-called 'higher orders' allot them. Are these not the very souls you and your colleagues at the Eccentric Club are sworn to defend?"

He hoped that his spasm of alarm was not too obvious. "You are disconcertingly well-informed, my lady."

She waved that away. "Too many of Whitehall's finest are prone to ill-advised babbling when in proximity of a well-filled corset. Worry not. Your secret is safe enough with me."

"Speaking of safety, where might the formidable Reginald have gone to?"

"No doubt taking up station in the proper spot for maximum surveillance. If I need him, he is easily called."

He eyed the box on her wrist. "Via your wireless telegraph?"

Lady Kalmaar favored him with one of her arc-light smiles. "Clearly I am not the only well-informed one here. Shall we go, then? The remaining acts pale beside your Miss Tilley."

Lady Ambergris stood to go. Paragon noticed her fan for the first time. No fragile affectation, it had ribs of the stoutest iron. His mystery woman carried a tessen, a Japanese war fan. When employed by a skilled practitioner, it could be lethal.

*My interest in you grows exponentially, madame. As does my wariness.*

She took his arm, elevating his pulse and his trouser seam. "I really ought to get Reggie home and into his rewinding cabinet."

Paragon led the way out. Halfway to the door, Reginald appeared behind them as if summoned by magic, which was near to the truth. Outside, he spied Vesta hiding in a crowd of Arsethetes. She appeared to be following them at a discreet distance, remaining in male guise. *Is Phoenix so fearful of my emotional state that I must have a nanny at all times? How is that likely to calm my rages?*

Beyond all expectation, they found a hansom. In its relative silence, seated side-by-side in delightful proximity while Reginald clung to the rear, they could breathe without aid. But what the sealed cabin kept out, it also kept in. Lady Kalmaar's alluring sea-scent, as attractive as a siren's song, captivated Paragon just as it had the night before. In his weakened state he now had much less resistance to it. It did not help matters that her warm ripe body pressed up against his. His pulse pounded so loudly that he wondered that she did not complain about the noise. Adequate breathing required opening his mouth to reach for great gulps of air. And once he began to dwell on mouths…

Later he would reflect that any other woman would have used that deadly tessen to put him in his place, particularly as a weapon of no less firmness was rudely prodding her hip. *Blast! That's bloody embarrassing. Yet it **is** her fault, after all.* But Ambergris Kalmaar hardly fit the mold of any other woman. Like a trained jiujutsu master, she met his attack and redirected his energy while subduing him with minimal force of her own. Said subduing, with warm lips and tongue, took the better part of two minutes. *Making dead certain the enemy cannot rise. In this case, however, that may be an inaccurate term.*

"You have the advantage of me, sir," she said from half-atop him as she broke the kiss.

"I beg to differ. You could cut my throat right now and I would send you a thank-you note."

"A gentleman to the last. How charming."

*To the last?*

She straightened his crooked cravat and gave it a pat. With an ease and elegance – and unexpected strength – she got them both upright. Paragon's head swam from a mix of sensation and concern. Her lips possessed intoxicating heat and promise. No amount of poppy had ever overwhelmed him so. This astounding woman had broken years of laboriously acquired ascetic self-control without any overt move to attract him. Since she was a chief suspect in the murder of a Member of Parliament, dallying with her was not only unwise and unprofessional, but potentially fatal.

"As delightful as that hors d'oeuvre was, perhaps we should postpone any main course to a more suitable time and place," she suggested.

"You are certain I cannot convince you to repair to an eatery?"

"I am not one of those little birds who starve themselves to squeeze into their corsets, but neither am I much of a champion eater. Indeed, I subsist on…fluids as much as anything."

"As you wish." *The lady is easy of maintenance. That dress, however, must have cost her a tradesman's yearly wage, to say nothing of her expensive mechanistic toys and combat clocker. Where might her funds come from?*

"How I adore hearing a man saying that. Particularly so handsome and charming a one. Her finger moved up to stroke his scar. "I do confess to being rather smitten with this mysterious token of your rugged past. War wound?"

"Hardly anything so exciting. Cut myself shaving."

She raised one imperious eyebrow at the joke. "Ah. Try standing farther away from the razor next time. Say, a mile?" One of her cigarillos appeared in a now ungloved hand. Ambergris leaned forward, the tight roll of tobacco between lush lips. Paragon gulped hard and found a match for her. Hand on his to steady it, she lit it with studied efficiency. Tangy cloudlets of smoke burst about them, as if a tiny locomotive were getting underway.

With the thick vapor obscuring his movements, Paragon took the opportunity to slide Phoenix's card from his waistcoat pocket and read it while fumbling with his silver flask. It read "*No record of her existence before eleven months ago. Title spurious. Do not trust.*"

The lady's nostrils widened as she sniffed his container. "Gin and tonic?" she asked with a note in her sultry voice that was not quite disapproval. "You surprise me. I would have taken you for a brandy or whiskey man."

"I spent a good portion of my life in the tropics, in some particularly unsavory climates. I find that a steady diet of palatable quinine helps to keep my malarial symptoms at bay."

*Not to mention the other symptoms, when they do not respond to chanting or Madame Bernays' wisdom.*

He shifted in his seat. "Gin is a botanical, you know. Made from seeds, berries, flowers. All manner of exotic ingredients."

"Does that sort of thing interest you?"

"It does, actually. Take the flower you wear. Though I am widely traveled, I have never seen its like."

She reflexively touched the bit of red pinned inside her cape. "No? Neither have I. Someone gave me a tiny pot of it. It takes so little watering that one might almost wave a damp sponge at it. I made the mistake of soaking it just after delivery and the creepers nearly devoured me in three days."

"You appear to have a fondness for wearing this gift."

"Yes, well, I must do something with it, else my rooms will be quite overrun. Perhaps I should donate the wretched thing to the Royal Botanical Gardens."

"I cannot imagine Kew turning down such a prize. It might interest you to know that I am somewhat of a keen collector myself." Paragon pulled out the crushed red sprig he had found beneath Grimsby's corpse. "I found it in a machine shop, of all places."

Lady Kalmaar's lovely face twitched not at all. To Paragon's amazement, however, something even more damning – and remarkable – occurred.

Her skin and *hair* flushed the same red as the odd flower, then as bright blue as a Hindu god, then canary yellow, and back again to her original creamed tea complexion…all in the space of two seconds.

Paragon's brow shot up into his hairline. Mastering himself immediately, he took a deep breath and sat back. *Did I just imagine that? Am I losing my wits again?*

Puffing furiously on her cigarillo, Lady Ambergris tried to continue the game. "Why, Mr. Paragon, have you been round to my house?"

"This particular specimen came from under the dead body of a murdered MP. It is most likely that whoever slew him dropped it there."

"What a sad Empire we must live in now if possession of a simple flower garners such a sordid accusation."

"What am I to think, my lady? You come to me out of the blue, warning of my imminent doom if I continue to investigate beast-men. You wear a Breaker ring. This morning I discover your charmingly unique decoration at a prominent murder scene. Please explain how this flower came to be at an Islington blacksmith's last night, along with a pair of winged monsters and a three-legged homicide machine."

Again, she changed color for an instant, this time to a white that rivaled a linen tablecloth. "You saw a tripod there?"

He kept an eye on her deadly fan as he pressed. "No, but we found its tracks. However, I did see one last night as I left the theatre. It stalked me with a heat ray. Then several toughs attempted to brain me in an alley as I sought its master. Another curious coincidence, wouldn't you say?"

"Coincidence? Tripods never appear on a whim." Now her complexion went olive green. "Did you see a large man, shoulders wide as a barn door, on a steam penny farthing?"

"I did. Lost him in Whitehall. Is he the machine's operator?"

"Perhaps. I do not know. I have seen a tripod only twice myself. Both times he was nearby. Beware that fiend." She rubbed an arm. "He is cruelty incarnate."

"We met this afternoon. Came near to dispatching me. Would you know where to find him?"

"Alas, no. If I could place you on his doorstep, armed, I would do so without a second's hesitation."

"In what circumstances, I wonder, did those tripod sightings occur?"

"My answer would mean little to you, without telling you more than I dare yet reveal…for your sake."

Paragon slapped this thigh. "For my sake! Always solicitous of my well-being. So that death-dealing little trinket last night had nothing to do with you? Likewise, the thugs with cudgels who sought my demise only a little later?"

"Upon my honor I know nothing of those incidents. I truly do seek your safety in all things. Of that you must assure yourself."

"Why? Why must I? Because I tell you candidly that from where I sit you are not merely my prime, but my only suspect in the murder of the Honorable Samuel Grigsby, to say nothing of the assaults on my person."

She flushed pink as a rose, then paled to her normal dusky skin tone. "I deeply desire…that no harm come to you, because I believe my own continued existence depends on it."

"Heretofore I have not noticed that you require defending. Your violent valet appears capable of repelling all assaults."

"Not all, much as I would wish it. Brass does melt. And a well-placed bullet to his left eye and I am defenseless." That fault had been built into clockers by Her Majesty's government in case one ran amok.

"The same could be said of me, and not just the eye. By the way, I am certain that you are violating the law there. Civilians are forbidden to possess battle automatons."

"I have Home Office authority for him. The papers are in order. Enquire all you wish."

"I shall. But I am more interested in the threat you fear."

"He fired an electro-compression pistol at you two nights ago."

"The fellow in the flight togs, whom the beast-men called father?"

"He is, in any sense that matters. Without him they would not exist. His name is Dr. Sebastian Moreau. One of Professor Huxley's brightest assistants, until circumstances forced him to flee."

"What circumstances?"

"The full tale is long and sordid. You may want to have another drink."

Paragon took her at her word, all the while keeping Dardanelles' warning note in mind. One eye remained on her while he pulled at the flask.

Lady Ambergris seemed to realize his concern, for her knowing smile and natural coloring returned, along with her refined composure. She leaned back with her cigarillo, indicating that Paragon should feel free to enjoy his pipe.

"Once the code of Huxley Cells was broken and the secret of life revealed, great advances appeared in rapid succession. Dreaded diseases nearly eradicated, child mortality reduced, natural life spans extended. For the wealthy, at any rate. And all of this in less than thirty years."

Paragon nodded. "I gather that a case can be made that Huxley actually re-discovered that secret, since apparently that Swiss chap, that Frankenstein, achieved remarkable success. Records destroyed, though, so we may never know precisely how he did it."

*I really should drop in on Adam Franklin again some evening and see how much he knows about his own creation. It may very well be applicable to this case.*

She fingered her wireless wrist box. "The explosion in learning since the late Fifties has been nothing short of remarkable. Historians shall struggle mightily to explain it."

"Pray continue. Your tale would cure deafness."

"Moreau worked diligently, toiling to develop wondrous cures, new varieties of farm animals, that sort of thing. This was all long before Parliament passed the Eugenics Act. Discoveries far outpaced legislation. Another great Age of Exploration, with industrialists competing against one another. Naturally, there were anguished losers as well as triumphant victors.

"One of the losers was a firm called Clerval and West. They had invested heavily in a process to regenerate dead tissue. Marvelous applications in medicine, as you can imagine. Developed by a Professor Percy Simple. Alas, the fellow turned out to be a charlatan. Took their money and vanished before the project could bear fruit. His conception proved to be of no value, though others have since been more successful."

"Yes, we've had to clean up the refuse left by some of those so-called successes. Re-animated tissue often gets out-of-hand as it degrades. Violent, even." He recalled the hanged man he had re-killed that afternoon.

"The directors panicked. They spun spurious tales of phenomenal progress to their investors whilst searching for a new, and legitimate, genius, hoping to find someone with few scruples and much need. In Moreau, their prayers were answered. A wizard with a microscope, some said. More privately, they despaired that his tool of choice was too often the scalpel."

"A vivisectionist?"

"Yes, among other even worse proclivities. It seemed that the exchange fate made when awarding him his scientist's talent was to withhold empathy. Other than wife and child, the man cared more for knowledge than for the lives of those he studied. He just had to **know**. It was like the love of the pernicious poppy, which so often consumes a man's will." She blew a smoke ring at him and raised one elegant eyebrow.

If Paragon had been a lesser actor her sudden thrust might have struck home. As it was his parry barely sufficed. "So I have seen, yes, in my time in the Orient."

"While under the watchful eye of the Ministry for Natural Philosophy, Moreau's weaknesses were held in check. But events intervened. His wife and child both contracted a pythogenic fever. Despite all his advanced knowledge of disease, they expired in a matter of hours. Distraught as only a man with a single love can be, he succumbed to the blandishments of Clerval and West. Free rein to investigate any problem he desired, so long as he saved their regeneration project. No one inquired as to the ethics of his experimentations."

"I take it that things did not, alas, proceed according to plan?"

"At first they did. He corrected and completed Simple's work, managed to develop a formula that would resurrect newly dead tissue. But his monomania drove him to seek not only to revive his deceased wife and daughter, but to blend the Huxley Cells of man and beast in unique ways, in order to create a higher order of man. This new being would be wiser, stronger, resistant to all disease and aging."

"Clearly he has been successful in those endeavors."

"Somewhat. But the grand design eluded him. Worse still, his regenerative formulation proved to have a fatal, and much less profitable, flaw. After a few weeks, the cells began to regress to their animal nature again, and then die. Clerval and West turned to ruthless men to forestall a repeat of the Simple affair. Forewarned by a sympathetic creation of his, he managed to flee England, just ahead of the assassins. They stayed on his scent across France, Switzerland, Italy, even Egypt. But eventually he eluded them."

*Doesn't this sound painfully familiar?* "Where has he been?"

"A remote island far west of the Galapagos. You will recall that it was in there that Huxley first identified the cells which bear his name.

"Moreau established a supply chain, under assumed names and fictitious companies. Once a year a ship docks to drop off technical equipment, as well as the necessities of living. No one from the ship is permitted to go further ashore than the dock. It is not a difficult rule to enforce, with the terrifying rumors of monsters roaming the jungle."

"So, Dr. Moreau has filled the countryside with his less-successful attempts at species manipulation?"

"Correct. Many perish in the Petri dish or on the vivisection table, of course. Those capable of fending for themselves live in a rude village, under a leader who maintains order with a kind of law. The good doctor administers stern justice with his own hand."

"I saw an example of Moreau's justice two nights ago. Not the forgiving sort, is he?"

"No. He feels rejected by civilized men. They hounded him out of Europe. Is it any wonder that he believes that he can improve mankind with a new bloodline?"

"I hardly consider a monomaniacal psychopath to be my first choice as deliverer." Paragon frowned. "Surely he cannot have managed to take enough money with him to sustain life and work for a decade?"

"Shrewd investments bring in impressive amounts. And he also engages in smuggling and other illicit trade via intermediaries throughout the world. He has built quite the impressive operation. Moreau is one of the great criminal operators of this century. The laws of the men who ruined him are no bar."

"And he has taught himself to pilot aeroplanes. But he could not have flown all of the way here in that light ornithopter."

"True. He owns a large Giffard steam-aerostat, the *Prosper*, one of the world's fastest. It even has rockets to assist it in escaping pursuit, as you saw today when he snatched your girl from you. It is painted like a standard commercial passenger ship, to deceive any authority that might challenge him. The craft is large enough to house several Hargrave 'thopters. But he prefers to remain on his safe island."

"Then something of importance must have driven him here. Can you think what?"

"Not thus far. He has been remarkably secretive of late."

*Perhaps. But that monstrous Giffard will not be easy for him to conceal. It must be close to three hundred yards long.*

"I presume not all of your intelligence is second-hand."

"I have had a direct connection with the man. Quite an intimate one, actually." She sighed. "Sebastian Moreau is my father. And I intend to cut his throat."

# Act Three

~

# Be Not Afear'd

*Above Hertfordshire*

*Millie crouched down in the corner and made her terrified body as small as she could. The other cramped laboratory cages held monkeys, rats, lizards, dogs. In a corner, lit from within, stood a tall glass case like an aquarium. It held the bodies of a woman and child, floating in some sort of golden fluid like medical museum specimens. When he had entered, the doctor had touched his forehead to the glass like it was a religious shrine. She was the only live human captive…other than the poor sod on the operating table, his quivering torso open like a sample case.*

*The awful man in the steaming breath mask cut away at something inside the gut with a long knife. Though the localized anesthesia dulled the victim's pain, it did nothing to allay his fear, as he was conscious, eyes wide. A sponge gag in his mouth muffled his horrified shrieks.*

*Now the doctor injected some purplish substance into the subject's viscera with a gleaming steel syringe. When the great airship hit a pocket of turbulence, he steadied himself with practiced ease and continued the hideous work.*

*Of course, she would be next. Why else would that disgusting white ape have scooped her up in its four brawny arms? Did they plan to dissect her, to see what made her wigglers work? Was this how she had come by them in the first place? It had been only two years before that she had awakened in her room with an ache in her head and a pair of wriggling additions. Pockmark Pete had behaved as if she'd been born with the things. Gave her a right good walloping every time she asked about them.*

*The laboratory door opened to admit a handsome dark-haired bloke in a gray uniform. He said, "No pursuit. Yorkshire by dawn."*

*"Excellent," came the metallic reply. "At least something is going to plan today."*

*"Lochmoor is becoming quite the thorn in our side. Paragon should be dealt with."*

*"He is merely a tool. I am more concerned with my erstwhile pupil."*

*"Jimmy Navita? Lost his prize today, he did. You plucked it from under his nose." He squatted before Millie. "Isn't that a wicket for our side, as you folks say?"*

*"Merely the first over. He shall send up another batsman."*

*"You expect him to follow us, then? Is his operation that good?"*

*"If it were not, I should not have crossed half the world to deal with him."*

*"Then I shall prepare a proper reception for him at the factory." He rose and turned to go.*

*"Do so. We shall host a business conference there in two days' time, at noon. Heads of departments. I have yet to meet some of them. We must take steps to destroy his Riot Army."*

*Captain Carter smiled and gave him a two-fingered salute. A sprig of the red plant was pinned to his collar. "Of course. I expect that the famed Dr. Moreau shall make quite the impression on them." He nodded toward a frosted glass door near the floating bodies. A shadow moved on the other side. "Will our…immigrant friend be there, too?"*

*"She shall."*

*Carter laughed. "You should have a photographer there to capture their faces. And a mop to clean up when they piss themselves."*

*Millie whimpered, a tear cutting a channel in one filthy cheek. She turned away from the grisly scene, not wishing for Moreau to see the paper that Carter had pushed through the bars of her cage.*

## 9 / "MISERY ACQUAINTS A MAN WITH STRANGE BEDFELLOWS"

Again, Paragon had to master his surprise. "Indeed?"

"Yes. I was a passenger on the annual supply vessel. A brain fever left me delirious and wasting away. Moreau took pity upon me. I can only speculate that the memory of his lost daughter softened his loathing of mankind.

"These particulars he informed me of at a much later date. I lost all memory of my life before awakening on the island some weeks later. No childhood recollections, no knowledge of my true parents. My life began on that sweltering jungle rock.

"I did not lack for education. Moreau's library was astounding. As he is a polymath, skilled in history, literature, geography, politics, law, languages, and science, of course, I did not suffer the want of a good, if terribly strict, teacher. Perhaps the injections he gave me every week assisted my mental development. That would certainly explain how I advanced so rapidly, from a cipher to a whole person in only three years.

"But Prospero could not shield his Miranda. I would steal down to the wharf when the ship came in, surreptitiously speaking to the crew and wondering what their world might be like, back in Kuala Lampur or Marseilles. Moreau often would return from one of his airship journeys and let slip some enticing tidbit about life on the mainland. Is it any wonder that I plotted escape from my little prison?

"I secreted money, food, and other necessities in the airship, a tiny bit at a time. By good fortune, Moreau had to dash off on some emergency and did not take his usual care to ensure that I remained behind. So, I managed to slink aboard only moments before the Giffard left the ground.

"I will spare you the rest. Two years ago, I found myself on the streets of Singapore. My observation of the aggression responses of wild animals and beast-men proved fortuitous, as did Moreau's lessons on proper behavior and civilized customs. With luck and cunning, I traveled to Europe, with only a few alarming moments. After that it was a matter of cultivating the friendship of the right people."

Lady Kalmaar paused to down a swallow from his flask as the hansom rolled to a stop. "And with that I shall have to leave you. Reginald needs to be rewound and I need to get enough rest so that I am not a public embarrassment tomorrow. You would not wish to see me in that state. These sturdy limbs of mine flop like India rubber. My skin becomes positively puckery."

*And multi-colored, also. Just what sort of new medical techniques did Dr. Moreau employ to save you? Is that why you desire his death? Because he made a monster of you? What are you so afraid of that you need a total stranger's protection from it?*

They took their leave in front of Largo House, a sandstone Regency masterpiece. Paragon kissed Lady Kalmaar's hand, proud of himself for stopping there. Squeezing gracefully out of the narrow carriage door like an eel out of a bottle, she turned back to him with that warm yet knowing smile.

"Thank you for a lovely evening. Just so that there is no misunderstanding, I thoroughly enjoyed every single moment of it." The manner in which she lingered over each word left no doubt of her veracity. Paragon felt like a songbird that had only just escaped the cat.

"The pleasure was all mine," he told her, inwardly reliving that rapturous kiss. "May I call on you tomorrow? I feel that we have much more to discuss."

"Please do. Not too early, though. A lady requires time to properly prepare herself for important visitors."

"Fear not. We actors are not known for being morning people."

She favored that with a warm chocolate laugh. Her beautiful hand came up, displaying the Breaker ring. "Since you are so concerned, let me assure that this was merely a gift...from a most grateful admirer."

"Yes? From where did this gratitude spring?"

"The gentleman seemed happy that he still drew breath." She blew him a tiny kiss. "Pleasant dreams. May they need no bottled assistance."

With that parting shot across his bow, she crowded on all sail and vanished through the hotel's ebony doors, Reginald pounding after her. For several moments Paragon stared at the closed portals as if mesmerized. His driver's whip handle pounding on the hansom's roof startled him back into awareness.

"Sorry. Up to Soho, please. Oxford Street."

"That's alright, mate. A bird like that'd stop a bleedin' racehorse in his tracks, she would."

All the way home Paragon pondered what Lady Kalmaar had told him. She could be an ally for Lochmoor and a potential trap for Moreau, presuming that she did not have her own separate hand to play. How much of that story was true? Though she appeared amenable enough, something did not sit right. *Possibly the way her skin and hair can turn every color of the bleeding rainbow, hmm?* For instance, where did all the stupendous amounts of money she was spending come from? A suite in Largo House cost as much per week as a City accountant brought home in a month. Yet he knew her to be no aristocrat, if her story of escaping the island of Doctor Moreau were true. She had no honest title, seemingly no income-bearing property.

*Time for a Hades conclave. We need to put our collective heads together and see what sort of tapestry all these various strands are weaving.*

He approached his dark house with care, hand on pistol, but no gargoyles leaped upon him. Thanking Providence for small favors, he entered and called out to Mervyn.

The clocker entered from his normal defensive post near the sitting room. His crystal eyes sparkled blue. "Welcome back, sir. Delighted to see you well."

"I am delighted to be well, considering my comprehensive thrashing this afternoon." That reminded him afresh of his bruises and cuts, so soothed by his time with Lady Kalmaar. He winced. "Any threats?"

"No assaults or infiltrations have been made."

"Good. I'm going to bed. Too knackered to stand upright."

~

Paragon's dreams were of something he had thought was dead to his sleeping mind. Had Madame Bernays unlocked it to force him to confront that grim episode in '79? It would hardly have surprised him.

The images were a patchwork rather than a complete narrative, but he knew the plot. Lower leg shattered. Tourniquet barely keeping him alive. Face bleeding. Crawling in a fevered haze. The old Zulu woman's hut. Screaming as she sawed his limb off. Healing him with some native potion. Telling of her only child, slain by the British though she begged him not to fight. Believing Paragon's arrival was a sign from her gods to forgive.

A lieutenant from Paragon's own regiment, some wealthy lord's son, a cruel ass, riding up. Accusing Paragon of desertion. Was that why he was alone? Guilty of his own charge? Attempted arrest. His savior intervening. Fighting. Her dead on the ground. Paragon lashing out in a rage. The officer down, clutching a ruined eye, vowing revenge if it took him the rest of his days. "Sleep with one eye open, Parsons," and laughing madly at his joke. Chased off with his own pistol.

Paragon making a crutch and fleeing east to the coast. Taking the first ship he could get. Going east, always east. How the bastard's assassins found him was unknowable, but they did. The reward must have been staggering, for a new one was forever at him. Seven desperate years of running, hiding, new identities, developing survival and life skills through any master he could persuade. Finally tiring of it and returning to England, adopting his present persona, and gaining the protection of the ECS. But the boy was the Earl of Moura now and the price still lay on his now-aching head.

He woke in exquisite misery from the damage he had incurred in his Whitechapel scrap. It required all of Mervyn's considerable expertise as physician, chef, and drinks mixer to get him out of the house and off to the Eccentric Club.

"Normally I might say 'look what the cat dragged in', but no self-respecting feline would bother with such a sorry specimen," sneered Wilde from behind the *Times*. Vesta read the same paper from over his shoulder in Lochmoor's waiting room. With her black-rimmed monocle she resembled half an owl.

Paragon glared at Wilde. "Oscar – and I mean this with all of the loving sincerity my soul can muster – bugger off."

"Careful what you wish for, old bean," Tilley muttered.

"I heard that," Wilde said with a firm elbow nudge.

She smiled and returned his jab with a hip bump. "You were meant to, silly sod."

Phoenix' cloying gardenia vanguard appeared before the rest of him did. From his office door he said, "Let us postpone the buggering until I can send out the invitations. Gather in the parlor, please."

In the parlor, Paragon remained on his feet, fearing he would fall asleep otherwise. Their leader cradled a tiny cup of rare and hellishly expensive white tea from the Chinese mountains. How Phoenix managed to obtain it was anyone's guess. *Relays of airships across the Himalayas to Goa, probably. Your Imperial taxes at work.*

Phoenix said, "If this grows any more confusing, I shall need the Wizard Shop to invent some sort of helmet that cures the headache. Oscar, Vesta, how went your sojourn to the Royal Society?"

Tilley said, "Natural philosophers seem to have an aversion for clearly marking their doors. But by the application of my manly charm, I convinced a giggling maid to escort us to the proper wing and floor."

"The poor vacant girl nearly swooned from longing," smiled Oscar. "Never a clue." He sighed. "And might I add that the place is a dreadful Palladian monstrosity. How England ever achieved an empire with that sort of architecture is quite beyond me."

Vesta went on. "Oscar's pick-set convinced the door to yield. It was a document room. All the walls had shallow wooden drawers built into them, full of Dagron images. Tens of thousands of miniature photographs, dozens to a sheet, all a sixteenth of an inch square. Naturally, we despaired, having no solid idea as to just what we were looking for.

"But Lochmoor luck was on our side. Though the room showed little sign of recent visitation, by which I mean since Cromwell was in nappies, in the northern corner the dust had been disturbed. We examined the handles of all the trays in that vicinity. Only one was clean and it had not quite been closed all the way. Someone had done us a favor, probably Dr. Jekyll. I used the magnifying lens of my Stanhope ring to peruse its contents. The documents in question concerned a secretive 1878 investigation into the nefarious activities of a biologist named ---"

"--- Dr. Sebastian Moreau," said Paragon.

All eyes turned to stare at him as if he had just pulled a dragon out of his arse. Tilley seemed put out that he had ruined her ending flourish. Paragon clung to the mantle and related the details of his late-night meeting with Ambergris Kalmaar, omitting the more labial bits.

Wilde confirmed that the Dagron files agreed with Lady Kalmaar's account. "Except that your mysterious lady misled you about the wife and daughter," he said. "They did not succumb to a fever. It is ever so much juicier than that, if you fancy sordid and exotic domestic tragedies."

Paragon raised an eyebrow. "Do tell."

"Moreau's assistant was a younger chap names James Mapp. Utterly brilliant, I gather. Came up with devilishly clever medical marvels that astonished even his mentor. What astonished Moreau even more was finding his beloved in Mapp's arms."

"Sordid, yes, and sadly common. How exotic?"

Vesta jumped in. "Moreau had been experimenting on himself in his pursuit of a superman. It did not go well. Organ failure, nerve damage, skin lesions, muscle atrophy...and mental decline. He wears that breath mask because without it he would die, to say nothing of showing the world that he looks like a walking plague corpse. If he weren't regularly injecting a special serum, he would have died years ago."

"What sort of serum?"

"All that the documents say is that it is an orange liquid that seems to heal insanity, with the added benefit of rapidly curing physical wounds. The latter is permanent, but the mental improvement wears off in a week or so. And greater and greater doses are required."

"So, our man is mad and dying, just more slowly than he might otherwise. How does that concern our love triangle?"

"It is pertinent because the enraged husband fired a flechette scattergun at them. The daughter flung herself in front of the offending pair, but one of the poisoned darts missed her and struck the mother, as well. As the instantly repentant Moreau tended to his dying family, Mapp fled before he could shoot again."

"What a charming display of courage for his beloved."

"It would have been vain and suicidal. Moreau's venom was his own creation and has no antidote."

"So, Mapp now lives a secure life in Switzerland?"

"Alas, no. Moreau's reach is long. One of his lackeys, a disgraced army colonel with an air gun, infected Mapp with a variant of the same concoction that is destroying Moreau, causing homicidal insanity. Intended as a long and miserable revenge that would end in disgrace on the gallows. But he did not anticipate his protégé somehow acquiring the same temporary cure that Moreau himself employed. Mapp has survived, the deadly urges suppressed by the injections."

"And no one knows what this wonderful drug is or where it comes from?"

"If any medical man knows, he isn't talking. Too bad. The mental cure could be sprayed by airship over Whitehall."

Paragon snapped his fingers. "What does this Mapp look like?"

Tilley consulted her notes. "Medium height, stocky, dark brown hair, blue eyes, remnants of an Irish accent."

"Too bad. I was hoping that tentacled bloke was him. He was spying on us in the breakfast room the other day."

"Out of luck there, it seems."

"Just what is Moreau doing in London?" Paragon wondered. "He would not be cutting throats and shooting up the East End merely for a lark. Island solitude has kept him safe from those who wish him imprisoned or dead. Why abandon that now, so suddenly and so publicly?"

"Lady Kalmaar said that once before he'd left with little notice, as if it were a great emergency," offered Wilde. "Perhaps his criminal enterprise had been found out and he needs to apply a tourniquet."

"A possibility," conceded Paragon. "But she says that Moreau controls a web of efficient lieutenants who could manage that. I fear that something rather more dreadful than mere chastisement of beast-men is afoot. Perhaps a scheme akin to the late Jubilee plot."

Phoenix said, "To that end I have set to work several teams probing the world for unexplained funds transfers, unusual gang activity, 'monster' sightings. Do not concern yourselves with that drudgery. What we need you to do is to act upon whatever they turn up. Until then, let us concentrate on some of the more bizarre elements, as that is our Home Office brief."

"Why would a dollymop have tentacles?" asked Paragon. "They seemed natural as breathing to her. She behaved as if she had possessed them all her life. That is clearly impossible, given her age. Huxley Cell Attributes have only been manipulated in the last fifteen years."

Wilde shrugged. "Unless someone succeeded before Huxley and we never knew about it."

Phoenix nearly choked with delicate outrage. "I beg your pardon! I happen to be apprised of the state of the Shah of Persia's nether regions. Do you think that such a monumental discovery as HCA's would have escaped our notice? More likely they tampered with the poor girl's brain so that she has no recollection of it. I posit that she was an experiment that succeeded all too well. Not only was the transplantation effective, but the recipient escaped and went straight back to plying her trade."

"That makes sense," said Vesta. "They probably expected her to die, like so many other Huxley patients."

Paragon set his cup down on the sideboard. "Perhaps that explains her kidnapping. The minions of Dr. Moreau may have simply been instructed to recapture an escaped laboratory specimen. Having her saunter about London waving those wigglers as an advertisement for her charms would only call the wrong sort of attention to his other, even less savory, operations."

"Quite possible," Phoenix muttered. "Though one does wonder why the operation was done at all. And by whom? Moreau has been a near-recluse in the South Pacific. Someone he knew must have done it against orders, to spark such outrage that he flew here to mop up the mess. That would explain the gargoyles. Not Moreau's style at all."

Wilde stood to help himself to another scone. "Moreau's very existence is centered on reanimating – or reconstructing – his dead family. Implanting tentacles hardly fits in with that scheme."

A faint voice croaked from the doorway, "And that is not the most fantastic aspect of all this."

Vesta rose to shake the hand of Henry Jekyll in her bluff masculine manner. "So glad you could come, sir."

"This hearty young fellow assured me that this affair is of the utmost interest to the Empire," said the handsome professor as he limped painfully into the room. Paragon noted that he wore a linen bandage beneath his high wing collar, and another on his forehead, as well as a nasty bruise on one temple. His voice sounded as if he had poured acid down his throat. "Sorry I'm late. Would you believe it? Fell off my ruddy bicycle."

Paragon joined in that, but also took note of the way the man favored his left abdomen. "Those penny-farthings are deathtraps, aren't they?"

"They certainly ---" Jekyll stopped short and gave him a queer look. "Yes, one has to be alert at all times."

The group expressed their sympathy. Jekyll adjusted his spectacles and opened his black leather bag. Out of it came the tentacle tip and white hairs Paragon had found in the garret, as well as the red weed and original tissue evidence. "Fascinating, the things you chappies bring me."

"How so?" Phoenix asked. "When last you were here you enthused about the first set of remains. This new sample is different?"

"Completely." The anatomist indicated the bone shard from the fire. "This is standard, though exquisitely-crafted, HCA tinkering, animal cells into human ones."

Dr. Jekyll pointed a long finger at the hairs and shook his head. "But these...after submitting them to every test I know, I actually understand it less than when I began. It is neither human nor animal."

All mouths gaped.

"Astounding, no? I so disbelieved my findings that I brought in several outside experts to review them. They concurred." The physician sat back, waving his hands like a triumphant magician. "You see before you something that cannot exist. None of its cells originated in any life form on earth."

No one spoke for a long moment. Eventually Wilde said, "The same has often been said of me, you know."

"Let us snip off the end of your tentacle and compare, shall we?" Phoenix shot back.

Rolling her eyes, Vesta brought the conversation back. "Was it created out of whole cloth in a laboratory?"

"Unlikely," replied Jekyll. "That is the sort of advance we have yet to make. The head-spinning conclusion is that if the seed cells do not originate on this planet, they must have come from another one."

The previous silence was an eye-blink in comparison to the stunned response that this news brought. All the room's occupants exchanged glances that ran the gamut from worry to mirth to fear.

"A suggestion worthy of Monsieur Verne," Oscar Wilde chuckled.

"Let me be absolutely clear," said Phoenix. "You are convinced that these hairs, or at least the parent cells and the knowledge to grow them, came from another planet entirely?"

"And the red plant, as well. When one has excluded all other explanations, the one which remains – however implausible – must be the truth."

That brought Paragon forward. "Consider what else we have already seen. Are men from beyond the stars so much more improbable than some of the other phenomena we have encountered? Re-animated corpses. Golems. Werewolves. Giant Sumatran vampire rats. The universe is a bloody strange place."

Wilde raised an imperious eyebrow. "The learned gentleman's theory casts light on several other mysteries with this case. I speak of the deadly little tripod and the weird machinery in Islington. Both seem to violate earthly physics."

"Do we have any idea yet of the purpose of those devices?"

Phoenix shrugged. "Queue says the Wizard Shop is drooling over them like Scrooge in a bank vault. They are not powered by steam, nor by electricity. Some seem to be for manufacturing devices so small as to require the strongest of lenses. Others apparently weld without heat. Most are still mysteries."

"Might they be used for manufacturing the tripods?"

"Possibly. From your description of them they are clearly beyond any mechanistic capacity of which I am familiar."

After finishing his tea, Professor Jekyll picked up his bag, then stood with a pained grunt. One hand touched his throat for an instant. "I must ponder all of this." He made his way to the door. "But now I have a meeting with the astronomy boys about the current Orionid meteor shower. Spectacular stuff, they say…this year even more than usual."

Paragon escorted him to the exit, bumping into the doctor's left side as if by accident. Jekyll winced, but managed to control any other reaction.

*I have something to ponder, as well.*

When he had gone Tilley said, "If we accept his life-altering suggestion, where does that leave us?"

"It leaves me with a pounding headache," Wilde announced, standing. "I am off to wallow in vapid but remunerative prose. Phoenix, send round a pneumo when you have a task for me. Montague, may your Caliban terrify ladies into near-miscarriage. Vesta, I trust that you will have the expected total of confused matrons swooning after you. God bless British theatre! Long may it reign! Good-day, all."

Wilde breezed out. Paragon and Tilley turned to Phoenix with the look of children seeking paternal guidance. He raised his palms to the heavens. "Stare all you want, that is unlikely to procure wisdom from my arse."

Tilley snorted. "If a lady were present, your statement would shock her to the core,

Mr. Dardanelles."

Phoenix tittered with her. "Vesta, perhaps you can make inquiries amongst your music hall contacts. Discover if any of them has noticed peculiarities of the sort we are searching for. Monsters, people with odd body parts, weird machines. They will tell you things that they would never dream of revealing to a constable or detective."

Tilley adjusted her monocle. "I shall perambulate amongst the unwashed masses and dislodge their secrets." She procured her stick, gloves, and hat and exited.

Paragon said, "I could go back to Whitechapel and snoop about. It has been a while since I have disguised myself as a dock worker or butcher, but I fancy that I ---"

Phoenix waved that off with an elegant hand. "Not necessary. Go home. Sleep until your makeup call tonight. You look like hell. I cannot have my best instrument out of tune. Rest and recuperate. That is an order. I will send a plainclothes officer round to your house in an hour with instructions to verify your presence with the ever-truthful Mervyn."

*Bless you, Phoenix.*

Paragon raised the head of his cane in understanding and left the parlor. Queue waited for him at the outer door in a brocaded white Chinese blouse. In lieu of a braid, her lustrous hair was pinned up with what looked like a chopstick. It was really an iron-hearted fighting tool. That knowledge had been painfully acquired by way of a bruised temple and a wicked pressure lock on his wrist.

"Does the Empire still stand, with at least one remote corner proudly warmed by the sun?"

"A bit wobbly here and there, but no imminent toppling is contemplated."

"Unlike you. I would wager that you are mere inches away from falling slap onto your manly dimpled chin. Did all of my toys perform as planned?"

"They did, indeed. Your galvanic bumbershoot dropped a charging seven-foot-tall beast-man as if pole-axed. If there had been another jolt in the thing, I might not be in the state of decay in which you see me."

"We are working on that." She fiddled with the earpiece of her round spectacles, eyes lowered. "And the leg?"

He gave her the details of the fracas in Whitechapel, including how well the flash heel had worked. "The new structure of the limb is superb. Despite the extra weight, it moves more naturally and easily. Strikes hard as a Farquharson rifle. Congratulate the wizards for me."

"I shall." Her slim hand patted his cravat in a hesitant, awkward manner. "And I congratulate you in coming home alive. Pray continue to do so."

He echoed her earlier smile. "Why, Priscilla, you do have a heart, after all."

The blur of her fist hammered against the door an inch from his nose. That lovely face darkened like a summer thunder cloud. Paragon feared that he was in for an epic thrashing. But she spun on one heel and fled back into her training room instead, muttering, "Bloody useless man!"

His head sagged against the steel of the door. *My, my...you cocked that one up, Monty.* After covering half of the distance to her lair he froze. *Best to let her boiler cool, old man. Too many lethal objects in there.* He lay a hand on his bosom. *And in here, I daresay.*

Paragon returned to his home unassailed. Mervyn greeted him with a brandy, though it was not yet noon. "Delighted to see you back so soon, sir," said the brass giant.

"I'm delighted to be able to." Paragon took a warming sip and sighed with bliss.

"All quiet on our flanks, then?"

"As the grave, sir."

"My preference is for a more reassuring simile."

"Understood, sir."

After a periscope survey of the front, Paragon dragged himself upstairs. *Oh, for a dose of Moreau's magic medicine.* He hurled himself onto his bed to sleep like one of the righteous dead, awaiting re-animation.

Awakening somewhat refreshed, though stiff, he meditated for nearly an hour. Then he donned a dark green double-breasted waistcoat. The Webley's shoulder holster went atop it, then a chocolate-brown Prince Albert coat and gold ascot. After a hasty dinner, he gave Mervyn the evening's defensive instructions. Then he selected a stout black stick and a low topper and headed to the Ogilvy.

The performance seemed slow to him that evening. Perhaps the absence of Lady Kalmaar contributed to that. Her box held a young married couple. More likely it was only a combination of pain, fatigue, and settling into the role. At the curtain call the audience gave no sign of disappointment, rising to their feet with the accustomed enthusiasm. He even had to politely reject the advances of a romantically adventurous mother-daughter team in the lobby. But the actor had other game in mind.

He hailed a steam-growler and directed it to Largo House. There the clockwork doorman spoke to him cheerily.

"Mr. Paragon, sir?" He wore an out-of-date Dickensian topcoat and John Bull hat. "You are expected."

*Am I that predictable, my lady?*

The automaton tipped his hat and opened the door. "Third floor, sir. Last door on the left. The Gold Bond Suite it is."

Inside, Largo House proved to be as lush as its spectacular exterior. Compared to it the Eccentric Club was a mere tradesman's hovel. Everywhere precious materials had been employed in tasteful understatement. Great swathes of imported Italian marble were in evidence. Equally valuable Asiatic and African woods comprised the walls and furnishings. The expense of it stunned Paragon.

*You've come a long way from the bleak Yorkshire of Michael Parsons. The boys in the old district would wet themselves to see this... and then set about stealing everything not nailed down.*

Before her white paneled door, he paused to take stock. Just why was he here? What did he expect her to do? Blithely confess to killing Grigsby and hold out her wrists for the manacles? Fling herself weeping onto a fainting couch, then explain every bizarre fact of the case? At no time had she shown any inclination to tell him a single blessed thing unless it served her purpose. Even the previous night's incredible color shifts, no doubt a result of some nefarious biological cruelty on Moreau's part, may have been calculated to communicate some message he did not yet comprehend, rather than to reveal any weakness on her part.

Or did he have other reasons for visiting at such an obscene hour? Motivations having more in common with the breathless episode in the hansom than with safeguarding the sacred British Empire? *My old guru would thump me soundly for it. 'Attachment causes suffering', he always said. But what a way to suffer.*

With the head of his stick, he rapped thrice. After a half minute with no response, he repeated his knock. Still, no one answered. Had she sent all the servants to bed? Where might the redoubtable Reginald be? More out of Lochmoor habit than anything else, he tried the doorknob before departing. It turned with barely a sound. Before he could talk himself out of it, he slithered inside. His ears detected some vague muffled sounds from the far corner of the suite, but nothing nearby or threatening.

He scanned the suite from the small entryway. A single rose-shaded gas table lamp was the only illumination. Lady Kalmaar's living quarters were not quite what he had expected after passing through the rest of Largo House. To be sure, there was a certain richness, but nothing like the breath-taking opulence seen elsewhere in the building. Though not austere, her sitting room was bereft of the expected clutter of classical busts, vases, paintings. Not a single image of any kind was in view.

The love of purple she displayed upon her person was not much in evidence. Rather, the room's color scheme tended toward green and rose. Patterned wallpaper – small gold diamonds – matched well with the jade draperies on the windows. An expensive Turkish tapestry divided the sitting room from the billiard room. Paragon left the entryway in search of the lady of the house…and ran smack into Reginald.

Paragon prepared to either defend himself or ingloriously fly, but neither proved necessary. The fearsome automaton stood in a glass-fronted mahogany cabinet. No light showed in its crystalline eye sockets. A brief examination showed that it was being rewound, as all clockies required. At the cabinet's rear a small steam engine, exhaust pipe running along the wall and into the hearth, turned a crank inserted into the base of Reggie's thick neck.

A modest bedroom lay along the left side of the hall, with the master bedroom on the right. In the first he found the missing maid, sprawled awkwardly across her plain narrow bed, still dressed. One sniff told her story. Laudanum, and not a small dose. The lass barely breathed. His sense of danger perked up like the ears of a wolf.

A gasping cry came from the other bedroom. He dashed across the hall, pistol in hand. All that he could see through the half-open door was the foot of a huge canopy bed with gauze curtains. Beyond sat a dressing table with mirror and washstand. An unseen candle lit the room with flickering gold. More muffled cries could be heard now, as well as the unmistakable noises of a struggle. Paragon employed the mirror to see what was causing the commotion.

A man crouched on the bed, straddling a woman and throttling her.

With three strides, Paragon rushed unseen into the room and clouted the fellow behind the ear. He collapsed onto the far edge of the mattress as if shot dead. Bare from the waist up, clad only in light army trousers, the attacker looked to be a young and hearty specimen with a thin moustache and short hair.

His victim was Lady Ambergris, naked as the day she was born.

Paragon was not so much the gentleman as to avert his gaze. That would have been a sign of death or dementia. Lady Kalmaar's exquisite form would have shamed Aphrodite. Not for the first time did it occur to him that she might have been designed in a laboratory by a cadre of lusty scientists. The woman could have aroused a months-old corpse.

Only the slick tentacles slithering between her legs ruined the impression.

Paragon felt his groin contract. The rest of him shrank back as well, from a mix of fear and revulsion and, frankly, disappointment. It was a truism that a single flaw in a beautiful woman served to accentuate her attributes, but there were limits.

It seemed that he stood staring at her nether region in horrified amazement for hours, but it could have been only seconds. When he finally shook his head clear, he saw that Lady Kalmaar lay in a profound trance. Fixed and glassy, her half-shut eyes focused on nothing. So shallow was her breathing that those stunning breasts hardly rose or fell. Her mouth hung slack as an opium addict's.

Paragon sat on the silk sheet and touched her brow. The skin was hot and moist, almost feverish. A wave of his hand before her face brought forth no response. Fearing for her health, he felt at her throat for her pulse with one hand while pressing the other over her bosom.

She sucked in a deep breath with a great gurgling gasp, as if breaching the surface of the ocean after a tremendous dive. He nearly wet himself in surprise. Panting, she blinked hard several times and clutched at the duvet. Consciousness flared in her eyes and she drew her knees up. Rising at the waist, she hissed, gripped his throat with a taloned hand, and hurled him onto his back with a tiger's strength. Her sleek caramel skin turned the gray-brown shade and rough texture of a lizard's scales. Astride him in all her uncanny naked glory, hair hanging in his face, she growled, "What? WHAT?!"

Darkness was pressing in at the sides of his vision from her choking hold, he rasped, "Amber... it's me...Paragon. He was killing you. And you're killing me." He made a weak wave toward the man he had clubbed.

With frustrating slowness her grip began to relax, the reptilian pigmentation washing out. The tension in her muscles gave way. Completely mindless of her nudity, Ambergris rested on Paragon and looked at the prostrate man. She let out a whimper of concern. "Fisk!" To Paragon she snarled, "What did you do to him?"

"I knocked him over his bally head, of course. The bastard was trying to strangle you."

As if speaking to a small child, she threw up her hands in frustration. "He was not attacking me. He was feeding me!"

When she sat back on her haunches, making a display that at any other time would have had Paragon adjusting his trousers and baying at the moon, he saw the tentacles again. Thick as his thumb, they lived in slitted pockets high inside each thigh. Dark pink and smooth all around they were, not suckered like the others he had seen. Now he noticed that they leaked blood... from tiny, toothed mouths.

*By all the ten thousand devils, Amber, what are you?*

She saw him staring and, despite her moist womanly display, knew what he was thinking. Like cables on a spring reel, the sinuous arms retracted into her body and vanished.

"Better? Not the sort of thing one reveals to a man she hardly knows, is it?" A spot of blood stained one thigh. With the tip of a little finger, she scooped it up and popped it into her mouth.

Paragon gulped and said, "So... how does that happen, exactly? Because it certainly looked like he was ---"

"I have little control over myself when taking blood. He was restraining me so I wouldn't drain him." Lady Kalmaar stroked the hapless Fisk. "That would be unfortunate. He tastes of purity and strength."

Paragon croaked, "This pinning and draining. Does it happen...often?"

Her sly smile noted his concern. "Only once, long ago. Now I choose my vessels with care, training them. They are volunteers all, so pray calm yourself."

"Do I, ahem, not look calm?" *I think my acting skills have reached their limit here.*

"You look like a rabbit cornered by a she-wolf, truth be told."

He aimed his head at her vessel. "What does he get out of the arrangement?"

Ambergris Kalmaar raised a single patrician eyebrow as if he had taken complete leave of his senses. She spread her arms wide, then tangled them in her black locks while arching her back. Her strong hips ground into his. Letting her hair drop until it reached the center of her back, she leaned her unashamed naked form over him until her spiked nipples brushed his waistcoat. From deep in her furry core, that captivatingly musky sea-scent pinioned his will as if she were his dungeon master.

Her warm lips brushed his ear. "My vessels never seem to want my bank notes."

*Lord, just kill me now. Om mani pedme hum...*

Despite the male force in his tailored trousers, which threatened to hurl the poor woman to the ceiling, he eased her back into the position he had first found her and turned away. From her amazed expression, this was a new experience for her. Sympathizing with that, he struggled to a sitting position. Several gray moments passed before the blood returned to his brain.

"You will pardon me if I express a certain level of anxiety about being sucked dry like a bug in a spider's web."

Lady Kalmaar pouted and sat up. "But I told you that I have control ---"

His voice gained force and impact, silencing her. "That is not what I wish you to tell me! I have a Member of Parliament murdered! I have citizens kidnapped! Men, and worse, have tried to kill me. Impossible... things... are running about my city. And now this!" He gestured in exasperation at her. "What in bloody hell is going on?!"

For the first time all pretense left her features. Understanding replaced it. "You think I killed Grigsby." She sounded hurt, like a schoolgirl falsely accused of stealing from her classmates.

"Your strange red weed was found beneath his body."

With a sigh, she rubbed her eyes, now more sad than enticing. "He was already dead when we arrived. And the blossom was doubtless his own."

"We? You and your clocker?"

"Yes. I received word that Grigsby was headed to Islington, to receive money from Moreau, so he thought. They have long had dealings."

"What sort? When? Where?"

"That was why I went there, to find out. But when we got there, the place had been shut up and the black smoke pumped in. Grigsby was beyond saving then."

Paragon grew dizzy from all the fresh turns. "What black smoke? All we found was dust."

"That is the remains of it. The tripods use black smoke as a weapon. All who inhale it die instantly. Breath masks fail after perhaps two minutes exposure. Rots the filters. After five minutes the stuff becomes inert. Because of the size of the machines, the smoke is of minimal effectiveness in the open. But in an enclosed space such as that shop, with all avenues of escape blocked..."

"So, you just left him in there to choke to death?"

"Wisps of black were already leaking from the door. Nothing we could have done would have changed the outcome. It would only have overcome me as well." She stroked his thigh. "Would you have welcomed that?"

*Is there a bit of that black smoke in here? All of a sudden, my breathing seems to be impaired.*

He grasped her hand, intending to remove it from contact with his suffering self, but she intertwined her fingers with his and kept it in place. "You might have sent in the indefatigable Reginald."

"I might have done, but I repeat that Grigsby would nonetheless have died. And a tripod's heat emitter can melt a brass man. Reggie cost me too much in gold and favors to part with him so casually."

Accepting her explanation for the moment, he moved on while his brain remained relatively unfogged. "And did you see Moreau there?"

"We did not. So far as I can tell the entire meeting was but a lure to dispatch Grigsby."

"But why? It seems a needlessly complex and colorful method of murder. Why not just shoot him in the street, or smother him as he slept?"

"I can only surmise that this was more of an execution, intended to not only slay a traitor, but also to send a warning."

Paragon admitted to himself that her theory made sense. From what little he knew of the dead MP the man was much condemned for an itching palm. Plus, the murder might have been a test of the black smoke's effectiveness.

"You say the red flower was Grigsby's. Why? Some sort of membership badge?"

"In a manner of speaking. I am not certain what it signifies. I wore it to fit in, to try to discover what he and others knew about my father's whereabouts."

"The unusual machinery in that shop. Beyond anything I've ever seen. What is it for?"

Amber's thumb was caressing his hand while still maintaining a firm grip on it. "They are as mysterious to me as they are to you. But Moreau values it above gold or gems."

"Methinks my Lady Kalmaar has been less than forthcoming to me." Paragon dropped his eyes to her lap, shiny with dew. "About a great many things."

Her free hand slid up his other thigh as she parted her own even more. "I indulged in no mendacity. Moreau did rescue me from the sea and rear me as his own daughter. But he proved to be a less-than-ideal parent. As you can see, he installed some of his own particular improvements." She seemed to fade into near invisibility, taking on the color of the sheets until only her outline remained. Paragon's amazement was tempered by the shifting in his loins. *Om mani peme hum.* "Like an octopus, I can adapt my coloration to my surroundings, even alter my skin texture."

"Permit me to point out that it requires you to be, um, naked for full effectiveness."

"Well, yes." She leaned in closer to him, natural pigment restored. "But don't you find my nakedness effective?"

Paragon let out a weak moan in his head. "Quite. But what of your other adaptation? The one for dining."

The pinkish tentacles slid out of her like fast-growing vines, twining up his arm. Warm as blood, they felt no different in texture than the hand he held. Now their fanged mouths were sealed tight. "He changed my anatomy significantly. I do not know why. Mere cruelty, perhaps. Or testing vile new techniques. But I may not consume normal human food, only blood."

"Human blood only?"

"Yes. I have tried that of animals, but my system violently rejects it. The fluids of men… strong, virile men, preferably… seems to provide the best nourishment."

The fleshy creepers reached his face and neck. He shrank back. "I thought you said that your vessels had to be volunteers. More mendacity?"

"Not at all. I fed well from poor Lieutenant Leight-Eire. But his reward might as well fall to you. You have no idea how arousing it is. Makes my flesh burn, it does. Perhaps that, too, is one of Moreau's little enhancements. As is this." Her erotic scent flooded the room like a storm wave into a beachside cavern… and it was from Lady Kalmaar's own cavern that it came, finally smothering his every objection and all his remaining reserve.

*By all the heavens…why would anyone corrupt the flesh of such a splendid woman? What could Moreau have hoped to accomplish? And furthermore… oh, to hell with that! Abandon hope, all ye who enter here!*

With her extra set of nimble fingers, the shedding of his clothes required less time than shuffling a deck of cards. That gambler's image seemed painfully apropos to Paragon as the predatory woman skinned him as a cook might an eel. As to his own eel… she took particular care not to peel it, which relieved him immensely.

Sometime during the proceedings, the unfortunate Fisk must have awakened with much head pain and even more confusion. At any rate, he disappeared. That was all to the good, for Ambergris believed in making use of every acre of her immense canopied four-poster. The lady displayed a gleeful aggression Paragon had previously only associated with tiger sharks. With inhuman strength, she pinned him on his back. Her first kiss echoed that in the hansom, hot and probing, tongue teasing. This time, though, other mouths also explored him. Tiny teeth gave him playful love bites along his flanks and belly. When they coiled about his most prized possession like a sultry fist, nibbling and sucking at the same time, he jerked and gasped.

"Ah, you like that, hmm?" Ambergris asked with a wicked chuckle. "I thought Harriet and Vesper repulsed you?"

His own voice came out weak and hoarse. "You named them?"

"And I suppose you have never named your willie?" She snickered in disbelief. "Please…" Her branding-iron kisses trailed down his neck and chest.

*I suppose I have. Deuced difficult to recall the name right now, however. Hell, I'm not sure about my own… nyaaahh!*

Every cell in his brain fireworked as her scalding mouth took him in. The tentacle tips, so like long loving fingers, continued to stroke him at the same time. Like nothing he had ever experienced in his many years of wandering the fleshpots of Asia and Europe, the total effect could only remind him of taking opium while being struck by lightning. And when she cupped his too-sensitive pouch with an insistent yet gentle hand, he feared that he had smoked a fatal dose and this was all a mere pipe dream.

*Why did I come here, again? Ah, yes, to interrogate her. Then I imagined that I had rescued her from danger. That's an impressive set of delusions for only one evening.*

One of his hands tangled in her hair and yanked her head back. Pretending to struggle, she writhed full against his length. It was manifest that she surpassed him in brute strength if it came to a true contest. *Another of Moreau's little gifts?* She danced lustily atop him with exquisite slow undulations. Ambergris scored his bruised chest with her nails, still kissing him like a wife sending her man off to war. The tentacles slid between his legs and climbed up to his shoulders to add delightful toothy scratches.

Paragon stroked her face with one hand and the other explored the center of her sweating back. What he felt there alarmed him but was driven out of mind by the volcanic sensations building. Their rhythm increased in pace and intensity. Ambergris' hauteur began to fade as the fuse inside her grew short. Her almond eyes locked with his as she nearly crushed the life out of him and hit her screaming, moaning zenith. Seconds later Paragon's joined her, praying that the top of his skull had not actually blown off.

For several long moments they lay there, dampening the fine bedclothes and catching their breaths. Harriet and Vesper flopped away from Paragon and disappeared into her still-quivering thighs. He ran a slow finger along her smooth cheek. She almost seemed to be in the same state as he had found her after feasting on Leight-Eire's blood... dazed, almost catatonic.

When she returned to herself again her first words were decidedly unromantic. "I plan to kill him with my bare hands, you know."

He frowned. *Not the pillow talk I expected.* "Who?"

"Moreau. My doting foster father. A knife's too merciful."

He had no glib answer to that. Ambergris could hardly be expected to thank him for vivisecting her into a circus freak, however lovely and sensual a one.

She let out a single snorting laugh. He felt it all the way down to their delicious connection. "Is this your idea of a probing interrogation of the murder suspect?"

"It was not my idea at all, as you well know," he protested, nuzzling the soft space between her breasts. "All I did was beat your meal senseless."

"Yes, and thank you for that. If poor Fisk refuses to be my vessel after this, I shall knock at your door come mealtime."

"Is that so? Why do I already feel devoured, then?"

"Poor Paragon. You can best every foe of the Empire but cannot handle an ally."

"Oh, you are an ally now? And just when did that happen?"

"I have always been on your side. Though now I seem to be more on your front."

He slid out of her, eliciting a frustrated little cry, and rolled onto his side, examining her back with pretended nonchalance. Long white scars intersected all over it, raised up from her skin in ugly puckered welts. Paragon had seen such before, on escaped slaves.

Though he could not see her face, the sadness in her voice was enough. "Papa's justice bites deep. Even his own kin must not transgress the Law. Control the monsters. For are we not Men?"

Paragon recalled his earlier thought about how a flaw might emphasize a woman's beauty. "I see no monsters here. Moreau, however, certainly is. This is like slashing a Renaissance portrait. Shall I kill the wretch for you, my lady?"

Ambergris turned over to face him, a queer look on her face, as if no one had ever spoken to her with even that much tenderness before. "My, aren't you...sweet." She traced his lower lip with a slender finger. "Love and death in the same breath. Is that not always the way?"

He tenderly caught the tear easing down her cheek with his thumb. "I meant every word."

"All the better." She kissed him full on the mouth and slung her legs over the side of the bed. "But Penny will soon awaken from her dance with the poppy. And I would prefer that she not see too many scandalous things during her employ. I am the talk of Largo House as it is."

She gave him a sidelong glance and that evil little smile again. "You know, I could have another go at you. I doubt you could resist. And this time I might feel a bit peckish in mid-embrace." Hot breath from her tantalizing lips made his tired soldier twitch anew.

"Oh, no, you don't." Paragon backed away, just far enough to avoid hand or tentacle should she be so inclined. "A reborn Torquemada you are." Donning his wrinkled clothes as quickly as he could – Mervyn would weep oily tears at the sartorial carnage when he returned home – he kept a wary watch on her in case she pounced. Lady Kalmaar took pity upon him and behaved herself. She aided his dressing, giggling as a little girl might when putting her dog in one of mama's frocks.

Throughout the entire delightful episode, she had never made mention of his artificial limb. In fact, not once had she even given it a curious glance. He had forgotten what that felt like. Being whole, not seen as a curiosity. At least his new lover had the benefit of being able to cloak the attributes which could make her an object of scorn or terror. Until Queue had provided him with this marvel of modern mechanistics, not even well-cut trousers and clever boots had been able to hide his deformity. True, Queue also apparently paid it no mind. But she had designed the limb, considered it almost more a part of herself than of him. In the back of his mind lurked the constant thought that she never forgot what kept him upright, what made him seemingly normal.

*How might she behave in this circumstance? Probably halt mid-way to pen a detailed memorandum outlining specific areas of possible improvement. I would find myself put on a strict regimen of physical culture exercises for my poor John Thomas.*

Paragon fell into a laughing fit as he envisioned the very proper Queue with a clipboard, counting off repetitions as he 'improved himself' below the waist. Lady Kalmaar tweaked his nose hard and glared at him, though the twinkle never left her eye.

"In the best circles of London society," she said in a grand dame tone, "it is considered bad form to chortle at a naked lady."

That only increased his crippling mirth. He fell onto one knee and positively cackled, certain that he would die from loss of breath.

She placed both hands on her perfect hips and stared down at him, flushed breasts swaying, still in character. "Rise, sir, from that semi-recumbent posture!"

Rise he did, in every sense of the word. Abandoning all his earlier thoughts of reserve, Paragon scooped her up in both arms and spun her about the bedroom until they nearly collided with the dressing table. He kissed her face as if it were about to be banned by royal fiat. Now she was the giggling one, muttering insincere protests.

"Take me back to bed," she begged, nuzzling his throat.

Instead, he hurled her beneath it.

## 10 / "I DO BEGIN TO HAVE BLOODY THOUGHTS"

Naturally, she shrieked and cursed. Paragon dove after her, gun in hand, as two pistol shots shattered the mirror. A quick glance along the floor showed the feet of the attacker whom the mirror had betrayed, moving with inelegant power.

Reginald was trying to kill them.

"Stay put!" he commanded. "Your darling Reggie has a wee malfunction."

Paragon grabbed a remnant of the mirror that had saved them and used it like the shield of Perseus. The clockwork man scanned the room. Grey-green smoke leaked from the back of his neck. His left eye was bright red, his right was blinking blue and white.

"Berserker breakdown," he whispered. "He's been over-wound."

Two more bullets from the heavy Colt revolver thudded into the mattress. Paragon felt grateful that Lady Moura had not scrimped on her bedding.

"How many cartridges in that pistol?" he asked.

"Just six."

Reginald's feet stirred. In a moment he would clump his way around the bed and have them dead to rights. Paragon acted first. With the false leg he grunted and shoved the prodigiously massive four poster up and onto its side, away from them and directly into the murderous automaton mid-stride. Despite its metal strength, the unprepared assailant staggered back. Paragon popped up, blasting at the thing's face with four rapid shots. His only hope was to shatter the crazed left eye and destroy the controlling mechanism. The bullets threw sparks as they ricocheted from the shining brass, but none struck home. *Damnation!*

He dropped back down behind the overturned bed just as his foe resumed its advance. "Push!" Throwing his shoulder against the right side of the bed frame, he began to pivot it like a great door on a hinge. Though naked, Ambergris flung herself at the base of the frame. Both grunted as their combined might drove the canopied monstrosity into the advancing automaton. Before the lethal machine could react, they had pinned it against the wall and opened an avenue to the door.

"Run!" Paragon cried. She raced out of the room and down the hall. One step behind her, Paragon ran backward, guarding their rear. As heavy as the four-poster was, the battle clocker would fling it aside with a single swipe of his iron arm.

Ambergris fiddled with the lock on the hall door. Beside her, Webley aimed back down the hall, Paragon wondered how long it might take for the house staff to hear the gunfire and alert the police.

A crash came from the bedroom. The automaton lumbered out on his stiff legs. Shiny streaks on his impassive face indicated where Paragon's futile bullets had struck. Once he had stomped closer, the implacable arm would rise and they would be dead.

"The lock is jammed!" Ambergris wailed. "Someone's frozen it from the outside. A sort of glue."

"Your vessel Fisk, I imagine," Paragon said, eyes firmly set on Reginald's gun hand. "My instincts were right when I clouted him. Leave it. Billiard room! Go!"

They rushed out of the line of fire, through the sitting room. Ambergris snatched her handbag from the mantle. *Really? I will never understand women.* Paragon reached into his coat for a new clip. But Reginald had increased his pace. He batted aside the furniture Paragon had shoved into his path.

Though certain of its futility, Paragon called back to Ambergris. "Try giving him a Stand Down order!" Even if it only made the behemoth hesitate, that might serve to give Paragon a clear shot at the controlling left eye.

From her crouch behind the ponderous oak table Lady Kalmaar yelled, "Reginald! Inactive! Imperative!"

A hitch appeared in Reginald's step, but he recovered nearly instantly and maintained his inexorable advance, giving Paragon no clear shot. Nothing was left except to close with the enemy and hope that he could kill its eye before it did the same to him. That was a prospect he viewed with a decided lack of relish. Both previous encounters with berserkers had left him in the hospital.

*But first I need him to waste his remaining rounds. That means playing the hare.*

Clockwork men were cool shots, but they were not particularly accurate. That was why the citizenry were generally not permitted to arm them. Innocent bystanders suffered. So Paragon had not completely taken leave of his senses when he hopped onto the immense pool table and waved both arms. But his timing needed to be perfect.

Just as he had planned, Reginald swerved his thick arm and pulled the trigger, aiming dead center as all his kind did. The bullet struck only air and the corner window as Paragon flung himself onto the carpet. Now he had half a ton of wood and slate for cover. If the assassin marched in his predicted fashion and bumped up against the table, he might be frozen there long enough for an aimed shot that would put him down. *First, though, is the small matter of that final cartridge.*

Paragon looked around for Lady Kalmaar. No sign. *What the devil? Did she slip out while her dear Reggie shot at me? Only the one door.* Cold night air leaked in through the broken window. The hole, however, only the size of a fist, would not have served to give her an escape.

Giving up on her whereabouts, he popped up into Reginald's view with a shout, then dropped down again. This time Paragon felt the breeze of the bullet past his ear. *Damned near thing, that one.* The repeated click of the hammer confirmed that his foe had emptied his revolver.

After a pair of relaxing breaths to flush the tension from his system, Paragon calmly stood and aimed at the fiery left eye of his would-be slayer. Waiting until that dead space between heartbeats for maximum stillness, he squeezed off all four rounds in a single breath.

And missed.

Reginald had proved more resourceful than the run-of-the-mill automaton. He had grabbed a cue stick from the table and whipped it at Paragon's hand. All the bullets went high and wide as the Webley flew from his grip. *Jesu Maria! I need to invest in a lanyard.*

Though he reckoned his odds as something less than zero, he nevertheless snatched the other stick from the table, laughing as he did so. *I'm about to be killed by a brass butler. A sorry end after managing to get out of Isandlwana alive. What might my guru have to say about this? Something about an overdue payment of karmic debt, most likely.*

He jabbed at Reggie's face with the stick, taking care to keep the table between them. Raising both great arms above his head, the clocker brought them down with tremendous force. It gave way like a dynamited bridge, leaving the automaton a clear avenue of advance.

As he backpedaled, Paragon tripped over an ottoman and went down. The servant from hell jerked Paragon upright by his lapel. An instant later his face was squashed against the diamond-patterned wall, the cue stick choking his life out. As darkness began to cover his sight, all Paragon could think of in his final moment was how lumpy the paper next to his face looked. *Shoddy workmanship. She should have it seen to.*

The bad spot in the wall faded away, transforming itself into the fine face and figure of Lady Kalmaar. She had color-shifted to hide there. Both of her hands wrapped around the stick, pulling it away from Paragon's throat just enough to restore breathing. Her fleshy tendrils rose like cobras and spat thick black ink into both of Reginald's eyes.

Clutching at his face, the killing machine stumbled rearward into the remnant of the billiard table. Before it could wipe the blinding fluid off, Lady Kalmaar raised her folded iron fighting fan and plunged it deep into the left eye. A spark shot out, followed by a sickening spurt of thin blue-green fluid. With a tremendous dust-raising crash, the maimed berserker fell over backward onto the table wreckage, never to rise again.

Paragon swallowed hard to restore the use of his throat. With more grace than he felt he croaked to Ambergris, "You appeared right on... cue."

Her first reaction was to curl the corner of her mouth in mocking disbelief at the verbal atrocity. What followed hard upon was the fervent application of that same delicious mouth to his. Her arms and tentacles all wrapped around him as if fearing that he would flee. Paragon worried that his coat buttons might damage those superb breasts.

Breaking the kiss she said, "You have no idea what it took to remain against the wall until the perfect moment, all the while watching you being ---"

"Sshh," he said, caressing her hair. "It's all over now."

"Is it? We still have no idea how this happened, or who is responsible."

"This sort of thing happens to me all the time. My stock in trade, love. Worry not."

"If that is true, you earn every penny of your salary."

He ran his fingers lazily over her flesh. "Occasionally I receive payment in kind."

That got him a playful slap on the chest. "Is that what I am? A stalwart lass doing her part for the brave boys at the front?"

"If it's your front, yes." The back of his hand ran along the side of her breast.

Harriet and Vesper nipped sharply at his hand as they relaxed their hold on him and returned to their nest in her loins. "I ought to hide it away in a corset and await the inevitable arrival of the Metropolitan Police."

"I should go, then. No need for me to end up in a sergeant's office explaining why I was in a proper aristocratic lady's bedchamber." Paragon steered them toward the door.

"That is quite the set of assumptions you are stringing together but thank you." She turned into the hall. "You may have to saw your way through that thing to leave. The lock is quite ruined."

Bending down to peer through the lock, he raised an eyebrow. Whatever had been poured into it was rapidly dissolving like wax in an oven. He examined the winding cabinet. Just as he had suspected, an ice pick had been thrust into the controlling linkage, preventing the automatic fail-safe from interrupting the windup. The missing Fisk would have much to explain.

Paragon reloaded the Webley, then wandered about the sitting room, awaiting Lady Kalmaar's return. The warning about her from Phoenix had not been forgotten. He had experienced enough metaphorical, and real, knives in the back from supposed lovers to always keep a wary eye out for a smiling betrayal. Though she seemed to have confessed all and thrown her lot in with him, nagging concerns remained.

Her sitting room did not trumpet any of the answers. It seemed sterile. *Almost like a stage set.* None of it spoke of a life fully lived.

*Where are the bills? The little hand-scrawled notes on scrap paper? No ashes in the grate, in late October. Good Lord, my lady, are you even partly human?*

Ambergris returned with his hat, her memorable form now hidden beneath a soft violet silk dressing gown. He informed her of the clear sabotage of her rewind cabinet. Upon hearing that her trusted vessel may have tried to kill her, she bit her lower lip and shook her head.

"I would find that difficult to credit. Because I am so helpless during the process, the tendrils inject a substance which mimics first love. Harming me is quite impossible, I should think. Moreau claimed to have tested it on animals which were mortal enemies. A starved serpent refused to devour a mouse, preferring death."

"What about a threat to himself or to his family? Might that, or even mesmerism, interfere with it?"

"That I do not know."

"But if the vessel is fooled into thinking that he actually protecting the host…?"

"Ah. That could be a different story entirely."

Paragon kissed her lightly and lifted the battered topper onto his aching head. *Neck and throat will need tending, too. The late Reggie didn't do things by halves.* "I trust you will have a splendid story for the constables when they arrive."

"I shall. It would do credit to Mr. Dickens himself, if he were to come out of retirement."

"If you are wearing that robe when you give testimony, the officer will believe anything you say. The décolletage opens alarmingly."

The lady pantomimed distress. "Why, sir, I had no idea!"

"Vixen!" He kissed her again and tested the door. It swung open with ease. The viscous substance had entirely evaporated into the ether. "Beware your vessel. I still believe you may be compromised there. Surname?"

"Leight-Eire. A cornet in the Royal Dragoons."

"That should make him easy to find. The junior officer with the sticking plaster on his head, and another about his throat."

"The last is unlikely. Healing secretions, you see."

"Is there any end to your wonders?"

"Come back to my bed again and you shall see such stuff as dreams are made on."

Paragon backed into the hall, hands up in alarm. "Take pity, lady. You see this poor ruin of a body? It smells of mortality."

With that she blew him a kiss and closed the door. He sagged against the wall. *By all the powers, I am drained. What must an evening as her vessel be like?*

He reached the front exit just as a half dozen armed constables rushed past. On their heels was Inspector Weybridge Shepperton, pipe between his teeth. Paragon made sure to hide behind the imposing doorman as he passed.

"Damnably glad I am those fellows aren't after me," he said, swaying a bit as if drunk.

"Strange, isn't it?" the clocker said. "First time I've ever seen the doctor arrive at the scene of the crime before the police."

"That is a bit odd. I fancy I saw him as I came down. Stout chap, long face, about sixty?"

"Oh, no, sir. This fellow was no more than forty, I'd say. Blonde bloke. Blue eyes as pale as water, with madness in them. Slight limp. Black doctor's bag. And can you believe it? He arrived behind a steamer penny farthing, driven by the biggest bloke I've ever seen."

Paragon dearly wanted to dash back in and find the fellow, but with Shepperton there it would never do. *Probably ducked out the back already. And how is he walking so soon?* He dragged his outraged body home. Mervyn met him at the door. Without a word, Paragon draped the savaged coat across his great arm, hanging the punctured top hat on the end of the thumb, and climbed the stairs. Perhaps the poor clocker would burn the offended items on an altar while chanting pagan hymns to the gods of Saville Row.

In his bedroom, the scent of daisies stung his nose. That instantly recalled his little sister, who had worn crowns of them, giggling, to the last. Hearing tiny feet in the hall, he dashed out, pistol in hand, to see a small girl wave and at him and run through a solid wall. The floral scent faded as she vanished.

*Lovely. Now the house is haunted? What will that do to its resale value? Or has my mind finally gone?*

After a long hot soak, and a brandy to drive the disturbing vision away, Paragon slept till noon, for once untroubled by any dreams worse than Ambergris Kalmaar's tentacles singing siren songs to him.

*London Medical College sub-basement*

*"The lady may be playin' a double game," muttered Humphrey Littlewit.*

*The fair-haired doctor let out a harsh giggle as the long needle slid into his neck. Between a series of pained gasps, he said, "Of a certainty…if not a triple one." His rubber-gloved assistant thumbed the plunger to send sparkling orange fluid into his master's body. "Don't we all, though? I feign an alliance with the monsters who keep me sane with this foul stuff. Blood-sucking bastards."*

*"To say nothin' of makin' a show of love to the Confederacy."*

*"Easy to fool, they are. Foul slavers. It will be a cold day in hell before I provide them with reanimated soldiers. Even the Bonaparte of crime has standards." He swatted the man's arm with the damaged tentacle as the needle was yanked back out. His arms were strapped to the chair. "Have a care! I'm not one of your corpses."*

*Humphrey Littlewit cringed. "So even carnal relations didn't loosen Paragon's tongue?"*

*"She says he clearly knows too little to be a bother to us. And if congress with that goddess can't relax the man into carelessness, nothing will."*

*The long-faced minion set the syringe beside a gleaming yard-long cylinder. "Just so long as Lochmoor don't learn about these beauties and who's sendin' 'em." His gloves came off. "Who tried to slay the lady tonight? Moreau? Or somebody else?"*

*Navita's face twitched with involuntary spasms as the exotic serum began to circulate in his damaged brain. "Unclear. She has made many enemies in her brief time in England. Numerous backs bear her blade-marks. I doubt that Moreau wants her dead until he can discover what she has been up to. He may even harbor hopes of rehabilitating her so that he may employ his lovely weapon to the purpose for which she was created."*

*"And she still has no idea about her origin?"*

*"No. The lady believes that tall tale he spun her on the island. Not that it is of consequence. Lady Kalmaar still burns to throttle him for what she thinks are merely a few mad manipulations of her HCA."*

*"Another cylinder arrives tonight. The boys are waitin' for it in Cornwall."*

*"They had better be watchful. We only beat the other side to the last one by a whisker. But the false plans did sabotage their little murder machine, though not thoroughly enough, more's the pity."*

*"I reminded 'em. Eddie Hyde was supposed to be their muscle, but his dodgy elixir just wore off. He's back at his other self's house, sleepin' it off."*

*"Inconvenient, that. I may have cause to remind him of what he risks if he fails me. The law takes a dim view of physicians who aid and abet the poisoning of other doctors. But I've put another team onto Paragon and his lady. If they make a move against Moreau before it is convenient, then our boys will act. I want to be the one to look Sebastian in his mirrored eye when his empire is wrenched from him, not Dardanelles."* He eyed the end of the bad tentacle. *"One of his, er, large, imported fellows has thrown his lot in with us. Apparently, we use the lash with less gusto than his former employer."* Navita laughed. *"He is 'well-armed.'"* The uninjured tentacle rubbed at the sore injection point.

*"Will the missin' tip grow back, do you think?"* Littlewit asked.

*"Who can say? It's not like I installed familiar earthly cells into myself. 'Tis already itching, though, as is the leg. But I do know that I am in a better condition than that fool Moreau, rotting away inside his rubber mask like months-old carrion. At least I proved that rejection of alien tissue is preventable, though at a cost."* He glared at the needle.

*"So has he, if the stories are true."*

*"That remains to be seen. His lovely subject may decay at any time."*

*"I hear he's taken to the air and is escapin' north with our prize."*

*"So he thinks."* Navita laughed like a boy squashing insects. *"Our intelligence is the equal of his. We will snatch Fthosa back and force her to help us destroy her own people."*

Navita stood, put weight on the leg Paragon had shot. Nodding, he walked on it with the barest hint of a limp. *"Give those squiggly buggers their due, this stuff works."* He collected his coat, hat, and stick. Patting the pocket where the lock-binding fixative lay, he smiled to himself. She had proven her worth...this time. The clocker might have dispatched her, too. If Navita had not been so certain that she could outwit it, he might never have overwound it on the whim brought on by his damnable illness. True, the inconvenient Paragon had also survived, but his luck could not hold forever. Did she preserve him, against orders, or had his own cursed talent done it? If she grew attached to her prey, that could ruin everything. Her test would be if she played her part honestly when their furry foreign friend arrived on her airship. Paragon had to be removed from the board. The Jubilee affair had proven that he was too formidable. Lochmoor could not know who was providing the advanced knowledge that had inadvertently changed the world. Not yet. Once Moreau was dealt with, then Navita could swoop in and dramatically foil the cylinder-senders' plot as publicly as possible. Victoria would probably give him a knighthood. But before he dared do that, he had to unlock his formula's secret. If all went as he hoped, no more shipments would be falling from the sky. And his departed darlings could rest in peace.

## 11 / "THE TRUTH YOU SPEAK DOTH LACK SOME GENTLENESS"

"Is that some new cologne?" asked Queue, sniffing at him like a terrier after a rat.

Paragon frowned. "Er, no. Why?"

"You smell funny. A bit like fresh fish, but also like…a starry night… smoke… and other things. Odd."

Her 'shag sense', he called it. To forestall it, he had not only scrubbed himself raw with his strongest soap but had also donned a brand-new suit. Even his wing-collar shirt and drawers were virginal. But despite his precautions, her hackles were up. And to make matters worse, this was a personal combat training day.

*I should have pneumoed in sick, like any sensible man. Now she'll make me pay for my sins. I had been better off playing rugby against Royal Marine clockers.*

He had given Phoenix the expurgated details of the night's activities, voice hoarse from Reggie's attack, though it had involved a bit of creativity to explain how he knew that Lady Kalmaar was tentacled. Dardanelles had immediately sent out orders to find Lieutenant Leight-Eire and Eddie the giant.

"I would wager my best suit," he said, "that this cyclist knows the creator of the tripods and gargoyles. How someone so large, traveling in that absurd manner, manages to avoid capture baffles me. It's like he changes his skin. But it's certain that this Moreau is not the only maker of monsters in town."

"Perhaps he returns to his spaceship near the moon each night," Paragon smirked.

"Or maybe he is Spring-Heeled Jack and bounds over the rooftops. Speaking of space, you ought to have seen that meteor shower last night. A marvelous display. There were reports from the Royal Observatory that some interplanetary shards actually fell to ground in Cornwall."

"I was… otherwise engaged."

Phoenix cackled. "In every sense of the word, I would imagine."

"Have you any other pertinent information?" Paragon asked, holding his aching head. "I am particularly interested in the Honorable Samuel Grigsby's activities."

Phoenix pushed a paper across the desk with a single manicured finger. "As is the Clandestine Investigative Arm of the Commons."

"Didn't know they had one."

"Thus, the term 'clandestine.' I'll spare you the full reading of it. Their prose is less than Ciceronian. Grigsby had his hand in every till he could wedge it into. Smuggled weapons into the Confederate States of America, despite Her Majesty's professed embargo. I admit that our own government played a double game there, but he never consulted with the Crown. He did meet, however, with the German, Russian, and Chinese espionage services on many occasions. Rumors abound that he was thick with the Breakers, despite railing against them in Parliament. If that black smoke hadn't laid him low, we would have. The noose was tightening, and he knew it."

"Yet he did not flee the country, he went to Islington to meet with Moreau. Why?"

"That is still a mystery. Perhaps he hoped to book passage on Moreau's airship."

"Lady Kalmaar says that he betrayed powerful people and was executed for it as a warning to others." Paragon snapped his fingers. "Riot Army."

Phoenix raised one eyebrow. "An apt description of my last party. Someone has been telling tales out of school."

"Oh, shush. You know what I'm talking of."

"I do, indeed. They enjoy scrawling their name on things, generally at the scene of very public lawbreaking, even if they aren't the perpetrators. Beyond that, not much is known, except that other entrepreneurs of crime are scared witless by them. Shadowy. Fingers in many pies. Envious of competition. Creatively violent. Their boss is accomplished at remaining invisible."

"Put a man on it and let me know more."

"I did. Philip Draxx. He is the chap who was slain by his own brass valet. Berserker breakdown, funnily enough. But I shall pry some more. Coincidences disturb me."

After reading the report, Paragon judged that the late Samuel Grigsby was a singularly inept traitor. He took very little care to avoid discovery. *It looks like he was so certain of protection that he saw no need to worry. But how could he be? What was his escape plan? Or did he hope to stay here as part of a new government? Is this part of a coup d'état? Or even worse, invasion?*

He changed into a white singlet and black pajama bottoms. Queue waited on the mat wearing ominous scarlet.

At first, she took pity on him, seeing his throat painted in purple bruises. "You move like an aged monk," she noted, launching light punches at him.

"I feel like a dead one," he admitted while employing forearm blocks.

"Perhaps a bit more reliance on what I teach you here would have lessened the toll."

"You would be attending a memorial service for me if I had done anything but."

"Good to know." Without warning, she aimed a sharp hopping kick at his center. It struck nothing as he pivoted out of its path and sent an elbow to her jaw that fell purposefully short. After a praising nod, her hands and feet blurred in random assaults. He forgot his aches as all his concentration went into defense. When she broke off, they both huffed from the exertion, he rather harder than her. Just as he congratulated himself, she smiled and purred, "Right. So much for your warm-up."

She snapped a slim hand out at him in a full-speed face punch. As her arm reached its limit, he wrapped her hand in both of his and bent it back in toward her, twisting as he did so. Landing hard on her face, the arm locked out straight with Paragon pulling against her elbow joint. With an appreciative grin, she slapped the mat twice. He released her and she sat up.

"Be sure to apply the same techniques on the strategic level, as well," she said, springing to her feet. "If you are forced to defend yourself against an unexpected strike on the street, that is one thing. But if your opponent is always one move ahead of you, keeping you confused as to his intentions, then perhaps you should blend with him as you did with my strike."

They moved back toward the wall, to the rack of weapons. She handed him a rattan walking stick with a crook handle.

He accepted it with a bow. "So, I should endeavor to get inside his organization? I had thought of that, but first we shall need to discover where he keeps his recruiting office."

Queue pulled on a quilted jacket. "Moreau will be wary of strangers who are suddenly desirous of a place at his side. But there is another way. His new base is likely part of his existing criminal operation. Some mostly innocent front business. He will scarcely have had time to construct a new one. He left for England precipitately."

They put on leather-backed fencing helmets. She took up a straight stick. "You need not become a minion to get close."

He bowed to her and took his guard, stick held high. "I could appear as a potential client."

"Precisely." Queue assumed the attitude of some ill-paid thug with minimal fight training. Her stick sliced straight down at his skull while she bulled her way toward him.

Paragon pivoted on his front foot. Her impetus as the blow missed took her past him. He stepped on her knee joint from the rear, buckling the leg. A painless tap to her shoulder ended the first exchange. "That will necessitate some quick action once we discover it. He shan't linger after that spectacular daylight raid in Whitechapel."

"Of course." This time she swung her stick with both hands, like a batsman trying for six. Not so easy to avoid as a vertical attack.

Knowing this, Paragon did not attempt evasion. Instead, he slid directly into her, letting the stick swing beyond him. Adding his own force to hers, they spun like a top. He simply bent his knees as they went around, causing her to fall forward. She landed on her back with a boom, his stick against her throat.

They met for a third time. Now she feinted another head cut, but as he raised his stick to parry, she shifted to a spiking bayonet-style strike at his chest. Paragon pivoted like a toreador, with a simultaneous left cross to her jaw. Despite her armor, the impact sent her sprawling.

Paragon cast his stick aside and rushed to the small immobile form. Queue's eyes remained closed, her breathing shallow. "We need some help in here!" he bellowed. "Priscilla is ---"

The room swiveled as if on ball bearings. Before he could comprehend his predicament, he stared at the ceiling lamps. A leg made of cast iron clamped onto each side of his outstretched arm, one heel boring into his much-abused throat. Jolts of pain shot along his limb as Queue bent his elbow across her thigh.

*I'll be damned if I'll tap out for her satisfaction. She's unlikely to inflict more pain than dear old Reggie.*

Another three seconds showed him how much in error that belief was. Queue yanked on the arm as if trying to pull a locomotive down the track. "What did I tell you about calling me Priscilla at work?" she asked, more glee in her voice than he thought right and proper.

A pair of gleaming shoes appeared next to his face. *There's been a lot of that lately.* "I could have sworn that he said 'we' need help, Oscar," said Vesta. "Did I mis-hear?"

Tilley's face appeared next to Paragon's eye, the monocle examining him as a natural philosopher might a bug. "Ah! He is probably seeing double since he is too bloody stubborn to tap the mat."

Oscar sighed. "Oh, let him up, Queue. Whatever sin he committed, I doubt he'll repeat it."

That intolerable pressure on arm and throat eased. Paragon coughed and sucked in air. It took a full minute, but his breathing and vision did return. He sat up and glared at his torturer.

"And just what sin did you commit, white-faced Western demon?" she asked in a childish Chinese stage accent, eye twinkling.

*Spending time in the wrong woman's bed? No, best keep that one to myself.*

"I let my opponent get too close with a ruse of defeat...Miss Ang."

Queue gave him some light applause. "Bravo. A lesson in the tactical and the strategic."

Paragon snorted and stood. *Running out of body parts to injure.* "Here's a lesson for you, then. Breaking your students in two is bad policy. They aren't dogs you can train with whipping." He stormed off to the changing room.

To his surprise, she followed him. Clad in only his trousers, he backed up against the cold wall. For a moment he feared she was about to administer the coup de grace. Her hand flashed out to his throat. But the movement ended in the lightest of touches as she ran her trembling fingers over the ugly swellings and discolorations. The digits felt their way upward, over his cheek, along his scar, lingering on his stunned lips. A quiver began on her own mouth, which moved into her eyes. His amazement peaked when a single crystal tear appeared there. Before it could roll more than an inch down her smooth cheek, she obliterated it with a ruthless swipe of her sleeve. She vanished out the door as he reached out, touching only the air's memory of her.

He finished dressing in a silence broken only by the rapid pounding of his pulse. If this was a mating dance, then he needed instruction as to the proper steps. Whatever was happening, little good could come of a workplace tryst. *Makes mad the guilty and appalls the free.*

Paragon opened the parlor door. Dardanelles, Wilde, and Tilley all crowded before a wall map of Britain, usually hidden behind a portrait of the Queen. It was cluttered with paper labels, pins, and ink markings.

"Ah! You're back with us," said Phoenix. "Come look. We've had rather a breakthrough, I think."

A plump red pin had been thrust into a spot in north Yorkshire. Deep in his stomach he felt the first stirring of an old fear. Aloud, though, he made a show of breezy insouciance. "Quite a long way from recent affairs."

"Agreed. But one of your dirty yet effective street lads just brought us word that his network has spotted Moreau's airship there."

"Makes sense, actually," said Vesta. "He could hardly keep a ship that size near London. I daresay he neglected to register with Foulness Aerial Coordination."

"We're endeavoring to confirm the report," Wilde said. "Telegraphed our people in that barbaric region of the realm. Have you seen their shirt collars? And the waistcoats!" His shudder spoke volumes.

Paragon inwardly shuddered. In his village many of the poor had been fortunate to have a single suit of patched clothes, him most of all. On the rare occasions when his garments had been laundered, he had sat on his bed, shivering, a prayer on his lips to keep Peaceful Manners ignorant of his nakedness.

"Looks like the North York Moors," he said. "Mostly empty, is it not?"

"What better place to hide an extra-large Giffard?"

"But where could he set it down and hope to avoid detection by the RAF? There is little cover there unless he brought a cracking great camouflage net with him."

"That is the beauty of it," Vesta said. "According to your Griffin, an enormous clockwork accessory factory has just been built there. Putting it in the middle of an empty moor makes no sort of business sense, so that is suspicious in itself. And it is much too large for its purpose. Not fully operational yet. Licensed to add cosmetic mechanistics to clockwork servants, under strict supervision. Faces, eyes, specialty hands for certain types of work, that sort of thing. Their first roof was damaged by a storm and had to be replaced. At present, it is only canvas."

"It would be nothing to pull back the fabric, drop the ship in, and cover it all up again," said Wilde. "And as work is stalled, there are no inconvenient Clockwork Ministry inspectors. The sales office is open, however, to meet clients and receive orders."

"There is only one direct route to the factory," said Phoenix, "a fifteen-mile private pneumatic rail spur from Goathland Station. I have men heading there from York, disguised as a shooting party, to try to get a better picture of the situation. But getting into the factory itself will not be easy."

"Bomb the whole bloody place on mere suspicion," ventured Wilde. Everyone else turned to stare at him. "Well, is that not the purpose of a Royal Aero Flotilla?"

Phoenix shook his head. "Such bloody mindedness for an Aesthete. Would you like us to explode it in an especially artistic manner? Multicolored munitions, perhaps? No, obliterating him might solve some problems but create a host of others. We need Moreau alive, if possible, to get his schemes out of him. I'm certain he did not dash across the world merely to chastise an old associate. Something else is afoot."

"The factory is not operational yet, but the office is?" Paragon asked. "They ought to be accommodating to a wealthy man and wife looking to hurl baskets of guineas at them."

"I'll have to invent an excuse for your absence from *The Tempest*. A flare-up of the Somalian pox might do." Phoenix seemed to enjoy that rather too much. "And just who will your beloved spouse be?"

Everyone turned to stare at Vesta Tilley, cigar in hand. "You must be joking. I am pathetically out of practice. They would spot me in a trice."

"Even in a bustled skirt," said Oscar, "as soon as she held the door for Monty the game would be up."

Phoenix frowned. "Most of our women operatives are on assignment. I suppose I could call in Misses Galore or Masterson."

Paragon shook his head. "No, those beacons of crisp efficiency will not do. I need someone who is all woman, who can wear money lightly, think on her feet, play a role, yet defend herself if all goes wrong."

Dardanelles responded with a knowing chuckle. "And why do I feel that you already have a candidate in mind?"

"Truly, Phoenix, you are the very modern model of a modern model manager. I do, indeed."

~

Lady Ambergris Kalmaar stroked her cue stick and pouted. "Married, but no honeymoon? You distress me immeasurably."

Paragon assured her, "Nothing would give me greater pleasure than to 'dis-dress' you, but time is of the essence."

She had managed to clean up the Reggie wreckage. A Clockwork Ministry team had swarmed in like efficient ants an hour after the attack and put things right. They had even replaced the billiard table already.

Ambergris leaned enticingly over the corner of the table in a sea-green Worth polonaise day dress. "We shall have to employ considerable makeup skills to pass muster up there," he told her as she pocketed the six ball.

With a puckish smile, she strolled to the other side of the table. "To cover those spectacular love marks Reggie gave you?"

"Er, no. I was speaking of you, seeing as how Moreau will recognize you in an instant. Wig, paint, putty, a thick veil. Perhaps a bit of padding to make your figure appear more...matronly."

"Sounds dreadful." The nine-ball shot across the green surface and dropped. "As for the wig and paint..."

Beginning at the top of her head, the black hair turned bright blonde as if a bucket of golden dye had been poured there. At the same time, her dark complexion faded into clotted cream with roses damasking her cheeks. As a final touch the eyes became a deep blue.

"My cosmetics expenditure is minimal."

Paragon swallowed. If possible, the lady's beauty had grown. "I can well believe it."

"As for padding, my dresses are all carefully fitted, and I would venture to say that there is little room in them for...augmentation."

*Truer words were never spoken.* "We shall have to provide you with a new nose, at any rate. I shall meet you at the Eccentric Club in two hours." He consulted his watch, careful not to engage the wrong sequence of hidden triggers. Her lodgings had suffered enough without the added indignity of one of Queue's bombs. "Where is your abigail?"

Ambergris drained the final two balls into a single hole with a masterful combination shot. "I am unfortunate in my serving girls. This last one awoke from her poppy-slumber, took one look at the lamented Reggie's remains, and promptly gave two seconds notice."

"Such a sorry state the servant class is in nowadays. And the state of your bedchamber?"

She took her burning cigarillo from its tray. "No better. He knocked my four-poster all asunder. I am making do with a lamentably ordinary bed from the late Marchioness of Auric's rooms." A perfect smoke ring oozed from her lips. "They say she expired of exhaustion in it one night, just before dawn."

Paragon returned home by cab, congratulating himself in having not dropped his clothing onto Lady Kalmaar's floor again. After reminding Mervyn to keep an eye out for dangers, Paragon changed into appropriate traveling clothes for a wealthy gentleman. That entailed transferring his Lochmoor-issued specialty articles to the new suit.

"Envenomed stickpin...gelignite cufflinks...garrote wire hatband...acid-tube buttonhole...sap gloves." Paragon completed his self-inspection with the items stored in his artificial limb. "Spyglass...flash bomb...stiletto...lock picks, and the rest."

Mervyn lifted the luggage as if it were made of sea foam. "Sticks and brollies, sir?"

"Queue's electrical stunner, of course. It brought down that gargoyle easily enough. The pearl swordstick. And that new one I haven't yet tried. More than that would be gilding the lily."

The Eccentric Club's glass-fronted carriage waited for him. He opened the door and waved to the driver, old Ian Goodnight. Mervyn took the bags out and packed them with efficient ease. After pulling on his gray tweed Ulster, its detachable cape full more of Queue's surprises, Paragon climbed into the carriage. Mervyn handed him a small black velvet box.

"A selection of wedding rings, sir."

"Ah! Good show."

The clockwork man closed the door and raised one great metal hand. "Bon voyage. Enjoy your honeymoon. Do English manhood proud."

Impossible as it was, Paragon would have sworn that Mervyn winked at him.

## 12 / "THE MISTRESS I SERVE QUICKENS WHAT'S DEAD"

"Should you not get down on bended knee?" asked Lady Kalmaar when he presented her with a gold band in the Eccentric Club's lobby. "A girl needs time to think. This is all so sudden."

"Oh, hush," Paragon smirked. "We are doing this backwards as it is. My understanding is that the consummation traditionally *follows* the exchanging of rings."

"Well, um, yes. You make a valid point, husband." She admired the glint on her finger. "I would suggest that you declare your intentions to my father, but as I am en route to slay him that might be socially awkward." Though her tone was flippant, she kept running a finger across the band, head down, eyes wet.

After dabbing her eyes with a violet-trimmed handkerchief, she linked her arm in his and gave every indication that they were happily wed. A respectable upper-middle class lady she seemed to be, in a practical dark brown wool dress with just enough fashionable bits to indicate her status. Lady Kalmaar was as conservative and covered as it was possible for such a beauty to be. With her white-blonde hair pulled up tight and her skin now pale as fine china, no casual observer would have recognized her. But Paragon knew that Sebastian Moreau could not be so easily fooled.

"Can you affect a different mode of speech? Perhaps a bit of Welsh?"

She considered for a moment, then asked in deep liquid vowels, "Shall I serve your wedding breakfast with my dress on or off, good husband?"

*By Jove, I would pay dearly to share a stage with this one. Beatrice and Benedick, perhaps. Phoenix would drool at the prospect. We would run for years.*

"Bravo. We shall concoct an appropriate background story for us based on that. There will be abundant time. The journey takes all night."

Her ringed hand slid down to cup his rump. "All night? Is our newlywed room soundproofed?"

*God help me.* "Do you call this proper matronly behavior?"

"If you are speaking of separate bedrooms like most of the married couples in London, I shall hurl myself into the Thames here and now. What is to be our married name?"

"Mr. and Mrs. Robert Llewellyn, married four years. A tragic past. Select a suitable Christian name for yourself."

"Always fancied myself a Margaret. You can imagine what a burden Ambergris is."

"Ah, my little Maggie Muffin, apple of my eye."

"And you, Bobby Biscuits, pickle of my loins."

That forced a weak groan out of him. "Well, I was going to order cucumber sandwiches, but now you've put me right off them."

After taking a table and ordering tea, they settled on their story. He would be an ex-soldier from an old Welsh family, invalided out of the army with a crippling leg wound and now enriched by coal mines. Ambergris would play the dutiful wife, mourning her lost child and now unable to conceive more. In lieu of a real son, she hoped for a clockwork boy.

Paragon excused himself. He had spied Wilde in the foyer. Before the Irishman could make his exit, he found himself recruited as companion for Ambergris.

"Despite the sordid rumors, I do have a home life, you know," he complained.

"You need to keep her at the table, and don't permit her to communicate with anyone else until I return. I'm popping down to sort out mission details."

"Sounds like your new wife has been less than successful in capturing your heart, old boy."

"She has snared other regions, I will admit, but not that one. I cannot say if she is an ally or an exquisitely clever foe. Go see for yourself."

Oscar took a step toward the dining room, then froze. His eyebrows launched themselves ceiling-ward. "Oh, her."

"Can't say as I like the sound of that."

"The wig and makeup are well-done, but I'm not mistaken. Her notoriety is fast eclipsing my own. Surely you have heard the stories?"

"Enlighten me, but quickly. I have an airship waiting."

"She has been seen in the company of the late unlamented Mr. Grigsby on more than one occasion, as well as departing from the German consulate at two a.m., to say nothing of her frequent intercourse – a word I do not use unadvisedly – with the infamous weapons trader Ernst Klebb. The dubiously titled Lady Kalmaar has several other equally unsavory friends. She seems quite eclectic in her presumed treachery."

Paragon sighed. "Forewarned is forearmed, they say. I'll be back in two ticks. I expect you'll have a grand time volleying double-entendres."

Soon Paragon was in the Lochmoor parlor with Phoenix. "Is all in readiness for my pleasure cruise to the enchanting sights of Yorkshire?" he inquired.

"Indeed. The hand-picked crew awaits your arrival aboard HMAS *Henry Coxwell*."

*Coxwell? Is Wilde writing the scenario for this little adventure?*

"Who is pilot?"

"Your favorite, that daft Commander Farnborough."

"Clement Farnborough? He nearly killed us all. Flew his ship into the mother of all storms to escape those Russian Hargraves. I still weep whenever it rains. He's a crazed swashbuckler."

"As are all military airship captains." Phoenix handed him an envelope. "Passwords, maps, etc." Paragon tucked the packet inside a zippered inner coat pocket.

"Naturally, you have a plan for getting Moreau out of a guarded airship that is worthy of Napoleon?"

"That depends. Did he ever pull one out of his manly ass on the spot?"

That earned him a smirk, but Phoenix rose above it. "Where is your blushing bride?"

"In the dining room, doubtless evoking blushes from Wilde. I daresay he has met his match there. And when were you planning to tell me about her ties to the Germans and to international criminals?"

"Hearsay, mostly. All social occasions with others nearby. Even the late consulate episode followed a long night of Fasching revelry. There is no concrete evidence of her having any nefarious dealings with Her Majesty's enemies. But smoke tends to be accompanied by a certain amount of fire. That's why I agreed to her being a part of this, mad as it is, so that you can watch her. She's no doubt less dangerous to us that way than on the loose." Phoenix grew deadly serious. "Dispatch her if she proves treacherous. No remorse or second chances. I would keep one eye open while experiencing the delights of the *Coxwell*'s honeymoon suite."

"The Royal Aero Flotilla has love nests on its ships?"

"Have you seen how they outfit the cabins for their Air Marshals? You may have naked golden putti on your ceiling."

Phoenix disappeared, whistling "Fare Thee Well, Attractive Stranger" from *Iolanthe*. Rolling his eyes, knowing that in the opera it was sung by the Fairy Queen, Paragon passed into Queue's work area. She squinted hard through magnifying spectacles at a palm-sized metal box on the cluttered bench.

He peered at the object. "What do you have for me? The barking mad Commander Farnborough awaits."

Her voice came out as a snarl. "Not to mention the charming Lady Kalmaar."

*Ah...I might have known.* "You neglect her other appellations: mysterious, unnatural, mendacious, deadly, likely criminal, and potentially treasonous." *I suppose I could add vindictive and vampiric, as well...*

"In short, your idea of the perfect woman."

"Do you really wish to have this conversation now? I already have an alienist."

A grumble deep in her throat served as an answer. Queue held up the box. Perhaps an inch thick, it was made of riveted bronze. "Grasshopper telegraph. Very experimental. Stolen from the personal papers of the murdered Edison. So termed because its signal can hop a short distance through the air, via Hertzian waves, to a nearby telegraph wire."

"What range can I expect?"

"Hope for two hundred yards, settle for half that."

*Is this how Ambergris' wrist box works? Was she involved in Edison's demise?* "I can send a signal to anyone with a telegraph receiver?"

"You can. And receive. Slow, cumbersome, and insecure, though." She smirked as if she had just described his prime faults.

Paragon tucked one into each coat pocket. "What else do you have for me?"

She held up full-moon clips for the Webley. Unlike the soft lead bullets he normally carried, the noses of the new ones came in a variety of colors. "Reds are incendiaries. Blues carry an anesthetizing agent. They will put a hippo to sleep in just a few seconds. Greens make eye-stinging smoke. It will defeat most breath masks, so shoot downwind. Yellows are armor-piercing. Use both hands, they kick like a bee-stung carthorse. Will not penetrate a land dreadnought's hull but will likely punch through thin iron."

"Might they bring down a clocker without the need for an eye shot?"

"Perhaps. Don't wager your life on it."

"And the lovely purple ones?"

"Explosive. I would avoid using them in an enclosed space. We nicked the formula from Nobel's laboratory. So powerful that he will not sell it. Reassuring to know that even death-dealers have standards." The final clip appeared in her hand. "Black nose. Frangible ammunition."

"Ah, you know how your elevated vocabulary sets my heart to racing."

Her face assumed a homicidal aspect. "Full of tiny little bits. Expends a tremendous amount of shallow energy into your target. Trust me, he will go down hard and fast, with a very large hole in him. But the round will not pass through to strike anything else."

"Such as an airship's hydrogen bag."

"Precisely."

"Anything else for your favorite operative?"

"He isn't here, so you will have to suffice. No."

"As always, your destructive propensities are much-appreciated. Thank you."

She touched the back of his hand with two fingers without looking at him. "Come back…whole. Please."

Paragon rotated his hand until he held hers. "I shall."

He headed for the door. She called after him, "I do not trust her."

Without turning back, he replied, "Then we are of one mind about that."

Back upstairs, Lady Ambergris rose at the sight of him. His trousers responded in kind. "Shall we go, darling?" Just to be cheeky, she filled the air with her enticing scent.

*Well, there goes my hope of being rested when I confront the enemy.*

Wilde gathered his gloves, seemingly unmoved by her scent. "Bon voyage, you lovebirds. I shall repair home to embrace my own Constance and dandle my progeny upon velvet knee." He saluted them with his stick. "Good hunting."

Paragon steered his new spouse out the club's front door and into their carriage. "Let us practice our Welsh accents. Invent a gorgon of a mother and remind me of how we overcame her fierce resistance to our union."

After enduring the polluted London streets, they arrived at Her Majesty's dirigible tower in Whitehall just after sunset. It loomed above Horse Guards and St. James's Park like a great railroad spike plunged into the earth. Prince Albert had brought in the Frenchman Eiffel to construct it. The Prince Consort loved mechanistics, and for good reason. Clockwork and HCA had combined to rebuild him after a series of riding accidents, illnesses, and assassination attempts. Standing on four great lion's paws, the airy iron lattice structure swept in at the waist and rose straight into the sky with a pronounced twist. As might be expected, the regiment keeping guard over it had a less-than-respectful name: the 'Imperial Tallywhacker.'

A brace of Grenadier Guards privates helped transfer the luggage to the steam lift which would take it up to the *Coxwell*'s hold. "Here, darling," Lady Kalmaar said. She offered Paragon a palm-sized leather packet, decorated with the Eccentric Club owl in gold. "My wedding gift. I saw how you lusted after mine." A touch of her gloved finger opened it up like a flower blossom.

The impossibly light and compact breath mask, a masculine copy of hers, weighed less than a thought. Paragon brought it up to his disbelieving face. It embraced his skin like a lover, sealing in an instant. His first breath was a revelation, sweet and effortless. Ambergris helped him to adjust the brass-rimmed eye protectors.

"No blurring," he told her in the blissful tone of a religious convert. "No headache." His voice contained only the barest hint of voice-emitter buzz.

She had put on her own mask. "Wonderful, yes? I would give up Swiss chocolate before I would part with this beauty."

"I can well see why. Where on earth did you find them?"

"Oh, I know a large clever chap. A mutual acquaintance, I expect. Lives in

Bloomsbury. Just brilliant, he is."

If his jaw had not been restrained it would have dropped. *"Adam Franklin made these? Well-done, old man. And to think that some still call you a monster. But how does she know about you? It's a state secret.*

Paragon gazed up at their transport. The *Coxwell* resembled a whale floating in dirty water. 300 feet long and 60 feet in diameter, she was a light scout craft and often served as a command ship for Air Marshal Glaisher. Paragon had been aboard her once before, when she had extracted him from the sea after the messy Volante affair. The twin engines rumbled and snorted like enormous iron bulldogs. Her exhaust funnel angled down and rearward, mixing steam with the hot exhaust to reduce the risk of a spark igniting hydrogen. Despite the long success rate of Her Majesty's airships, Paragon still preferred to travel in contact with the ground, though he was Lochmoor-trained in piloting them and all other aircraft.

"An entire evening aloft with several dozen rugged men," Lady Kalmaar mused as she stepped into the lift cage. "I must have done something right."

When they bumped to a stop, the captain waited. Ambergris stiffened upon sighting the aeronaut who would hold their lives in his grease-stained hands. Well over six feet in height and as thin as a starving greyhound, Clement Farnborough's wild-eyed demeanor, gold front tooth, and sharp black Van Dyke beard suggested less a disciplined military man and more a pirate. He dressed like a big game hunter serving time with a traveling circus. Khaki jodhpurs, knee-high brass buckled boots, tight double-breasted blue leather shell jacket with fringed gold epaulettes. A waxed moustache with upturned tips. For added effect, Farnborough sported an 18th century lace jabot of white cambric at his throat. On his head sat a standard naval peaked cap, white with glossy black brim, trimmed with an ostrich feather. Green-lensed goggles gave him a bug-like appearance.

"Montague! As I live and breathe!" he bellowed, his voice an octave deeper than might have been expected. The man spoke in a rapid single rush as if fearful of forgetting all that he wanted to say. "Still killing undesirables for Queen and country, eh?" He snatched up Ambergris' kid-gloved hand and bestowed a bristly kiss upon it. "Clement Farnborough, HMAS, at your service. Charmed, I'm sure. Lovely perfume, by the way. Well, must run. Enjoy your stay on my ship. Toodles!"

With that breathless declaration the lanky force of nature scurried away. He shouted over his shoulder, "Monty! Why don't you show your lady a bit of the old *Coxwell*, eh? I seem to recall that you have a talent for that sort of thing." His laughter could be heard long after he was out of sight.

"We're doomed," Lady Kalmaar stated with the same certainty one might reserve for predicting the next sunrise.

"Perhaps," said Paragon. "But it shall not be because of him."

A pink-faced young crewman, much more properly attired than his captain in bloused black trousers, starched gray roll-neck jumper, and blue beret, requested that they follow him. Lady Kalmaar took Paragon's arm and clutched her skirt to prevent it tangling in the confusion of cables and struts in the passage.

"I somehow imagined it to be roomier," she said.

"Built for speed. Purely utilitarian, without many amenities, excepting the Air Marshal's cabin."

"Dare I hope that it is our destination?"

"You may. It even has a bathtub with hot running water."

"A splendid recruiting tool for the RAF."

"I imagine the ordinary crewman has infrequent access to the same amenities."

"Pity. I shall make every effort to enjoy my bath in their stead, then. The least I can do for our brave lads."

"Always thinking of the little man, you are."

She cast a downward glance at him. "In every way, good sir."

In order not to faint from lack of circulation to his brain, Paragon forced himself to think of cricket statistics and reorganizing his pantry shelves. He counted the rivets in the airship's structure. *The bloody Zulus had more mercy than she does.*

Their guide stopped before a windowless door with three white stars. Giving it a sharp series of two short and two long raps, he stood aside as it opened to permit Lady Kalmaar to enter. Inside another crew member barely old enough to shave held the portal. He saluted, told them to freely ask for any assistance needed, and left.

When the door closed again Paragon turned about to familiarize himself with the room while Ambergris shed her cloak and hat. Most berths on an airship tended to be generous coffins, but this was a major exception. Twenty feet square, it resembled a White Star liner's first-class stateroom. The azure-and-gold walls matched the lush carpet. A fine sleigh bed of impressive acreage filled the far corner. Rose-shaded lamps powered by the new Gassner zinc electrical battery provided safe illumination.

Ambergris purred as she reclined full-length across the down bed. "Mmm... delicious. Morale must be high in the RAF."

"Clement does not believe in doing anything by halves. Though I daresay his own cabin is resolutely spartan." Paragon spied a bottle of champagne in a silver bucket. "Veuve Clicquot,'61. Comet vintage."

"Pour me a glass *a tout de suite*."

"Patience, dear wife. I am off to meet with our equally effervescent pilot and re-acquaint myself with the ship's topography. Make yourself comfortable."

He made his way forward again through the cramped corridors. All seemed to be in order. No nefarious devices could be seen. Satisfied that Moreau had not managed to sabotage his transport, Paragon hurried down into the control room.

"Ah, Monty!" boomed Farnborough. "Just in time to watch the old girl spurn her suitor Earth and leap into the clouds' embrace."

"All is in readiness, then?" Paragon inquired with more savoir-faire than he felt.

"Capital! Clear weather, no enemies in sight. Soon we will be above this breath of Tartarus. Then you shall see the Pleiades and be smiled upon by Orion."

"No incipient thunderstorms, if I take your meaning."

"Still on about that? Did I not deposit your less-than-grateful carcass safely upon terra firma?"

"That you did, though I confess to having to burn my ruined drawers."

"Bah! Never wear the damned things! Keep one's gents free and clear, that's my motto!"

"Thank you for that indelible mental picture."

Farnborough pointed to his map. "Since your superiors are so terrified of a bogey man no one has actually seen, we shall take a devious route, just in case your fellow has laid an ambush."

"Complicated. Why not just float out into the North Sea and fly like an arrow?"

"The bloody Germans have posted reconnaissance ships out there. I was ordered to avoid an engagement. But you should be on the ground by eight in the morning. One refueling stop."

"Excellent. I am off. I shall sleep like the righteous dead."

The entire cabin burst into laughter.

"That won't do, mate. Word has gone 'round of your lady. Cleopatra on the barge, she is."

The First Officer announced that the *Coxwell* was ready for departure. "Smashing! Let us wrench free of this great iron willy and get back into our element." Farnborough gave Paragon a saucy wink. "Time for you to return to Mrs. Paragon, before she seeks solace elsewhere. No shortage of eager volunteers amongst this lot."

Paragon gave them a sardonic two-fingered salute and left the gondola, eager to remove his leg and have his wife-of-convenience massage some liniment into his thigh.

*Never thought I could even think this…but I need sleep, despite the goddess in my bed.*

Sleep might have been possible, if Lady Kalmaar had not been waiting for him wearing only black silk stockings, a matching choker with cameo medallion, and – incredibly – a violet wedding veil. The suppressed thrum of the steam propellers seemed to fade away, unable to compete with pounding pulses and labored breathing.

He never did remove the leg.

# Act 4

~

# The Isle is Full of Noises

*Above Lincolnshire*

*The opaque face plate of Moreau's mask caught the wardroom's light, making it seem to glow. A soothing thrum from the airship's engines made for a relaxing atmosphere. Captain Carter leaned back in his chair, a bourbon in hand, and advised, "We daren't linger here."*

*"We shan't." Moreau coughed. With a trembling hand he unscrewed the end of his staff and pulled a roll of paper from it. "Once we snare Jimmy, off we go."*

*"If they snare him. He's proven to be damned slippery."*

*"Not this time. We have an ace. A double pair of great white arms will hold him fast."*

*The Confederate shuddered. "I've fought those things on their home ground. Wouldn't like to be in his shoes when it jumps him."*

*"I'm eager to see Jimmy meet our long-distance visitor face-to-face, mind unprotected."*

*Spreading the document across the table, Moreau pointed to a complex diagram that resembled a lunatic's scribbles. "From our most recent cylinder, at Brighton. We snagged it before our foes could get there. Our friends upstairs included the plans for the device we need. We assembled it in their magical shop, like the little tripod and the other toys. We will test it before we leave this chilly, foolish island."*

*Carter peered at the paper. It showed a sort of iron suit, with bizarre weapons attached. An oblong tank rested on the back, two nozzles facing down. "I swear, warfare is passing me by."*

*Moreau nodded. "As so many other fields are, thanks to the gifts from the stars. It's unfortunate that so many of them have been stolen or leaked to the world at large. Our masters wanted their allies to have this power, not Earth's defenders. But our Breakers have dulled the advantage that they might have gained."*

*"Surely they don't share their truly formidable items with us. That'd be bad strategy."*

*"Unlikely. Makes one terrified of what they may bring when the dance begins." He coughed again and returned the plans to his staff. "As it is, just the knowledge they've shared that's in here keeps one up at night. You ought to make sure that your government is the highest bidder for this new one. Wouldn't do to have to face the Union Army if it builds regiments of them."*

*"I've already informed them that they need to marshal their bullion."*

*"Excellent. I prefer doing business with people I know. Can't trust the Germans or Russians. They have an undeveloped sense of honor when it comes to death machines."*

*The masked man leaned heavily on the staff, making a pained sound. "Time for another orange pick-me-up. Gather everyone here at noon tomorrow. I need to learn the status of my corporation. With Navita gone, we'll swoop up his gangs in a very hostile merger."*

*When Moreau had left the room, Carter began writing in code on a tiny paper, keeping one eye on the door. Finishing, he tucked it into a little metal capsule, like the ones worn by messenger pigeons.*

## 13 / "A MOST RIDICULOUS MONSTER"

Distant shouts and thumps awakened them from a sticky yet satisfied slumber. The cabin gave a slight lurch. No light came through the porthole.

Paragon slid out from under the satin duvet and left Lady Kalmaar to her dreams. Harriet and Vesper lay along her thighs, only half-withdrawn. They had done themselves proud and deserved their rest.

He donned a green quilted dressing gown. Wearing it nude felt like a full body embrace from a pair of Bengali courtesans, a youthful experience that made him smile. After bolting on his leg, he peered out to see what the crew were up to.

The airship lay below treetop level, atop a barren ridge near a telegraph line, where dozens of men clinging to ropes were holding it in place. Squinting through the murk, he could make out a line of coal wagons leading up to the cargo ramp.

Warm hands snaked around to caress his bare flanks. Paragon tensed every muscle in surprise. He had yet to fully adjust to her pale skin and golden hair. She wore a sheer violet chemise trimmed in white lace which perfectly complemented her new look.

"The air is so clear out here," she said. "I can't recall the last time I could see stars."

One of the horses kicked over its traces and become ensnared. In a moment, the whole team was thrashing about. All three men on the vehicle leaped clear. Soon the chaos settled and the dull routine was restored. They would finish in a few minutes.

Paragon turned away from the window, then frowned and returned. He looked hard at that wagon again. Certain, he set his jaw, and yanked on trouser and boots.

"Where are you off to?" Amber asked, hand at her bosom.

"Chasing a wild goose, I hope." He loaded his pistol with the fragmenting bullets, slid back the barrel/cylinder mechanism to cock the weapon, and handed it to her. "Here. Lock the door. Admit no one but me." On the way out he snatched up his swordstick.

"Why are you so suddenly alarmed?"

"Because when that wagon team went wrong there were three men on it. Now there are only two. And the missing bloke was the size of a bear." He opened the door and checked to see that no one lay in wait. "The password is *namaste.*"

"Namaste. Very well, then. Take care." She kissed him lightly. "Try not to explode the ship. I imagine it is expensive."

With that he was gone, gliding down the narrow passage toward the service hatch two decks down. The opening was crowded with men coming and going with their coal loads in wheelbarrows. He accosted an officer who supervised the proceedings from the very edge of the ramp, giving the fellow a light touch on the shoulder with the tip of his stick. The bearded young Lieutenant Blanchard turned to look Paragon up and down in puzzlement and mirth.

"Shouldn't be here, sir. Captain will have my bollocks if anything ---"

Paragon cut him off with a curt wave. "No time for that. I believe you have a stowaway on board, and a dangerous one, too."

"Begging your pardon, but that's not possible. We are very thorough about that sort of thing. Weight ratios and all, you know."

"He only snuck on in the last few minutes."

"We have sentinels, sir. I suggest that you go back to your ---"

Paragon slammed the tip of his stick onto the deck with exasperated force. "That fracas with the horses just now was a diversion."

Blanchard sighed with a growling undertone. "Sir, I am in the midst of a sensitive resupply operation. We will send word to Commander Farnborough of your request in due course. Who shall I say is raising this alarm?"

The poor lieutenant's answer was a clenched fist in his face, owl ring clearly visible. "I am Paragon of the Eccentric. I am your sole reason for being aloft this night!"

That made Blanchard gulp. "Lochmoor, is it?" He backed away and called out, "Sergeant Bland! Assemble all refueling hands. Possible enemy infiltration."

Booted feet stomped across the ringing plates as the crewmen formed up in ranks. In minutes, the non-commissioned officers reported that all were present and accounted for. No one had seen anything amiss. Blanchard turned with a glint of triumph in his eye.

"Satisfied, Mr. Paragon? May we get on with our real work now?"

"Thank you, Mr. Blanchard. You have been more than patient. Please carry on."

He gladly left the freezing gangway and headed back. That took him past the main coal storage compartment, where the airmen had resumed dumping. Their boots had left black smudges. Halfway up the second stairway he froze. His grip on the pearl-headed stick tightened.

*What is it?* While he pondered the situation, the whole ship trembled and tilted as the engines got back up to speed. They were climbing again. Paragon slid his hand along the smooth railing and resumed his travel up the stairs.

Again, he paused. But this time he knew why. He wiggled his fingers. Coal dust covered the banister.

*He's stolen a march on me. The bastard hid in a wheelbarrow. Let them dump him into the bin, then snuck out during the roll call.*

He took the steps two at a time, head whipping to and fro, anticipating an attack from any direction. When he arrived on the berth deck, he crouched in a corner to watch and listen, rather than charge into who knew what. A funk stung his nose like as if a rampant monkey had mated with a rotting lizard.

Paragon crept along the corridor. The smallsword was out now, leading the way like a narwhal's tusk. In case something dropped from the rafters, he kept the stick body aimed up in a saber defense. Now the air was so noisome that he longed for his new breath mask. But no enemy did he spy. What he found sent ice water down his spine.

His cabin door had been knocked half off its hinges by a blow which had split it down the center.

Abandoning all caution, Paragon dashed at it, remembering to call out "Namaste!"

in case Lady Ambergris waited with his Webley. But the room was wrecked and empty. The pistol lay on the bed, unfired. No blood or other worrying sign could he see, other than overturned furniture. The thing had taken her.

Though mad with worry, he took the time to don his shoulder holster and thrust the Webley and a small spring-powered torch into it. A search of Amber's effects produced her opera glasses. After fumbling with the mechanism, he managed to turn the things on. To his amazement, they did indeed permit him to see in the dark, in hues of green and yellow. With spare shoelaces he tied the glasses to the holster and returned to the corridor to track his quarry.

His bride of convenience had proven her resourcefulness yet again, for tiny double scratches along the wall leading to the left indicated which way he should go. Fine tooth marks. Harriet and Vesper were active in their host's survival.

The trail led him up a circular stair, through a hatch, into the bowels of the gas bag. *I'll wager he expected to catch me asleep and dispatch me with no fuss. So, he snatched a hostage instead. The fiend expects me to pursue him.*

His breath fogged the air in the lifting chamber, which was as dark as Satan's belly. Luckily, the miraculous opera glasses amplified the weak light. Impossibly thin supports, made of a new alloy formula 'liberated' from the Germans, crisscrossed the enormous space. Steel cables from the command gondola moved to and fro, controlling the tail surfaces. The engine noise could not be heard so well up here, but the rush of wind, the snap of stretched fabric, and the creak of stressed metal were just as loud.

Oiled gray sacks the size of omnibuses filled the space. Contained by netting, they were full of the dangerously flammable hydrogen gas which kept the vessel in the sky. Service catwalks ran below and between them. Whatever it was he had tracked here would have no difficulty hiding.

Every sense on its highest alert, he closed and locked the hatch to deny his foe an easy exit. That would not deter his lady's kidnapper for long, but an extra second or two might be all Paragon would require to fall upon the fiend.

*Of course, if I am the poor sod trying to get out…*

Shivering, he secured his Webley in the holster. There was no telling what hydrogen leakage there was up here. Any combat engaged in would likely have to be with blade or bone.

Frozen as he was, Lady Ambergris had to be in a worse state. He had left her in next to nothing. And as she had been living on a South Pacific island, he doubted her constitution could withstand sustained exposure to these temperatures. With the image of his lady turning as blue as her new irises, he began a systematic but hurried search.

Ten minutes of painstaking hunting, every shadow causing him to react with a slash of the sword, took him to the rear of the chamber. There was no place left for the monster to be than behind the final gas bag.

Muttering a chant to calm his nerves, Paragon eased forward, deadly steel sting leading. He took tiny sliding steps to minimize the noise of his advance. His thumb rested lightly on a small bulb at the base of his swordstick hilt.

A careful stretch of his neck around the corner showed him a dangling feminine hand. His knuckles whitened around the sword. In her senseless state Lady Kalmaar had reverted to her natural coloring. Her abductor had hung her in a cluster of ropes as if in a hammock. From the slight movement of her bosom, he could tell that she still lived.

*A lucky thing for you, my abominable friend. Now come on out and play. I'm damned cold and need my tea.*

As if their minds had been joined, the thing scampered down the netting to launch itself at him. He barely had time to dive forward and roll out of danger. A heavy body smacked into the catwalk plating, making it quiver. Rising to his feet, blade before him, Paragon gained time to take the creature's measure as it hesitated to rush his defence.

The head was ape-like, but with a carnivore's tusks and pale reptilian eyes. Soft white fur, patched by coal dust, covered every inch. Amazingly, the monster had four arms, all as brawny as a circus strong man's, with taloned fingers. Too-tight trousers covered its lower limbs. A hole in the back allowed for a ridged and scaled tail eight feet long. Paragon found himself unexpectedly laughing aloud, for the abomination wore a royal blue top hat.

"Ha-ha-ha!" the creature rumbled, mimicking him.

Paragon wondered if it was as sensible as the beast-men Moreau had slain. "You violate the Law. Be off, before your master's justice scars you."

One of the white arms scratched the broad skull. The head cocked to one side and its eyes narrowed. Paragon began to have hope that his gambit had worked. But the thing only laughed again.

"Ah, well…it appears that I shall have to kill you, then." *Bold words, indeed. Have you any idea how to handle a double helping of arms, old boy?*

He needed to keep himself between the beast and the insensible Lady Kalmaar. Anticipating that his foe's simian qualities would lend it prodigious strength and leaping ability, Paragon made a screaming feint at it and then retreated. The thing cackled and bounded dead at him, the quartet of fearsome arms clutching for a lethal embrace. With exquisite timing, he dropped hard onto his back and jabbed one great thigh with his sword tip, squeezing the hilt bulb as the behemoth flew past.

The ape squealed. It landed with a crash and spun about. One paw rubbed at the spot where it had been stung. Another rubbed its jaw as it considered Paragon's fate. With the barest hint of a limp it began another rush.

*Blast! He's too bloody big. I'll have to needle the stuff into him more than once.*

This time the creature employed some cunning. It hurled itself sidelong up the gas bag, nimbly running along the netted surface. If Paragon had not noticed one eye stealing a glance at the planned route, it might have worked. As the monster flew through the icy air, Paragon deftly sidestepped and gave the howling thing a blast in both eyes from his spring-torch, averting his own. Again, the creature smote the deck with a heavy thud. The top hands pawed at its face. Paragon stepped back against the bag and gave the searching lower arms one neat prick each with South American frog poison.

Queue had sworn that the South American poison would relax the muscles of a man in short order, eventually suffocating him. Of course, she had never considered a thirty-stone impossibility. But now that frenzied movement had set the monster's blood to racing, the toxin was speeding through his system. The bottom arms hung nerveless. Like a ship's anchor, the poisoned leg held its owner to the spot.

However, the deadly tail had not been subdued. Paragon managed a weak parry of its blow, but the muscular tail slapped the insult away. The blade clanged against distant struts. That fearsome whip advanced, clearly intent on snaking around his throat and throttling him.

Just as in Lady Kalmaar's billiard room, Harriet and Vesper were his salvation. Her surprisingly strong tentacles seized the tail near its tip and restrained it, though Amber showed only the slightest whisper of returning consciousness. They strained with the effort, though, and could only perform their life-saving task for a moment. Even worse, the creature mustered its final reserve of strength to drag its failing bulk forward to crush him with the unparalyzed arms. One long horrid roar, and rank breath, added to the terrifying effect. A frantic search revealed that the sword lay two dozen yards away, hopelessly out of reach.

*Damnation! Let us hope that Clement's hydrogen vent is doing its job.*

Before he could talk himself out of it, Paragon hauled out the heavy pistol and shoved the barrel into the beast-man's terrible-toothed maw. When the muzzle stopped against the palate, he pulled the trigger, flinching against a massive hydrogen fireball.

But Queue's ammunition did its job. The heavy hollow bullet, filled with disintegrating shot, splattered the monster's brains inside its thick skull in a gory firework that did not exit the head. Blackened scarlet fountained across Paragon's arm. Gurgling, the body slumped onto the catwalk, a long final breath wheezing out of it.

"Crikey!" whispered the groggy Lady Kalmaar.

Paragon drew his dressing gown over as much of her as he could. His fingers had grown stiff from the cold. When they arrived at the hatch, he vainly tried to use his elbows to slide the bolt free. Just as he began to despair, the hinges screeched and he fell onto the spiral staircase, to be caught by the hands of Farnborough's search crew.

The captain addressed the squad attending to Lady Kalmaar, who was pale and golden again. "Get those blankets on her! Gawk later. Have you never seen a woman before?"

One old hand muttered, "Well, I'd always thought so, until now."

Several armed men pushed past Paragon. "He's on the stern catwalk," he told them. "The only four-armed bloke up there." Paragon laughed and quoted *Hamlet*. "'He will stay till you come.'"

Commander Farnborough held out a blue RAF blanket to him. "One may only speculate upon your daring choice of ensemble for this night's revels."

"On the return trip I shall wear sealskin drawers and an ermine overcoat. Make sure they fetch back my swordstick, will you? And take care. 'Tis unbated and envenomed."

"Truly? You Lochmoor lads get to play with all the fun toys." Farnborough laughed and slapped Paragon on the back. "Go warm her up. But try to sleep, too. You'll have a guard the rest of the way."

Paragon was amazed to see that damage-control had already replaced his shattered cabin door. On either side of it stood a brace of burly corporals, each with a queer-looking sidearm. The weapons resembled Very pistols with long barrels, a rear stock, and a bulbous chamber below the muzzle.

"Compressed-air stun gun, sir," one of the men explained. "12-gauge India rubber slugs. They'll take down a charging ox, they will, without blowing a hole in the ship or combusting gas."

Inside the cabin, order had also been restored. Hot tea, biscuits, and soup awaited. To stop his shivering, he changed into a cabled pullover of black Irish wool. Then he climbed under the duvet to share warmth with the woozy Ambergris.

"Just like an old married couple, we are," she said, wiggling against him.

"Absolutely. Romantic airship holiday...champagne..."

"Lovemaking..."

"Hellish multi-limbed monstrosities..."

"Frozen brutality…"

He kissed her blonde hair. "Who says I cannot show a lady a good time?"

"Well, you certainly did not hear it from me." She paused, looking out at nothing. "It…burst in so quickly, I never had a chance to shoot at it. What was that wretched thing, anyway?"

"One of Moreau's pets, I presume."

She shook her head. "I have never seen him experiment in that way. He makes humans out of animal tissue. This creature seemed to be more of an attempt to animalize a man." Her head rose to look him firmly in the eye with unfeignable sincerity. "At any rate, thank you for Lanceloting, my love."

*Love?*

They fell upon the food and drink like wild animals. They might have done the same to one another, but stress, terror, and exposure conspired against them. Both succumbed like Sleeping Beauty after pricking her finger on the spindle. And that was all the pricking that happened the rest of the voyage.

## 14 / "WHERE THE BEE SUCKS, THERE SUCK I"

They were dressed and ready just before the *Coxwell* touched down. As they wore unremarkable tweedy traveling clothes, any casual observer would not favor them with a second glance. Unusual bright morning sun made them squint. Paragon wore his smoked spectacles, armoured bowler pulled down nearly to his nose. Ambergris took his arm and they strolled down the ramp, where a one-horse phaeton awaited them.

Farnborough met them there, resplendent in a snakeskin Jacobean doublet and purely ornamental clockwork eyepatch, a bright yellow scarf about his neck. He fought the sun's glare with a pith helmet like the one Paragon had used in Zululand. At his hip hung a new Enfield rapid-fire steam pistol, powered by a small, insulated boiler on the belt. *Ah, good old Clement, always wanting the newest impractical thing.*

"Sunny Yorkshire welcomes you," he said, twirling his mustache. "Enjoy that while it lasts." He kissed Lady Kalmaar's hand. "I shall remain on station, passing this spot every four hours, beginning at noon. We will be on watch for signal by mirror, lamp, fire, or smoke."

"Righto. Did they tell you our man has a trans-oceanic Giffard? His ship could carry half a dozen pursuit craft."

"Those could be trouble. Nimble buggers. But fragile. Get a message out as soon as you know for certain. Wouldn't do to run into incendiary rounds. Scorch my new suit, it would."

Ambergris interrupted, shivering. "Not getting any warmer, dearest husband. Perhaps I shall snuggle with the crew a while. My patriotic duty and all that."

That earned her a sympathetic laugh at Paragon's expense. They approached the carriage and its freckle-faced driver.

"Top o' the mornin'," said the fellow, his Irish words fogging the air. "Seamus Flanagan at your service. But please call me Quarrel, everyone else does. I came by it honestly enough. The fragrant Mr. Dardanelles sends you his warmest regards. Might I admire that splendid ring of yours, sir?"

"Not at all. I purchased it in Threadneedle Street, in the autumn."

"Did you now?" The Irishman squinted at it. "I find myself partial to the shops in Tottenham Court Road, but only in the spring." He nodded once and winked. "I reckon that'll do, Mr. Paragon. Who makes up these silly secret identifier scripts?"

"Some poor underpaid sod in a windowless office, I imagine." Paragon happened to know that Oscar Wilde wrote them.

"Whoever it is knows bugger-all about how real folks talk. Who's the bit o' skirt, then?"

Paragon stiffened. Lady Kalmaar laid a gentle hand upon his arm and stepped between them. "Margaret Llewellyn," she purred. "Pleased to make your acquaintance, Seamus. Do call me Maggie."

"Me gran were a Maggie. Right welcome, you are." Turning his head about, he called to a short fellow who stood near the freight wagon. "Help her aboard, Desmond. Hop to it! The lady's quality."

Desmond spat at the ground and trudged forward to offer Amber his grimy hand. She took it with as much gratitude as if he had been Sir Galahad. He gave her a shy toothless smile while she ascended. Quarrel shook the reins and clucked the chestnut horse into motion.

Most of the few trees had turned color or were already leafless this late in October. Bracken, heather, and gorse covered landscape. Black-faced sheep roamed. It all burned violet-gold from the attentions of the still-sleepy sun. Behind them the *Coxwell* rose, its shadow shrinking like a snowball in a spring thaw.

"We're five miles south o' Goathland," Quarrel said. "Your factory's another fifteen west of that."

"What have you learned about it?" asked Paragon.

"A legitimate enterprise, maybe. Only the lord Jesus knows why they built it way the hell out here, fifty miles from any customers. They'll be bankrupt in a month. Upgradin' and repairin' of clockwork servants. New faceplates, better eyes and ears, windin' mechanisms. That sort of thing. They do have a handful of clockies as examples of their work. The Ministry has a team on site to monitor compliance. But as the factory itself is dormant, they're huddled in a cozy pub in York."

"Phoenix said that a guard is still present, however."

"True enough. Hard-lookin' lads. Not local."

Ambergris frowned. "Who owns it?."

"The Tredegar brothers of Virginia. They hope to one day convince Her Majesty's government to permit 'em to construct automatons from scratch, as well as to manufacture other modern mechanistic marvels."

"The Tredegar name is unfamiliar to me," said Amber. "How came they by their engineering acumen?"

"The Great War Between the States, that's how. When the North had Richmond on the ropes, it was the Tredegars who invented the war machines what turned the tide, with aid from a still-unknown benefactor. It was their submarines, armoured trains, explosive bullets, and other wonder weapons that saved them. After the Treaty of London in '71 gave the CSA its independence, the Tredegars decided to go into civilian business."

"And just how do these brothers fit in with us?"

"Their nation is of recent vintage, fragile, and an international pariah. They gained the support of Britain and France during the war by falsely forswearin' slavery. Now they only survive through their cotton trade, their armaments, and guile. I doubt that these clever gents are actin' without the knowledge and assistance of their government."

"You think that President Beauregard is personally involved?"

"Unlikely. The old boy is a figurehead, installed as a pawn of commercial and political interests beyond his ken. No, this seems altogether too shrewd for him."

Paragon asked, "What of the layout of the factory? Have you any idea what we shall face?"

"The front entrance opens onto a waitin' room with a reception station and clerk. Straight to the front, behind the clerk's desk, is the factory floor." Left is the manager's office. To the right is the room where clients are received. Behind that there's a telegraph room, infirmary, and a small office for the security men. Farther on's a row of workshops and storerooms."

"How many guards?"

"Eight. And that many again on the monorail from Goathland."

"And the factory staff?"

"Right now, only the assistant manager, sales manager, and clerk."

Lady Kalmaar asked with undisguised eagerness, "And Moreau?"

"Stays on his airship mostly. It comes and goes. Just got back an hour ago. The 'thopters do go out from time to time. Only at night. Them pilots must have bollocks of pure brass to fly such balky machines in the dark." Quarrel cringed a bit. "Beggin' your pardon, Missus."

"Oh, you needn't apologize. I find talk of bollocks rather refreshing." To emphasize her point, she laid a hand upon the crotch of Paragon's trousers and gave it a friendly pat, as one might a dog. "What is the crew complement on a Giffard that size?"

"I wouldn't think less than eighty."

"Any particularly odd-looking fellows amongst them?" asked Paragon.

"Nothin' but, to my mind. All Lascars and other Asiatics, 'ceptin' for the truly queer ones."

"Do tell."

"Like somebody bred the scum o' Limehouse with a menagerie. And there's talk of even more terrifyin' specimens, hidden away."

"I would wager that some disturbing occurrences have taken place in the vicinity?"

"And you'd win. No less than three street people have gone missin' from their usual haunts. Many more sheep. The farmers have taken to patrollin' with shotguns."

"Any idea of the number of these beast-men?"

Quarrel shrugged. "A quarter of the total crew, perhaps."

"A couple of dozen?" gasped Lady Kalmaar. "That would mean he brought much of his island's population with him, unless he has been breeding elsewhere."

Paragon shook his head. "Not good, either way. Let us hope this does not come down to a fight."

Paragon relished the clean air and sun, though being so close to the scene of his boyhood nightmares gave him pause. For nearly ten years he had managed to avoid returning, not wishing to dredge up old memories of strife, starvation, and Peaceful Manners.

Ambergris' finger ran along his cheek. "You look pained."

"Do I? Well, we are sneaking into the proverbial lion's den, after all. With real lions, too, more or less."

"Believe it or not, when he crosses lions with men he ends up with the most adorable and docile fuzzy fellows."

"And here I was pumping myself up to battle fiendish monsters."

"Oh, those would be the baboon-men. Nasty brutes. But enough of man's cunning to make them formidable."

"How well has the Law controlled his creations?"

"Almost flawlessly. He manipulates the brain's Huxley Cells to create amenability to command. Only rarely does that fail."

"I saw it fail spectacularly in Whitechapel. Nearly had my throat cut. But I also saw his so-called justice. He did not even have to do the deed himself. They slew each other without hesitation."

"That is part of the design. Unquestioning compliance to his commands. But no one else receives the same veneration."

"But away from his influence some few do stray from the Law?"

"I have seen it happen, though seldom. There seems to be a correlation between his proximity and their civilized behavior."

Quarrel kept up a run of rural witticisms lasting all the way to the hotel. He had just explained that a Welshman with forty wives was called a shepherd when they stopped before the Hotel Sayers. As if by sorcery, Lady Kalmaar enslaved the staff with her charm. They fought over her luggage as if it held the key to eternal life. A few minutes later, Quarrel shut the door of their room and grinned.

"Maggie, I swear you could convince a Turk to eat a pork sausage."

Paragon smiled to himself. He looked in her direction to see if the same risqué thought had occurred to her.

Ambergris lay on the carpet.

Strictly speaking she sat on it, propping herself up with one arm while a gloved hand covered her brow. Paragon knelt to support her. "I'm quite alright," she protested in a weak voice. "Just a wee bit light-headed."

They helped her to the sofa near the porthole. Quarrel fetched a glass of water while Paragon loosened her high collar. She lay against the sapphire-blue upholstery, smiling in embarrassment.

"Dreadfully silly of me, collapsing like a breathless schoolgirl."

"All the changes in altitude, perhaps?" asked Quarrel. "I've seen airship sickness strike down even strapping lads."

"Possibly," Paragon replied. "Or a too-tight corset."

"No, no," said Ambergris, "I imagine I am merely ill-nourished."

Quarrel moved to the bell pull. "Easily remedied. Some good English beef will ---"

Her too strong "No!" stopped him cold. He turned back to frown at her. "Thank you, Mr. Quarrel, but I am on a rather restricted diet."

She traded significant looks with Paragon. At once he grasped her dilemma. "All too true," he said. "I shall apprise the hotel chef of her special needs."

Quarrel shrugged and sat at the side table. From the satchel he pulled an Ordnance Survey map of the area and a hand-drawn one of the Tredegars' factory floor plan.

"Rolling country, as you've already seen. Heather and hills. Believe it or not, the factory is called A Man for All Seasons."

"...Of an angel's wit and singular learning. I know not his fellow," Paragon recited in his best stage voice. *I expect Wilde would declare Wittington's remark to have been a prophecy about his own splendid self.*

Quarrel jabbed a finger at the map. "They've run a bloody-expensive private elevated rail spur from here to the factory. Runs on compressed air. The staff watches you so hard you fear they can see through your garments."

Amber chuckled. "Harriet and Vesper would frighten them out of a year's growth."

"Who?"

"A private joke," Paragon said. "What specific security measures?

"A uniformed guard in each car. The blokes look like CSA veterans to my eye, as do the engineer and the two porters. Rear car holds a wall full o' weapons."

"All of this for a simple clockie factory? Do you have anyone inside?"

"We did. Bob Dorian. But he disappeared a week ago. No trace. Then they closed everything up tighter than a nun's thighs. When we tried to get a new man hired on, they told him that local chaps need not apply anymore."

"Clearly they caught on to you. Let it not be in vain then. Show us his map."

The two men leaned over the table so that Quarrel could explain the floor plan. "The façade is built in that absurd Gothic Revival nonsense. All pointy spires and gargoyles. Looks like a madman's idea of Chartres. That's where the offices are in the front. Beyond is your standard red brick warehouse, only immense. It's nearly a quarter mile front to back and a hundred yards wide."

"Crikey!"

"Well, a Giffard liner is 250 yards long if it's an inch, ain't it? Not many places you can hide one o' them."

"How many automatons on the premises?"

"One or two samples of their work, and at least two servants for staff and clients. Moreau may have some."

"Unlikely. He prefers biology to engineering. But he is gadding about in a Hargrave and brandishing a ray gun, so perhaps he has broadened his outlook."

Paragon held up the ground plan. "Leave this with me, if you please. I need to memorize it."

Quarrel stood. "As you wish. I need to get back and coordinate my team's next move. Snoopin' on our bellies in the heather, most likely."

"Do they search the train passengers?"

"No, they just glare at them like shopkeepers suspicious you'll nick the merchandise."

"That is precisely what we intend."

Quarrel laughed and took his leave. Paragon familiarized himself with the factory map while ensuring that Amber consumed abundant water. In the absence of a human blood source, a role for which he did not intend to audition, that was all that could be done. It revived her somewhat, but she remained on the couch to conserve her resources.

To establish his credentials as a moneyed man, Paragon strolled about Goathland, enriching the shopkeepers while getting a feel for the town. Standing at the door of a shop enticingly named Sweets Galore, he saw a group of cyclists, which reminded him of the mysterious chap who had thus far eluded him. *I owe you something, my man...you and that arrogant bloke with the wigglers.*

A bony street urchin approached him with uncombed blonde hair, a torn pinafore, and a toeless boot. She was perhaps eleven years old.

"Good day to you," she said in a hoarse voice. "Be you Mr. Paragon?"

He looked about for spies, then leaned toward her. "I confess that I am."

"Got a message from the Griffin."

"Quite a long way. Did he send you a telegram?"

Her jaw set and her nostrils flared. "Don't muck me about, toff. I ain't here to explain our ways to the likes o' you. If the Griffin hadn't said you'd done him a turn, you'd be missin' that fine watch already."

"My apologies for patronizing you, Miss...um?"

"Selkie. A seal what sheds its skin and becomes human."

"Is that so?"

She paused, looked a bit embarrassed. "I saw one, you know."

"What? A real selkie?"

Her jaw clenched again. "You laughs at me and I'll boot your shin, I will!"

That made him bite down on his lip. "Where was this selkie?"

"In the river, of course. Do you think they amble about in the high street?"

"What did she look like?"

"Pointed snout with whiskers. Sharky teeth. Spiky hair on her head and all along her spine. Webbed hands and feet."

"You only saw her once?"

"That were enough. Give me nightmares."

"Are you aware of the disappearances here lately?"

She nodded. "Folks gone missin' from the street."

"I am fairly certain that your selkie and her kin are the ones responsible. You don't want anything to do with them."

"As if I would anyhow." She rolled her eyes to indicate that she was speaking to a complete idiot.

"Excellent. You are a young lady of discretion and sagacity."

Selkie raised her fist to him. "Watch your mouth! I'm proper, I am!"

Paragon raised his hands in token of surrender. "Of course, you are. I merely meant that you are of good judgement."

That calmed her. She leaned against the wall of the shop. "That I am. This is me patch, you know. Anybody tries to run me off it, I gives 'em a right good hidin'!"

"And a prime location it is. Are there many who try to take it from you?"

"Not any more. There's lads hereabouts what's missin' some teeth 'cause they tangled with Selkie."

"I have no doubt about your formidable pugilistic skills."

"Here now! What did I tell you about that saucy mouth?"

"Pugilistic means boxing...fisticuffs."

"Alright, then."

Paragon was reminded of his own sister, poor long-dead Dotty with the daisies in her hair. Selkie's age, a reckless carriage had run her down in the street. The wealthy young driver had never even stopped, merely cursed her for endangering his horse with her broken little body. Though dozens had witnessed it, his single word had counted for more than all of theirs when Michael Parsons' mother had dared to accuse him before the law. *The same would happen with the Earl of Moura and I now.* All her courage had earned her was a sacking at the mill. That had begun their awful spiral into the gutter. Poverty, starvation, prostitution. Then the dubious rescue by Peaceful Manners. *At least Dotty was spared that horror. Small favor from the Almighty, that.*

"You havin' a fit?" asked Selkie.

"Fit?"

"The way you clutch your stick and shake so."

*Careful.* "I am concerned about someone who is also missing. Her name is Millie." He described her to Selkie.

"Hydra and Arachne found her, yesterday, 'round tea time. They was down by the new fact'ry, huntin' for scrap. Saw her dragged into a back door. Kickin', screamin' threatenin' 'em all with nine kinds o' hell."

"And you are all certain it was the lady we seek?"

"Lady! Never heard any sort o' lady use that language. It was her, alright. Who else'd have snakes growin' out o' her head?"

"You see? I was right about your sagacity."

"Yeah, well, me saggy city don't come for free." Her dirty palm stretched out at him, fingers snapping with impatience.

"Professional services should be properly remunerated." He gave her two bob. "Buy yourself a sweet, but also some proper food."

"One and the same, to my mind." She turned toward the shop door. "Mrs. Glidrose gives me soup every now and then."

He handed her his card. "If you ever need to reach me."

She squinted at it. "The Eccentric Club? Sounds like lodgin' for loonies."

"There's that saggy city again."

She left to spend her fortune. Paragon did the same in a few more shops, using all his performing skills to portray a brainless man of means. He limped rather more than necessary. Doubtless the news of his harmlessness would reach the factory offices ahead of him.

After spreading a goodly portion of Her Majesty's expense money about, he returned to the hotel. Amber slept atop the bedclothes, the pale coloring having reverted to her natural tones to preserve her strength. He settled down to commit the factory floor plan to memory, transforming it into a detailed three-dimensional image. It was a knack that he had been forced to develop while on the run.

He raised his trouser cuff and checked the cargo hatch of the metal limb. Amber spoke in a drowsy voice from the bed, "If you are hoping to get a leg over, dearest, I am afraid your wife is just too knackered to oblige."

"I see someone's sense of humor has not withered for want of nourishment. How are you feeling?"

"Somewhat better, I think…for now. It comes and goes before I completely collapse."

"How long can you continue?"

"Another day, perhaps. By then we should be home and I can find a new volunteer. It has never proven difficult."

"I can well imagine."

She nodded at his leg. "It looks like some lost portion of an ancient statue of Apollo. Other such legs I've seen have little or no shell, merely the exposed inner workings."

He began to unbolt the appendage. "When I was first injured, I presumed I would never survive to need one. It was a miracle that I did." *And I've been paying for it ever since.*

Her fingers touched the mounting points. "Are these actually…part of you?"

"Yes. The pins are screwed into the bone. Makes the whole business much more secure than straps. I can walk on it for hours longer, too. It can do nearly anything that a real limb is capable of." A knock on the door made his lady start. "That will be the items I bought while you were resting. You may want to resume your disguise."

After ensuring that no ambush waited, he admitted three of the hotel staff. They lay the parcels upon the table. By the time they all turned for their remuneration, Ambergris had risen and become a blonde vision again. After they had finished admiring her, they backed out.

"They will found a religion around you by tomorrow," Paragon chuckled. "Human sacrifices in the lobby, possibly a henge in the back garden."

"This is none of my doing," she protested. "I barely have the strength for a proper attractor scent right now."

"The scent is superfluous. Do you really have no idea of your effect on men?"

"Their behavior does tend to be rather odd. And I confess to being shamelessly willing to use that to my advantage."

"Which makes you a typical woman in that regard."

"What else are we to do? We have no political rights and cannot compete with men in contests of strength."

"Says the woman who slew a combat automaton while stark naked."

They rehearsed their Welsh accents and their cover story. Paragon hit upon the idea of obtaining an invalid chair from the hotel. That would permit her to rest and reinforce her weakness in the eyes of those at the factory.

The wicker-backed chair proved just the thing. With a blanket across her lap and some sallow adjustments to her complexion, Lady Kalmaar presented the very picture of English ill-health. To set her infirmity in the minds of the locals, they went to the station to purchase their tickets and inspect the situation.

Obtaining the tickets caused no concern, but the pair of unsavory men lounging in a dark corner did. Paragon recognized their bearing as that of former military men. *Likely they did not leave Her Majesty's service with all due honor. The smaller one is a drinker, and his bulky mate looks to be a bully.* Though they did not approach the disguised couple, they were always nearby.

"Shall we confront them?" asked Ambergris.

"Not necessary. I have new resources at my command."

He wheeled her to Sweets Galore. The redoubtable Selkie still occupied her patch out front, a smear of chocolate around her mouth.

"Good afternoon, Miss Selkie. You put your wages to good use, I see."

"As much choccy as I could stuff in me gob."

"May I present Lady Kalmaar?"

Ambergris and Selkie exchanged greetings. The girl seemed impressed by only one thing, the veiled black velvet confection of beadwork and feathers atop the sick lady's head.

"Nice bonnet."

"Do you think so? I shall give it to you if you do something for us."

Selkie's eyes widened. "Pull the other one!"

"There are two rather rough-looking chaps pursuing us. If you can redirect them to a secluded spot, the hat shall be yours."

"What, them two blokes down by the pub there?"

"The very same."

"Humph! Two ticks."

She dashed down the alleyway behind the shop. In less than a minute she appeared at the other end of the street with a couple of ill-fed boys. The mysterious men from the station did not know that the children were near until their hats had been snatched. Laughing, Selkie and friends danced circles about them. Paragon pushed Ambergris into Sweets Galore. Watching from the window, he saw the toughs race off after the children.

"Rest and have some tea," he said, relieving her of the coveted bonnet. "Won't be a moment."

He rushed back around to the alley. Selkie's naughty band kept him alerted to their position with exaggerated shrieks. Catching them up in a cul-de-sac of sheds, he crouched out of sight, stick at the ready.

"Alright, brats," growled the smaller of the two. "You've had yer fun. Now hand 'em over."

Selkie slapped his flat cap onto her head. "I don't know 'bout that. I think it makes me look right distinguished." She punctuated her statement with a huge wink.

With a roar the other man, a broad fellow with a shaven head, rushed at her. His companion followed. Selkie stood her ground, only evading them at the last instant. Both men crashed empty-handed into the wall. Whirling, they discovered to their shame that they had been gulled.

Three more small figures appeared atop the roof and dumped barrels of ashes, whooping like red Indians. Howls of indignation came from inside the boiling mass of gray dust, instantly replaced by choked coughs. They clawed at their eyes.

"Thanks for the hats," grinned Selkie. "Your generosity shall be rewarded in heaven."

Paragon entered the dead end. He handed Selkie her well-earned bonnet and a shilling for each of her troops. She beamed and led them all out laughing. Then Paragon approached the sightless men, who blued the Yorkshire air with nauseating profanity.

"For shame! There are children present." He swept the larger one's knee with his stick, taking him to the ground. A hard shoulder knocked his partner into the wall. While that one slid down it with a groan, Paragon used his arm to choke the big bloke to sleep.

He had to act with decision, because the shorter man had regained his feet and was heading for freedom. Paragon's thrown stick tripped him up, then his knee pressed him into the earth, one arm twisted up behind in a nasty manner Paragon had learned in Siam.

"Sod off!" his victim growled. "Who the hell are you? What're you about with them damned kids?"

"Damned they are not, but I suspect the same cannot be said of you. I shall, however, offer you an opportunity to earn your way out by choosing right action. In the East they call it karma."

"Let me up! I can't bloody see!"

"I shall serve as your eyes and guide you toward nirvana."

"Nerve? You're cuttin' the nerve in me arm in two!"

"It is you are choosing to do that by resisting. Surrender to the will of the cosmos and all will be well." Paragon's prisoner grunted and relaxed a bit. "Better, yes? You are well along the path to enlightenment."

"What do you want?"

"There is darkness in my mind. I wish you to share knowledge which will dispel it."

"Speak bleedin' English, why don't you?"

"Who sent you?"

"I just wanted me hat back."

Paragon twisted his arm a bit more. "Following me across town, your hat was set firmly upon your vacant head. Every corner I turned, there you were. Try again."

"You know how it is. Somebody gives you a few quid to keep an eye on any bloke buyin' a ticket on the monorail..."

"Why would anyone spend pounds in that fashion?"

"Times is hard, mate. We didn't ask questions."

"So you work for the factory owners, then?"

"Those slavers? Hell, no. They already know who's comin'. The ticket agent pneumos your name and description to 'em."

"Careful, are they not?"

"You'd be careful, too, with the bally Clockwork Ministry watchin' your every move."

"Who pays you, then? Give me a name and you can go your merry way."

The graying man laughed. "He's a lot less forgivin' than you are, mate. The worst you can do is kill me."

Maintaining his submission hold, Paragon went through the fellow's clothing. Though he searched the likeliest places to hide documents, none came to hand. A similar survey of the other attacker yielded similar results.

As concerned voices and running feet approached, Paragon abandoned the pair and made his way out back to Ambergris. While he pushed her back to the hotel, he revealed what had transpired. As he finished, a syncopated drum chorus of small feet rushed up from their rear.

The gaggle of chattering children surrounded them, all talking at once. When he had managed to calm them, he pointed at the stolen cap that Selkie still held. "Might I admire your spoils of war?" She handed it to him, but yelped when he cut open the lining with his pen knife.

"What you doin' that for?"

In reply he pulled a £10 note from inside.

"Blimey! How'd you know that was in there?"

"I didn't. But he went to a great deal of risk to recover it." More excavating rewarded him with a railway ticket and a scrap of soiled paper.

It read, *N's orders are not to be questioned. As soon as you find the man from the Eccentric Club, send an encoded telegram with his precise location. We will dispatch him and give you the rest of your money. Do not disappoint us again.* The remainder of the message was a jumble of letters and numbers.

"Why is no one ever happy to see me?"

Ambergris raised one saucy eyebrow. "Your memory is faulty, I think." He showed her the note. After a strangely long moment she asked, "Um, what are these numbers and such at the end?"

"Telegraph address. More secure than revealing the name of the recipient, who is this N person."

Paragon held out the money to Selkie, who stared at it as if it were a pagan idol. "Here. You and your team earned this. Buy yourselves proper shoes."

"Don't dare!" she protested. "Peelers'll think I stole it."

"Very well. I shall purchase shoes on your behalf. All of you, give Selkie your sizes."

After arranging for delivery of the treasured footwear, Selkie led her Myrmidons off, crowned with Lady Ambergris's feathered bonnet. He found the previous owner grinning at him. "What?"

"You are the rankest fraud. Clothing street urchins. St. Francis was a loathsome worm compared to you."

He gave her a sad smile which hinted at his own dreadful childhood. "Tell a soul and I swear you shall walk back to London."

Back at the Hotel Sayers, Mr. and Mrs. Llewellyn enjoyed a perfectly chaste nap, then worked on perfecting their characters and cover story. Paragon threw surprise questions at Lady Kalmaar, testing her ability to react to unforeseen danger. She handled each one with perfect poise.

"You have a suspicious facility for lying, if I may say so," he said.

"I could say the same of you," she retorted, "and I doubt that yours is entirely due to theatrical training."

*True enough. And the longer we remain in Yorkshire the more falsehoods I may be telling.*

He set his makeup kit on the table and began to subtly alter Ambergris's face. The nose changed from the Platonic ideal of what a nose should be into more of a somber housewifely affair. A careful application of paint made her eyes sag and appear red. He flattened her breathtaking cheekbones and gave her a hint of crow's feet. Paragon turned his talents on himself, masking the cleft chin with a Van Dyke beard and covering the scar.

Quarrel knocked in their pre-arranged code. "Time to see how good my handiwork is."

He admitted Seamus, who had changed into black clothing and carried a small satchel. His eyes shot up on seeing them, particularly Ambergris. "That's well-done and no mistake. It should have no trouble foolin' Moreau."

Paragon told Quarrel about the brace of men who had followed them from the station, handing him the note from the cap.

"Who's this N? Don't look like he's in with Moreau or the Tredegars."

"Get Lochmoor to trace that address. It might help, but my guess is that it's probably vacant by now."

"Righto. Me and the lads'll lie out by the fact'ry and see if we can chart the security pattern. Guard changes and whatnot."

"Your signal system?"

"A green flare means all clear and your airship is on station. Yellow says hold your position but trouble's brewing. Red means bugger out of there, there's been a cock-up."

After confirming some other details, Quarrel took his leave. Lady Kalmaar excused herself to bathe. Paragon ordered ice for his innumerable aches and pains. If he accumulated any more damage, he would have to submerge himself in the stuff.

Ambergris appeared from the bath, uncamouflaged and purring. The violet lace garment clung to her damp skin in such a luxurious fashion that Paragon grew light-headed. *One would expect that a chap would grow at least somewhat accustomed to the sight of her by now.*

She smoothed her wet black hair, which fell to her narrow waist like seaweed from Poseidon's personal garden. The slow feline motion made her breasts stand out, which was certainly her intention.

*I begin to suspect that this truly is some clever scheme of Moreau's to slay me with biological combustion.*

He swallowed hard. "You seem quite… revived."

"Do you think so? I feel less enervated, despite having gone so long without feeding." She lingered on the final word.

*Can a man die of an erection? One would think not, and yet…*

"Have I mentioned that blood is not my only means of sustaining myself?"

"I believe you have not done so, no." His mouth was full of sawdust. Somehow, he knew that no part of her would be so dry.

"The male essence will suffice for a time, though it is a poor substitute. I am sorry if that is painful to hear, but it is the truth."

*Not half so painful as my male essence-maker, woman!*

"Still, it will energize me for a few hours. And it will not involve the risk of addiction from Harriet and Vesper."

*I beg to differ.*

She oozed onto the bed where he sat with the dripping towel of ice. When she took it into her hands, he half-expected steam to hiss from it. He prayed that she would dump the frozen stuff into his tormented lap.

She tossed the towel into the wash basin. Paragon worked his torso back and forth. It was stiff and sore, but he could still move it. *Should still be able to maintain appearances tomorrow.*

"All shipshape?" Ambergris asked. "Splendid. That will make this so much easier."

Before he could react, she was upon him from behind, tugging his shoulders onto the bed. Her frenzied feeding did not take long. Ambergris devoured his stem as if it were the last morsel on earth. He feared he would spend until his poor heart burst. For several minutes after, he lay beneath her, toes curled, knees trembling.

Eventually pain replaced joy in his throbbing groin. Her mouth slid from his abused organ. Variegated hues of passion flowed across her skin like current through a wire. He stared at the ornate plaster scrollwork on the ceiling, willing it to stop spinning.

Paragon laughed, but it came out as a feeble croak. "That was supposed to be non-addictive?"

She rolled up on one elbow to favor him with a satisfied smile. "I may have overstated my case a bit."

He tapped the corner of his mouth and then pointed to hers. She ran her tongue out to scoop up an errant pearly drop. Vesper rose and plucked it off her tongue with a quick kissing motion.

"That is certainly something one does not see every day," Paragon observed.

"Speak for yourself, sir."

"So…that is your emergency feeding technique, eh?"

"It is. I admit to injecting somewhat more enthusiasm into it than is my wont."

"Any more injecting and you would be sending a pneumo to the Goathland undertaker."

She cuddled next to him, tugging the duvet over them both. They slept for several hours. Eventually Paragon discovered powers of recuperation he had not realized he possessed. She applauded his performance with appealing vigor and rafter-shattering shouts of joy.

*Above south Yorkshire*

"*We lose confidence in thee,*" *thrummed the eerie voice. It sounded like angry hornets in a pool of electrified blood.*

*Across the airship's laboratory, as far as he could physically place himself from the frosted glass door, Moreau listened through a weird sort of crystal-and-leather helmet, connected to her chamber by a segmented copper hose. Built from her design, it translated the otherworldly thoughts. It also, thanks to modifications she was unaware of, filtered her terrifying mental control, the same way the structure of her cell did. Otherwise, no one within ten yards of her would be safe from enslavement. If he had not been denying her the full measure of her dreadful food, the range would be twice that. He would have had more exsanguinated crew than he already was cursed with. In fact, it was time to leave her door ajar again tonight.*

"*Your words wound me,*" *he said into a brass transmitting device.* "*How have we not given satisfaction?*"

*Fthosa Woldrarwe reminded him,* "*Thy promises were large and bold, but have yet to come to pass. Control of government and commerce is most incomplete. Dangerous men of learning and creation, who might thwart us, still live. Our science, lent to thee to aid in weakening thy planet's defenses, hath escaped thy charge and instead hath given the Terrans knowledge and power they would not otherwise possess. This hath made our inevitable conquest more difficult and costly. Thy protégé of old battles thee to a standstill, interfering with our great work in preparing the battlefield. And now this Lochmoor creature stings and taunts thee. Should we cast a wider net for more effective allies?*"

*Moreau licked suddenly dry lips.* "*None would be found. Your Excellency already resides with the most powerful organization for your needs. Granted, we humans are flawed and imperfect in comparison to ---*"

"*Spare us thy bootlicking. Thy welcome rescue of us from the Navita captivity was proof of thy worth. Yet past laurels gain us nothing. The fleets of Omos Rab near completion. We must ready the Terran soil to receive its masters. Thou art our eyes and limbs. Must we pluck out the weak ones, as my people do, and let stronger ones grow in their stead?*"

"*All will be as you wish. No battle plan ever survives intact. The enemy always has some say. But we have reacted and adjusted. I have drawn Lochmoor to us. He will be a threat no more. The London traitor has met justice. His replacement will be compliant and loyal, the election shall be simple to manipulate. Tesla is on the run and our hounds snap at his heels. As for my former friend, his supply of your remedy is nearly exhausted. He has failed in synthesizing it. Soon his mind will crumble again into cruelty and murder. Our own law will disgrace and dispatch him.*"

*"See that thy declarations do not ring hollow again. If, in the next lunar cycle, progress has not been made ---"*

*"Understood, Your Excellency. The law of Omos Rab is harsh but fair. Our deeds shall be our defense."*

Moreau cut the power of the communicator and removed it from the door plug. He swallowed and fought the nausea that always accompanied his conversations with the envoy. Though she was caged for their own protection, she was nevertheless his mistress in this business. It would not do to lie to her or provoke her. Others of her kind were en route to Earth as advance parties. One had proved difficult to control. Several would no doubt overcome him. Then his wife and child would never live again.

The other child, the recalcitrant one, must be reminded of her place. She spent too much time with his enemies. Her leash had to be tightened, and he knew just how.

## 15 / "WOULD I MIGHT BUT EVER SEE THE MAN"

The next morning, Ambergris was up and dressed before he had even stirred in the bed. With a moan, Paragon announced that his every fiber, down to his damnable Huxley Cells, was declaring a holiday, Empire-preserving secret mission or no. That earned him a flung pillow.

He hopped to the washroom while she applied her disguise. While drying off, he gazed into the mirror and marveled at the collection of scars he had accumulated in a decade of wandering. His skin resembled an aerial photograph of a bombed battlefield.

*Knives, bullets, spears, even a bally crossbow bolt. Perhaps I should just stick with the acting.*

Then the sturdy young man dissolved into a scrawny runt wearing filthy rags and the eyes of a terrified rabbit. Michael Parsons, poor Dotty's brother, unable to save or avenge her. In his ear he heard the wicked snort of Peaceful Manners, ridiculing Michael's every dream and desire.

*Ah, yes. That is why I do this.*

He knelt on the cold tile floor and chanted. For a quarter of an hour, he cleansed his mind and soul of every distraction, doubt, and fear. Meditation often was all that prevented stunted young Parsons from fleeing the sordid past and plunging into the lethal present.

A dark blue morning coat and charcoal gray trousers were his choices for the day, accented by a monocle on a satin ribbon. With the beard he looked like a sober man of business, abetted by false documents identifying him as Richard Llewellyn of Cardiff, owner of Imperial Export, world-wide dealers in coal, timber, and other profitable materials.

Lady Kalmaar, wearing a conservative dress of gray and black, handed him the armored bowler. "Have you all of your lethal toys, dear?"

"Well, the dynamite in my drawers is somewhat diminished, but otherwise…"

Into Paragon's valise went one of the grasshopper telegraph devices, hidden inside a hollow Bible, as well as the identifying papers. A false panel concealed his Webley and holster, along with a few other handy tactical items. He chose the electrical umbrella. He gave Ambergris a crook-handled cane of ivory and ebony to indicate her frail yet wealthy status. Before the porters arrived, he showed her how to activate the stick's special features.

A spacious landau carried them to the station. Wearing his armored bowler, Paragon pushed the feeble Mrs. Llewellyn onto the narrow platform. Above them, on iron pillars, rose the monorail. Steep stairs, with a steam lift beside them for baggage and invalids, led up to the gleaming new train. Unlike the locomotive on the lower track, no steam or smoke poured from the oblong green-and-gold cars. Nor did any appreciable noise assault the ear. Incredibly, it had no visible wheels, either.

"We are traveling to the factory on that?" asked Paragon in character. "Perhaps we should wait until they finish building it."

He pushed her into the lift along with two others. One was a balding mutton-chopped old gentleman of great height who looked every inch the man of business, while the other was a slight young fellow in a sack coat altogether too light of weight for the frosty morning. In a few seconds they rose to the top on a silent column of air.

A trio of black-clad security men already stood at the top. Their uniforms resembled those of prison overseers, but with black berets. No firearms to be seen, but they did carry truncheons on their belts. From their manner, he gathered that they would not be shy in using them. All of them spoke with the soft drawls of southern America, all looked tough and capable. Of the four passengers, only Paragon could be taken as a credible threat. But the security chaps eyed the lot of them as if fearing a violent uprising.

*This is hardly the welcome a legitimate concern should offer to clients seeking its expensive services.*

One of the guards approached him with a tight smile and a nod. Paragon returned it. Too late he sensed another man coming upon him from the rear. That one lightly bumped into him.

"Beg your pardon, sir," said the offending guard. "Clumsy of me."

Lady Kalmaar asked in a near-whisper, "What was that all about?"

"Checking me for a weapon. His hands patted me so intimately that I almost had to marry him."

"Inform him that you are spoken for."

"That was a professionally managed. Excellent teamwork, nothing to cause alarm. We need to be careful with this lot."

The passengers took seats in the front car. Little expense had been spared in the appointments of their carriages. Tooled Moroccan leather seats, curtained windows, heated floors...all was calculated to make a positive impression upon the customer.

Ambergris examined the other passengers. "Quite a few customers for a factory which is not even in operation yet, and on a Sunday."

"If they are customers. The large old gentleman with the whiskers seems likely enough. Looks to have the resources to afford clockwork vanity services. The coatless lad in the corner, however, is problematical."

"Clearly too impecunious to be a client."

"Seeking employment, perhaps?"

"A good deal more likely, though what skills he would bring that the owners have not been able to hire with their millions is beyond my ken."

The landscape outside their window began to slide backward. From their vantage point thirty feet above the ground they watched the gray slate roof of Goathland Station float away, followed by the tank house and treetops of the town. *No jerkiness, no noise, no odor. Like being on a boat in an impossibly calm sea. I could grow accustomed to this.*

They played their little scene for the waddling conductor. Unlike the security detail, he showed avuncular concern for Mrs. Llewellyn's comfort and health.

"We thought we might be the only people on the train," Ambergris told him.

"And any other week you would have thought rightly. But there has been a steady stream of folks in the last few days. Some special meeting, apparently."

"Is that so?"

"Not many people from hereabouts, either. Londoners, Frenchies, Russians, even some Asiatics, believe it or not. A few Americans, of course." He waddled off to visit the other passengers.

"From what I know of Moreau's activities, this could be a gathering of his lieutenants."

"In that case the meeting will most likely be on his airship."

Ambergris put a hand to her temple. "My resources may be exhausted by tonight, I fear."

"Then we shall have to be sure to finish our business quickly and make good our escape."

"How? We cannot reasonably expect to board this train with a captive Moreau and calmly sojourn back to Goathland."

"Clearly not. We must evaluate the circumstances as we find them at the factory, particularly in light of this mass arrival of suspicious personages."

"In other words, you hope to pull a rabbit out of a manifestly-empty top hat?"

"You know me well, good wife."

In only a few minutes the spires of the Tredegar facility came into view. Just as Quarrel had said, its front had been built in lavish imitation of a gleaming white Gothic cathedral. Ten stories or more its twin towers soared. Every square foot was covered with elaborate scrollwork, statuary and, ominously, gargoyles. Though half-scale to its historical pattern, no excess of detail had been spared.

"Only Americans would erect something that pretentious," Ambergris snickered. "And as you know, I am something of a connoisseur of erections."

"Welcome to A Man for All Seasons!" bellowed the conductor.

Paragon pushed Lady Kalmaar to the open door. Out on the platform he saw that the rear car had been opened to let out five more security men. A quick glance revealed a wall rack full of rifles, pistols, and shotguns. But a guard hastily closed the door, while another firmly escorted Mr. Llewellyn and wife inside the building. At no time was anyone given an opportunity to sneak away from the group. Paragon did, however, notice the sharpshooter in each belfry.

*Detracts somewhat from the ecclesiastical effect. They have every inch of ground covered for several hundred yards.*

"What are you looking at up there?" asked Ambergris. "Quasimodo?"

"Not quite. This is not the sort of church in which I would seek sanctuary."

Once inside they were not blessed with a glorious nave. Instead, they stood in a perfectly ordinary waiting room. Expensive, but uncomfortable, furnishings abounded. The carpet spoke of a lost battle between taste and cost. Images of gleaming clockwork men making one's life ever so much easier covered the beige Lincrusta walls. Behind a counter to their front stood a pleasant morning-coated young man with a dark receding hairline and pince-nez upon his long nose.

"Good morning!" he sang out. "I am Pelham Grenville, senior clerk of this firm and your guide through the process of augmenting your Man for All Seasons." He consulted a large leather notebook. "Mr. Oliver Savage? Are you with us?"

The tall old fellow with the impressive whiskers raised his hand. "I most certainly am, my man." His voice was refined, elegant, and held undertones of the west of the country.

"Excellent! Please be seated, sir. Mr. Richard Llewellyn of Cardiff?"

Paragon tipped his hat. "That would be me."

"Splendid! I see that you have your lovely wife Margaret with you."

"That I do. She is somewhat under the weather, but do not despair, she is eager to do business with you."

"I am glad to hear it. It says here that you represent Imperial Export."

"I am the founder and sole owner."

"Ah! Now then…Mr. Walter Rossum?"

That brought a tiny nod from the poor young fellow. "Here I am, sir."

"You may look me in the eye. I am no lord."

"Of course." But he did no such thing.

"You are a late addition to my manifest. Much pertinent detail is lacking. Occupation?"

"Crystal eyeman."

Grenville narrowed his gaze and gave Rossum a thorough appraisal. "You, an eyeman?"

The object of his unspoken scorn seemed to shrink and squirm. "I am. Times have been hard, sir, I will not deny it."

"You are not here as a client, then?"

"No, sir. I seek a position."

"You have a character, I presume?"

"That I do." Young Rossum produced a worn envelope from his inner pocket.

With a dubious air the clerk accepted it as if it might contain worms. Seconds later his supercilious attitude vanished. He looked at Rossum with the air of a true believer meeting Saint Peter in the flesh. "This is from Sir Miles Lambert."

"It is, yes. He was very kind to me."

"Am I to understand that you were eyeman to the Minister of Clockwork himself?"

"For a time, yes. Specifically, for his children's automatons."

The atmosphere in the room brightened. Rossum's estimation rose in the eyes of all.

Grenville sighed in that snippy officious way that in bred into all clerks. "Yes, well… any offer of a position will be up to our manager, of course. I will inform him of your arrival." A guard appeared at his gesture. "Mr. Rossum is in need of tea, biscuits, and a wash-up."

The escort nodded and led Rossum through a door to the right. Grenville forced a smile. "If you will excuse me, I should ensure that he is properly attended to."

No sooner had he followed the unhappy couple through the door than a perfectly turned-out automaton entered, resplendent in green velvet tailcoat, with a tray of food. Lady Kalmaar's hands clenched hard, digging into Paragon's arm. She gasped.

It was Reginald.

Not literally, of course, but his twin, at least. The same cool eye, strong brow, and mirror-polished brass complexion. *Why do they need a battle clocker to serve dainties?*

"Relax. Just the same model, is all," Paragon told Ambergris.

"You should talk," she whispered. "Your hand was halfway to your pistol."

Paragon accepted a double helping of the delectables on the tray, giving some to Lady Kalmaar for appearance's sake. "We will soon be taken to Grenville's office. Hopefully, he will not have guards there. Once we are spinning our story of loss and woe, it should be simple enough to subdue him, lead pursuers astray, and find Moreau…and Millie."

*If she is still alive, that is, and not having her Huxley Cells harvested.*

Grenville returned and Paragon went back to fussing over his poor sickly Maggie. In the other corner Oliver Savage snapped shut his book of poetry and began to stand. With an apologetic gesture the clerk indicated that the frail Mrs. Llewellyn's condition required her to have pride of place.

"Hmph!" the older man snuffed, grudgingly waving acquiescence.

Paragon pushed the wheeled chair across the hideous carpet. Grenville led the way, taking them down a dark corridor to another door, an armored one like a bank vault's. He opened it with a long key which he went to much trouble to hide from them. But Paragon saw just enough of it to feel a shock of recognition.

It was a twin of the weird corkscrew key which opened the equally bizarre glass room in Islington.

The next chamber proved to be a perfectly orthodox room: a large oak desk, two overstuffed chairs for customers, ferns in large vases. A tall, narrow window of stained glass let in muted light. And directly behind the desk…a door. Not another steel one, but a plain wooden office door.

Through it came a sleek-haired man of middle age in a black frock coat and wing collar. He looked so perfect for his assigned role that Paragon immediately suspected that he was a mere actor.

"Mr. Llewellyn, I am simply delighted to make your acquaintance!" he gushed. Paxton Barbellion, at your service. And this is your lovely wife?"

His speech bore every indication of a fine public school education. *And too perfect by half. This one will bear careful watching. He is not what he seems.*

Barbellion oozed behind the desk, accepting papers from Grenville. Lochmoor had transmitted the falsified documents from a convenient Cardiff address via the new scanning phototelegraph device. That the Tredegars possessed such a rare and expensive bit of mechanistics spoke volumes about their commitment to the Industrial Age.

"I see that you have lost two infants and are unable to conceive more. Such a tragedy. And you wish to examine the possibility of our augmenting a mechano-boy. That is a significant step to take, sir. Pardon me, but I must ask. Have you already considered adoption? The orphanages are full to bursting with fine lads eager for a loving home."

"We have," answered Paragon, patting Ambergris's hand and letting his lip tremble. "In point of fact, we came very near to adopting a handsome fellow named Barrie, from a well-recommended establishment in Great Ormond Street. But Maggie…"

Ambergris leaned forward. "The truth is that I cannot bear to lose another child. I believe it would put me in a madhouse. Typhoid or cholera could claim him. He could be struck down in the street by a runaway tram, or fall into the river, or…" She sobbed and fell back into the chair. Paragon embraced her in a calculated display of mournful comfort.

Barbellion nodded. "My apologies, but it was my duty to ask. Since it is time-consuming and expensive to augment a mechano-boy, we prefer to trade only with committed parents."

Paragon sniffed and wiped a tear. He took Ambergris's hand. "I wish to see her smile again, to warm our home with it. I would give my last penny to make that happen."

"Um…yes. About that…"

With a bluff wave of his free hand, Paragon became a wealthy man. He handed Barbellion his papers. "Imperial Export is the second-largest shipper of coal in Britain. Our chemical and manufacturing concerns are of similar value. If it will make my Maggie happy again, I shall sing as I write the check."

Since Imperial Export was owned by the Home Office and existed solely as a source of funds and cover for operations such as this, Paragon knew that money was literally no object.

"You are able to demonstrate your wares? Though I am here to spend, I am still desirous of seeing what it is that I am buying."

"Of course. We have just one boy at the moment, a spry chap named Winston, to serve as an example of our craftsmanship. You are aware, of course, that we do not manufacture the basic clockwork figure. That is absolutely the purview of the Ministry. But your fee covers our acquisition of the little fellow from Norfolk, as well as any needed personal touches."

"We understand perfectly. And we are eager to meet the little chap."

£ signs lit up in Barbellion's eyes. "Pelham, if you would be so good as to fetch him?"

Grenville exited through the rear door, which was secured with an ordinary key.

"He is a charming boy," said Barbellion. "Excellent manners. We are proud of him." Their host produced a cigar. "Feel free to smoke."

Paragon pulled his straight-stemmed briar from his pocket. "A bowl of Izmir will be welcome."

Soon Grenville returned with an automaton not quite four feet tall, wearing a sailor suit top, knee breeches, and ribboned boater. His crystal eyes were a dark caramel color with flashes of light behind them which made his expression warm and friendly. Winston's skin was natural brass, hand-rubbed to a high sheen. Thin eyebrows had been etched on the boy's chubby and cherubic face, and the mouth was set in a cheerful smile.

"Good morning, Winston," said Barbellion.

"It is a good morning, sir," the lad replied. "The weather is crisp and I saw sheep in the meadow." He had an educated accent. The voice had the usual metallic buzz to it, but in this one it was barely detectable.

"I would like you to meet Mr. and Mrs. Llewellyn. They have journeyed all the way from Cardiff to see you."

"That is a great distance." The little fellow bowed to Paragon and Ambergris. "I am pleased to make your acquaintance. My name is Winston and am ten years of age."

Paragon could not help smiling. "Greetings, Winston. I am Richard and this is my wife Maggie."

Winston's head cocked to one side. A whirring could be heard inside of it. Finally, he said, in a low embarrassed voice, "Do your legs not work, madame?"

Ambergris smiled even more broadly than Paragon. "They work, after a fashion. I have just been unwell of late."

"I am sorry to hear it. I do hope that your vigor returns." When Grenville took him back out, Paragon slapped his knee.

"Astounding! By gad, Barbellion, you have made a believer out of me. The lad is a delight, just a delight! Is he not, my dear?"

"Truly," Ambergris agreed. "That is the first time I have smiled in months."

The contract was signed, and the breath-taking check written. After consulting the transmitted information to assure himself that his customer did have the funds he claimed, Grenville took it over to a framed painting of Windsor Castle. It swung open to reveal a wall safe. While he fiddled with the combination lock one of the guards entered through the factory door. The manager rose.

Paragon put his hand to his cravat. Lady Kalmaar immediately gasped and fell out of her chair.

"I say!" The manager half-caught her but went down beneath Ambergris. The guard came toward them to assist. When the guard reached them, he slapped at his hand as if a mosquito had landed. Five seconds later he lay asleep on the carpet. Grenville rushed to the distressed group, but he, too, felt the sting of Paragon's stickpin. Barbellion made for the door, but Paragon felled him with the guard's truncheon.

"Might you move this great sack of potatoes off of me, kind husband?" Lady Kalmaar requested.

Paragon pulled the inert man around to the other side of the desk. "Block the iron door with his chair. Jam it under the latch. That may buy us some extra time."

He took Grenville's keys and all the bank notes from the safe. From it he also snatched up some documents, including a packet from the Tredegars themselves and another written in strange symbols. After pocketing them, he kicked out the window and scattered some of the money on the grass.

"If they think we are simple robbers and escaped outside, they may be less inclined to search the factory for us."

Paragon opened the hidden panel in his bag to take out the Webley and his holster. With his electrically charged umbrella at the ready, he approached the factory door. Ambergris was a step behind with her stick.

Just as the ground plan had indicated, they crept into a hall running thirty feet to another door. They rushed to it, where he used a tiny telescoping mirror to peep beneath the new door. It was a windowless sitting room for the staff. And empty. Luck remained with them.

Paragon burst in. On the right-hand wall a notice reminded the staff that Barbellion was seeing clients until eleven in the morning. At noon he would be attending an important managerial meeting 'in the airship' until 3. No one should interrupt that gathering for any reason short of a conflagration.

Paragon blew down a speaking tube to activate the whistle at the other end. A rough voice answered. "Guard Room."

In a passable imitation of Barbellion's voice, Paragon yelled, "Some job of guarding you are doing. I just saw two strangers break out of a window and run off north, trailing £50 notes!"

"Mr. Barbellion, sir? Are you certain?"

"Young man, I may be twice your age, but these old eyes can still spot someone nicking my money! Get after them!"

They raced to the Guard Room entrance. But their good fortune evaporated. With five paces to go, a man exited through the steel door and headed straight for them.

Lady Kalmaar's walking stick coughed. A thimble-sized packet shot out and burst against the young fellow's chin just as he took a breath to call out. The thin paper burst, sending a small cloud of quicklime into his lungs and eyes. He gagged and clutched at his throat with one hand while the other desperately wiped his burned eyes. Paragon ended his agony by choking him to sleep.

All the other security men had obeyed Barbellion's supposed call to action. The place looked much like any barracks room, full of worn furniture, old magazines, a billiard table, and a rack of weapons and ammunition. *Can't leave these beauties here to be used against us.*

Paragon locked the armored door with the corkscrew key. He pulled down the sock on his aluminum leg and opened a panel. Out of it he took a small glass eyedropper. A single careful squeeze went into the breech of every gun.

"Melts and bonds the metal," he explained. "If they attempt to fire those weapons, they shall fill their infirmary with their own wounded."

He moved to the next door. "From now on we shall have Moreau's rather more formidable men to watch out for, as well." He checked his umbrella connections. "I advise you to keep that stick ready. But the less fighting we do the safer we shall be."

"What is the next room?"

"Workshops and parts storage on the right, against the north wall. Dead ahead will be the factory floor, empty except for the airship."

The first workshop was filled with brass and ceramic faces. So many not-quite-human visages arrayed on the wall made for a disturbing sight.

"Like a sort of mass grave," Ambergris whispered. "Chilling."

"I spent a very long night in one of those, hiding from a pack of pariah dogs. This is a holiday in Brighton by comparison."

The next shop, even more eerie than the first, contained jars of crystalline eyes; the next held hands, fingers, and toes. As they continued along the line, a great mass loomed on their left. Like some leviathan which swam in ether instead of water, Moreau's trans-oceanic airship, thrice the length of the *Coxwell*, inspired dread. Ambergris shuddered at the sight of it.

"I bow to your experience as to getting aboard undetected," he told her as they hid in a shop for voice emitters. "How did you manage it?"

"I merely picked up an empty box and pretended to be a worker loading the ship's stores. That will not be possible here."

Paragon agreed. From their hiding spot they could see that a disciplined cordon of guards patrolled the factory floor. He counted at least eight, all of them carrying weapons which resembled the rubber slug guns used on Farnborough's vessel.

"We might try to enter with those attending the meeting."

Ambergris shook her head. "Moreau is very careful about that sort of thing where his business is concerned. No one gets in without identification or personal recognition."

"Where is the cargo door?"

"Behind the gondola, about thirty feet. It will be soundly locked."

"Well, it's either go in and get him, or lure him out here away from his protectors. Either is daunting." *Well, Paragon, time to start rummaging in that manly arse, eh?*

"I can offer an alternative, however. I doubt that you will like it very much."

~

As it turned out, Lady Kalmaar was prescient on that point.

Fifteen minutes later Paragon lay just beneath the great building's makeshift roof. Enormous sheets of white canvas popped and strained in the breeze. An elaborate support system of beams and lines ran along the factory perimeter to permit opening of the cover, which he had climbed to reach his terrifying perch.

Being over a hundred feet above the stone floor was not what had upset him about Ambergris's plan. He had performed more hazardous stunts. Riding a clockwork shark halfway across the Bay of Bengal to elude a pair of 'thopters. Posing as a human cannonball in a circus. And as for the pugilistics atop the runaway locomotive, in freezing rain, at night...

No, what distressed him about Lady Kalmaar's sudden scheme was that it called for her to stroll straight up the gondola's ramp and embrace Moreau as her father again, feigning a contrite mien. And he was not permitted a veto.

*Why did I bother disguising her, then? Foolish woman! Was this always her aim? She had better not stab him on sight.*

She had accomplished her part with ease, gliding up as her natural self to the first guard she saw, insisting that she be taken to see her father. She declared her loyalty and intimated that she had precious intelligence about his enemies.

Now she was somewhere on that great ship, waiting for Paragon to sneak aboard and locate her. But unlike the factory, where he had the benefit of Quarrel's ground plan, he had only the barest idea of the layout of Moreau's airship.

Some forty feet directly below him lay his objective, just forward of the great vertical tail. Impossibly tiny.

The airship's gas vent.

Several people approached the gondola ramp, led by an irate Barbellion. They appeared to be some of the expected guests. Tredegar guards now moved with quiet efficiency among the workshops, looking for Barbellion's attackers.

Paragon's brows shot up when he saw the last guest. Though he had cleaned himself up, there was no mistaking Walter Rossum. To add to his astonishment, Paragon also recognized the stuffy Oliver Savage. The First Officer ushered them into the gondola. Paragon set his jaw and plunged from the canvas roof to achieve the same.

If he had not brought the umbrella it might have been his final act on earth. Landing with more than expected force, he bounced against the tail fin and began sliding to his certain demise. At the last possible instant, he snared the lip of the open vent with the brolly's crook handle. With speed and strength born of desperation he hauled himself back up until he lay panting beside the vent. He noticed the ship's name on the tail: *Prosper*. After laughing at that as Caliban might, he contemplated the essential tragedy facing him.

*I lost my hat.*

He grasped the metal edge of the vent with both hands and went in, surveying his landing area before letting go. Though larger, it very much resembled the same place on the *Coxwell*. Thankfully, it was ever so much warmer...and lacking homicidal monsters.

Paragon cracked open the first hatch he came to and risked a look. All clear. This was not his first time on a Giffard. Two primary decks there would be, plus the gondola. The latter he could ignore. Moreau would not have his gathering of criminals and freaks in front of the crew. The officers mess was most likely.

He kept a slow pace to avoid unpleasant surprises. Only twice did he have to seek cover to avoid airmen. Most were either at duty stations or sleeping until their watch.

Sneaking down the crowded circular stair proved more difficult, but he managed it by boldly feigning a bad sense of direction and asking where his friend Mr. Barbellion might be. A young fellow with pointed ears and a low brow growled how to get to the wardroom. Two sentries with stubby spring-guns stood on either side of the door, acting as ushers. They gave those queuing up to enter a careful examination, then waved them inside as each showed the passport of entry.

A sprig of the same red weed Lady Kalmaar wore.

Retreating into the shadows beneath the stairs, he considered possibilities. It was not absolutely essential that he ensconce himself in the wall and eavesdrop. After all, Lady Kalmaar was inside. But Paragon still did not fully trust her to tell him all. Plus, Moreau might simply throw her in the brig and return her to his island. Many lives might depend upon the information about to be discussed.

A crewman opened a maintenance hatch in the bulkhead behind him and disappeared inside. It ran just behind the wardroom wall. Resolving to burn hecatombs to the Goddess of Fortune, Paragon followed. He found himself in a narrow service area. Ahead, the stranger slunk along a catwalk.

The man took a knife from his uniform jacket, thrusting the tip of the blade into a wall joint where two panels met. A section some three feet wide and six feet tall came loose, revealing the wardroom wall behind. Paragon swooped down upon him while both hands were full.

His intended victim proved to be no fool. The wall section flew at Paragon, stopping him dead and giving the other man time to leap back, knife raised.

"Stay back or I'll do you!" he snarled. Paragon saw that he had a pointed snout and whiskers.

"I rather doubt that. You want to listen in on that meeting as much as I do. A battle on these rattling plates will call down the guards."

The shrewish face frowned. His knife dropped an inch.

"A word of advice, my friend. Gardenia scent is difficult to scrub off completely."

"Eh?"

"Excellent make-up, by the way. I commend you, Phoenix."

The beast-man's entire demeanor changed. He grew taller, less hunched over. With an exasperated sigh he whispered, "Bloody hell! What are you doing here? I might have cut you up."

"And would that not be an embarrassing report? 'After I brutally dispatched my own operative ---'"

"They would all stand me drinks for ridding us of your insufferable 'humor.' You knew it was me all along?"

"Not until I bumped my nose against this panel and smelled you."

Phoenix sniffed and shook his head. "Christ, you have the nose of a bloodhound, then." He pointed toward the entrance. "Do us a favor and bolt that hatch. Don't want to host a bloody convention."

Paragon did that while Phoenix sliced a tiny hole. Immediately voices could be heard. Both men bent an ear to listen. Barbellion's topped the others.

"They attacked me in my own office! And now you tell me that there is no sign of them? More armed guards than the Bank of bloody England, all to no avail!"

"Calm yourself, sir," said another man, speaking in cool pedantic tones with a metallic whir. "They cannot escape the grounds. We have stopped the train and our searchers are on the hunt."

"I trust you set the dogs on them."

"Oh, I assure you we have done better than that. My hunters are hardly man's best friend."

Others in the room laughed in a mordant fashion that chilled Paragon's blood.

"We'll not tear them to shreds too soon. We must interrogate them first. Someone had a great deal of intelligence and support to accomplish this. If they can steal cash from us, they can do much worse. That is why we are taking to the air."

"Unless they are already aboard."

"A most remote likelihood. But if they have managed it, then they shall be unable to escape."

"One of us needs to get off and warn the *Coxwell*," whispered Dardanelles.

"That should be you," Paragon told him. "Coordination of effort is your bailiwick. Lunatic manly action is mine."

"True enough. You will be sure to bring your partner back in one piece?"

"If I can. After all, she chose to stroll into this pit of vipers."

"Well, she is your concern now, old boy."

Phoenix shuffled off to the hatch, snorting in character. Paragon secured it after him, then returned to his spy hole. Moreau was speaking. Little could be seen due to a bushy fern blocking the view. From his shoe heel Paragon produced a collapsing periscope with which he could scan the entire space below. With his Victorinox knife he drilled a hole and poked it through.

A long table with many chairs took up most of the room. The only door was at the other end from Paragon. Along the far wall sat a sofa, sideboard, and bookcases. It held Oliver Savage and a fidgeting Oriental woman of indeterminate age. Dressed in chic Western clothes, she behaved as if the man beside her carried a dread disease. At the head of the table sat a sulking Barbellion, with Grenville at his elbow, both looking unwell. On the other side of him was a dapper little turbaned fellow in rich Indian garments. In the rest of the chairs were a generously proportioned matron, a somewhat younger mulatto woman, two prim fellows who appeared to be a matched set of Swiss bankers, and a perky gent in checked sack coat and oiled hair. Little Winston pushed a tea cart crowded with cakes, biscuits, jams, and the like. He teetered about the room, taking orders and dispensing tea in Chinese cups.

Four others stood. One of them was Walter Rossum, pacing with the agitation of a mouse that has blundered into a snake's den. Near the door a dark-mustached fellow proudly wore the uniform of a Confederate captain of cavalry, ivory-gripped saber at his hip. Two guards remained near the door.

Moreau peered at a notebook. By his manner of standing, Paragon judged him to be in great pain. His breath mask covered his face in midnight-blue leather with silver fittings. Its single mirrored oval lens wrapped around to the temples. Near the pointed chin its voice emitter resembled a shining metal honeycomb with wisps of steam dribbling from it. He wore formal attire, down to fine kid gloves. No bit of skin showed. A heavy, yet expensively made, staff some five feet tall leaned against the wall behind him.

Moreau snapped his notebook shut. "Let us return to business. I have been reviewing the latest figures. Our overall operations are still profitable, but some of your individual franchises have been under-performing, particularly on this wretched island." He stopped, his mirrored face aimed at Rossum. "Forgive me, but you are not one of my regional managers."

"Rossum, his name is. Our new eyeman," said Barbellion. "He has worked for the

Minister's own family and could tell us much."

"A splendid acquisition, but why have you brought him here?"

Barbellion stood and gestured for Rossum to join him. He put a friendly arm around the small man's shoulders. "He is so special that I thought you should meet him personally." With no warning, he smashed Rossum face-first onto the table. Ladies screamed and shoved themselves away. Holding the little fellow down with one hand, he peeled the false moustache and rubber chin away. "Dr. Moreau, may I present to you...a spy."

Paragon gasped, at once surprised and chagrined.

It was Vesta Tilley.

## 16 / "DO NOT INFEST YOUR MIND WITH BEATING ON THE STRANGENESS OF THIS BUSINESS"

While the surprise still held, Vesta reached up, grasping and twisting Barbellion's hand in a jiu-jitsu lock as she threw herself up. She used him as a shield as she backed to the door, then she shoved him at Grenville and Moreau. A guard bear-hugged her from behind, but she wrenched his bollocks and head-butted him away. When the other raised his stun-gun, she snatched up Moreau's staff and bashed the weapon out of his hands. The stick's end came off with the impact and several documents burst out. Vesta jabbed and cut at the security men, but more guards came in and swarmed her to the floor. Even then she struggled, twisting atop the papers, and howling insults.

Moreau shook his head as he examined her. "A woman! I confess that I had no idea."

"I admit to having been fooled myself," Barbellion said. "But one of your hound-men sniffed her."

"He has earned live meat as a reward. The Law should be relaxed in such a case."

The Confederate knelt beside her, almost nose-to-nose. "Perhaps your work would be better served if she were in the laboratory."

Moreau chuckled, his voice emitter turning it into a dreadful gurgle, as she was hauled to her feet. "You are right. Another delivery has arrived amidst the meteor shower. There are new tests to conduct. My dear, you are about to serve the cause of scientific advance. Few of your sex can say as much."

Vesta tied to lunge at him, teeth bared. "Come see what one of my sex can say to your throat!"

"Oho! Spirit...fire! That is just what our masters wish for this new device. We shall see if it can pry the name of her employer from her mind. Search the ship down to its last rivet. She may have accomplices. Gather up those documents and put them back into the staff. They are worth more than the lives of any of us. Please take your seats, all. We may now safely resume our proper business."

Paragon felt torn. *Vesta wants rescuing. But I am in desperate need of the intelligence Moreau is about to give. Who are his masters? And what advanced mechanics are they providing to him?*

Moreau spoke again. "Captain Carter, do you have an explanation for your nation's depressed production?"

"War and rebellion, sir!" cried Carter. "Is that not enough reason to see costs rise? We are freshly independent. It will require time to ---"

Moreau's palm came up. "I am aware of your political situation . Must I remind you that unrest, misery, and despair are precisely how we are funding our grand enterprise?"

"But we are protecting a thousand-mile border from Yankee aggression. They do outnumber us."

"But thanks to the aid of our special friends you have superiority in weaponry."

"Which you did not provide gratis, as I recall."

"Would you rather that there was no Confederate States of America?"

"I merely am pointing out why our financial contributions are not all that you might wish."

That chilling laugh returned. "Your government should consider the result if the United States receiving plans for an armored earth-borer, or even a full-sized fighting tripod?"

*What the devil is he talking about? And what do meteors have to do with any of it?*

Carter froze like a patrician gamecock. "We do not respond well to threats, Moreau."

"Nonsense. Everyone responds to threats, even me. That is how the entire planet is run. And not only this planet. Do you think I made that statement without prompting from…above?"

The room fell silent as all its inhabitants absorbed Moreau's words. Everyone but Paragon seemed to know precisely what they meant. Captain Carter sagged a bit.

"I shall, of course, convey the need to redouble our efforts. The slaves, African and brass, shall sweat all the harder."

"That is all that I wish." Moreau's mask puffed steam as he turned to the icily handsome Chinese woman seated on Savage's sofa. "Madame Mou Sha, your gains in the opium and extortion trades are most encouraging."

The woman stirred, eyes like a cobra. She spoke in an educated Eastern accent, but with hints of European schooling. To Paragon she was what Queue might be if turned to evil. "My clan are grateful for the poisons supplied by your worthy self. The black smoke has proven quite efficacious in chastising malefactors and enfearing the reluctant."

"I am gratified to hear it. Mister Savage, a pleasure to finally meet you. Your Liverpool and Manchester gangs have been quite active. From your dock operations alone we have managed to fund several new surgical procedures."

Savage set down his book of verse. "You flatter me, sir. My lieutenants manage things on your behalf. I merely…encourage those who shirk their duties."

"Your modesty does you credit, but tales of your methods of encouragement would freeze the blood of my most brutish experiments."

"Even in my part of the world," added the dark woman at the table. "And we are no amateurs in the realm of suffering."

"Ah, the formidable Mistress Uvalo. Is the Cape Town shipwreck business truly as lucrative as my reports indicate?"

"It is, though diamonds and gold are beginning to supplant it. Naturally, we are taking our share of the that, but an even greater income will be made from selling naïve prospectors supplies at inflated prices."

"How are the submarine boats faring?"

"Some of them leak a bit, but they enforce our toll-taking much better than the surface ships ever did."

"Excellent!" Moreau nodded to the prim fellow beside her. "How goes the Jewel in the Crown, Mr. Yatna?"

The Indian answered in a Calcutta accent. "Thanks to our enormous population, we are profiting handsomely by extorting tiny amounts from the citizenry which do not raise suspicion. We anticipate much growth."

Moreau spoke in this vein to all his criminal representatives, announcing that they would speak in more detail at dinner. Then he announced his larger purpose: treachery.

"Those whom we serve are not tolerant of failure. We must not slack in our duty. Else when they arrive to claim their place here, we shall be treated as the rest of the human cattle."

*What is he on about? Invasion? Who might hope to achieve such an aim against the British Empire? Germany? Russia?*

"One of my most trusted subordinates dared to sell my secrets to a mere criminal, once a valued friend, who is creating abominations to do his bidding. Freaks of nature with no knowledge of the Law and of no use in the higher calling of the defeat of death." A great thick mass of steam boiled from his mask. "Gargoyles! Repugnant reptilian follies! The very thought clouds my lens!"

After a few moments, the vapor diminished. "This traitor Grigsby forced me to leave my precious work and rush back here to deal with him. But others have bought his stolen learning. All over the globe these advanced mechanistics keep appearing, despite our slaying leading inventors. A master criminal in London has created enough mischief with it that the government has noticed. Those who have dared to infiltrate this ship and the factory might well have been sent by them, by Lochmoor."

"Or merely thieves," said Savage. "Is it not just as likely that this criminal is responsible?"

"All the more reason to wrench the truth from the brain of our new prisoner. And why we must not permit that safe-cracking couple to escape us."

"This chap who is so high in the London underworld…who is he? Can we not remove him?" asked Yatna.

"He now calls himself Professor James Navita, of London Medical College. I blush to confess that he is a former student of mine. A mathematician and biologist of the first rank. His talents have been turned to the mere acquisition of money and power. But he is greatly interfering with our own operations in England, particularly London, even attacking and killing our people. For this, also, I hastened here. It must be stopped. He calls his enterprise the Riot Army. A childish name."

Madame Mou Sha said, "We have heard of it even in the East. He is no mere pickpocket. You would do well to not underestimate the trouble he can bring."

"I assure you, I do not. Jimmy has manufactured his biological mercenaries with admirable speed and ability, to say nothing of corrupting my own creations. I had to discipline a pair of wayward children mere days ago. If his hirelings had not been so eager to breed tentacled harlots for a quick profit, I might not have learned of his activities. One of the streetwalkers is in the laboratory. I am eager to dissect her and see how he has adapted my secrets."

Paragon smiled. *Millie! And in the very spot where they have taken Vesta.*

"Surely this fellow can be hurt," said Carter.

"The Riot Army has proven its loyalty and resourcefulness. In these past few months, I have lost valued assassins to knife, garrote, bullet, poison, even air guns. There are many layers of protection and deception to penetrate. He has even bred simple-minded twins of himself as decoys. We must draw out Dr. Navita with some enticing bait."

The door opened. "And here is the lure, right on cue. Permit me to introduce my foster daughter, Ambergris."

Lady Kalmaar had changed into a royal blue dress trimmed in gold, low-necked and bustled, with chinchilla fur at collar and hem. She had swept her hair up and secured it with a pearl-trimmed comb. Both alluring and elegant, she had never looked lovelier.

Paragon nearly dropped his periscope. Every male fawned over her. *She must be scenting the room. Moreau's mask will protect him from the effects.*

"She has been studying abroad," Moreau lied. "Heidelberg, Paris, Rome. A remote island hardly provides the proper environment for a modern young woman."

"On the contrary, Papa," she said meekly, "my only dream is to return there and walk amongst those simple, kind people once more."

Ambergris affected an entirely different demeanor than Paragon had ever seen. Much more reserved. *I wonder what colossal falsehood she spun for him. Whatever it was, he seems to have accepted it. Is he that gullible, or just pretending to play her game? I should ask myself the same question. Those guards behind her indicate that he is hedging his bets. So must I.*

"And so you shall. Just as soon as my business is completed here."

"Splendid! Will we spend some time in society before we return?"

"You are prescient. I am making those plans this very moment. Would you like to visit London and mingle with the best sort of people, even the royal family?"

"Certainement!"

Moreau kissed her hand. "You shall charm the gruffest of them. Your quarters are adequate?"

"Very comfortable. Rather less sand and crabs than I am used to."

Everyone laughed politely at that. If Ambergris had ordered them to leap from the portholes right then, they would have fought to be the first to go. She gave them a sweet bow and bid them farewell. When the door had closed behind her, the atmosphere seemed just a bit darker.

Her father sighed steam. "A delightful girl, though still naïve in the ways of the world. But she has a gift that compensates for that. You have noticed a feeling of enrapturement, gentlemen? A desire to serve her? Come, come, do not be embarrassed. If I were not forced to wear this device, I would be enthralled myself."

All the men nodded with varying degrees of sheepishness. "Ambergris was found at the point of death. I was compelled to save her life by surgical and chemical means, manipulating her HCA in a more sophisticated manner than ever before."

Moreau chuckled. "That is what she believes. I fear that the actual truth would be rather more than her psyche could bear."

"You blended her HCA with that of brutes?" asked a shocked Savage.

"Nothing so crude, sir. I do that sort of experiment every day in my search for the secret that will restore my lost loved ones to me. No, she is a much different case. My crowning glory. Believe it or not, I grew the girl in my laboratory…from scratch, as the cooks say."

This time Paragon really did drop the periscope.

# Act Five

~

# All O'erthrown

*Above north Yorkshire*

"*Blimey, it's creepy in here and that's a fact.*"

*None of the other guards dared enter Moreau's flying laboratory. Being the new man, he did not know this, of course, which is why they had insisted that this was the traditional initiation into their brotherhood. 'We all had to do it. Just ten minutes inside and you'll be one o' us, mate. We'll stand yer a round o' drinks afterward.'*

*If he had heard their hoots and wagers after he had entered, he would have known where he stood with them. But all unaware, he now stood with his back against the door, surveying the clutter of cages, glass, and metal in subdued light. The operating table, a ceramic and steel tool worthy of the Spanish Inquisition, took up most of the space. A missed bit of blood crept down one edge. Attached to it were clamps, hoses, and terrifying sharp gadgets that were so odd they made his head hurt. Wooden cabinets, animal cages. Monkey stench soured the air. In at least one cage a person lay sleeping. More disturbing, a floor-to-ceiling glass tank full of pale green fluid held the motionless bodies of a comely woman and a child. His guts lurched at the sight. Finally, to the left, a frosted glass door four feet square.*

*"Ten minutes. Just hold yourself together that long and you'll be home free."*

*His plan had been to remain against the entrance until his friends told him he could bolt. But with two minutes to go, something bumped against the translucent door. He half-jumped out of his skin and saw something dark moving there. Abandoning all thought of his status with the boys, he reached behind, fumbling for the latch. A terrible buzzing filled his head, though, making him approach the glass instead. Every step increased the pressure in his mind. Standing before the door, which had no obvious knob or handle, the guard vibrated as if electrified. It was both pleasant and utterly…wrong…at the same time.*

*Steam hissed from the door. Strange that it would be open. Everything else was locked tight. Through the fog he made out a large round form that resembled an enormous brain. Two great black eyes, unblinking, like a snake's, transfixed him. On either side of the wedge of a mouth horrible tentacles wriggled. The buzzing faded and a soothing sound, not quite language, replaced it. He relaxed as it invaded his entire being.*

*In the bar later that night, his fellow guards drank wordlessly, downing whiskey after whiskey in a vain attempt to wipe the sight of his shriveled corpse from their minds.*

## 17 / "POOR WORM, THOUGH ART INFECTED"

He had the presence of mind to snatch it back before it fell through the hole. Such were the gasps of astonishment and outrage below him that no one noticed. There was no concealing the confused pounding in his brain.

*Ambergris is one of his creations? Not even born of woman? Impossible. Even he does not possess that sort of skill. No human does.*

"Pull the other one," said Savage.

"I am quite serious," Moreau insisted. "She is but five years old. Our otherworldly friends provided me with the tools and techniques, as well as their own HCA."

Captain Carter stared as if he were looking at a freak show exhibit. "You are calmly telling us that your daughter is a…Martian?"

*Martian? What sort of madness is this? Do they know I am observing? Are they toying with me?*

"A hybrid, to be precise," Moreau corrected. "She has HCA of both, as well as of cephalopod, panther, and a few other creatures. Carefully designed and reared to seduce any man on earth."

"And you are disgusted by Navita's gargoyles?" sneered Savage.

"There is no moral equivalency. His creations are mere tools, unloved."

"I fail to see the difference."

"The difference is that I love her as much as any father ever has a child. It is true that I have manipulated her memories, not told her of her birth. Her fragile mind could not accept the facts."

"Yet you plan to use her as bait, to entice Navita here to his destruction."

"And it has worked splendidly. What wouldn't a daughter do for her papa? He is en route this very moment, no doubt to dispatch me as I would him, while believing he is rescuing an ally. She has been inside the Riot Army for months."

Paragon dared no longer stay. This had to reported, fantastic as it was. Particularly the bit about her being a spy inside Navita's gang. *When were you planning to mention that, Amber?* He grasped the hatch lock. Before he could throw open the bolt, someone tugged on the handle. Swearing, he dashed back along the passage. As he ran, he pulled off a cuff button and climbed back to his wall perch. On the other side of the hatch something immense rumbled like a locomotive and hammered at it with a great hoof.

A sharp rap on metal made the button spark. Dense yellow smoke boiled out, stinking like all the sewers of London. Breath mask on, Paragon poked the bubbling button into the wardroom. Panicked shouts of 'Fire!' rang out. It was the worst thing imaginable on a hydrogen dirigible. Paragon watched Moreau and his lieutenants flee. Only Savage remained calm. Handkerchief over nose and mouth, the old chap gazed at the ceiling, laughing.

Bells rang throughout the ship. Paragon felt along the narrowing service passage until he discovered a hatch. He dropped to the deck, stowed the mask, popped in his monocle, and assumed an air of upper-crust confusion. A gullible crewman gave him directions to the laboratory.

It boasted a particularly beefy guard. Paragon leaned heavily on his umbrella and hobbled up to the fellow, grimacing. "Help! A spy...attacked the wardroom! Barely...escaped...with my life."

The guard raised his spring-gun. "Let me confirm your story. Don't move."

Paragon groaned and pretended to faint, causing the tip of the bumbershoot to catch the gun's muzzle. It discharged its solid-rubber slug into the deck plates between them. His shoulder caught the big man in the armpit, knocking the gun loose. The umbrella's crook hooked the guard's neck and spun him hard into the bulkhead. He fell with a groan.

Cocking the spring-gun, Paragon knocked on the door. When it opened, an unwary guard received a fist-sized rubber punch to his belly and collapsed like a broken doll. Paragon charged the weapon again and entered, dragging the man in from the corridor and locking the door. A pair of white-coated technicians stared at him in shock. He made the threat which would carry the most weight.

"Do not alert anyone, or I shall smash all of your equipment and destroy your notes." With expressions of abject horror, they gulped and collapsed onto wooden stools, quaking like dandelions in a gale.

It resembled any university's biology lab, save for the disturbing tank containing the bodies of the wife and child Moreau hoped to revive. An operating table was locked at a nearly vertical position, and the subject strapped to it had countless wires and tubes connecting her to devices that resembled those he had seen in the glass room in Islington.

Vesta was semi-conscious, but her earlier fire still burned. "Ah! Young Montague, here to play the dashing hero. I had hoped that the role would go to me, but it seems that my understudy shall be forced to appear this evening. Gave it the old college try, though." Between her lips was a picklock. God only knew how she'd managed that.

Paragon grinned as he looked for the safest way to remove the apparatus from her flesh. Needles had been plunged into both arms and her neck. Electrodes covered her skull. A gleaming metal orb obscured one eye. He turned to Moreau's technicians. "Get her out of this...safely!"

"Mister Paragon, sir!" a weak voice called out from a cage. "Is that really you?"

He rushed to open it. Millie looked like a starved little dog. She crawled out, too weak to stand. "What have they done to you?"

"Aw, nothin' much. Pokin' and proddin', is all. But they were talkin' about a vivi-somethin' or other. Didn't much like the sound o' that."

He set her on a wheeled table just in time to catch Vesta as she fell from her restraints. "Did they manage to see into your brain?"

"Not yet. They were waiting for Moreau to arrive and supervise the fun."

Paragon stripped the largest technician of his white coat. After locking all four of Moreau's men in cages, he lay each woman on the table, limbs entwined, and daubed their faces with disgusting fluids from specimen jars. A sheet went over them. He donned an emergency breath mask as a disguise and took the evacuation map hanging with it. Then he pushed the table out the door.

The 'thopter hanger and refuse bins were located next to one another in the belly of the ship. After several confusing turns, and a thrilling descent on an unexpected ramp, they arrived at the double doors to the bay full of flying machines.

This time the guard was not a formidable warrior. He was something even worse…a bureaucrat.

"No dumping on the schedule," he declared. "You'll have to take that straight back to wherever you brought it from."

"It won't be on the bloody schedule, mate," Paragon informed him in a gruff Cockney voice. "This is Moreau's lab business."

"I don't care if it's from the kitchen of Queen-Fucking-Victoria, if it ain't on this paper it ain't going down the chute."

"I'll tell you what. You can do as you like with it. Weren't my idea to cart infected dead anyhow." Paragon turned to go.

The guard stepped back as if shoved by an invisible hand. "Infected, you say! With what?"

"Who knows with Moreau? But I don't want to catch it, whatever it might be." Paragon pulled back the sheet to reveal the awful faces of his casualties. Both women held their breaths, eyes open and glassy. Vesta's tongue lolled. Millie's wigglers lay across her neck, stiff.

The guard gulped and jerked his head toward the disposal chute. As Paragon pushed the table, the sentry sprinted up the ramp to imagined safety.

No one else was in sight. Paragon locked the doors and informed the women that they were a miracle had just occurred. They rolled off the table, requiring a firm hold onto it to remain standing. Millie clutched the electro-shock umbrella. He handed his Webley to Tilley.

"If anyone but me comes through those doors, send him to hell. My password is 'namaste.'"

"Where are you going?" Vesta asked. "Aren't we flying out of here?"

"I certainly hope so. But I need to fetch my partner first. And her so-called father, if I can manage it."

With the map's help he worked his way back up toward the main berth deck. Ambergris's room would be there, likely next to Moreau's. Unfortunately, they would probably be guarded. But there was nothing for it. Getting there proved easy enough in the confusion. Disguised as he was, no one accosted him. In three minutes, he had reached a door marked *Guest Suite* and burst through.

A faint whimper came from beyond the bed. Between it and the wall lay a much-changed Lady Kalmaar. The honeyed pigment had drained from her face, leaving it white as a dead fish. Her eyes were clouded like cataracts. Those perfect cheeks were sunken and dark, while her once kissable lips were pulled back from her teeth in a rictus of pain.

"Are you the Angel of Death?" she whispered.

He remembered that he still wore the mask. Peeling it off, he knelt beside her to stroke her brow. Her skin felt like dead leaves.

Tearful astonishment welled in her eyes. "You…came back for me?"

*By Jove, she must have been horribly mistreated on that bloody island.* "How could I not? Till death do us part, remember?"

She made an apologetic face. "My love, I fear that your seed did not preserve me…as long as I had hoped."

"You need blood." He unfastened his collar stud.

She gave him a push as weak as a baby's. "No! I care too much for you…to doom you to that dependency. Let me go."

"Hush and obey your husband."

Paragon lifted her onto the bed. There was no time for any of the niceties. He pushed her skirts and petticoats up to her waist with ungentlemanly haste. The tips of her toothed tentacles peeped from their pockets. Harriet and Vesper tried to slither out, but only made it a hand's-breadth before stopping from exhaustion. It did not require much effort to pull them out far enough to reach his throat. Once they neared it, they gained new vigor and began almost to sniff at his neck.

*Are you certain about this, Monty? This is likely how Martians consume their prey.*

Another glance at the dying Ambergris settled it. No matter the risks, he would not let this rare jewel perish, even if she proved an enemy. The scene reminded him of his own mother, expiring of consumption in her green plaid dress, her Sunday best. Peaceful Manners had been getting blind drunk in a pub, leaving poor timid Michael to comfort his mum in her last hours. "Let me pass, Michael. I need a wee rest, don't you think?" Then she touched the tiny, knotted silver cross around her neck and left him with a sigh.

*By all the gods, it shall not happen a second time.*

As if they had read his thoughts, Harriet and Vesper latched onto his throat. Their scalpel teeth only pained him for a moment. An opiate-like euphoria flooded his system.

Ambergris's color returned with amazing speed as she drew his blood into her. That deadly shadow fled her beautiful face. Soon her eyes grew clear. Sea-scent flooded his nostrils. What had been a death rattle became a satisfied purr.

His concerns about self-control turned out to be justified. Just as the angel of discipline awoke in the back of his brain, the tightening of his trousers announced that the imp of desire had something to say. He weakly reached up to his neck to disengage the dining tentacles, but lost interest halfway there. Lady Kalmaar's legs snapped closed like a wolf-trap. One of her hands fumbled with his fly buttons. The other yanked his face to hers for a moaning kiss.

Ambergris' warning had been no idle threat. No mere mortal could resist her. Every drop of his essence, from neck and loin, would be drained. Whatever biological magic Moreau had worked could not be countered by force of will. Only one other power could save him.

Gravity.

The silken duvet shifted and launched them onto the floor. Their breaths left them with the sudden impact. Ambergris frowned, confused. Paragon seized that opportunity to slide fully ten feet away from her. Each lay back, gasping.

"I see quite a bit of that thing whenever you are about," she eventually said with a smile in her voice and a nod to his groin. "At this rate you may have to declare your intentions."

"My intentions are simple enough," he told her while tucking himself away. "Retaining a goodly measure of the blood in my veins."

Paragon helped her up, keeping a grip on her arm as her knees wobbled. His were little firmer. She kissed him lightly on his cheek. "Again, you are my Lancelot."

"As I recall, that did not end well, my Guinevere."

Moreau's cabin was, indeed, next door, but the door hung open and no one was inside. Paragon would have to get hold of him some other way. By judicious hiding in corners as guards ran past, they arrived at the hangar without incident. He accepted the Webley from Vesta. A look out of the nearest porthole revealed that the factory was just visible on the horizon. With the sun behind them, the great airship threw its long shadow on the moor.

A terrific blow crashed against the doors, as if a rhinoceros craved admittance. He looked about for options. The bay was home to baggage, as well as huge rubbish bins and flying machines. Lochmoor had given him a basic training in aero piloting, but he was no expert. When he arrived at the row of Hargraves, he despaired. Three were single-seat 300's, fragile little dragonflies covered in red canvas. Beside them sat a pair of blue two-seat 500 models, with a longer body to hold the extra cockpit. These boasted a pintle-mounted rifle in the rear. Tucked in a corner was an odd contraption that looked like two water tanks with shark fins, bolted to a seat and oblong storage compartment.

With the entry door about to give way, Paragon hurried past the unknown machine to examine the last aero. Here his spirits lifted as if provided with fresh gas cells.

It was a rich green Zaschka Orion gyroplane, made to hold three but with room for an uncomfortable fourth in the luggage area behind the second cockpit. Unlike the Hargraves, this craft had no wings to speak of, merely struts which supported rotating blades above. These glorified windmill vanes kept the thing aloft. There were two tails, running fork-like away from the body. As a means of locomotion, it used an airscrew, mounted between the tail booms at the rear of the fuselage. A gun poked out of the round nose.

Behind them one of the doors burst its hinges and clattered along the deck plates. Booted feet clumped into the hangar. "Do something, Paragon!" shouted Tilley.

In reply, he picked her up and tossed her into the rear seat. "Hide in the baggage hold!"

"Oh, right! Little Vesta is always the one. Story of my life. If it isn't a bloody closet, then it's a steamer trunk."

*Must be a cracking good story there.* He helped Millie up into the same cockpit, along with Lady Kalmaar. The first guard appeared, spring gun aimed at them.

Paragon aimed at the fellow's thigh. The light drugged bullet hit its mark. Five seconds later he swooned, dropping into the path of the two men behind him. A shot to the arm of one of them produced the same effect. "Poison!" cried the remaining attacker to those behind. All took cover amongst the baggage and the hangar's support beams. Their stubby weapons made chuffing sounds. To add to their difficulties, he sent a choking smoke round amongst them.

Keeping the Zaschka between him and the incoming slugs, he explained how to get the new-fangled coal oil engine working. While the women set to their task, he employed the Webley judiciously to keep the guards away. So fearful were they of it that they dared not rush him.

Soon Ambergris shouted, "Ready!" over the engine noise.

He yanked out the restraining pin on the hangar door. It banged open into a steep ramp position. Air roared in as he peered out. They must have been more than a mile above the earth.

Scrambling up the side of the Orion, he landed in the pilot's seat and donned the goggles there. With his head ducked low, he re-familiarized himself with the controls. Then he released the brakes and rammed the throttle in. The Zaschka crept forward as the airscrew whined. The ramp drew them down with stomach-churning speed into the late afternoon void. Shrieks announced that his fellow travelers had no experience with such a thing. Flying aboard an airship the size of a hotel bore little resemblance to this Icarian insanity.

Overhead the rotor spun as their speed brought it to life. It bit the air and slowed their plunge, holding them aloft like a wing. Paragon pulled back the throttle to stabilize the craft and let the alarmed women catch their breaths. As they put more distance between themselves and the dirigible, he examined the queer automatic gun. It consisted of a pair of horizontal spinning disks rotating inward at incredible speed, powered by the gyro's engine. A hopper fed half-inch round shot into the narrow space between the rotating stones, which propelled the bullets out the barrel when he pulled the firing lever. *With all of Moreau's advanced science, this was the best he could do here? Must have bought the aero with the silly thing already installed.*

Ambergris called out, "Here they come! Three of them!"

He jerked his head around. Sure enough, two 300's and one 500 burst from the Giffard like angry bees from a shaken hive. Their wings flapped furiously as they strove to catch the gyro. They had the advantage in speed and maneuverability. A look below showed no good place to set down. On the open heath the enemy guns would massacre them.

An air-fight it would be then.

"Heads down! Hold on!" he yelled, bringing the Orion hard about to place the sinking sun at his back and in the eyes of his foes. His aero, which could fly so slowly as to almost hover, gave him the more stable firing platform. Their flapping motion made accurate shooting difficult, so they would attempt to close to point-blank range.

The onrushing 300's split, intending to swoop in on him from each side, negating the sun. Paragon let them do it. They must have already looked at it long enough to be seeing spots. He turned into the one on the right, dead at its nose, and yanked the gun's toggle.

It made little noise as the balls spat out the end of the barrel at a rate of two per second. The heavy but low-velocity balls could not travel far, but would still do great damage to fabric and wood, to say nothing of bodies. He gave the oncoming 'thopter an experimental burst, missing high and right. While he adjusted, the other craft sneezed out a puff of white smoke like a little dragon. His shot threw sparks off a rotor strut not two feet from Paragon's face.

Before the opposing pilot could fire again, Paragon let fly. Expecting it, the 300 turned away. Only one ball hit, knocking a hole in a wing. The gyro pursued, knowing that the fellow's partner must be closing. Sure enough, glass exploded from the windscreen behind him. Millie cursed, Ambergris yelped, and a muffled Vesta complained that she could not see the action. A second later the 'thopter swooshed past him, funnel spewing black smoke. *These bastards are no tyros. More's the pity.*

To add to his troubles, the third machine, a two-seater with a gunner in the rear, arrived from overhead. Only a quick jerk on the control stick avoided the heavy bullet. Another round nearly took off Lady Kalmaar's nose. Its rifle could reload too quickly for Paragon's liking. Best deal with it now.

"Pistol!" he bellowed, holding a palm up behind him.

Ambergris slapped it into his hand. "Empty!"

He dropped it into his lap while giving the Orion full throttle, climbing after the 500. With desperate fumbling he loaded a clip of the purple-nosed cartridges. They drew close to the heavy 'thopter. Both were evenly matched in speed and turning. Paragon sprayed the enemy fuselage with auto-bullets. Some penetrated and struck the gunner in the legs, for he winced and reached down. Abandoning the automatic weapon, Paragon flew alongside the ship. Before the pilot even recognized his danger, the Webley barked once. Nobel's explosive charge did its work, blowing apart the joint of wing root and piston. Spinning like an oak seed pod, the ship crashed into the heath.

Its astonishing destruction made the remaining craft cautious. Paragon shoved the stick away from him, dropping into a dive that prompted more alarmed noises from the rear. Perhaps two miles away, the factory offered sanctuary. The pair of tiny flappers followed. To their rear, the great airship approached, as fast as any of the aeros. All would arrive at the makeshift hangar together.

Despite the impetus of his dive, the 300's closed. One was now only a hundred yards behind. A bloody streak against the silvery mass of the Giffard, it had built up too much speed.

*Excellent. My apologies in advance, old chap.*

Paragon yanked the throttle out and hauled back on his stick. The Orion seemed to stop in mid-air. The Hargrave blew past without even getting off a shot.

Not so Paragon. He sprayed the aero just as it crossed his nose. Heavy lead balls pummeled it, pulverizing its wings, tail, and, alas for him, the pilot's skull, which burst into a crimson vapor. The 300 crashed beside the monorail line, fuel tank ablaze.

Feminine cheers erupted behind him. Paragon smiled and looked for the final pursuit ship. But he had had enough and fled. With a relieved sigh, Paragon swooped low over the heather, avoiding the factory sharpshooters. Workers and customers clustered out front to gawk at the smoking wreckage.

The canvass roof covering had not been replaced, anticipating the quick return of Moreau. To inconvenience him, Paragon landed in the center of the factory floor. Then he leaped from the cockpit and crouched beneath the left winglet.

"Out, ladies!" he called to his passengers. "We are hardly safe yet."

Lady Kalmaar disembarked first, assisting Millie and then Vesta, who walked under her own power now. All hurried into the warren of workshops. Along the way, Paragon happily stumbled across his bowler. Moreau's ship came in like a falling mountain. The ground crew scampered out to haul it in. Two of them rushed to move the Orion. It exploded in their faces, courtesy of one of Paragon's specialty bullets. Black smoke filled the air with choking fumes.

"That will delay the removal of the thing," Paragon said with more bravado than he felt.

Ambergris said, "Moreau plans to depart tonight. He believes the Riot Army leader will come soon and that he will be dealt with. Then they will fly out of Imperial airspace."

Vesta frowned. "Then what are we to do? He will send men to hunt us down. You took two things he values and humiliated him before his underlings. Endeavor to escape back to town? Sell our lives dearly for queen and country?"

Paragon said, "Our mission has not changed. Moreau must be captured. It is imperative that we destroy his operation and discover how much truth is in his fantastic claims of Martian involvement."

He led them to the shop where he had left his valise. From the hollow Bible he removed the grasshopper telegraph and stuck it in a coat pocket. The other items he passed out to the women: pen, watch, pewter matchbox. This last went to Vesta, of course, which made her giggle at the joke.

"In case we are captured, they will possibly be left on your person as harmless. That would be to our advantage. None of them are as they seem."

Quickly he explained what surprise each object held. When he finished, Ambergris asked him what his plan for capturing Moreau might be.

"Because the hill is too high to climb," she said. "Even if he comes out of the *Prosper*, he will be surrounded by guards and beast-men, to say nothing of the sharpshooters. And if you did manage to snatch him, the only way out is either on his ship or the monorail, both chock-full of gunmen."

"Farnborough could drop in and pick us up," said Tilley.

"Not without a fight," Paragon said, "and likely heavy casualties. His orders are to engage only as a last resort."

Lady Kalmaar asked, "What about Quarrel? What can his men do?"

"Not a great deal. They are lightly armed."

"So…we're right fucked," pronounced Millie, her mouthed wiggler spitting onto the floor.

"Not necessarily. But we must come up with a way to lure Moreau out of that bloody gasbag."

"And if we cannot?" asked Ambergris.

"Then he will burn in it. We cannot permit him to escape to perpetrate more mischief."

"A capital plan!" exclaimed Vesta. "I vote that we proceed directly to that last bit and flee amidst the chaos."

"Tempting," Paragon admitted. "But if there is any way to entice him out, and not just his men, I am duty-bound to attempt it." His gaze shifted to Lady Kalmaar. "We do have something he wants enough to pursue it himself. That's why she went aboard and put on such a fine show." *If it was a show.* He held up the wireless telegraph. "Have you the other?"

She raised up her skirt to show it strapped to her thigh with a garter. "Of course. Though it does compromise the line of my dress."

"The sacrifices you make for England." He crouched down. "Listen closely. This is what we shall do."

## 18 / "FLOUT 'EM AND SCOUT 'EM"

Fifteen minutes later, Moreau's ship had been secured. Ray-gun on hip, he descended the gondola ramp. Six guards trailed him, plus two beast-women who looked to be a mix of greyhound and viper. Barbellion, Grenville, and Carter followed, little Winston bringing up the rear.

"We are compromised. Destroy any incriminating documents here," Moreau ordered. "You have twenty minutes. After that we depart, with you or no." As the manager and his clerk proceeded the down the ramp he added, "Oh, one more thing."

Pelham Grenville exploded with a wet plop which almost drowned out the eerie sound of the ray gun's discharge. Barbellion shrieked as blood, brains, and bowels showered him. The sight produced no reaction in anyone else.

"A wrist slap for your failure," said Moreau. "You have been...untidy."

The quaking Barbellion held up his gored hands. "I shall give satisfaction."

"Do. You would be well-advised to remember that our masters are even less inclined toward forgiveness. Winston, go with him." He turned to Carter. "Have a team sweep this place for my daughter. Arm them with real weapons, but take care she is not harmed. Leave her abductors in tiny pieces for my research."

The sun had set, and gloom filled the hangar. Paragon watched through Lady Kalmaar's opera glasses. They had stowed themselves behind barrels of brass chins and cheeks, just beside the security room. Four factory guards loitered in there. Vesta and Millie had already moved off on their separate assignment.

"How certain are you of your mechanistics?" Paragon whispered. "Disaster waits if they fail."

"Adam Franklin designed the thing." She fingered her small wrist-box.

Paragon recalled how helpless he had been against her rogue automaton. "You will pardon me, I hope, for regretting that I just gave my revolver to Tilley."

"Men so enjoy fondling their guns. What would your alienist say about that?" She made herself blonde again.

"She would blame it on a tragic childhood. I can hardly fault her there."

As Barbellion and his tiny brass shadow passed them, Ambergris plucked Winston by the sleeve. He slowed and bowed. "It is a pleasure to see you again, ma'am. I feared you were lost. I shall apprise Mr. Barbellion of your safe return."

Ambergris held up a finger to stop him going. "But first, may I give you a present?"

She showed him a brass disc with a lion's head on it. "Pretty, isn't it?" A gloved hand slapped it upon the back of his neck. Paragon gave it a whack with a workshop hammer, forcing the disk's spike through the brass surface. A half-second later, Lady Kalmaar turned a dial on her wrist box.

Winston stiffened as if holding a bolt of lightning. His eyes dimmed, fluttered, then returned to their normal brilliance. Ambergris addressed him while manipulating her controller.

"Winston, how are you feeling?"

"Dizzy, ma'am. And my head buzzes."

"That will pass. You are a very brave boy." Her coloring returned to normal. "My name is Lady Kalmaar. I am your new mistress. Do you remember this gentleman?"

"I do. He is wanted by Mr. Barbellion and Dr. Moreau. He abducted you from the airship."

"They are mistaken. Mr. Paragon rescued me from danger. Repeat, please."

Winston cocked his head a bit. "He...rescued you from danger."

"And you are to trust and obey him as you would me."

"I shall, my lady." He paused, his head still tilted. "The buzzing..." Ambergris fiddled with the ivory box. His head straightened. "Better. Thank you."

She leaned in close to Paragon's ear. "This experimental Gassner battery has little life in it. Perhaps only a quarter of an hour. When it fails, so will our hold on him."

Lady Kalmaar whispered instructions to their new ally. Paragon gave her the shock umbrella. "Here we go, then."

Moreau showed no sign of either leaving the ramp or returning to the air. Around the criminal leader stood Savage, Yatna, and Madame Mou Sha, hectoring him with considerable heat. *Apparently, all is not paradise aboard the good ship* **Prosper***. Splendid...*

With no one's attention on them, Paragon, Ambergris, and Winston hurried to the guard room door. Lady Kalmaar waved the metal boy through first. She followed two paces behind, with Paragon crouched behind her skirt.

"You're alive!" cried Barbellion. "Did that ruffian abuse you?"

"Thankfully not," she told him. "He informs me that he is reserving such treatment for those who deserve it."

Lady Kalmaar stepped aside to reveal a smirking Paragon. Sputtering, Barbellion ran for the other door. "Shoot them both! She is in league with him!"

That only played into his enemies' hands. A properly functioning civilian automaton could not harm a human, but defense of one's master was the exception. Winston knocked a guard down and seized Barbellion by his waistcoat. Ambergris shouted an order to subdue but not harm. Barbellion continued to squawk for aid as the chaos erupted.

Before the nearest guard's pistol could clear the holster, Paragon kicked him in the belly. Another's shot went wide, knocked off-target by Ambergris's brolly slapping his wrist. That exposed her to the gun of the third man. But the iron rim in Paragon's thrown bowler caught him in the neck. By then the kicked guard had recovered. He tried to backhand Lady Kalmaar, but she caught the strike with the umbrella, hooked his arm, and spiked her hatpin into his eye. Yowling, he pawed at his bleeding face.

A bullet whizzed past Paragon's ear, shattering the glass in the door behind him. Winston's victim had fired from the floor. Paragon remained too far away to engage the man, who thumbed the hammer for a final, fatal shot. Ambergris, too, was not near enough to stop him.

Seeing his new mistress in jeopardy, Winston hurled the shrieking Barbellion. The collision rivaled a train wreck. Bones could be heard to break. Blood flowed from the unconscious guard's mouth.

Lady Kalmaar snatched up the enemy weapons. "Winston, carry him to the infirmary. Do not let him speak to anyone." The brass child picked Barbellion up as if he weighed no more than a shawl.

After tying the fallen guards and taking pistols from them, they pushed through the far door to the communications office. It contained telegraph equipment, speaking tubes, pneumo ports, even a caged window for carrier pigeons. While Ambergris set about smashing the tubes and ports, Paragon underlined words in the telegraphic code book, leaving it open at the cluster of gibberish letters which stood for "ARMY."

"A false trail?"

"Panic is an excellent interrupter of an enemy's thinking."

They moved on to the empty waiting room. When Paragon donned his breath mask, Ambergris followed suit. He hefted his pocket watch.

"There's no fighting them all in the shops, so I intend to return to the train and make him come to us. Let's hope the ladies had success." He handed her a small ball of wax. "For your ears. Use all of it. You left, I right, at a sprint. Stay as low as you can. Take care you don't run into Reggie's twin."

He jerked open the outer door and tossed the watch. Someone cried out, "Grenade!", but there was no explosion. They dashed out, crouched low, turning to each side as soon as they left the building. A fusillade struck the empty doorway, but the train guards who had fired from ambush were immediately downed by an unholy mechanical screech from the watch. They clawed at their ears, teeth clenched.

*Pity about the watch. It complemented this waistcoat superlatively.*

Paragon tripped over a body with a Martini rifle strapped to the shoulder. Farther on lay an identical man. Each had plummeted from a cathedral belfry. Vesta and Millie had done their duty. The way was clear. He waved Ambergris toward the pneumatic train. As they neared the track they slowed, wary.

With a hiss the top hatch of the lead car popped open. Lady Kalmaar loosed a shot, which made the man duck back down inside with a Gaelic curse. "Just for that I'm chargin' ye double fare!" shouted Quarrel.

More craggy freckled faces appeared in the windows. They carried cudgels, knives, and a few pistols. If Paragon met this crew on a murky night, he would call for assistance. But now they looked as welcome as a water boy in the Transvaal.

"You took this train yourselves?"

"We rushed 'em while they were all gazin' skyward at your manly display of aeronautical insanity. Like baby birds waitin' for the worm, they were."

"Have you seen a rather unique brace of ladies hereabouts?"

"One a refined gentlewoman, despite her boyish apparel? And the other, er, not? In the weapons car."

Paragon climbed aboard, tugging Lady Kalmaar up beside him. "Heads down, eyes open. We shall most assuredly be pursued."

The monorail smoothly accelerated. No one fired at it. Behind them, the train's guards pounded their skulls, some vomiting. The *Prosper* remained in its factory hideaway. None of its 'thopters gave chase.

"We are away," said Ambergris. "No Moreau, alas. I should have strangled him when I had the chance."

"As far as he knows, you are my victim. He will come to us."

She wrinkled her brow. "What if he decides to simply drop explosives on us?"

"I would surmise that he would much rather add our Huxley Cells to his collection of freaks. Yours, particularly, when he learns the truth."

Ambergris shuddered. "I shall save the last bullet for myself before I permit him that satisfaction."

He led her to the guards' car, which was now in front. Amidst the weapons sat Vesta Tilley with a smug smile. Behind her stood Millie, sipping from a small silver flask.

"Top o' the mornin' to you!" she sang, saluting them.

Paragon said, "I see that you had little difficulty in persuading those riflemen to desert their posts."

"It proved simple enough," Vesta said with a shrug.

"Your chosen argumentative technique was...?"

"He unaccountably hurled his skull into my pistol barrel. After that he I believe he clumsily tripped over my hip and precipitated earthward." She tossed the gun back to its owner.

Paragon eyed the tipsy Millie. "I expect you approached the matter rather differently."

"Well, you didn't give me no gun, did you? I had to use what nature gave me." Her wigglers peeped out from beneath her hair.

"Nature, you say?"

"Me workin' girl's nature, anyhow. I popped his tallywhacker into me mouth. After that he couldn't think of a bleedin' thing to say."

"They rarely do, in my experience," Ambergris snorted.

"Just as he got started – for which you owe me two bob, I has rent to pay – me wigglers popped out to say hello. Give him such a fright he jumped back six feet and fell over the ledge."

"What now?" asked Quarrel, appearing in the door.

Paragon looked out of the window of the next car. "Any sign of pursuit?"

"Not a whit. Do you suppose they're cuttin' their losses and are glad to see the backs of us?"

"If this hound refuses to give chase, we shall just have to offer him more enticing prey. I believe that the time has come for daughter and papa to have a little heart-to-heart."

"I remind you that we are hurtling away at fifty miles per hour."

Paragon fondled her thigh. "Let us see if this marvelous instrument can perform as advertised."

It took considerable fiddling, and even more cursing, to master the grasshopper telegraph's operation. But once the dial's needle indicated that the machine was ready, all that remained was to send the message with the tiny telegraph key via the wires that paralleled the tracks.

"I cannot believe that this toy really works," Ambergris said.

"You and me both, my lady," muttered Quarrel, who eyed the box as if witches lived in it.

"We shall soon know," Paragon said. "Moreau will certainly reply to such an arch message."

"Oh? What did you say to the bastard?"

"'Dear Papa, I stole all your plans from the *Prosper*'s safe. Your employers will be most unhappy to hear that Her Majesty's government is in possession of them.'"

"Aye, that'll stick in his craw, all right."

*I expect that my true message will achieve the same end: 'I know that you grew me from a foul alien seed. I shall take my own life, but not before revealing all to the press and Royal Society. Huxley himself shall publicly dissect my sad corpse as proof. You are broken. I wish you luck in evading your monstrous Martian masters.'*

Paragon concealed any hint of that from Ambergris. He was still uncertain if he ought to reveal to her the true facts of her creation. *Not very different from Adam Franklin. Would the truth mar her psyche? Or is she strong enough to shrug it off like a bit of stray factory-soot?*

It was fully dark now. The miniature telegraph chattered. They all waited as he jotted down the letters. It was brief.

Paragon laughed. *"How sharper than a serpent's tooth it is..."*

Lady Kalmaar sighed. "I do not suppose he is planning to strip himself naked and howl at the lightning?"

"The real question is: which daughter does he see you as, Regan, Goneril, or Cordelia?"

"Hmm. And here I was hoping that I could be the noble and disguised Kent."

With markedly slurred speech Millie asked, "What the hell are you two on about?" Her tentacles drooped with the effects of her whiskey consumption.

"Dr. Moreau sees himself as the much-abused King Lear."

"The only leers I knows about is the ones I get from likely customers on the street. Few bloody kings among that lot. One time, though ---"

A heavy thump boomed atop their car. Paragon drew his gun. The others all seized weapons from the nearby racks.

Quarrel said, "What sort o' thing can jump atop a speedin' train?"

"And why would we want to scrap with it?" added Millie.

Paragon ordered, "Quarrel, ready your lads. Kill the lights." Backing into the first passenger compartment, Vesta right behind him, he kept eyes and ears fixed on the ceiling. Millie and Ambergris remained in the weapons car.

More rooftop bangs announced several new unnatural somethings. They ran to and fro, claws scratching the metal surface, seeking a weakness.

"Nimble bastards, eh?" laughed Quarrel.

An immense paw with six-inch claws smashed a window. The chap on guard there flinched and brought up his pistol but was snatched bodily out of the jagged opening. Despite Paragon's shouted warning, most of Quarrel's men rushed to that spot. Another fellow disappeared to his doom, broken nearly in half by the window frame.

Paragon jerked his head back and forth to watch all the unguarded windows. A screeching, tearing sound came from Ambergris's car. There something peeled away the top as easily as one might open a page of the Sunday *Times*. Millie sent caustic London invective up at the creature but that did her no good. A hairy hand the size of a nail keg scooped her up. Ambergris's pistol barked, but it might have been shooting soggy peas for all the notice her foe took of it.

Just as Millie was about to disappear forever, the beast-man's shoulder joint exploded in a spray of meat and bone. The limb dropped away from the body like Grendel's. Howling, the monster leaped from the train as Paragon aimed another specialty round at it. Wind whistled through the roof gash. He poked his head out to see just what they faced.

A reptilian head hissed. Soulless yellow eyes were his last memory as an impossibly long tongue lanced out at him. A sting at his throat, blurred vision...and darkness.

*Two miles south of the factory*

*Two great winged gargoyles carried him slung on a wicker hammock affair. Navita clutched a white pigeon in a tentacle, while he used his gloved hands to read its message. It had been simple enough to snare Carter's message. The code had proven laughably simple to break. His treachery was scarcely a surprise but discovering that he did not serve Lochmoor was. Time enough to deal with him later.*

*Paragon, though, was a concern. The Lochmoor chap had certainly proven to be more capable than anticipated. He had spotted the quad-ape's ruse immediately and dispatched it, though without suspecting that the lady had been a lure and not a victim.*

*"At least we now know that her ruse has succeeded," he said aloud. "He must now believe that she needs his protection. A pity to lose poor Bernard, though, and on his maiden mission."*

*"This Paragon could be of value if we can turn him. White apes are formidable opponents. He has vulnerabilities. A haunted past he would prefer to keep hidden. And mental war wounds. Psychological torments and an exploitable poppy dependency should be all I need. I have created new servants with far less."*

*One of the gargoyles looked at him with a cocked eyebrow. "That's correct," Navita said. "Sometimes I prefer to create my minions the old-fashioned way. Set me down east of the factory. Let them wear themselves out battling one another before I give Sebastian the reunion he thinks he wants."*

## 19 / "CANST THOU REMEMBER A TIME BEFORE WE CAME UNTO THIS CELL?"

Fog…pain in every joint…nightmares worse than his dalliances with the poppy had ever caused…and hushed voices.

"Stay down," Ambergris whispered, relief in her voice betraying great concern. "They are waiting for you to wake before beginning the torture."

"You are splendid at raising morale," he said, voice hoarse. *Why am I always getting it in the neck lately?* "Where are we?"

"Factory cellar. In a literal cell."

"What sort of factory contains a jail?"

"Shush!"

Booted feet appeared on the other side of the bars. After half a minute the man spat and stomped off again. Paragon opened his eyes. His three stalwart accomplices looked back at him, haggard and bruised.

"Where are the rest?"

"Dead, mostly," said Vesta. She had that hollow gaze he had often seen on young men after their first battle, himself included.

"Quarrel?"

She stared at her toes. "Torn in two. And…eaten."

*Bloody hell.*

Ambergris explained. "Four of them. Like nothing I have ever seen back on the island. There the beast-men are mostly like children. These…" She shuddered. "You killed the biggest one with that explosive bullet. Then there was the snake-woman who stung you. She led the attack. The other two were ursine, but also possessed characteristics of cheetahs. Fast, agile, ferocious."

"Of late Moreau's Law seems flexible in the extreme," Paragon sighed. "Where is he?"

"He appeared when the train stopped. They turned off the air pumps just as you fell."

"He seems not to have tearfully clasped you to his paternal bosom."

"On the contrary, he slapped me with a loaded riding crop." She angled her beautiful face so that he could see a purple welt running across one cheek. "To be fair, I did try to kill him with my bare hands first."

"Ah. So, you are decidedly not Cordelia, then."

"It would appear not." She chuckled without mirth. "Nor Miranda, neither."

Paragon experimentally flexed his limbs. Nothing seemed to be damaged beyond repair. Already some of the venom's pain and nausea was easing. "I suppose the Martian interrogation device is now being oiled?"

"They desire you to be clear-headed enough to fully appreciate its tender mercies. Also working in our favor, Moreau has dissension in his ranks. Apparently, Mr. Savage is desirous of an immediate departure, leaving us here. Some of the others, such as Captain Carter, are starting to agree. They took your bait. The army's arrival is expected at any time. Files are being burned in a great pyre. He is planning to bolt."

"How do you know all of this?"

"Our guard is particularly sensitive to my aromatic persuasions. Alas, he has no key. Moreau is not a fool."

Millie hissed, "He's comin' back."

Paragon rolled his eyes up in his head and let his tongue loll. The boots appeared once more.

"Still out?" a gruff voice wanted to know.

"Yes," Lady Kalmaar replied, "no thanks to your friends. His pulse is irregular. I fear his heart may fail."

That produced a guffaw. "Like it ain't gonna fail anyhow once the boss has his way with him!"

Strong sea-scent washed over Paragon. It seemed as if Eros had invaded a florist's shop, cloying and enticing at the same time. As was always the case, his loins responded with ardor. *Let us pray that the guard overlooks that detail.*

"Perhaps if you return in, say, fifteen minutes instead of your usual five, he will have recovered sufficiently for you to safely take him. My father will be most piqued if you deliver him dead."

"I…I suppose so. But my orders are to take you all out on the next go-round, no matter his condition." The feet shuffled. "Make it ten minutes."

Full of unstated and perplexed yearning, he retreated down the dim and dirty corridor. With the aid of all three women, Paragon gained his feet, wobbly as a newborn foal. When the cell ceased to spin, he patted his clothing.

"They stripped you," said Millie. "Same with the rest of us. I should have charged 'em my usual rate, they was that thorough." She produced the folded paper she had been given in the laboratory. "There was one place they were too squeamish to check, though."

Paragon's smirked. "I don't suppose you have a gun in there, as well?" He opened it and read it, eyes widening. "I shall murder Phoenix, if we live that long."

"Why?" Vesta asked. "What's it say?"

"We have had a spy inside Moreau's coterie this whole time. That Confederate chap, Carter."

"Then why hasn't he helped us?"

"He answers to the Foreign Office, not Lochmoor. A long rivalry in these matters. Says his mission is too secret to risk him being found out, even now."

"Then what good is he?"

"He claims to have preserved Millie from immediate dissection. And he will give us what aid he can that does not unmask him."

Vesta shook her head. "Well, since we are sharing literally intimate secrets." A paper appeared in her hand, also. "They didn't look there on me, either. Who knew that murderous henchmen were so chivalrous?"

Paragon glanced at it. Though in bizarre Martian script, it seemed to be a chemical formula of some kind. "Should I lay all my money on this not being a cake recipe?"

"Unlikely. It came from Moreau's staff. I pinched it while they were piled atop me."

"One more puzzle to untangle. But it won't happen if we remain here."

He tugged at a thread on the lapel of his ill-used morning coat, pulling out some two feet of the cord, perhaps an eighth of an inch thick. His collar yielded a similar piece, though darker. Out of his leg came a brass sparking device and a bit of fuse.

"Here. What you doin'?" asked Millie.

"Posting bail, I hope."

He twisted the cords together and wrapped them around the cell door's lock. Then he tied one end of the fuse to them and clamped the sparker's jaws on the other.

He advised the women, "You should look away. The light is quite blinding."

With a squeeze on the sparker, blue-white flame flooded the gloomy cell like a newborn star. The powerful chemicals sizzled. After half a minute they faded, leaving tangy smoke in the mildewed air.

Paragon kicked the lock. It snapped like a brittle twig. "And the wizards take a wicket."

They all squeezed out. Dim gaslights provided fitful illumination in the passageway. A steep set of stone steps led up to a trapdoor.

"These go to the guard room," Ambergris told him.

"No hope of simply slinking away in the night, then?"

"I fear not. Are you capable of antagonistics in your present condition?"

"I hope so." In truth he felt like a rabbit run over by a train. "But we are not without resources." Out of his leg he took a six-inch black metal tube.

"Resources?" said Ambergris in a dubious tone. "Some marvelous new death ray?"

With a snap of his wrist the steel baton expanded to its full eighteen inches. "Rather more primitive than that, but effective, nonetheless. Apply it to any offered skulls, wrists, or knees." He looked at Vesta. "Remember your training. Queue's lessons shall serve you well. Millie, I do not have to tell you how to control a man, do I?"

The dollymop waved a dismissive hand. "It's me stock in trade, ain't it?"

Paragon burst up through the hatch before the nearest man could do so much as raise his eyebrows. A jab feint at the nose made the man bring his hands up. Then Pargon snared a wrist, twisted it while spinning, and drove the guard's head into the stone floor. He lay unmoving, as if shot point-blank.

Shouts. Blurred motion. Chaos. Curses and threats. Six other men reached for weapons. One gun clattered onto the floor when Ambergris's baton broke its owner's elbow. He shrieked and backed into Vesta, who seized his abused arm to whirl him into another bloke who had raised his billy to strike at Lady Kalmaar from behind. Little Tilley, fully invested in her male persona, used her fists to jab the next chap in the nose and throat. A savate kick to his belly sent him down the hatch. True to her promise, Millie simply reached down to take hold of her man's bollocks as if crushing walnuts. When he raised a hand to bat her away, a fanged tentacle bit into his palm and worried at it like a terrier with a rat.

Someone wrapped Paragon from behind to immobilize him so that another could swing a bludgeon from the front. A vicious stab of the Apache ring into the hugger's hand made him loosen his hold, while a low kick from Paragon's invincible foot broke his partner's knee. He turned his hips and pulled the man behind him over and into a wall.

Millie's victim proved to be made of sterner stuff than at first supposed. After elbowing her away, he snatched up a shotgun from the wall and leveled it at her. She squeaked in anticipation of her imminent demise, but the sabotaged weapon exploded in his face. Lady Kalmaar confused the final foe by turning her skin as red as cooked lobster, adding brilliant yellow eyes with purple pupils and a leopard-spotted tongue. When he blanched at that, as did Vesta and Millie, she rapped him soundly atop his head. It proved to be the cell guard she had entranced.

"So sorry, my love," she sighed. "We are from different worlds, you and I. It could never be."

After forcing the defeated guards down the hatch and locking it, Paragon collected his Webley and bowler, as well as Ambergris' fan and their sticks, from a corner table. He brushed dirt from his expensive clothes. *At least I shall be properly attired for my trip to hell.*

Vesta said, "We must bustle out of here."

"Easy enough for you to say," Ambergris retorted. "You are not wearing one."

Paragon inspected his pistol's load. "Front's no good this time, if they are mounting a defense against the troops they believe are en route."

"Back into the workshops then," Lady Kalmaar said.

"Yes. Ladies, procure a fallen revolver, if you would. Don't touch any in the rack."

They moved to the exit. A truncheon-wielding guard stood in the corridor. Confronted with four pistols and a scarlet-skinned woman, he embraced discretion and fled. But he pulled a lever on his way out. Clanging alarms rang from the belfries, then shouts and running feet burst from the airship.

Paragon's crew ducked into a storage area stacked to the ceiling with crates. A side doorway led to a forge and smelter. Millie and Vesta stacked heavy boxes as barriers. The voices of guards and the grunts of beast-men grew louder as they searched the workrooms. Now merely escaping looked to be dubious, let alone capturing Moreau.

Vesta checked her revolver for the fourth time. "Selling our lives dearly then, is it? Romantic, but distressing. I was just beginning to enjoy this job."

Childlike sobbing interrupted them. Paragon and Ambergris pulled hard on a corner crate to reveal little Winston crouched between two barrels. Ambergris changed into Mrs. Llewellyn again and knelt beside the brass boy, who looked as confused as an albatross in a desert.

"Hello, Winston. You seem distraught. May I assist you?"

Winston looked up at her with sputtering eyes. "Thank you for your concern, my lady, but no. I am lost. My soul is unmoored."

Ambergris and Paragon exchanged puzzled looks. Clockwork men could not cry. Nor did they possess the capacity for speaking of their souls.

"What has happened?"

Winston sniffed. "My master is no more."

"Mr. Barbellion, you mean?"

"Yes. His injuries were too grievous. And I am to blame."

"Nonsense. You were protecting your mistress. Do you not recall?"

The little eyes dimmed. Tiny white lines like shooting stars darted across them. "I...I...perhaps..."

"At that time, I was your mistress. There was an exchange of authority."

"I fear my memory cogs are faulty. Can one such as I have dreams?"

"What dreams, exactly?"

"I was in the infirmary. Poor broken Mr. Barbellion coughed blood. He seized my lapel and claimed I had killed him. Then he breathed no more. Surely that was a dream such as humans have."

"I fear it was no dream. Do you remember nothing before that?"

"I do not. There is a gap." He pounded his forehead onto his iron knees, making an echoing clank. "They shall hurl me into the smelter for this!"

Ambergris took his cold face in both her hands. "No one would be so cruel. You are a fine boy, and no murderer." She brushed his coat with her fingers. "Will you stay with me? Let me look after you?"

The odd flashing in his eyes ceased. "A generous offer, my lady. I think...I should know you, and know this man...yet I am doubtful."

"Yes, you do. You preserved my life this night. I intend to return the favor."

"Might I call you...mama?"

Ambergris's jaw dropped. Paragon stared. Automatons did not, could not, behave this way. Emotions? Utterly impossible. *Has he been tampered with by Moreau? Is this a trap?*

Lady Kalmaar's skin tone subtly shifted back to her natural tawny shade, her eyes moist. "Why...you certainly may, my darling boy."

They embraced as if Winston were flesh-and-blood. Paragon began to wonder if Mervyn might suddenly behave in a like manner. *Might become too self-aware. Join a trade union. Demand better hours and conditions. Where would it all end? And who would press my trousers?*

Loud bangs nearby interrupted the touching scene. The *Prosper's* troops had entered the forge room. In seconds they would be pounding upon the makeshift barricade. Paragon turned his mind into knots trying to think of a way to survive, but nothing came to him.

"Time is up," he informed Ambergris. "Would that I had that other watch now."

Lady Kalmaar smiled and reached into Winston's coat pocket and pullet out the watch. "It seemed important to you, so I thought it best to take precautions. Though a man who carries two of them seems guilty of the sin of pride...or punctuality."

He gave her an enthusiastic kiss. "My transgression is of a homelier nature. Self-preservation." He hefted the gold timepiece. "Can you persuade your newly-adopted son to punch a small hole high in that wall?"

At a soft word from Ambergris, the little automaton clambered atop the stacked boxes. With his iron fist he knocked out two square feet of bricks. Through it a few stars could be seen. He made his way back down to lean against the crates which barred the door from the forge room. With his knees locked, and with the three women's combined weight adding to the effort, the wall ceased to shift inward. On the other side, men swore.

Paragon climbed to the punctured wall, pulled out the stem of the watch five times to charge the device, then wound the spring until it tightened and stopped. That gave him half a minute to set it properly and get to safety. He reached through the wall gap to set the watch upon an ornamental ledge. Hurriedly he bounded down and joined his straining team at the barricade. "Heads down!"

The small bomb burst with less noise than a typical grenade, but with a great deal more light. Brilliant scarlet tendrils flew in all directions. One lonely finger flew up and out from the wall as if guided toward the loitering *Coxwell*.

"What the devil was that?" demanded Tilley.

"Incendiary bomb. Magnesium and strontium nitrate, says Queue. Designed to start fires, but in this instance, it serves as a bully signal."

"If that loony Farnborough tears himself away from his looking-glass long enough to see it."

A bestial roar shook the very floor. Before it died away, a tremendous impact struck the other side of the barrier. The entire mass moved inward some six inches. Another ferocious crash shoved them all back again. At the other entrance, more attacks came, though blessedly of a more human nature. A dark shadow of doom seemed to dim the already meager light.

"Shall we solicit inspired notions at this juncture?" asked Vesta. Despite her plucky demeanor, she looked pale and frightened.

In a deflated voice Lady Kalmaar said, "I shall give myself up to him again. Perhaps I can barter for your freedom."

"Moreau knows that we possess enough knowledge to destroy him," said Paragon. "He will not be in the giving vein today."

"You are not the only actor here. I can weep and wail and make moan. Possibly shame him into a gentle rain of mercy."

Winston spoke, tinny voice full of childish frustration. "I want these bad people to leave us alone!"

Like some sort of magical incantation, the pounding ceased. No more angry shouts could be heard. In fact, the only sound Paragon's sensitive ears could detect was that of booted and hoofed feet running away.

"Oi!" cried Millie. "They knockin' off work for the day or what?"

"I doubt that they belong to a henchmen's guild," breathed Paragon. "Surely Farnborough cannot have responded already?"

A young and arrogant voice called out from high above them, "Evenin', Mr. Paragon! Peach of a night, ain't it?"

A soot-smudged little face grinning at them from the scorched hole. Paragon laughed. "Why, hello, Selkie! A bit far from your patch, are you not?"

"We just wanted to see what all the fuss was about. 'Thopters shootin' at one another, aeros burnin' in the fields, red sparklers like it's Bonfire Night. I won a shillin' because I bet that you was in it up to your eyebrows."

"Well-played. That I am. You brought reinforcements then, did you?"

"Three of 'em are holdin' me up here like circus acrobats. The rest are hard at it."

"Where?"

"Give a listen."

Though faint, the sounds of high-pitched children's taunts and shrieks were audible. Deeper, angrier adult voices acted as counterpoint to that melody.

"Them fool grown-ups are easy to mystify. They're all dashin' about the factory floor, tryin' to collect me mates. Might as well try to shovel flies."

"How the devil did you all pass through the defense line?"

"Is that what they call it? Barely a man every three yards and not one of 'em with the night-eyes of a gnat. We walked right past 'em when that pretty red boomer of yours went off."

"Well done! But have you a plan besides twitting our enemies for a few minutes?"

"That's all we was asked to do."

"By whom?"

"By the handsome lad what floated from the sky and landed almost on top o' me.

From that little airship that's right above me head."

Paragon slapped the side of a box. "Look alive, all! We are back in the graces of Dame Fortune!"

"How so?" asked Ambergris.

"Farnborough has arranged a clever diversion. Nothing derails the adult brain like the shrieking of children."

Paragon peeked out the door. At the other end of the cavernous building some two dozen men flailed about, attempting to gather a bunch of ragtag children. Occasionally one of them would let out a triumphant cry as he collared an urchin, only to make an entirely different noise as sturdy teeth chomped on his hand. On the gondola ramp Carter, Mou Sha, and Savage still stood with Moreau, who waved his staff about as if it could magically organize a defense against the filthy little hellions. Presently he grew so irate that he stormed back into his ship, leaving the Confederate officer in charge of vanquishing Selkie's force. Captain Carter hesitated, then drew his saber. He moved to rush down the gangway and enter the fray.

But he never made it. After glancing up at the canvas roof and then, inexplicably, directly at Paragon, Oliver Savage reversed his heavy-headed stick and clubbed the gray-clad American on the skull. Carter's inert form rolled down the ramp and lay still.

*What on earth? Have we a palace coup? And why did you clout my only ally out there?*

Madame Mou Sha's black eyes grew wide as train tunnels. When Savage raised his stick to pay her the same compliment, she hissed and backed away to the gondola. He tipped his hat to her, then turned to survey the chaos below. In that instant, the Oriental woman yanked out one of her steel hair sticks. She flew at him, but he had lured her in with a ruse of defenselessness. His hat batted away the undoubtedly envenomed little dagger. Before she could strike again, his huge elbow smote her jaw with a terrific blow.

Paragon crept from the storeroom, followed by the others. They moved with increasing speed toward the *Prosper's* gondola, taking care to use every available doorway or stack of supplies as concealment.

In a voice only slightly less powerful than naval ordnance, Savage cried out, "Dr. Moreau has placed me in command! Ignore the brats, fall in, and prepare to move! The army approaches and we must augment our defense out front!" In an eye-blink three ranks of eight stood at attention, weapons holstered and eyes on their new commander.

Selkie's gallant mob had also vanished. Paragon scanned the factory for the wild creatures. Just as he had decided that they must have scarpered, Ambergris pointed up. All of them had climbed the tie-ropes which secured the vast canvas roof. They were happily working at the great knots like monkeys feasting upon fruit.

When a gap some eighty feet long opened, Paragon sprang out of his crouch and rushed the Giffard. The ranks of enemy he paid little heed to, for he knew what would happen next.

A squadron of giant dragonflies soared through the opening roof. They were no Huxley Cell monstrosities, but rather Royal Aero Marines from the *Coxwell*, Farnborough in the lead. Each soldier flew in a triangular kite-like affair, employing his Enfield carbine to deadly effect. Half a dozen of Moreau's men fell before they even realized there was a danger.

Two of Farnborough's Marines went slack before touching down as their fire was returned. Farnborough landed, shrugging off his harness and engaging the enemy with his steam-pistol. A brisk and deafening exchange commenced.

Paragon caught Farnborough's eye and wordlessly requested cover fire, earning a wink and a nod from the splendid peacock. With that Paragon dashed into the open, sprinting for the ramp. He safely reached it, though his coat tail gave its life to a bullet. Savage backed up into the gondola, stick ready for a vigorous defense. The man wore an unaccountably mirthful expression. In no mood for it, Paragon pointed his Webley at the man's smirking face.

"Careful, old cock," said Oscar Wilde, "you could put someone's eye out with that thing."

*Oh, bloody hell. I shall be a Lochmoor laughingstock for this.*

"Just keeping up appearances," Paragon lied. "We don't want to expose your excellent disguise."

"Pray do not pretend that you knew it was me. You had no inkling."

*Best to be a man about it.* "I bow to your superior skill at hoodwinking the public. Now, shall we sally forth and finish this?"

"By all means." Wilde pulled off his bald pate, moustache, and false teeth. "Ah! Much more aesthetic."

They rushed into the control cabin. Bullets shattered the gondola windows, forcing them to dive onto their faces. Wilde's expression said much about the insult suffered by his bespoke garments. "Someone shall pay dearly for this."

He turned his wrath upon some half-dozen of the airship's company who poured pistol fire at the Marines from portals amidships. Bursting onto the promenade deck, Wilde and Paragon caught the squad of gunmen in the rear. Their sticks, fists, and feet made short work of Moreau's unsuspecting men. With that fire removed, Farnborough ordered a full assault. When the Marines charged, the remaining guards threw their hands into the air. A whoop of triumph came from the RAF commander. He led his team into the airship, leaving a force outside to secure the factory. Paragon greeted them from the captain's chair.

"Good show!" crowed Farnborough. "Bully!"

"Let us not rest on half-grown laurels just yet," advised Wilde. "Dr. Moreau is still at large...and still dangerous."

"This ship is ours. There is nowhere for him to ---"

His boast died as the *Prosper's* engines belched clouds of steam. In the space of a breath the entire hangar filled with opaque white mist. A ramp near the tail dropped with a boom. Paragon sighed. "He is pulling one last rabbit out of his topper."

Two odd vehicles clattered down the aft gangway. The things had a pair of tall tires in front and a smaller wheel in the rear. Each rider sat atop his boiler on an upholstered seat. Before him was a small cannon, a protective iron plate riveted to its breech. The escapees made for a wide service door.

"The blighter's making a run for it!" cried Wilde.

Dr. Moreau was indeed aboard the lead machine, long hair flying behind his mask. The reptile-woman followed him on the other. Just as they passed, Paragon leaped through a bullet-shattered window onto the trailing vehicle.

He almost overshot. But his left hand just did manage to snag a bit of the frame. Dragging behind the armed cycle, he despaired of his trousers...to say nothing of his joints.

Moreau's cannon barked. An explosive shell demolished the door. He bounced into the heather and vanished. His reptilian ally followed, unaware that Paragon still clung to her stern.

That happy state of affairs did not last. She turned to see if she was being pursued.

When she spotted Paragon, who fumbled for his revolver, she spat her venomous tongue at him.

*Not this time, lassie.*

Just as when Queue flung wooden daggers at him in training, he snatched the deadly thing. It felt slimy and repulsive in his fist. The tongue's pointed tip leaked a yellowish fluid.

"Pardon me, madame!" he shouted. "I believe you are in my seat."

With that he jerked her into the night. Clothes half-shredded, he climbed aboard and barely managed to avoid a tree. He found the throttle and brake while hurtling into the murk. The path Moreau had taken through the vegetation was clear. Since his prey dared not travel at full speed for fear of gullies and boulders, Paragon would catch him if he remained in his track. He opened the throttle as far as he dared. Bracken slapped against his knees.

A huge spray of dirt and vegetation came near to capsizing him. He reflexively returned fire, then commenced a series of sharp random turns to spoil Moreau's aim. Two more enemy shells went well wide. But their muzzle sparks plainly revealed they came a small clump of trees. Paragon skidded his machine to a stop and fired.

His shell detonated beneath the machine, tumbling it backward in a shower of metal fragments. One or two small fires burned in the dried leaves. Moreau's broken and twisted form still moved, dragging himself on shattered legs. Paragon drew his pistol and crept in. In the dim firelight he could make out a decrepit shed with a sagging roof. He ensured that no gunman lay in wait and rushed up to the creeping man.

"That will do, Moreau," he declared. "The game is over."

No response. Burnt fingers scratched at the earth. Pained breaths puffed from the mask, accompanied by sad strings of steam. After a long moment, the wounded man coughed, then rolled over. Paragon pointed his pistol straight at the heart.

"Let us see what you have done to yourself."

With a sucking sound the mask came off. Beneath was a pasty-white, lumpy mass of flesh. The nose was a rat's snout, with yellow eyes like a lemur. Most horrible of all was the round tube-mouth full of needle teeth. It wore a white wig. What lay before him was not Sebastian Moreau, but a beast-man decoy.

*Blast! Outfoxed again.*

As he remonstrated with himself, a terrific blow struck him on his right shoulder, numbing the whole arm. His pistol disappeared into the grass. Something roared and bashed him into a tree. Cloven hooves appeared beside his bleeding face. The thing lifted him by his lapels with frightening ease until he stared into three rows of sharp teeth. Rank breath threatened to asphyxiate him.

It was not the same gargoyle that he had electrified in Whitechapel. This one was much larger. He struggled, but he had spent his last reserves of strength. Too much fighting, too much venom, too much bleeding into Ambergris.

"Not yet. You must learn to enjoy your work more. That's what will make you human."

Through pain-blurred eyes Paragon saw a man in a fine black overcoat and matching trilby appear from behind the shed. It did not surprise him to recognize his blonde tentacled troublemaker, still smirking. Paragon now saw that he was not as young as he had supposed. He was close to fifty years of age, with some gray streaking his golden hair. His blue eyes held a cold, hard, barely checked madness which infrequent blinking accentuated. Also present was keen intelligence and considerable cunning.

"My friend, I don't like trouble, unless I give it. I do relish games, but 'tis time for me to take your queen and move on." He nodded at the false Moreau's vehicle. "Fine shooting, by the way. Pity it wasn't old Sebastian. That would have simplified my life enormously."

"Who…?" Paragon blinked, trying to clear his head. "Who have I the honor of addressing?"

"Ha! You Limeys…I swear, you spout poetry even while you shit." The stranger tipped his hat. "You have the honour of addressing your better. James Navita, MRCS. Try to keep it in your failing brain while my toothsome friend here eats you…alive."

"You're lying. James Mapp is stout, has dark hair and eyes."

"Mapp is dead and gone. Moreau murdered him. As for appearances, my bespoke pharmacological treatments have eaten the fat and faded everything else."

Navita took two steps away, then turned back. "I suspect, trained scientist that I am, that you aren't too keen on this whole devouring business. Perhaps you would like to leave your pathetic employer and come play with the Riot Army instead? Oh, I know, it's such a cliché. 'Mad scientist tries to lure the intrepid hero over to the dark side.' But I am legitimately insane. Barmy. Unfortunate tendency to slice up whores into tiny bits. Sometimes I fry and eat those tiny bits. As I said, Moreau murdered Mapp. I literally thank my lucky stars that I have means to hold it at bay…mostly."

A tentacle raised a post-mortem knife and carved at the tree. "Better to have you with me than against me, I confess. You've seen the sad specimens in my employ. We pay better than Her Miserly Majesty. You **will** have to conquer your inconvenient scruples about stealing and murdering, though you show a promising flexibility on the latter. And our ideals aren't totally at odds. For one, I am diligently warring with those invading Martian bastards, just as you are. They have yet to find out that I'm not really aiding them."

He moved close to Paragon's swollen face. "As an added inducement, I can offer solace from your nightmares. A drug that actually benefits you, for once. Think of it: no more Zulu dreams, no more re-living those sordid evenings with Peaceful Manners. He's alive, you know. A Southwark whoremaster. Still speaks of you with a fond longing. At any rate, I can do no worse than Madame Bernays."

Paragon's world spun like sewage down a drain.

*"Your skin is so smooth, Mikey. Like a girl's. I could touch your bum all night. Aw, don't cry. We're just havin' a bit of a lark."*

*"Run, lad! Save yourself! Live a long happy life and make me proud!"*

*"Let me pass, Michael. I need a wee rest, don't you think?"*

Tears oozed from his eyes. His nose ran. He made no reply, mired in an even worse place than a monster's jaws.

"No, then?" Navita shrugged. "Au revoir, Paragon…or should I say Parsons? I'm off to take over a rival firm. My poisoner has outlived his usefulness…"

Paragon was fading. Before everything could darken completely, he heard Albert Brutte again…from directly in front of him. Forcing his eyes open, he saw his old friend, comrade, ersatz father. He stood between the gargoyle's great arms, leaning against one like he was relaxing at a pub. In his regimental uniform, torn from bullets and spears, still sporting that magnificent black moustache and eagle's beak nose, pipe in his mouth, rolling a cracked shilling across his knuckles, he was the very image of the British Empire. Only the bloody gash in his throat took away from the effect.

*"Bit of a sticky wicket here, eh. Mikey?"* he grinned. *"But I fancy you can still swing for a six."*

His mother, pale and wasted, in the dress she died in, appeared outside the monster's other arm, holding it like a lover. But her face was not the same. Now it was happy and wholesome. *"Look at you, all grown up. Successful. I could just bust. Now you bust right out of this snare, you hear me?"* Her hands touched his throat, making it tingle. *"You still have work to do."*

Little Dotty popped up between the arms, cheerful despite her broken and dislocated bones, a crushed white daisy in her hair. *"Hey, big brother! You gonna let this big lummox push you around? I've seen tougher lizards in our back garden."*

Brutte told him, *"Time to show some guts, lad,"* and took his pipe from his lips. He pointed it at Paragon's belly in a significant manner.

*Oh, bless you, Albert, you always did know the perfect solution for every problem.*

Navita was still talking. No time had passed. "…as has his double-dealing, lab-bred, bitch-spawn."

The threat to Ambergris roused Paragon to action. His struggles availed him nothing as the gargoyle pinned him to the tree. Those horrifying teeth moved ever closer, thick drool dripping. But as the beloved phantoms faded away, he forced one hand down to his waist, to his thick brass belt buckle, and just managed to press a hidden switch. The explosion knocked the breath out of him, but the gargoyle fared worse from the .44-caliber bullet.

It did not slay the beast, which had shifted to one side as it moved in for the kill. But it blew a hole through the thing, just above the right hip. With a screech, it stepped back, releasing Paragon. And right then the monster grew a new set of legs, a black pair which appeared at the base of its shoulders and wrapped around its muscled throat.

His devourer released him as the new limbs tried to snap its neck with a ferocious twist. On a human that would have certainly killed, but its sinews were just too powerful. The mysterious assailant raised a long dagger. Before he could spike the thing, it seized his foot and flung him away like a child's rag doll.

Paragon's senses were returning. This proved fortuitous, for Navita pulled a ray gun from his coat pocket and aimed it at the mystery man. From the ground, Paragon kicked him in a knee, spoiling the shot. Blue-white energy struck the shed, melting part of it like candle wax. Snarling, Navita turned on him, only to yelp as the man in black hurled an object that stuck into his arm. Before Paragon could rise to engage him properly, Navita pulled out the spike, tipped his hat, and vanished into the night, snatched up by another flying horror.

Crawling like an infant, Paragon patted the underbrush for one of the guns. While he did so, the stranger closed with the monster. Though no match for the gargoyle's strength, he demonstrated an agility Paragon could scarcely credit. Each time the creature snatched at him, the dagger opened a fresh wound. Even its bullwhip tail struck only air, save for a single whack to a shoulder. For two full minutes the unreal combat continued, bellowing beast against weirdly silent human. By the time Paragon's hand touched his Webley, the creature bled from a dozen wounds. Now it clutched at its tormentor with painful slowness, as if under water. He held his fire as the unknown man rushed into the thing's deadly embrace, only to slide beneath its grasp to deliver a killing blow to its belly. With a sad moan, the leathery beast watched its entrails plop out onto the grass. A pair of brain shots from the Webley put an end to its suffering. Before their echo ended, his savior had vanished.

More reports echoed them. Lady Kalmaar stood above the false Moreau, pumping vengeful bullets into it. She kept pulling the trigger until the useless clicks finally registered. Then she hurled the gun at the corpse and shrieked to the heavens.

As if her voice possessed some rough magic, the factory exploded in a ball of yellow-orange flame.

Two bits of flaming red debris roared directly overhead, against the wind. The shed burst asunder, showering Ambergris and Paragon with its shattered bones.

"Just a parting shot from papa," said Ambergris' sour voice. "It is fortunate that he could not aim properly while strapped into that thing."

"Which was…?" asked Paragon.

"Emergency escape device. Steam jets out, propelling him at unbelievable speed. The other one was probably Carter."

"But it cannot contain enough fuel for a long trip, surely."

"Correct. But three minutes is more than enough time to reach a concealed gyro."

"You seem distressingly familiar with his plans."

"It is his standard procedure to have several such contingencies in place. Else he would not have survived this long." She nodded at the tree Navita had carved. "And there is the parting shot from our other professor."

Paragon turned to look. RIOT ARMY was easy to see even in the dark.

Lady Kalmaar squinted at him. "I thought you were a Buddhist?"

"Yes. So?"

She lay a finger upon his neck. "Is this standard issue for them?"

He felt where she had touched. Something small and cold hung there. He held it out and looked.

A little knotted silver cross. *How in the ---?*

After a long moment, ice creeping up his spine but then turning into warmth, he said in his old Yorkshire accent, "It was me mum's. She believed in…salvation."

They returned to the burning cathedral, holding one another upright, passing soldiers running toward the ray gun blast. Paragon had despaired for Selkie's children and the *Coxwell*. But Farnborough had landed her several hundred yards away. He had rewarded the children with sweets and sent them back to town. They found him near the monorail, supervising treatment of the wounded and collection of the dead, assisted by Oscar, Vesta, and Millie.

"Nasty bugger, that Moreau," he scowled. "Set off a bomb just as he flew himself to safety."

Ambergris was bustling amidst the survivors, asking everyone if they had seen her son. Most of them gave her puzzled looks. Finally, a badly scorched Aero Marine on a litter said, "Last I saw of him he was standing on the ramp of the *Prosper*, not two minutes before she went up."

She sagged as if Winston had been her living child. Never good at comforting women, Paragon left her alone to mourn. Soon the curious and the official would arrive. But for now, they had the site all to themselves. As he passed the corner of the charred factory wall, a naked blackened figure rushed at them. Two dozen bullets struck the fellow, clanging uselessly off its brass flesh.

"Winston!" Ambergris squealed, hugging him. "We thought you had perished in the inferno."

"Blown mostly clear, my lady."

"And I am glad of it. But your clothes are quite burned off. We shall have to return you to decency. Come along."

Which is how Paragon found himself back in the Admiral's luxurious bed, sticking plaster on his hurts and Lady Kalmaar embracing him in her sleep, a freshly polished Winston gleaming like gold as he stood guard in a too-large RAF uniform. Dreams of monsters kept Paragon awake, as did worry about the devilish Navita's whereabouts, to say nothing of Moreau's. Curiosity about the black-garbed rescuer also did nothing to help him sleep, to say nothing of finding an old, cracked shilling in his coat pocket. But eventually sheer exhaustion did the trick and when they awoke, they saw that they were above Horse Guards once more.

## 20 / "NOW OUR REVELS ALL ARE ENDED"

"Quite the master of the secret mission," grumbled Phoenix at the Eccentric Club two days later. "My creativity is being stretched as thin as an MP's conscience covering your trail of devil-may-care devastation."

"Exploding a few million cubic feet of hydrogen was not my doing," Paragon said.

"Nonetheless, I may have to turn Wilde loose upon the gentlemen of the press to explain this."

Paragon sighed and nodded. "Lady Kalmaar."

"Got it in one. I dared not show our ace to a player who might have been holding the other team's cards. So might she still. We now know that she has been a spy in Navita's army. Just for herself, or for Moreau?"

"So, my trust in her was meaningless to you?"

"No, but you will admit that Moreau declared that he bred her to seduce and control men. How many couplings were there? I ask merely for information."

"Would it reflect badly on me to say that I lost count?"

Phoenix cackled. "Paragon blushes! I shall inform the *Times*."

"I swear that even you would have succumbed to her charms. Dr. Moreau knows his business, I can admit that much."

"Do not presume to know the depths of me. I am more broad-minded than you give me credit for." He looked about the room. "Speaking of the literally intoxicating lady…?"

"She's downstairs with Patel, being debriefed."

"I hope Patel's wearing a breath mask. Pity that Martian mind-reader machine melted in the fire. Then we would know for certain, eh?"

Phoenix gathered his hat and stick. "One thing we do know for certain…Moreau has not left the country yet. Our valuable Captain Carter has rendezvoused with him and managed to sneak out at least that much to us."

"Did Moreau get the bodies of his family out?"

"So it would seem. They were nowhere to be found when we searched the wreckage. Your former spouse says Moreau escaped in a sort of rocket vehicle large enough for them."

"Millie says there was a monster in the laboratory, as well. Trembles like a leaf in a gale when she speaks of it."

"No monsters found, though there was a sort of environmental chamber that housed something unusual."

"He smuggled quite a bit out on such short notice." As he turned to depart, Paragon stopped. "About Lady Kalmaar..."

"Yes?"

"She would be a great asset to us."

That made Dardanelles cackle again. "To you, you mean."

"Do not presume to know the depths of me. I am less of a bounder than you give me credit for."

"Touché. Pray continue."

They moved toward Hades. "She has nerve. After all, she killed a rogue automaton with a fan while as nude as the Venus de Milo. And, as you say, was inside Navita's circle. She says she was forced to aid him to receive Moreau's location. With his knowledge or not, a dangerous game to play. To say nothing of her keen intellect. She had abundant opportunities to do me in and chose not to. And she controls a considerable intelligence network."

"A network which she employs for selfish and possibly treasonous ends, is that not so? How do you think she can afford her lavish lifestyle?"

"I am not ignorant of that. But holding her close to us is a sounder policy than pushing her away. And who of us is pure as the driven snow? A transvestite entertainer, an opium-loving fraud, a pair of ---"

"Inverts?"

"Misunderstood souls, I was about to say."

"Of course, you were. And I like to think of you, too, as a lost soul, struggling toward the light."

"On one sound leg and rather less of a whole psyche."

"At least no one mistakes you for a monster, offstage. Quite enough of those this week, yes?"

They descended the circular stair in silence. At the bottom Phoenix said, "Lord knows we could use some help. Lost too many good agents lately. I may have to engage an employment agency. Though there is that clever young chap over at the medical college. I hear he can look at you once and tell what your mother's maiden name was. Disturbs the other students." He sighed. "The sin be upon your head, then. I give you the benefit of the doubt, for now. But the lady has only the one innings. If she is bowled, then out she truly is...permanently."

In the waiting room, Vesta Tilley peered along her nose at Paragon like some superior monocle-wearing bird.

"She is nearly finished. Then it shall be my turn to face the dread Inquisitor."

Paragon snorted. "Patel? Pshaw! Scratch her belly and she'll purr."

Phoenix slapped his arm with folded gloves. "Shush, you! Give the game away and all of my authority melts like the spring snow."

In the training area Queue and another operative sparred. Poor Wilkins was out of his depth. She held him in a wrist lock, foot on his neck.

"Ah! back from the wars, are we?" she chimed. "I trust that the miscreants have been well and truly chastised?"

"If by that you mean, have I been pummeled within an inch of my life while permitting the mastermind to escape, then yes."

"Which would go far toward explaining how you come to sport such marks of success upon your rugged physique."

"These trifles? You should see the other fellow." He nodded toward her bare and bruised shoulder. "One of your students get lucky?"

Queue released her victim and shrugged the garment back into place. "Something like that." She collected her spectacles from her workbench. "Happy, as always, to see you alive and well. Perhaps you should have become a chartered accountant."

"I think we both know that such a life would kill me more quickly than any number of beast-men. Have that shoulder seen to. Also, that nasty mark on your ankle. It almost looks as if a great hand took hold of it…while tossing you across half of Yorkshire." He set the hair stick she had thrown at Navita on her workbench.

Her mouth gaped like that of the ornamental carp he had seen in the Shogun's water garden in Nippon. Paragon kissed her tenderly on one lovely cheek. He winked at her and mouthed 'thank you.'

"What was that all about?" asked Ambergris, taking his arm, Winston trailing behind. Neither of them noticed the distressing effect the simple action had on poor Priscilla Ang.

"She likes to play dress-up sometimes. And bloody glad I am that she does."

"It is none of my business, but if you two would just do the deed and be done with it you would both be much happier for it."

"You know, you will never be received in polite society if you continue to spout such shocking statements."

"I would last about as long in polite society as you would in chartered accountancy."

"I bow to your superior wisdom in such matters."

They passed out of the waiting room through the great armored door. When it thumped shut behind them, she asked about her Lochmoor status.

"The estimable Mister Dardanelles is of the opinion that you may well sell us out if circumstances dictate."

"But…?"

"But my powers of persuasion are legendary."

"Meaning you begged?"

"Just so."

"I expect that I am on the most probationary status imaginable? Assassins at the ready and all that?"

"Right again."

She kissed him lightly on his cheek. "Thank you. How shall we mark this auspicious occasion? Champagne? Caviar? Lovemaking till dawn?"

Paragon twirled his stick and kissed her hand. He saw a crushed daisy in her hair and smiled. "Actually, I was thinking of venturing into a few dens of vice to see if we can prod this Navita chap out of his lair. *And to see where your allegiance truly lies.* What say you?"

Her skin and hair flushed into Union Jack colors, while her eyes turned golden. "Why, Mr. Paragon…what an eccentric notion."

## ABOUT THE AUTHOR

Despite having leapt out of perfectly functional Army aircraft, scuba dived with sharks, lived with Crips & Bloods on a wagon train, and been paid actual money to portray both William Shakespeare and Chuck E. Cheese (though, thankfully, not at the same time), school districts still let Terry teach their children English for 30 years.

Somehow a winner of the Colorado Gold Literary Award for *Paragon of the Eccentric*, he has appeared in 3 Rocky Mountain Fiction Writers anthologies: *Found* (Colorado Book Award winner), *False Faces,* and *Broken Links, Mended Lives* (both CBA finalists). He claims to be the only author to appear in all three, and wonders why that doesn't seem to impress anyone.

The first volume in his ongoing tongue-in-cheek fantasy series (*Brimstone and Lily, Jasper's Foul Tongue, Jasper's Magick Corset*) was a finalist for the Colorado Gold Writing Award and won a Bronze Medal at the Independent Publishers Book Awards. His story about Broadway musical-loving nanobots in the President's brain, "The Day the Earth Couldn't Stand Still," won the Colorado Short Story Contest. Please note that he did not get to quit his day job after such stunning successes (though he's now retired, which amounts to the same thing).

Visit him on the web at www.terrykroenung.com before WordPress realizes their mistake and evicts him from their site.

If you loved *Paragon of the Eccentric* (or if you wouldn't even bother to wrap fish with it), please leave a review on its Amazon page. The more reviews, the more Jeff Bezos' overworked little elves are likely to recommend it to other unsuspecting readers.

# Coming soon

# *Rapiers, Rogues, and Romance*

An old-fashioned swashbuckler,
featuring d'Artagnan's father in his youth,
alongside the future captain of the Musketeers

Treville had to admit that the Protestants took their murdering seriously.

No threats, no boasting, no warning. The tall one had stopped him in the dim street, pretending to ask directions, while his squat comrade had slipped in behind with a business-like dagger. If it had not been for his elk-hide buff coat he would have bid good-bye to a kidney. As it was the wicked point punctured the expensive jerkin just below his red officer's sash and plunged into his side, just above the hip. Luckily Treville had caught the triumphant anticipation in the first fellow's eye as his friend came in for the kill. A quick twist not only preserved his life but trapped the blade in a fold of the thick leather. Before its owner could retrieve it Treville seized the set-up man's collar and jerked him close as if to kiss him. Snapping his own head to the left, he smashed his new friends' faces together. With a vicious elbow to the rear and a front boot to the bollocks, he managed to free himself from their attentions and plunge into the crowded market.

He ducked into a hatter's stall, browsing the merchandise while keeping a sharp eye out for pursuit. Had they penetrated his disguise or were they merely reacting to his speaking Spanish to that fruit seller? Hard to say if they merely wanted to dispatch an officer of the occupying forces or if they knew that he was spying for the French. Either one was a splendid reason for killing, in their eyes. After all, one only had to give Ostend a cursory glance to see what the army of Spain had done in its three-year siege. Close to a hundred thousand dead on both sides. They said that Queen Isabella had wept when she had seen the destruction wrought by her own troops. Six months later the town had hardly recovered. Buildings were burnt-out shells. Disease savaged conqueror and subjects alike. A stench of unburied dead competed with the gagging reek of sewage flowing in rivers. Only a handful of civilians had returned.

*Just my luck that two of them came out hunting Spanish troops today.*

He winced as he leaned out to scan the narrow street. The wound throbbed like a hoof-kick from Lucifer. Clearly it had been a nastier thrust than he had first thought. If it grew any worse, he would have to find a doctor. That could be a problem. It would not do to lie in a Spanish military hospital, growing delirious with fever and blurting out God only knew what secrets. Then this little pinprick would be the least of his concerns. Their interrogators were notorious for mixing devilish creativity with their enthusiasm for torture. And if he managed to see a local surgeon the man might just poison him out of spite, not knowing that he only impersonated a hated invader.

Both assassins came into view, peering into every stall for him. The tall one walked with a limp and the stabber's nose bled. As gratifying as that was, they seemed perfectly able to pursue him. Judging from their grim faces, they were intent on doing so until the Last Judgment. Now that he got a good look, they seemed suspiciously well-fed and free of sickness. Their garments were simple and had seen hard use, but these men did not have the bearing of siege survivors.

*How did they even get back in? It's not like the Spaniards have thrown open the gates and welcomed men of fighting age to repopulate the place.*

Questions would have to wait on answers. A well-placed Dutch coin bought his whereabouts from a ragged urchin, who was more than happy to earn it by pointing directly at him. With the ill will that the Spanish had earned with their bloody siege, the killers could probably have gained the information gratis. He would find few friends here if it came to a stand-up fight. Gripping his rapier hilt to narrow its profile along his leg, Treville snaked through the crowd and headed for any place that offered escape or at least a more defensible position. Now the wound was stiffening as well as hurting. Warm blood trickled inside his breeches and pooled in his tall riding boot. *No doubt about it. Going to need a doctor.*

*Or an undertaker.*

Masking his limp as well as he could, Treville adopted the haughty manner seemingly installed as a permanent feature on all the Spanish lieutenants he had seen since arriving two days before. His moustache curled into a hard sneer and he glowered like a rabid dog to make civilians get out of his way. He stomped into the nearest grimy alley as if he were the Habsburg Emperor. Once there he surveyed his new kingdom and found that it was populated by a bony cat picking through garbage and a snoring drunk. Beyond them lay the next street and the safety of his rented room. Freed from observation, he relaxed his assumed character and screwed up his face in pain while dragging his half-paralyzed hip and leg behind him. In a few more steps he would be behind his own door and could take stock of the damage.

Naturally, God punished him for such hubris. The light from the far end of the alley grew dark as someone entered it. At the same time heavy footsteps crept in behind him.

*Well, this is going to look bad on my report.*

He toyed with the idea of trying to over-awe them with the majesty of the Spanish Empire, threatening them with all manner of dire consequences for assaulting the King's officer. Such bluster had worked before. But one look at the dark faces before and behind him said that that would be wasted air. They had cast their dice already and would accept whatever the roll brought them. Treville sighed and drew his rapier, pulling the matching main gauche as well. Though he settled into his best guard, back flat against the wall so that he could keep both in sight, he had few illusions. One against two was nearly always a losing proposition. No sense letting them know that, however.

"Gentlemen," he said, trying to sound cheery though the wound felt decidedly wider than a church door now, "I'm so dangerous that it requires the pair of you? I'm flattered."